the BELIEVER

the BELIEVER

a novel

STEPHANIE BLACK

Covenant Communications, Inc.

Published by Covenant Communications, Inc.
American Fork, Utah

Printed in Canada
First Printing: January 2005

11 10 09 08 07 06 05   10 9 8 7 6 5 4 3 2 1

ISBN 1-59156-700-9

To Brian

Acknowledgments

Thanks to my husband Brian for his constant support. Special gratitude also goes to my mother, Kathleen McConkie, who assisted me in so many vital ways, from the early stages of the novel to the rush to the finish line.

For their feedback and help, thanks to my father, Stanford McConkie, and my siblings and their spouses: Dianna and Ken Hall, Suzanne and Jason Lucas, Stan and Amy McConkie, Marshall and Sue McConkie, and Bonnie and David Overly.

I'd like to express gratitude to all the people at Covenant Communications, with particular thanks to editor Angela Colvin—not only for her professional expertise, but also for her enthusiasm, encouragement and unfailing patience.

Prologue

Now this secret combination, which had brought so great iniquity upon the people, did gather themselves together, and did place at their head a man whom they did call Jacob . . . and he was one of the chiefest who had given his voice against the prophets who testified of Jesus.

Therefore, Jacob seeing that their enemies were more numerous than they, he being the king of the band, therefore he commanded his people that they should take their flight into the northernmost part of the land, and there build up unto themselves a kingdom, until they were joined by dissenters, (for he flattered them that there would be many dissenters) and they become sufficiently strong to contend with the tribes of the people; and they did so.

—3 Nephi 7:9–10, 12

CHAPTER 1

With the first unfeigned enthusiasm he had shown all evening, Ian Roshek leapt from his seat, determined to exit the conference room before he got trapped in a group of colleagues slobbering praise over the latest list of academic restrictions. Two hours of listening to Dr. Sheldon's harangue had already given him a skull-splitting headache.

Lavender twilight softened harsh angles of brick and steel as Ian hurried across the University of Tremont campus. He peeled off his blazer, hoping the September breeze would cool his frustration. If Sheldon was going to be so insanely picky, why didn't he just write the lectures himself and replace professors with computers?

Weaving through groups of students en route to Friday-night activities, Ian headed toward the tree-lined path that curved down the hill to Maddox Road. Students in yellow sweatshirts milled around the entrance to the path, peering up and down the sidewalk with an arrogant, alert air that prickled Ian's nerves.

More kids in yellow shirts lined the handrails of the path, studying each pedestrian as if trying to spot faces from the police bulletins. Ian forced himself not to quicken his step. What were these kids up to tonight?

He rounded a bend and stopped short behind a logjam of people. Several yards ahead, two tables blocked the path and students in yellow sweatshirts were rooting through backpacks, jackets, and computer cases.

"Oh, hi, Dr. Roshek."

Ian nodded at the boy's shaky greeting. He couldn't think of his name. A freshman, certainly, looking pale and edgy.

"What's going on?" Ian asked.

"They're hunting for, you know, illegal stuff. I guess there's been a lot of it around here, so the police got the student government to do a search."

"That's a new one." Ian tried to ignore a gush of adrenaline, but couldn't hold back a frown. Students deputized to stick their hands in backpacks and pockets?

"I think it's a good idea," the boy said loudly. "Can't be too careful, huh?"

Ian didn't reply. He'd already applauded enough idiocy tonight.

At the tables, a searcher shone a flashlight meticulously along the seams of a backpack like she thought the owner might have a warehouse of contraband hidden under the stitching. Sweat dampened Ian's palms and he squelched an urge to check his own pockets for anything illegal. He had nothing to worry about.

Footsteps clattered behind Ian and came to an abrupt halt. "What is the *problem* here?"

People stared at the student who had spoken—a girl with long auburn hair and a leather backpack slung over her shoulder.

"There's no *problem*," snapped a boy in front of Ian, a gangly kid with peeling skin from a recent sunburn. "Unless your pack is full of anarchist trash."

The girl reddened. "Idiot," she returned.

Massaging his aching forehead, Ian refocused his attention on the search. Fifteen or twenty kids in yellow shirts were leaning against the handrails near the search area or mingling with the waiting crowd, but only six were actually conducting searches—two dumping backpacks on tables, two emptying jacket pockets, two checking computers. Another kid in a yellow sweatshirt was forming the crowd into a line as he moved back along the path, scanning forearms with a portable ID scanner. Ian moved into the line as he presented his own ID chip. Apparently they were making sure no one left without going through the checkpoint.

Chilled now, Ian slipped his arms back into his blazer, fervently regretting that he hadn't chosen to stay in his office and get some work done. They couldn't keep this search going all night, could they?

How much contraband had they found? The searchers worked with rough, eager motions, almost ripping bags apart. A middle-aged woman in a yellow jacket, obviously the supervisor, watched impassively. No police officers were there, at least none that Ian could see.

The line inched forward and the auburn-haired girl shifted restlessly, inadvertently knocking her pack into Ian's ribs. "We're going to miss our bus," she grumbled to her companion.

"You're welcome to go ahead of me, if that will help," Ian offered.

"Thanks." The girl squeezed in front of him, dragging her friend with her.

The sunburned boy raised his voice like he was making a speech. "If you really cared about keeping campus safe, you'd wait your turn."

"Give me a break," Ian said, irritated at the boy's second attempt to draw attention to the girl and create a breach of behavior out of nothing. The boy turned away.

A searcher dumped a backpack with such vigor that the contents scattered. "Careful!" the owner yelped, grabbing for a falling thermos. The searcher laughed.

Losing patience with his role of captive audience member, Ian yanked his computer from his pocket. Perusing history journals wouldn't do much for his headache, but it might help his sanity.

Before he could open the case, a girl in a yellow shirt was at his side. "Put that away."

"What?"

"You have to put your computer away until it's been checked."

Everyone within earshot goggled at Ian like he'd been attempting to delete plans to assassinate the president. Face hot, Ian shoved the computer into his pocket.

The sky darkened and the pathway lighting flared on. The line behind Ian continued to grow. The supervisor finally gestured another handful of searchers toward the tables, but the line still moved slowly. Weary of watching the searchers, Ian stared with glazed eyes at the surrounding trees and resisted the urge to check his watch.

When the auburn-haired girl was able to rush forward and hand over her backpack, Ian felt a feeble stirring of relief. Soon it would be his turn . . . the search wouldn't take long since he wasn't carrying a briefcase . . . forty minutes to walk home . . . within an hour he'd be sprawled on the couch with a cup of soup, a couple of aspirin, and the evening news—

"Hey. *Hey!*" The searcher attacking the auburn-haired girl's bag flapped a folded white paper above his head. "Check this out!"

The girl's mouth dropped open. "That's not mine!"

"Did you think you were smart, sticking it under the lining? That's the oldest trick around."

"That trash isn't mine!" The auburn-haired girl whirled toward her friend. "Tell them it's not mine, I'd never read that stuff—"

Her friend shrank from her. The auburn-haired girl spun toward the supervisor. "I swear I didn't—someone must have stuffed it in my bag—"

"Yeah, sure," the searcher said. "Like one of your anarchist pals?"

The girl planted her fists on her hips. "It's *not mine*. Did *you* slip it in there so you can get a prize for finding it?"

The searcher slapped her. Ian winced as she staggered into the sunburned boy that had been standing next to her at the table.

"Scum. I knew it." the sunburned boy shoved her away.

Tears glittered on the girl's face. "I don't know what's going on here, but I did *not* put that trash in—"

"Listen to her!" the searcher shouted. "The anarchist sneak is blaming *us!*"

Anger arced through the crowd. People pressed against Ian, crowding forward to get a better view of the girl.

"A traitor!" the searcher yelled. "A terrorist, a Garrett follower—"

"No! That's a lie—"

The sunburned boy grabbed the girl's hair and yanked her backward. She screamed, arms flailing.

"Traitor . . . Tremont-hater . . ." the sunburned boy spat.

Ian looked anxiously at the supervisor, but she was stowing the contraband in an evidence envelope and didn't seem to be paying attention to the altercation.

"Thought you were too smart to get caught, huh?" The searcher wrenched the girl's hand into the air. "Here she is, the school genius! Who wants to shake her hand?"

Students began to yell. They surged past Ian, closing in around the girl.

Stop! Ian wanted to shout the word, but fear sealed his mouth. The police would be here any second, someone must have called them— these kids knew better than to hurt the girl too badly—

A shrill scream made Ian flinch and he stumbled as the crowd pushed him closer to where the girl struggled in the grip of the searcher and the sunburned boy.

"One shot per customer, don't be greedy!" the searcher shouted. "Break a finger, get a bonus point. Kneecaps are worth double—can't pray with broken knees." Laughter exploded from the crowd. The girl's former friend waved a handful of auburn hair that she'd ripped from the girl's scalp.

How can I let this happen? The thought roared through Ian's mind on a wave of panic. *They're torturing this kid and I'm acting like I approve—I'm a coward—a hypocrite—*

A grinning boy, rancid with sweat, wriggled past Ian. "Little trash-reader—"

At the glee on the boy's face as he reached for the girl, Ian shoved the boy aside so roughly that the kid tripped and crashed into the handrail. Grabbing another student by the shirt, Ian felt fabric rip as he jerked the attacker away from the girl.

"Back off! I said *back off!*" Ian's roar lanced through the hollering of the students. Everyone froze, gawking at him through still-frenzied expressions. Even the supervisor looked startled.

Ian pushed toward the girl. Blood streamed from her nose and trickled from swollen lips. Flesh gaped open across her cheekbone. Fingernail marks raked her throat.

"Back *off.*" Ian yanked the auburn-haired girl away from the boys holding her. Confused, they released her, but her former friend seized her wrist.

"She's *scum!*" the friend shrieked at Ian.

Ian knocked the friend's hand aside. "This is a police matter." He could no longer see the supervisor. Where had she gone?

The injured girl clung to Ian, her blood staining his jacket. "I didn't . . . didn't read . . . never *touched* . . ."

Ian used his shoulder to ram a path through the crowd, speaking loudly as he went. "We'll take her to the campus police station." Uncertainty throbbed around him, everyone wanting to challenge him, no one wanting to be first.

Finally, an anonymous screech, "He's helping her escape!"

"Follow me, if you're stupid enough to think that," Ian yelled. "We'll *all* take her to the police."

A hand reached from the crush, polished nails clawing at the auburn girl's face. Ian slapped the hand away.

"He's protecting her!" hollered a voice Ian recognized as the sunburned boy's. "He's her *friend*. He probably gave her that stuff to read in the first place—and we let this guy teach us?"

Ian's mouth was parched, his shirt drenched. He wasn't going to make it out of there without getting his ribs kicked in—

The crowd swished back, leaving a ring of space around Ian and the girl. Relieved—confused—Ian glanced over his shoulder and saw gray uniforms just as a shove hurtled him forward. Unable to catch himself, he spun to the side to avoid crushing the auburn-haired girl beneath him. His shoulder slammed into the ground. The girl tumbled out of his grasp.

Two police officers jerked Ian to his feet. Choking on pain, Ian couldn't breathe, let alone form words to explain. Another officer dragged the auburn-haired girl away, and Ian's escorts hauled him along the path toward Maddox Road. They stopped next to a patrol car parked at the curb and flung Ian facedown. His head struck the sidewalk with a jolt that ignited dizzying sparks of pain. An officer twisted his right arm up behind his back and an ID scanner beeped.

"He is the one who was protecting the anarchist?" A woman's voice, icy and authoritative, accompanied black boots that stopped several paces from Ian's face.

"Yes, Lieutenant." The officer checking Ian's ID chip released his wrist and straightened.

"I wasn't . . . protecting her." Ian struggled to speak. "Was taking her to—"

"Name?" the lieutenant asked.

"Ian Roshek," the officer filled in promptly. "He works here as a . . . let's see . . . assistant professor of history."

The black boots stepped closer. "Do you wish to explain your behavior, Dr. Roshek?"

Ian tried to look up at his inquisitor, but the attempt to turn his head sent pulses of fire through his skull. He caught only a brief impression of black hair, pale face, black clothing. "I thought the students were—going to kill that girl. I didn't think the police wanted that."

"She is one of your students?"

"No—I don't think so—please, I don't even know her—"

The woman stepped back and stretched out her hand. "Profile?"

Another pair of gray-clad legs marched into Ian's view. He braced his palms against the ground and tried to stop trembling.

Cheers erupted from the pathway. Had the students found another criminal, or were they still celebrating the capture of the auburn-haired girl? Ian's interrogator was speaking to an officer, but through the clamor from the hill, Ian couldn't hear what she was saying. He strained to listen and caught her last order. "Arrest him."

Terror slashed through him. "Look, this is just a misunderstanding—"

Handcuffs bit into his wrists. Dizziness blinded him as the officers yanked him to his feet and shoved him into the patrol car. The door slammed.

CHAPTER 2

The cot Ian was lying on felt cold and damp, and he shivered, wishing for the blazer the police had taken, along with his tie, watch, belt, wallet, and computer. Not that his jacket would have helped— the cell could be steaming like a crowded bus on a July afternoon and he still would have shivered.

He'd been a fool to help that girl. A brainless, interfering idiot. He should have stayed back and kept quiet—*"God hath given a commandment that all men should have charity, which charity is love—"*

Ian sat up so suddenly with the thought that his headache felt like a wrecking ball demolishing the contents of his skull. There was no reason to panic. Protecting a kid—even an alleged anarchist—from attack wasn't a crime. Maybe the police just wanted to talk to him and verify that he hadn't been involved with the girl's treason.

No reason to panic. He probed gingerly at his bruised shoulder, so hyperaware of the pain that it seemed he could sense each damaged capillary.

A mirrored panel formed a narrow rectangle in the upper third of the door—a one-way window, Ian assumed, so a guard could walk the corridor and easily monitor a large number of prisoners. Ian glimpsed his face in the mirror—skin bloodless, dark brown hair disheveled, fear emanating from stunned eyes. How was it possible to look so guilty without saying a word?

A clank from the door made him jump. It opened, and two officers stalked into the room, a brawny man built like a grizzly bear and a skinny kid who looked fresh from the police academy.

"Get up," the brawny officer said.

Wondering if his legs would support him, Ian obeyed. The officers led him along a dank corridor lit by a wan yellowish light from dirty bulbs in metal brackets. Numbered steel doors were set at frequent intervals along the wall. Was the auburn-haired girl here?

Two levels up, they entered a wide, white-tiled corridor where the air smelled fresher. The officers prodded Ian through a doorway marked *S7* and shoved him into a chair in the center of the room.

The skinny officer unbuttoned the cuff on Ian's right sleeve and rolled it above his elbow. Moving swiftly, the officers fastened straps around Ian's chest, ankles, and wrists while Ian grappled with a new burst of panic. If they just wanted to talk to him, why the restraints?

The officers stepped back, and Ian cautiously inspected his surroundings. The room was small, square, and windowless. Opposite him was a table or desk of some kind, a solid black cube with a surface that slanted away from Ian. By craning his neck, he could see it was a computer station, with various screens and keypads. An empty chair waited at the console.

The brawny officer picked up a tray containing four small black discs. He pressed one of the discs against the back of Ian's neck. The disc adhered to his skin, its gummy clutch making him shudder. The second disc went on his left palm, the third on his bare right arm above the crook of his elbow. The officer unfastened the top two buttons of Ian's shirt and attached the last of the discs to his chest, just above the restraining strap.

A woman entered the room. Was she the one who had questioned him at the university? Her hair was glossy obsidian, her features graceful, her skin as smooth as marble. Ian searched her surprisingly beautiful face for any hint of compassion, and met the darkest, coldest, most impenetrable eyes he had ever encountered. *Oh, Father in Heaven, please help me.*

The woman sat at the console. The taps of her fingers striking a keyboard hammered against Ian's eardrums. What was she typing? *Interrogation of Ian Roshek, suspected anarchist—*

"He's ready, Lieutenant," the brawny officer said.

"Dismissed."

Ian recognized that glacial voice. It *was* the woman who had ordered his arrest. She was younger than he had realized while lying prone at her feet, his vision blurred by pain.

The two uniformed officers filed from the room. The door closed.

"Dr. Roshek." The woman's gaze skewered Ian. "I am Lt. Kent of the Sedition and Treason Division. This is a preliminary screening. If you are not involved in any criminal activities, then you have no need to worry. We will speak briefly and then I will release you."

"This is all a misunderstanding," Ian said. "I don't even know the girl who was caught with the contraband—"

"What is your full name?"

Ian swallowed, but his mouth remained dry. "Ian Jeffrey Roshek."

"How old are you?"

"Uh . . . twenty-seven. No, sorry. Twenty-eight."

"What is your address?"

"Uh . . . 374 Maddox Road, #509, Tremont."

"Family?"

"One sister." Fear wrenched Ian's gut. Would the police try to drag Jill into this? And why was Lt. Kent asking him for simple facts that were surely already recorded in his file? Was she trying to throw him off guard before she got to the hard questions?

Kent's dark eyes focused on the console in front of her. "You've been teaching at the University of Tremont for how long?"

"Two years."

"Do you enjoy your work?"

"Yes."

"Do you have any complaints about the functioning of your Education Regulatory Committee?"

An avalanche of frustrations crashed through his mind at the mention of Sheldon and his cronies. He took a breath and managed to keep his voice level. "The Committee does its job thoroughly and consistently."

"Do you have any complaints regarding them?" Kent repeated.

Ian swallowed. He would have traded ten years of his life for a glass of water. "No."

"You teach history," Kent said. "What is your specialty?"

"The United States in the years leading up to Separation. New America in its earliest years."

"What sparked your interest in that field?"

"A . . . desire to understand our national roots."

Kent's penetrating gaze made Ian feel she could extract his thoughts and hold them up to the light for examination. "Why did your family follow James Tremont?" she asked.

"My grandparents—my mother's parents—" To cope with nervousness, Ian slipped into the rhetoric of the classroom. "During the struggle against the international terrorist groups that plagued the United States, my grandparents, like many others, came to feel that changes were necessary to protect their country in the future and to revolutionize an outdated and unwieldy form of government. They admired the work of Senator Tremont."

"What appealed to them about his work?"

"His goals of strengthening and centralizing the government—protecting the people—"

"Many felt the need to strengthen and protect, but they did not all join with Senator Tremont," Kent interrupted.

Ian flushed. Kent clearly wasn't impressed with textbook answers. "My grandparents also supported the movement to reduce the power of religious organizations." He tried to keep his voice neutral even as revulsion stirred at the thought of his grandparents applauding the tactics employed by Tremont and his friends: flagrantly false and horrific accusations brought against religious figures and organizations, arrests based on nonexistent evidence, trials before judges who ignored the law and ruled according to their own agendas, the thwarting of the appeals process, executions that amounted to judicial murder.

Kent remained silent, so Ian stammered onward. "When—the, uh, complaints came against those who were working to weaken the influence of religious organizations, my grandfather had a lawyer friend who was helping defend the judges accused of abuses of power. This friend drew my grandparents into Tremont's efforts to . . . break down and rebuild the government." Now he sounded *too* neutral. Kent would expect him to be proud that his grandparents had joined in the pact that shattered two and a half centuries of government and threw a nation into chaos.

Burying his discomfort, Ian continued, "After the assassination of President Hayden and the social and political fragmentation that followed, my grandparents stood by James Tremont. When he gathered his people and founded New America, my grandparents came with him, bringing my mother. My father had been dating my mother for a couple of years. He came with her family."

Still Kent made no comment, and Ian feverishly reviewed his answer, wondering if he'd said something wrong. *Assassination* had been a poor choice of words; it made it sound like he disapproved of the murder of President Hayden. What was the matter with him? He lectured on these topics all the time, and now in front of a police officer he was tripping over his tongue.

"Your parents and grandparents stood with James Tremont," Kent said at last. "What is *your* opinion of President Tremont?"

"He was—a brilliant political leader."

More cool, disconcerting silence from Kent.

"To gather millions of followers," Ian said hastily, "and to break off a portion of what was once the most powerful nation on earth— without civil war—and transform that territory into a vigorous, independent nation—"

"You study the United States," Kent said. "Do you admire it?"

"Well, they're not particularly admirable. They've rallied somewhat, managing to reestablish a semblance of government, but they're still socially and politically fragmented. About the only thing they agree on right now is that they hate us."

"They're not admirable," Kent said. "Yet we have citizens who *do* admire them—who want to revive the destructive traditions of the past. Do you sympathize with the aims of the anarchist groups?"

"I have no sympathy for people who seek lawless disorder," Ian said carefully, knowing he wasn't answering the question Kent was asking. She was using the term *anarchist* as the police always used it, to define a person who opposed, in any degree, the government of New America.

"Have you ever supported the anarchists?" Kent asked.

"No."

"Have you ever concealed treasonous actions committed by acquaintances or family members?"

"No."

"Are you acquainted with Megan Corill?"

"No."

"She is the girl you assisted at the university this evening."

"Oh."

"Perhaps you sympathize with Ms. Corill because you are also guilty of reading anarchist literature?"

"No."

"You've never read any of it?" An undercurrent of strain tugged at Kent's cold voice, and Ian had the brief, puzzling impression that she was not eager to pursue this line of questioning.

"I haven't read it," he said.

Kent glanced at the console. Ian could feel sweat forming clammy rings around the discs adhering to his skin.

"I ask you again," Kent said. "Have you read any anarchist literature?"

"No."

Kent's hand moved to the far right corner of the console and stabbed downward.

It was as though the blood coursing through Ian's veins heated instantly to a raging boil, scalding his entire body from the inside out. Screams tore out of his throat as he writhed in a crazed struggle to escape the pain. Resistance evaporated; he would confess anything, *everything*—

Kent lifted her fingers. Relief drenched him like cool water and he sagged, panting for air.

"You have read anarchist literature," Kent said. "Let us now get a brief overview of what you have read and if your reading has led you to commit other crimes. Then we will transfer you to the Detention Annex and proceed with Information Extraction."

Blinking sweat and tears out of his eyes, Ian strained to focus on the woman at the console. Information Extraction? What did she mean? Was this interrogation only a warm-up?

Kent displayed a small stack of folded papers. "All these pamphlets were found within the last six months, either on your university campus or in your neighborhood." She lifted the first pamphlet. "*Rise and Resist*. Have you read this, Dr. Roshek?"

"No," he croaked, immensely relieved that it was the truth.

"It was published by a Tremont-based gang called the Liberty Cadre. You've heard of the Liberty Cadre?"

"On the . . . on the news."

"Are you involved with the Liberty Cadre?"

"No."

"Do you know anyone who is involved with the Liberty Cadre?"

"No."

Kent flipped to the next pamphlet. *"Fight Oppression,"* she read. "This is another of the Liberty Cadre's publications. Undermine the work of your Neighborhood Security Watch and teach your children to resist the lies taught in the classroom. Also, a recipe for a home-made explosive device. Have you read it?"

"No." His head throbbed with nauseating pain.

"Freedom. This pamphlet came over the border from the United States. We don't know who is distributing it in Tremont. Have you read it?"

He answered quickly. "No."

"I ask you again." Kent's face was as blank as uncarved stone. "Have you read it?"

Acid seared his throat. He should just admit to reading it. That crime wouldn't net more than a couple of years in prison. But once he started confessing—

At his silence, Kent reached for the corner of the console.

"No—*please*—" Pain ignited his nerves and continued until he was certain he was going insane. When it finally stopped, he ached like his muscles had been ripped from his bones and his bones had snapped out of joint.

"That was thirty seconds," Kent said. "It can last much longer. You've read *Freedom.* Do you know who brought it across the border?"

"No . . . please . . . no idea . . ."

"Where did you get this pamphlet?"

Ian's thoughts were so scrambled that he couldn't remember. Someone had brought it to the meeting . . . Eric, probably . . . or was it Tim? But he couldn't give Lt. Kent any names—*Oh, Father, help me.*

"Very well, you are protecting someone. I will take the names of your friends during Information Extraction." One pamphlet remained in Lt. Kent's hand. Shiny white paper, blank on the front. A fresh torrent of adrenaline flooded Ian's body. *Please.*

Kent tapped the pamphlet against the edge of the console. She was looking toward Ian, but her eyes were glazed, her expression so immobile it looked frozen. "You have done extensive research on religious matters," she said. "Particularly on Christian religions."

Ian's vocal cords rasped like they'd been rubbed with sandpaper. "All my . . . research materials were . . . approved by the Education Regulatory Committee."

"Committee approval doesn't guarantee that research won't corrupt the historian or give him a taste for material that is not approved." Kent crinkled the edge of the pamphlet and flattened it with a jerky motion. "You've heard of David Garrett?"

"Yes . . . his arrest and . . . execution."

"Did you ever meet him?"

"No."

"This is the same pamphlet that was found in Megan Corrill's possession." Kent curled the pamphlet between her palms. "In it, Garrett writes that this continent has been cursed by a supernatural being who is offended by our rejection of him. Our only hope is to crawl to this being in hopes of regaining his favor. Have you—read it?"

Ian's uncontrolled breathing seemed to fill the room, painfully loud, jagged with terror.

"You've read it. Did you—did you believe it?"

Ian gritted his teeth, so terrified of the pain he could almost feel it already.

"You did believe it." Kent's voice was soft, barely brushing his ears. "And the—book he uses as the source of his teachings—have you read that as well?"

New terror pierced Ian like the fangs of a rattlesnake. Had she sensed his treason from the beginning?

"You've read that book. Did you believe it?"

Ian's tongue dried into useless, shriveled flesh. Seconds swelled into eternity as Kent stared at him, her eyes filling with hate. Pure, raw loathing, utterly without humanity.

Kent rose to her feet with a convulsive movement that sent her chair skidding across the floor. She snatched a phone from her belt.

A bewildering fog of relief and terror swirled through Ian. Kent was going to call her colleagues and tell them she'd discovered a believer, a Garrett follower who was ready for the next level of questioning. But at least she hadn't pushed the pain button again.

Kent gripped the phone, but didn't use it. As the silence expanded, Ian realized dimly that Kent's face was ashen, wet with perspiration. Was she ill?

She slapped the phone onto the console with a crack that made Ian jump. "You'd make yourself into another David Garrett, wouldn't you?"

Ian stifled a wild urge to laugh. David Garrett, the man who freely chose to return to Tremont, valuing the spread of truth above his own life. He'd never be like Garrett, never have that kind of courage.

"It will be much easier for you if you renounce your foolish book now." Kent spoke rapidly. "A reduced sentence . . . minimal punishment . . ."

Ian had a hazy sense that she was pleading with him, but he couldn't think clearly enough to consider why. He was too busy watching her hands, slender white fingers quivering toward the corner of the console where pain began.

Abruptly, Kent turned away from the console. She started toward the door, but stopped, her body rigid. For an excruciatingly long moment, she stood motionless, then wheeled to face Ian. Her eyes were balls of black glass.

"You are a fool." A ragged, malignant whisper. "A *fool.* Destroy yourself if you will." She moved to the console and jammed her finger against a button. Ian tensed, but the pain didn't begin.

The door opened and the brawny officer tromped into the room. "Lieutenant?"

Kent's lips were as gray as a Tremont winter sky. "He's cleared for release."

"Yes, ma'am." The officer peeled the discs off Ian's skin, unfastened the straps, and hauled him to his feet.

Ian's limbs felt weighted with lead and his head pounded with clamorous pain that pulverized his thoughts. The officer propelled him into the hallway at such a brisk pace that Ian kept stumbling. His head jerked forward and backward on neck muscles too weak to support it, and everything around him fractured into confusion. Gray uniforms, loud voices, the lurch of an elevator. The processing area where the arresting officers had first taken him, a rough hand forcing his arm past an ID scanner, a paper bag in his hands. A ramp sloping upward, another ID scanner, a door sliding open and clapping shut behind him.

A breeze chilled the sweat on his face. Across the street, spotlights illuminated the granite columns of the Executive Council Building.

He turned and looked up at the twenty-story, blue-glass building towering behind him. The headquarters of the Tremont Police Service. He was *outside* the gates of police headquarters.

Alone.

CHAPTER 3

A mistake? A trick? Ian didn't take time to think about it. He fled, his aching legs moving in an awkward, weaving jog.

Downtown Tremont was eerily quiet. Ian tried to look at his watch and realized he was still holding the paper bag someone had handed him in the processing area. He fumbled to open the bag and found his blazer, watch, tie, belt, and computer. Clumsily, he retrieved his watch. *Ten to midnight.*

Three blocks from police headquarters he collapsed onto a bus-stop bench and scanned the schedule board. The last bus would stop here in eight minutes.

He closed his eyes and gripped his head like he could squeeze away the pain. Any second now, a patrol car would zoom up to the curb and officers would drag him back to headquarters, saying his release had been an error. But no patrol car arrived—only the bus.

As the bus jolted him through downtown Tremont, Ian wondered blearily if it was a good idea to go home. Maybe the police were there, searching his apartment. *Jill.* Was she all right? He had to go home, had to check on her. Had the police bothered her? *Please, no.*

This late at night, no buses stopped in his neighborhood. He took the last mile on foot, hurrying, stumbling, frantic to get to Jill. Muscles burning, he yanked open the heavy glass doors to the lobby and staggered to the elevator. At his front door, he groped in his pocket for his keys. *Oh yeah, in the bag.* Before he could find the keys, the door opened.

"Late tonight," Jill teased. "Out with a cute girl, I hope—" Her smile disappeared. "What *happened*?"

Ian hobbled into the apartment. "You all right?" he asked her.

"You're hurt." Jill was staring at his shirt. He looked down to see red-brown blotches. The auburn-haired girl's blood.

"No—the blood's not mine." Ian scrutinized Jill from blond head to bare feet. "Has anyone been here tonight?"

"I just got home. *What happened?*"

Ian sank onto the couch. "I need some water."

Jill raced into the kitchen and returned with a glass of water that Ian gulped gratefully. His throat stung like the flesh had been clawed away.

Jill plucked the empty glass from his hand. "What happened?" she whispered. Her fingertips brushed his raw, swollen wrist.

"It was nothing, Jilly." Ian jerked his sleeves down to cover the marks left by the restraints. "A misunderstanding."

"A misunderstanding!"

Ian stuttered out a brief explanation about the search for contraband at the university and the auburn-haired girl. "It was just a mix-up. The police thought I was one of her friends."

"Did they . . . ?" she trailed off.

"They took me downtown, talked to me, then let me go."

Jill's face went milk-white. "They arrested you!"

"Jill, I'm fine. Don't worry."

"You were arrested!"

"It's all right. I'm all right."

"Ian—" She choked on his name, tears filling her eyes.

"It was a misunderstanding." Ian gripped her hand. "Everything is fine now."

"Your head—"

Ian prodded the lump on his forehead. "It's nothing. A bruise. I tripped and hit my head—it was an accident."

"You need a doctor. I'll call a taxi—"

"Jill, no. I'm fine. How about just getting me some ice?"

"Well . . . if you're sure . . ." Jill still looked half ready to lunge for the phone. "Let me help you to your room."

"I'll stay here." Now that his body was at rest, the thought of standing up was more than he could endure. He lay back on the couch and mumbled his thanks as Jill slipped a pillow beneath his head and brought him an ice pack.

Was he going insane? Why had Lt. Kent released him? She knew he had read and believed the Book of Mormon.

"Destroy yourself if you will."

What had she meant by that?

* * *

"Ian." Jill was leaning over him, her hair a mess of tousled waves, her eyes bleary from too little sleep.

"Wha—" Ian sat up, stifling a groan.

"Didn't you hear the doorbell? Eric's here."

"Sorry," Ian mumbled.

Eric Vettori glowered behind Jill. He was dressed in the olive green T-shirt and shorts he wore every Saturday morning when he met Ian for their racquetball game at the university gym. Morning. It was morning.

"You look like a corpse," Eric growled. "What happened to you?"

Ian dug through the mud in his skull in search of an answer. "Sorry—overslept—sit down, will you? Back in a minute." He shuffled into the bathroom. Maybe a hot shower would clear his thoughts and loosen stiff muscles.

He stood under a spray of steaming water and tried to figure out what to say to Eric. He'd have to tell Eric about last night, but how could he explain it when he didn't understand it himself?

Ian stepped gingerly out onto the mat. Every muscle ached and his hands were so awkward that running a comb through his hair took the concentration of a brain surgeon.

A knock at the door made him drop the comb. "Are you all right?" Jill asked.

"Fine." Ian tried to sound like he meant it. He dressed in faded sweatpants and a long-sleeved shirt that hid his battered wrists, then trudged reluctantly into the living room.

"You can't possibly play racquetball this morning." Jill twisted the narrow gold band she wore on her right hand.

"I'm fine." Ian had no intention of swinging a racquet, but he needed to talk to Eric alone. Let Jill think they were heading to the university as usual. He smiled at her, and his brain finally registered that her hair was cropped to chin length. "You cut your hair." Jill had been anxiously contemplating that change for weeks.

"Yes." Jill pushed a blond curl behind her ear. "Yesterday afternoon."

"Jill told me what happened last night." Eric's angry gaze scoured Ian. "You ought to see a doctor. I'll take you to the clinic."

Ian opened his mouth to protest but closed it as he realized Eric's intention. Eric was on the same track he was, hunting a plausible excuse to get out of the apartment. "You've got the truck?"

"Yeah."

"You have a car?" Jill asked.

"It belongs to Tremont Electronics. They just switched me to the mobile repair team, so I need it for service calls." Eric stood. "Let's go, Roshek."

* * *

The tires crackled on the wet pavement as Eric turned left on Maddox Road. "What did they do to you?"

Ian gazed absently at the apartment buildings crowding the street. Brown or gray brick, sharp vertical lines. "Let's go to the lake. No one will be there in this rain."

"Why the lake?"

"I don't know. It just feels like the city is breathing down my neck."

"Fine, the lake. Just tell me what happened last night."

Hoping that speaking the tale aloud would help him make sense of it, Ian related the details of his interrogation and release. Eric's hands clamped around the steering wheel like he would snap it in pieces and his tanned face paled to sickly beige.

Ian finished speaking, and Eric drove in silence until Lake Serena came into view. The trees lining the shore blurred in mist and an overcast sky darkened gray-green water to black.

"That story sounds like a load of garbage," Eric finally said.

"I know. But it's what happened."

"You think a police officer would release you, *knowing* you're a Garrett follower? She'd chuck you behind bars just for looking at that nutty book. Or are you saying she's a traitor too?"

Ian didn't answer. He supposed it was possible for a police officer to turn traitor and start releasing criminals she should condemn, but Lt. Kent's attitude toward his treason had seemed anything but sympathetic.

"David Garrett," Eric said. "The stupidest guy on the planet."

"What's that supposed to mean?"

"Fifteen years hiding in the U.S. and he comes *back* and scatters his trash right under Edgefield's nose? Why didn't he stay where he was safe?"

"Maybe he wanted to give us a shot at learning the truth."

"Yeah, sure. If that lieutenant called you another David Garrett, she had it right. You're both idiots."

"Thanks," Ian said sourly. He'd been accustomed to Eric's brusque manner since they were kids, but right now, it grated.

"You know what?" Eric continued. "I don't think she mentioned Garrett at all. I don't think she knew you were a traitor."

Ian was startled. He'd expected Eric to find the story puzzling, but he'd never thought his best friend wouldn't believe him. "What are you talking about?"

"You've got Garrett on the brain because of all those news reports. And because of that pamphlet, and because you think he's the one who brought your book into Tremont. You were so scared last night that you're mixing up memories with nightmares."

"I'm not imagining things," Ian said irritably, but doubt flickered. *Could* he have imagined it?

"That's a nice lump on your head. You were probably woozy when that lieutenant talked to you. You probably hallucinated half of what she said."

"*I wasn't woozy.*" No. He hadn't imagined it.

Eric scowled. He drove into the parking lot for Jensen Beach and stopped near a grassy hill sloping down to the sand. A triangular monument towered in the center of the grass, and Ian's gaze traveled automatically to the rain-soaked granite. He had read the inscription so many times that it drifted in fragments through his throbbing head. "*. . . in honor of President James Tremont's beloved wife, Serena Jensen Tremont . . . death at the hands of terrorists . . . new haven of security where his vision of peace and—*"

"Are you listening to me? *Roshek!*"

"Huh?"

"You think you remember last night? You can't even pay attention now."

"Sorry," Ian mumbled.

"How could you be that stupid? To jump in when those kids were going crazy?"

"I couldn't stand there and let them tear that girl apart."

Eric shook his head. "They had a supervisor, right?"

"She wasn't doing anything."

"Yeah, she was smart enough not to jump into the middle of a mob. You're getting crazier by the day, you know that?"

"Eric—"

"Does that book kill brain cells?"

"Eric—"

"God visiting some teenage farm boy, books made of gold, angels popping in and out? You don't even make sense anymore. I guess you think God told you to help that twit?"

Ian looked out to where wind chopped the surface of the lake into foam-tipped waves. "Should I have attacked her instead? Maybe brought you a handful of hair for a souvenir?"

"No one was asking you to attack her. Why didn't you just mind your own business?"

Ian's anger rose as he remembered the girl's screams. "You're the one who always says we should get out there and take *action*. Now you're saying talk is all we're good for?"

"*You're* the one who always says we need to be patient, and that doing stupid, random things won't make a difference," Eric shot back.

"I was talking about fighting, Eric. Not about helping—"

Eric cut him off. "Did you stop to think what would happen to *us* if you got arrested?"

Ian's anger crumbled into fragments of anguish. "I didn't think the police—"

"Meetings are off," Eric said. "They must be watching you now, even if you did dream up most of that interrogation. I'll tell Tim and Sherry. You stay away from us."

A bleak feeling of isolation settled on Ian like the storm clouds lowering over the lake. "I'm not saying we should continue the meetings, but I'm not sure it's wise to avoid each other altogether," he said. "Shouldn't we just act normally?"

"Don't tell me how to handle this. You've probably already destroyed us. Did it occur to you that maybe they released you so you'd lead them to your criminal pals?"

"It occurred to me," Ian said. "But if that's what they want, why didn't Lt. Kent pretend she didn't know I was a traitor? If I thought I was safe, I'd be a lot easier to track."

In response, Eric only rammed the key into the ignition. "I'll drop you a couple of blocks from your apartment. I don't want to be seen with you. You're crazy, or that lieutenant is crazy, or the police are playing some sick game."

* * *

Music poured from Jill's bedroom as Ian trudged into the apartment and locked the door behind him. Jill was playing her violin so rapidly that the notes were a gush of sound. She played like that when she was worried, relieving tension through the sawing of the bow and the motions of her fingers. *Worried? She must be terrified.*

The phone rang. Grumpily, Ian swiped up the handset and croaked a hello.

"May I speak with Jill, please?" It was an unfamiliar baritone voice, each word as smooth and precisely carved as the wood of Jill's violin.

"Yeah, just a second." Ian headed down the hall to rap on Jill's door. The music stopped.

"Phone for you," he said.

"Thanks." Jill opened the door. Her eyes were bloodshot. "Did they do anything for you at the clinic?"

Oh yeah. That had been his excuse for going with Eric. He handed her the phone. "Uh—I decided not to go."

Frowning, Jill lifted the phone to her ear.

Ian returned to the living room. He was hungry, but he didn't feel like standing up long enough to find something to eat. He stretched out on the couch to rest, but the more he tried to clear his mind, the more he saw Lt. Kent's face, merciless, rigid with hate.

Light footsteps padded along the hall. Ian slipped his hands under him to hide their trembling.

Jill swished into the living room, smiling, her cheeks bright pink.

"Good news?" Ian asked, relieved to see Jill looking cheerful.

"Just someone I met last night." Jill hung up the phone, her smile waning. "Why didn't you see a doctor?"

"I didn't feel up to the wait. And they wouldn't do anything for me anyway."

Jill pulled at a stray thread dangling from a button on her dress. "You're so pale."

"I'm fine. So you met someone last night? Did he come to your concert?"

"Not a concert. Councilor Brannigan's dinner."

"Oh, right. Sorry." How could he have forgotten? Jill had been talking for weeks about what an honor it was to play in the string quartet at a dinner honoring the newest member of the Supreme Executive Council. "Tell me about this guy you met."

Jill perched in the drooping, dirt-brown armchair, a sheepish smile returning to her face. "I feel stupid talking about it when—"

"I *want* to talk about it," Ian interrupted hastily. "No topic is more entertaining than your social life. By the way, I like your hair."

"Do you?" Jill stroked her fingers over her bobbed hair. "You don't think it's too short?"

"It's perfect."

"You'd say that no matter what."

Ian began to laugh, but stopped because it made his throat burn. "So who'd you meet last night?"

Jill's smile widened, creating dimples in both cheeks. "Didn't you see his name when you answered the phone?"

"I didn't look. Do I know him?"

"Know of him, maybe. Daniel Lansbury."

"Lansbury?"

Jill smirked.

"As in Councilor Marcus Lansbury?"

"Yep."

Ian felt like he had just gagged on a mouthful of rancid meat. "Who's Daniel? His son?"

Jill apparently didn't notice his disgust. "Right. He has these *gorgeous* eyes. Clear gray, almost silver."

"Silver eyes. Sounds creepy. How'd you meet him?"

"Well, after the banquet ended, he came to tell the quartet how much he liked our performance. I talked with him for a while. He's a musician himself. A pianist."

"Professionally?"

"No. He's a doctor, like his dad was."

"I didn't know Councilor Lansbury was a doctor."

"He was the director of the Tremont Research Laboratory before getting appointed to the Council. Did you know he was only thirty-six when he was appointed?"

"Impressive."

"His older brother, Andrew, was Councilor over Internal Defense, but when Andrew was murdered by anarchists, Daniel's father was appointed to take his place."

"Did his son give you this background or did you come home and look the Lansburys up?"

Jill blushed. "OK, I checked the news archives. What's wrong with that, Mr. Research?"

Ian forced a grin. "All right, you win. Did you meet Councilor Lansbury too?"

"Oh no, he wasn't there."

"Not at the dinner honoring his newest colleague?"

"Well—Daniel said something about his father not—" Jill bit her lip. "Well, he was probably busy. Daniel came alone. Daniel's known Spencer Brannigan since he was a child. He used to study piano with Councilor Brannigan's wife. Anyway, Daniel just called to tell me he's coming to the concert tonight and he'd like to take me to dinner afterward. I can't believe he'd even talk to me! His family is so . . . important."

Revulsion erased Ian's attempt at a teasing smile. Marcus Lansbury, the Councilor over Internal Defense, had the Tremont Police Service under his jurisdiction. The thought of Marcus Lansbury's son showing interest in Jill made Ian want to lock Jill in her room. "I can't believe you'd want to talk to *him*. Somehow a Lansbury doesn't seem your type."

The sparkle died from Jill's eyes. "You've never even met him."

"No, but—look, I'm sure he's charming, but it just seems kind of—"

"I'm not fifteen, Ian."

"I'm not doing the guardian thing. I just—"

"I'm not stupid," she interrupted. "I know Daniel could never get serious about me. It'll just be fun to go out to dinner with him—once."

"Hey, relax. I won't tell you who to date." He searched for another topic. "What did Councilor Brannigan say in his speech last night?"

"Councilor Brannigan?" Jill looked confused.

"He gave some kind of speech, I assume."

"Oh! His speech!" Jill's face brightened with an eagerness that surprised Ian. "It was—interesting."

"How so?"

She hesitated. "Well . . . it wasn't really a speech for the public. It was mostly government people who were there. Maybe I'm not supposed to—"

"If they didn't want you to hear the speech, they would have sent you out of the room. Come on, you can't get in trouble for quoting a member of the Council."

"I guess not. He . . . talked about the Health Services Department."

"An appropriate topic for the new Councilor over Health Services. What did he say?"

Jill picked at the fraying upholstery on the arm of the chair. "He . . . talked about the—" She glanced at the front door as though to make sure it was closed, "about the corruption in the Health Services Department."

"Corruption! He actually admitted there are problems?"

"Shh! You don't have to shout."

"What kind of problems did he talk about?"

"He said Health Services isn't . . . treating people fairly and things need to . . . change. Ian, I'm not sure I should be—"

"Hey, you're only quoting Councilor Brannigan. What else did he say?"

"Well . . . he said more resources should be channeled into medical research. He said our medical care is—" Jill lowered her voice to a whisper, "—primitive compared to the United States, and we've backslid since Separation instead of moving forward."

"He *said* that?"

Jill touched her mother's gold wedding band on her finger and pain tightened her face. "He—also said we're overusing the Euthanasia Centers."

"Unbelievable!"

"Maybe I shouldn't have told you . . . we'd better not talk—"

"You haven't done anything wrong."

"Do you want something to eat?" Jill asked. "I could fix you some soup."

"I'd appreciate that," Ian said, accepting the change of subject. He wanted to hear more of what Spencer Brannigan had said, but he didn't want to increase Jill's anxiety by pressing her.

Jill stood up and folded her arms tightly against her body. "Ian . . . you need to talk to Ms. Cluff."

A boulder seemed to settle on Ian's chest. He'd been so worried about the police showing up to arrest him that it hadn't occurred to him to worry about blacklisting. "I'm not sure what I'd say to her."

"Don't be an idiot! You've got to explain that what . . . happened last night was a misunderstanding. Otherwise, she'll think that you—well, you know she's already mad at you."

If Marta Cluff heard about his arrest, trouble with the Neighborhood Security Watch was inevitable, no matter what excuses he offered. "I'll talk to her." Ian manufactured a smile so phony that it felt like a pulled muscle. "Don't worry."

CHAPTER 4

Even under normal circumstances, the phone ringing at 4:30 A.M. on a Monday would have startled Ian, but after the events of the weekend, the sound was enough to hurl him to the brink of cardiac arrest. He leapt out of bed, crashed into the doorframe in an effort to exit his room, and staggered to the phone. His sleep-fogged eyes couldn't read the ID box to see who was calling.

"'Ello," he grunted, heart thudding like the boots of the police officers who had been pursuing him in a just-interrupted nightmare.

"Dr. Roshek. This is Dr. William Sheldon."

"Dr. Sheldon." Ian massaged his puffy eyelids with both hands. "Good morning."

"You will come to my office this morning at 6:00 A.M. sharp."

"Yes, sir."

Sheldon hung up.

"Is everything all right?" Jill's voice quavered from the hallway.

"Fine." Ian slapped the phone back in its cradle. "Just the history department's obnoxious Committee rep, enjoying his power to yank people out of bed."

"Ian!"

"Go back to sleep. I'm sorry he woke you up."

"What did he want?"

"Just to meet with me this morning."

"Why?"

"Probably to criticize the lecture I submitted last week. Don't worry, he does this to everyone. Go back to bed."

Jill retreated to her room. Ian dropped into the chair in front of the desk and waited for his breathing to slow down. Sheldon didn't want to hack apart a lecture. Even Sheldon wouldn't call before dawn on such a routine matter.

Ian had checked every news report about the university contraband sweep, but though there was extensive coverage on a handful of students who had been arrested for possession of anarchist propaganda, Ian's name was never mentioned. It didn't make sense—first the police released him, knowing he was a believer, and then they concealed the news of his arrest from the public? But he'd hoped, somehow, that this inexplicable media silence might delay the news of his arrest reaching Sheldon's ears.

Sheldon's rude summons had annihilated that hope. The Education Regulatory Committee was standing ready to grind Ian's career into hamburger. Ian tried not to imagine how Jill would react when he confessed that Friday night's "misunderstanding" with the police had gotten him fired.

* * *

At three minutes to six, Ian entered the fifth-floor suite of offices in the Matthew Ryce Social Sciences Building and stopped in front of Dr. Sheldon's open office door. Sheldon sat at his desk, pudgy fingers tapping relentlessly at his keyboard. He glanced up at Ian and resumed typing.

Ian waited for Sheldon to invite him in. When silent seconds began to accumulate into silent minutes, Ian spoke. "Would it be more convenient if I returned at another time, sir?"

Sheldon didn't look up. "If I wanted you to leave, I'd dismiss you."

Ian pulled the computer from his pocket. He wouldn't risk antagonizing Sheldon by walking away, but he'd use the time to grade some papers.

He was halfway through the first paragraph of an essay when Sheldon snapped, "Come sit down."

Ian stowed his computer in its padded case and sat in the chair facing Sheldon's desk.

Sheldon's belly strained against his white shirt as he leaned back and surveyed Ian. "You've been an annoyance to the Committee ever since we hired you. But I've been patient with you since you're new at your job."

"Yes, sir."

"But during the contraband sweep on Friday, you showed a blatant lack of patriotism when you were supposed to be setting an example for impressionable students. Anyone that stupid should not be teaching in a university classroom."

"Sir—"

"Save your excuses. I already know what happened. I got the police report last night."

Ian's flesh turned to cold wax. "The police report?"

"I'm glad to hear you're finally learning your lesson. I should have known it would take the police to get your attention. You've been slow enough to listen to the Committee." His flabby lips stretched in a smile. "Were they hard on you, Dr. Roshek?"

"They released me," Ian said.

"Oh, they released you, yes. After you were duly chastised for helping a traitor. As a loyal citizen, I, of course, have no idea what it means to be 'duly chastised' by the police, but I will say you look mighty pale."

Ian tried to visualize the report. *Duly chastised for his behavior.* He pushed the phrase around in his mind, trying to match it with what he remembered from his interrogation. Lt. Kent hadn't berated him over his conduct at the university. She had only used it as a springboard into other questions. And the pain she inflicted had seemed aimed at eliciting confession, not bestowing punishment.

Or was his memory faulty, as Eric had suggested?

"You're a lucky man. The police might have thought you were an anarchist for protecting that girl. *I* would have thought you were an anarchist." Sheldon removed wire-frame glasses and rubbed a nose that resembled a lump of mashed potatoes. "You'll be better behaved from now on, I'm sure. I expect that both your judgment and your patriotism will be impeccable."

Ian was too befuddled to speak.

"I would have recommended that you undergo a disciplinary hearing, but the police say that won't be necessary. That's more mercy than you deserve."

Relief coursed through Ian, followed instantly by confusion. The *police* had told the Education Regulatory Committee not to discipline him?

Sheldon's chin slopped over his collar as he yawned. "And the lecture you submitted last Thursday is unacceptable."

"My lecture?"

"Don't play stupid. You know better than to confuse your students by praising a document so innately anarchical."

Oh. "It is a neutral, historically verifiable fact that the Constitution of 1787 was unique in that it—"

"Don't try to justify yourself. The reference was inappropriate, and I deleted it, along with a bunch of other rubbish. I've never met a professor with such poor judgment as to what is suitable for an undergraduate classroom. Get out of my office. You've wasted enough of my time."

* * *

Ian felt like he had skidded into a surreal landscape where the grass was blue and the sky green. First, no news reports on his arrest. Now, the police had told Sheldon not to punish him.

Lt. Kent's voice seeped through his mind like poison. *"You'd make yourself into another David Garrett, wouldn't you?"*

Maybe Eric was right. Maybe nothing had happened as he remembered it.

Or maybe Lt. Kent was toying with him.

From the whispers trailing him through hallways and the frosty silence that greeted him when he entered a classroom, Ian knew rumors about his arrest had saturated campus. By halfway through his first class, he was checking the clock compulsively, hoping time would magically accelerate. By his second class, he had abandoned his planned lecture entirely and resorted to showing news clips illustrating the chaotic nature of U.S. politics prior to Separation. He usually waited until later in the semester to show the clips, but today he would have supplanted his lecture with anything up to and including old Bugs Bunny reruns to take the students' eyes off him.

The end of the day came as an immense relief. Weary of being gawked at, Ian bypassed the bus stop and began walking the two miles home. Each step tore at his stiff leg muscles, but he preferred sore legs to hostile stares.

Clouds blotted out the late afternoon sun and a brisk wind shook the geraniums straggling in planter boxes near the doors to Ian's apartment building. *Rain tonight.* At least it hadn't started pouring when he was halfway home. He limped across the lobby and heard a reedy voice call out from the manager's office. "Dr. Roshek."

Resisting an impulse to dash for the elevators, Ian halted in front of the office. He'd told Jill he'd talk to Cluff, but he knew it was pointless. Cluff would never believe his arrest had been a mistake.

Marta Cluff was teetering on a stepstool, stroking a velvet cloth over the James Tremont Patriotic Service Award that hung on the wall behind her desk. Ian doubted the plaque had ever harbored a speck of dust, the way Cluff obsessively cleaned it.

"I've been waiting for you." Cluff's eyes glinted beneath the line of her steel-gray bangs.

"What can I do for you, Ms. Cluff?"

"In my position as president of our Neighborhood Security Watch, the police keep me informed of any people in my chapter who present a danger to the community. *Personally* informed. The police rely on me."

"I'm sure they do."

Cluff refolded her dust cloth with toothpick-skinny fingers. "I knew you were heading for trouble after that appalling display at our meeting last month. Defending that greedy little parasite!"

"She wasn't blacklisted when I defended her." Ian tried to keep his tone polite. "According to the rules of the Watch—"

"And now, protecting an *anarchist*. Do you have anything to say for yourself?"

What could he say? It was useless to try to dissuade Cluff from recommending him for blacklisting. Unless—was it possible—?

"What did the police tell you?" Ian asked.

"Your appalling behavior has humiliated our entire neighborhood."

"I'm sorry. I didn't mean to embarrass—"

"Helping a traitor. A religious believer! And a Garrett follower at that!"

"They found a religious pamphlet in her bag," Ian said. "At the time I helped her, it wasn't clear if she was the one who put it there."

"So let's *protect* her! Coddle her so she can turn around and *destroy* us!" Cluff's nostrils flared in distaste. "Why don't you spit on your parents' graves and go crawling back to the United States if that's the kind of person you are?"

"What did the police tell you?" he asked again.

"Nothing that *surprised* me. I've been keeping tabs on you for a long time now. Hiding on the back row, all quiet and sneaky, like I won't *notice* that you're refusing to vote on blacklisting motions. You have sympathy for scum. But not anymore, I'll wager. The police taught you a good lesson."

"What did the report say?"

"I'm watching you. Any more trouble and I'll see you blacklisted."

"Any more trouble?"

"Do you think the police meant you were immune from black-listing forever? You may have paid for your stupid . . . your selfish . . . disloyal . . ." Cluff paused to inventory her vocabulary for a word strong enough. ". . . your *disgusting* behavior at the university, but if you do anything else so appalling, it's in the hands of the Watch." She turned her back on him and resumed wiping imaginary dust from the national seal etched in her patriotic-service award.

Paid for your disgusting behavior—duly chastised—Cluff was echoing the same message Sheldon had delivered—the police had found him guilty of nothing worse than bad judgment.

But that's not what Lt. Kent had said.

"You have read anarchist literature—we will transfer you to the Detention Annex and proceed with Information Extraction—"

Suddenly so shaky that it was difficult to walk straight, Ian hurried toward the elevator. At his apartment, he dropped his keys three times before he managed to get the door unlocked.

"You have read anarchist literature." A cold statement of fact, no traces of doubt. And no mistakes either, as Kent had deftly identified which contraband writings he had studied and which he had not.

Heart pounding with sickening force, Ian entered his bedroom and yanked open the closet. He kicked aside a worn pair of running shoes and dragged a box of hardbound textbooks out of the closet, exposing a patch of carpet stained long ago by a leaky pipe. He should have checked over the weekend, but he'd been too afraid that the police were watching him, that somehow they would know if he so much as touched—

Ian peeled the carpet back and popped loose a warped section of floorboard. He reached into the gap, gut twisting with a sense of desperation. It wouldn't be there—the police would have taken it—Kent *knew* he had it—

The box was there. Translucent plastic, smooth and undisturbed. Ian ripped the lid off and snatched the book that lay on top. Dizzy, he sat on the floor and braced his head against his knees, the book in his hands. *Oh, Father, help me. I'm going crazy.*

* * *

"Here's a tidbit from our University of Tremont contact." The man called One pulled a card from the inside breast pocket of his pin-striped suit jacket. "It's not much, but he thought it was interesting. A potential recruit, perhaps."

"Let's see it." Zero gestured at the computer resting on the vast surface of his mahogany desk.

One slipped the card into its port and accessed the file. The monitor displayed a picture of a young man with hazel eyes, a wry smile, and dark brown hair that looked like it would curl if he skipped a few haircuts.

"His name is Ian Roshek." One slid the computer toward Zero. "He's a history professor."

Zero typed a rapid series of commands. One knew better than to ask what Zero was doing.

A flare of interest lit Zero's face. "Investigate Ian Roshek."

* * *

When Ian told Jill he wasn't facing punishment in the neighborhood or at the university, Jill nearly wept in relief. Not wanting to mar her relief, Ian didn't admit that these reprieves eased only a small part of his worries. No matter how he tried to assure himself that everything was fine, he couldn't forget the fact that a police officer knew he believed in the writings of the church that had stood as one of James Tremont's strongest enemies prior to Separation.

Ian had studied his memories of the interrogation like he was examining a cup of sand grain by grain, hoping to convince himself that Eric was right—that many of his recollections were only nightmares invented by his traumatized imagination. But the more Ian thought about it, the more certain he became that his memories were accurate.

Lt. Kent knew he was a believer, and she loathed him for it. He recalled with inescapable clarity the hatred that had flooded her face when she realized his affinity for the book David Garrett had quoted so fervently.

Yet from the moment that hatred had appeared, she had not harmed him.

For the rest of September, Ian avoided passing the Tremont police complex if at all possible, chilled by the sight of the towering blue-glass headquarters and the stone-and-concrete Detention Annex behind it. Sweat rendered his palms sticky whenever he saw a gray uniform, but the police appeared to pay him no special attention.

By the beginning of October, Ian's neighbors and colleagues were treating him as though his arrest had never happened. Since he hadn't been officially ostracized by the Neighborhood Security Watch, condemned by the Education Regulatory Committee, or even mentioned in news reports, the rumors about him had withered. Only Marta Cluff still took the trouble to glare at him.

The autumn air was crisp with the scent of dry leaves before Ian could stop checking over his shoulder whenever he heard footsteps approaching. But though his fear of arrest was finally receding, he was constantly aware of how close he had come to destroying himself.

It was difficult not to wish that he'd kept his head down and his mouth shut when the auburn-haired girl was attacked. Keeping a low profile had always headed off the worst trouble. If he switched back to this longtime strategy, he'd be safe.

And he would despise himself. He already despised himself for his cowardice at his interrogation, lying as transparently as a child, thinking he could escape the consequences of his choices. He should have declared his faith, refused to name his friends, and endured his punishment with dignity. In the end, his frightened dissembling made no difference anyway. Lt. Kent had easily discerned the nature of his treason even without his confession.

He spent many hours behind the locked door of his bedroom, reading until his eyes burned, trying to draw courage from the histories of Nephi, Alma, Captain Moroni—all the people who had faced far worse challenges and whose faith had never flagged. When he prayed for courage, he felt answering peace, but his fear always returned—fear that he didn't have the strength to stand up for truth, fear of what the consequences would be for Jill and his friends if he were arrested again, fear that he'd choose physical safety over faith. He didn't have the courage of an Abinadi, and he knew it.

His acute sense of isolation didn't help matters; he hadn't heard from Eric or any other member of their discussion group. Even if they couldn't resume their underground meetings, Ian would have found it a great relief to meet Eric for a fierce round of basketball or to blister his feet on one of Eric's hiking expeditions. Countless times, Ian nearly called Eric, but he always stopped himself. He didn't want to make things worse. Eric didn't like to be pushed.

On a Friday evening in late October, Ian sat at the kitchen table grading midterm exams and listening to Jill hum as she prepared for her second date with Daniel Lansbury. After their first date, a brief out-of-town assignment had kept Daniel from calling back. Jill had feared—and Ian had hoped—that she would never hear from Daniel again. Now that he had called, Jill glowed so radiantly that Ian thought her face could have powered half the city.

Ian doubted Daniel Lansbury's interest in Jill would last—not for lack of charm on Jill's part, but because Daniel would eventually learn about Ian's arrest. The son of Councilor Marcus Lansbury would never knowingly date a girl whose brother had such a serious blot on his file. Ian was tempted to point this fact out to Jill, but he couldn't bring himself to erase the excitement in her eyes.

Jill danced into the kitchen, scenting the air with a light fragrance like honeysuckle. "Should I wear my hair loose like this, or should I—" she paused to demonstrate—"clip the front back?"

"Either way is fine."

"You haven't even looked at me!"

Ian glanced up. "Great. It's perfect."

"Which way?"

"Whichever way you want."

"Which way looks *better?*"

Ian rolled his eyes and gave an exasperated smile. "Give me a break, huh? It all just looks like hair to me."

Jill laughed. "Well, at least tell me if you like the dress."

"It looks like a dress, all right." Ian got up and ambled to the cupboard in search of a snack. "What's that tune you were humming? I don't think I've heard it before."

"Oh, be quiet."

"I swear I'm going to hide your violin if you don't leave Mr. Mozart and his concerto alone for a while. It's affecting your brain chemistry. Did you know you're starting to snore in D major?"

"You wouldn't know D major from a dog barking. And I don't want to talk about this tonight."

"Why are you so nervous? You've played a thousand solos."

"Not with the Philharmonic!"

"You'll be fantastic." Ian unearthed a bag of oatmeal cookies. "That's nice perfume. New?"

"You *noticed?*" Jill's cheeks dimpled. "It was a splurge, but I wanted something different. Can you believe *Daniel Lansbury* is taking me to dinner?"

"How can I not believe it when I've been reminded of it every twenty seconds for the past week?"

"I have *not* talked about it that much— Oh, I forgot to tell you. Eric called just before you got home."

Ian nearly sucked a chunk of cookie into his windpipe. He coughed and swallowed. "Did he leave a message?"

"You're supposed to call him back. Why hasn't he been around lately? You're turning into a lump sitting around on the couch reading all the time."

"He's—been busy."

Jill hesitated, and Ian knew she had sensed his discomfort. To head off questions, he said quickly, "What time will Daniel be here?"

"At six. Do you have to wear that old sweatshirt?"

"What's wrong with my sweatshirt?" Ian bit into another cookie and chewed more carefully.

"The neck is all frayed. Put those cookies away! You're getting crumbs all over you."

"You call them crumbs. I call them accessories." Ian spoke with his mouth full just to annoy her. He'd be meeting Daniel for the first time tonight—unless, as Ian hoped, Daniel got called away on a medical emergency and had to cancel the date. Preferably a medical emergency lasting until Jill had married someone else.

The doorbell rang.

"He's early," Jill moaned. "I'm not ready!"

"No problem," Ian said. "I'll just tell Daniel that due to a comb-and-brush crisis you can't go out tonight—"

Jill silenced him with a glare. "Go answer the door for me," she said sweetly, and breezed off to her bedroom.

Suppressing a sigh, Ian stripped off his ratty sweatshirt, ran his fingers through his hair, tucked in his shirt, and walked into the living room to answer the door.

Daniel Lansbury was tall and rangy, maybe three or four inches more than Ian's six feet, with a bony, elegant face, and neatly trimmed brown hair. Dressed in a charcoal-gray suit and maroon silk tie, he looked thoroughly classy—and thoroughly like his father.

"Come on in," Ian said pleasantly. "I'm Jill's brother, Ian."

Daniel extended his hand. His grip was firm, his smile a friendly row of perfect white teeth. "Daniel Lansbury. A pleasure to meet you."

"Likewise."

Daniel came into the living room and stood looking around at the furnishings. Ian was about to offer him a seat when Daniel walked over to the watercolor hanging above the desk and leaned close to examine it. "Jill mentioned that she painted. Is this one of her—ah." He gestured to Jill's signature in the corner of the watercolor. "She's very talented."

"Yes, she is." Ian tried not to stare at Daniel, but Daniel looked so much like Marcus Lansbury that it was unnerving.

"Very talented," Daniel repeated, studying the diamond-clear water sweeping over rippled sand. "This makes me want to visit the ocean again."

"Jill was in Newbold Bay with the Philharmonic last spring. She loved the ocean."

"Ah." Daniel gestured at the blank wall above the couch. "You should put the painting there. Right now, it's almost hidden behind the computer."

"Talk to Jill about it. She's the one who hung it there. I don't think she wanted to draw too much attention to it."

"She should definitely move it. It's something to be proud of." Daniel moved to the wall shelf that held a collection of photographs and picked up a family portrait taken a few months before their father died. "Jill tells me you teach at the University of Tremont."

"Yeah, history. And you're a doctor?"

"That's right. I'm at the Tremont Research Lab, mostly."

The Tremont Research Lab. So Daniel is following in his father's footsteps. "What kind of research do you do?"

"Work that we hope will assist the police in maintaining peace and security." Daniel replaced the portrait and selected a snapshot of Ian and Jill at Lake Serena. "You both look like your mother," he said. "But you've got your father's coloring and build."

"Ian took all the tall genes," Jill said from the doorway.

Daniel turned immediately at the sound of her voice, and the appreciation on his face made Ian wish Jill could have managed to look a little less attractive tonight. Her blond hair curled artfully, flattering the shape of her face and brushing against the soft skin of her neck. Her periwinkle-blue dress turned her eyes a brilliant sapphire, and the rose-petal flush on her cheeks advertised her excitement at seeing Daniel even more than her nervous smile did. Ian gripped the edge of the desk, resisting the urge to shove Daniel out of the apartment.

"Ready?" Daniel replaced the snapshot on the shelf.

"Yes. 'Bye, Ian."

"Have a good evening," Ian said, wishing the opposite. Daniel Lansbury held the door open for Jill and followed her out of the apartment.

Ian stared grimly at the closed door. *Medical research for the police?* That was worse than being related to Marcus Lansbury.

He trotted to the phone and called Eric.

"A few of us are getting together at Pepper's tonight, at eight," Eric said. "Want to join us?"

Ian smiled at the familiar code, feeling instantly better. "I'll be there."

* * *

At seven thirty that night, Ian unlocked the back door of Tremont Electronics, using the key Eric had given him long ago. The hallway was dark, and his footsteps clunked loudly in the deserted building as he jogged down the stairs to the employee lounge.

He flicked on the lights and admired the concrete floor, the scarred cafeteria table, the stained countertop and grimy sink. Savoring a breath of stale-doughnut air, he settled onto a creaky plastic couch.

He pulled his computer out, then put it away without opening the journal article he had planned to read while waiting for the others to arrive. He couldn't concentrate on history tonight. What would he like to discuss with his friends? For one, he'd tell them about Councilor Spencer Brannigan's criticizing the corruption in the Health Services system. Everyone would appreciate the rare gem of encouraging news from the Council.

Boots thudded on the stairs. Ian checked his watch. Seven forty. Eric was prompt to the minute tonight. Probably he was coming from the bar next door.

"Cold outside," Eric muttered, clomping into the room and brushing sleet off his denim jacket. "Thanks for coming on short notice."

"I was glad to be asked."

"We're all getting antsy. I was talking to Tim this evening. We decided we wanted to get together to blow off some steam." Eric tossed his jacket on the table and sprawled in a chair. "I kept checking the reports to see if you'd been blacklisted, but I never saw your name."

"Yeah, they didn't do me."

"Why not? People in my neighborhood have been blacklisted for a lot less than helping a traitor—and getting arrested."

"The police told the Watch to leave me alone. They sent a report saying I'd already paid for my idiocy."

"*The police* ran interference for you?"

"Don't ask me. I can't explain it."

"I can." Eric grinned triumphantly. "I *told* you that you dreamed up all that garbage at police headquarters. That interrogator didn't think you were a traitor. She didn't even think you should be black-listed." Eric tapped his forehead. "You get seriously kooky when you've got a concussion, pal."

Ian smiled blandly. If he didn't want to risk losing Eric's friend-ship again, then this was *not* a point on which to start an argument.

* * *

"He won't change anything." Sherry Mason twined a lock of pumpkin-orange hair around her finger. "The corruption is too entrenched."

Ian leaned forward in his chair. "Nothing's going to happen overnight. But just the fact that he was willing to speak about problems—"

Eric grunted. "Yeah, and how much of the Council thinks special privileges for their pals and lousy care for the rest of us are problems? Brannigan wants us to think he's a hero, but he'll never deliver."

"The guy may be for real," Ian said. "For one thing, he was speaking to a group of government people, and the news reports said nothing about the content of the speech. I don't think this was an attempt to woo the nation with empty promises."

Tim Sandring yawned and shrugged thin shoulders beneath his grease-stained work shirt. "Things don't get better. They get worse."

"Look at it," Eric said. "Brannigan's been a Council Assistant to Health Services for how long? Ten, fifteen years? Do we have the Appeals Board back? Are there better standards for the euthanasia program? Why do you expect instant change just because Brannigan's the chief now?"

Ian rolled his eyes at his friend's obstinate pessimism. "I'm not expecting instant change. But if Councilor Brannigan is willing to admit there are problems, that's cause for hope."

"So why doesn't he admit it to the entire nation?" Eric said. "Because he can't. Because the rest of the Council doesn't support him. He never would have been appointed at all if his father hadn't been President Ryce's favorite toady."

"That's right." Tim poked scrawny fingers into his pocket and came up with the handful of tiny magnets Ian had never seen him without. "You know what Robert Brannigan was like. He's the one who *axed* the Appeals Board."

"But who says Spencer Brannigan is anything like his father? Come on, folks. Won't anybody admit this is good news?"

"It *sounds* good." Sherry was eyeing the door as though finally remembering how nervous she got at these meetings. Ian could never figure out if Sherry truly enjoyed the meetings or if she came just because she didn't want ex-boyfriend Eric mocking her for losing her nerve.

"Sure, good news," Eric said. "If Brannigan really means it about reforming Health Services, he'd better watch his back or his Council pals will make him the victim of an 'anarchist assassination.'"

"Hey, did you hear about those people arrested for sneaking anarchists into the U.S.?" Tim asked.

"I did," Sherry said. "A couple of workers in the Travel Office and a couple of guards on the south border." She wound another lock of hair around her finger. "You'd think the police would be glad to let anarchists leave if they want out."

"Yeah, the U.S. will love it if we start dumping our criminals over their border." Tim was busily sticking the magnets end to end.

"Well, maybe the U.S. wouldn't even notice," Sherry said. "They're *all* anarchists there, right?"

Eric snickered. "Guess what, Sherry? Not *everything* the government tells us about the U.S. is true."

Pink spread over her freckled cheeks. "I was kidding, Eric. But it's not far from the truth. When we listen to those U.S. broadcasts, it's all the same—argue, argue, argue, kids shooting each other, everybody whining about their problems. I think it's amazing they ever cooperated long enough to stand up against James Tremont at all."

"It wasn't hard to stand up to Tremont, since he ran away the minute he saw he had more enemies than friends," Eric said. "The coward. If he'd stayed to fight, who knows what would have happened?"

"It doesn't take any brains to figure that out," Sherry snapped. "He was so outnumbered, he'd have been butchered."

"You sure?" Eric said. "When he carved out New America, the U.S. didn't have the guts to stop him."

"They didn't want civil war," Ian said.

"Yeah, and I never did get that. They let him grab a chunk of land, kick out anyone who didn't love him, and crown himself King Tremont rather than making him pay for wrecking their government and killing their president. Speaking of cowards . . ."

"It wasn't just Tremont they were up against," Ian said. "We're always taught that the reform movement was the brainchild of James Tremont, but that's more propaganda than truth. He was always one of its strongest voices, particularly in the persecution of religious organizations, but it wasn't until after the assassination of President Hayden that he assumed visible leadership."

"So?" Eric said.

"So many of the most powerful people in the nation were involved, including a large segment of the legal community. This wasn't a matter of getting rid of one man and a few fanatic followers. This was the very fabric of the government unraveling, with millions of citizens cheering the disintegration on. And consider that for years prior to this crisis, the U.S. had been fighting a difficult and discouraging war against international terrorist organizations. People were tired of war, and the last thing they wanted was to fight their own people. Allowing Tremont his New America seemed a sensible solution at the time. Borders were preferable to a bloodbath."

"Thanks, Dr. Roshek. Will that question be on the exam?" Eric grinned at Ian. "By the way—" He winked at Sherry—"I *did* bring the radio tonight if anyone wants to listen."

"Not tonight," Tim said. "Sherry's right. It's all the same. Just because it's illegal doesn't mean it's interesting." He tapped his heel against the concrete floor, knocking mud from the tread of his boot. "If you're going to tinker with that radio so it picks up stuff we're not supposed to hear, why don't you fix it so it plays decent music instead of political claptrap?"

"Wipe up that mud, idiot," Eric said. "You want people to know we were here?"

"Let's just talk tonight." Sherry stretched back in her chair like she was making a concerted effort to relax. "We haven't seen each other for ages. Anyone have any news?"

"Only bad news," Eric said. "My mom just got appointed to her Watch board."

"Finally got her dream, huh," Tim said.

"Yeah, her dream is right," Eric said bitterly. "She thinks she's queen of her neighborhood now, like that little rat-woman in your building, Roshek—what's her name?"

"Marta Cluff," Ian supplied.

"Yeah, Cluff. My mom even threw this big party to honor herself."

Tim held the magnet chain in front of his eyes to evaluate his craftsmanship. "She didn't invite you, did she?"

"Yeah, she did."

Tim gawked at Eric. "But I thought she always said you were the reason she—" He stopped abruptly and concentrated on adding another magnet to the chain.

Sherry studied her copper bracelet like she'd never seen it before. Ian examined a stain on the concrete, wishing Tim could manage to think before he spoke. It was always a bad idea to bring up the way Eric's obnoxiously ambitious mother had blamed him for not being patriotic enough, smart enough, or anything enough to bring honors to the family and boost her into the ranks of the neighborhood leadership.

"Yeah, she wanted me there." Eric's voice was harsh. "Now that she's finally royalty, she wants to show how generous she is by allowing losers into her presence."

"Did you go?" Tim asked.

"You crazy? I don't need that."

Sherry smiled nervously. "Well, if she wants to mend fences, you could meet her halfway. Invite her to one of our meetings."

Eric laughed loudly, and Ian drew a breath of relief.

"It'd be worth it just to see her face," Eric said. "But I'd announce it at a Watch meeting. She'd only care if the neighbors found out."

Sherry giggled. "Remember when she invited me to dinner and spent the whole time talking about how proud President Tremont would have been of Councilor Lansbury for starting the Watch?"

Tim wound the magnet chain around his bony wrist. "If Tremont would have thought the Watch was such a great idea, why didn't he organize the Nosy Neighbor Brigade before he died?"

"In Tremont's day, they didn't need to spy on each other," Eric said. "Since they were all down on the ground licking his shoes. Hard to believe people were stupid enough to follow him in the first place."

"Tremont promised them power." Ian knew he was inviting another gibe for sounding like a professor, but he was too interested in the topic at hand to care. "Power and the society of their dreams— peaceful, secure, stable, and purged of what they considered the corrupt and dangerous traditions of the past."

"And no one was bright enough to catch on to the fact that the only people who ended up with power were Tremont and his buddies," Eric said.

Ian smiled wryly. "Well, Tremont took it slowly. For instance, in the early years after Separation, he couldn't create anything as intrusive as the Neighborhood Security Watch because he knew the people of New America wouldn't accept it."

"I don't know about that." Eric kicked the leg of the cafeteria table, dislodging a hardened blob of ketchup. "People would have done anything Mighty King Tremont told them to."

"Sure, they admired him, they followed him, they believed it when he told them the rest of the United States would soon be crawling to their borders begging for admission, and they'd be the rulers of a nation that stretched coast to coast. He was a great flatterer. But remember, his followers anticipated being the controllers, not the controlled. Tremont and his inner circle were bright enough to realize they had to weave the rope one thread at a time."

Tim scratched his head through unruly hair. "They had neighborhood meetings when my parents were young, but you didn't have to join if you didn't want to and there wasn't anything like blacklisting."

"Hey, get this," Eric said. "You know what one of my mom's big responsibilities is? Deciding what kind of flowers to put on Tremont's tomb each week."

Tim gave a squawk of laughter. "They leave flowers at the tomb *every* week?"

"Yeah, they take 'donations' to buy them. Everybody's going broke buying truckloads of flowers. You remember what that neighborhood's like, Roshek. It's still the same as when we were kids, everybody trying to prove they're the biggest Tremont fan around." Eric reached into his inside jacket pocket and pulled out a dog-eared pamphlet. "By the way, here's your beloved David Garrett trash."

Ian reached eagerly for the pamphlet. "Thanks. I was hoping you hadn't . . . uh . . . gotten rid of this."

"Yeah, well, I should've burned it."

"So what did you think?"

"Hmph. At least it was easier to read than your book with its wacky dreams and brothers trying to kill each other and language from the dinosaur age."

"You might have gotten used to the language if you'd read more than twenty pages."

"Yeah, all right. But come on, Roshek. So what if God is real? I don't see Him helping us. So what if some angel gave that book to that John Smith guy?"

"Joseph Smith."

"Whatever. And the stuff Garrett's pamphlet was talking about— if God did choose this continent as some kind of special free land, He sure hasn't checked in on us lately."

"Eric, did you *read* the pamphlet or just skim the first paragraph?"

"I read it, I swear."

"The whole point of it was that this land is blessed to be a land of freedom, but freedom comes only when we're serving God. When we reject God, we lose His blessings. We've created our own captivity."

"Sure, all right." Eric tilted back in his chair. "Books and pamphlets are great if all you want to do is talk, but what we want is *change*."

"How are you planning to bring about this change?"

"Let's see." Eric grinned wolfishly. "A couple hundred thousand soldiers, some high-tech weapons—"

"A prophet taught that the word of God can do more to change people than anything else—including weapons. If you change people's hearts, you'll change the nation."

"Yeah, well, let your prophet friend chew on this one—we're stuck in the middle of ten million people who think religion is a disease that makes people crazy and gets them to rip each other into little blood-soaked pieces. Even if you could preach your book without getting arrested, New Americans wouldn't listen."

"So you take your soldiers and you overthrow the Council," Ian said. "How are you planning to fill the moral vacuum they leave behind?"

"What do you mean 'moral vacuum'?"

"When James Tremont founded New America, he gave complete moral control to the government. He established the rulings of the Supreme Executive Council as the only standard by which behavior could be judged—the only source from which rights could be granted. To suggest the existence of any other source of morality—such as the laws of God—became treason."

"So religion is treason because Tremont wanted to be the boss," Eric said. "You want God to be the boss. I say, let the people be their own boss."

Ian smiled. "Here, I'll put it in practical terms. In order for a society to exist in peace, there must be limits on behavior. Do you agree with that?"

Eric lifted one shoulder. "Yeah, I guess."

"Okay. So limits on behavior can come from within us, as we adhere to moral principles. Or limits can come from outside of us, through force. Right?"

"Yeah, I guess. But—"

"The only way to control a society which lacks an internalized morality is through coercion—limits from without," Ian said. "When you do away with Tremont's coercion, what will replace it?"

"Freedom."

"You won't have freedom. You'll have chaos. You're suggesting we could create a peaceful, stable, free nation simply by exerting force. I don't think that's possible. The political institutions of a free government can't successfully govern an immoral people."

"And you think the source of morality is God."

"If unchangeable principles exist, they have an unchanging source," Ian said.

"So you preach your word of God and that's just going to fix everything."

"It's going to fix a lot more than your advanced weaponry, my friend."

The muscles stiffened in Eric's jaw, then, abruptly, he laughed. "I missed you, Roshek. You don't make sense most of the time, but you're always good for an argument."

"Meet me for racquetball tomorrow morning," Ian said. "I'm sure you'd like a chance to challenge me in a contest you can actually win."

* * *

Early Saturday morning, One entered Zero's office. "News," he said. "It could be important."

"What is it?" Zero sat behind his desk, fingers interlaced, gold watch burnished by the sunlight shining through the bay window.

One extracted a card from his suit pocket. "This is from Seven. The bugs he planted on that history professor have picked up some interesting information."

Zero took the card and slid it into the port. He tapped his palms on the desk as he read. "Seditious meetings. Religious beliefs. A fool caught in David Garrett's net . . . Yet when he was arrested, the police didn't charge him." Zero's thin lips curved in a smile. "Thank Seven for his services and tell him to continue monitoring Ian Roshek. In addition, there is someone new I want him to monitor."

CHAPTER 5

"Thanks for the help." Peter Critchlow managed a smile as he switched off his notepad, but Ian could see that the remnants of Peter's migraine headache still clouded his eyes with pain.

"Congratulations on your midterm," Ian said. "I knew you could do it."

"Thanks to you. You explain things a lot better than the tutors. They're always in such a hurry." Peter peered at his too-large feet and shifted his notepad from hand to hand. "I mean, I'm not criticizing the tutors, I'd never criticize them, they're great—"

"Don't worry about it. But I won't be able to help you in math for much longer. You've about reached the limits of my knowledge."

"Anyway, thanks." Peter made no move to open the door. He looked around the tiny office, scrutinizing the peeling oatmeal-colored paint, the scratched metal desk, Ian's coat and umbrella dangling from a wall hook.

Ian waited. Peter always lapsed into clumsy silences when he was mustering courage for another request.

"Um . . . could we meet again next week?" Peter mumbled. "Sorry to keep pestering you."

"Glad to help. Same time?"

"Great, thanks."

"Not a problem. And I'm sorry it didn't work out about your medicine."

"Dr. Roshek, you were crazy to talk to Health Services for me." Peter fumbled with his notepad, nearly dropping it. "I mean, I'm really grateful, but I don't want you to get in trouble."

"I'm not in trouble. Have a good weekend."

"Thanks. I'm glad it's Friday night." Peter Critchlow shambled out of Ian's office.

Ian checked the time. The appointment with Peter had gone longer than he had anticipated, and it was already seven thirty. He was due to meet his friends downtown at eight thirty, so it wasn't worth going home now. He'd stay on campus, grade some papers, and endure the remaining minutes until he could leave for the meeting.

Three weeks and three meetings had passed since he and his friends had resumed holding their discussion group, and Ian appreciated his friends more than ever. Eric argued with him every time, even heatedly, but the farewells at the end of the meetings were amiable. And between meetings Ian was regularly nursing strained muscles; Eric had a tradition of confiscating Ian's computer, marching him outside, and shoving a basketball or football in his hands.

Ian retrieved a bag of pretzels from his desk drawer, propped his feet on his desk, opened his computer, and began the first research paper.

Two papers later, a knock at the door startled him. *Who would stop by so late on a Friday night?* He stood and reached for the doorknob, face composed in the guarded smile he favored when dealing with faculty and students.

A woman stood in the hallway. Her face was stony white, her eyes black holes.

Ian's smile froze.

"May I come in?" Lt. Kent asked in that cold voice Ian had heard so often in his nightmares.

Straining to bend a hand that seemed to have become a block of ice, Ian gestured her into his office, wondering why a police officer would ask permission, and wondering how he could have ever relaxed knowing Lt. Kent could come for him at any time.

Kent closed the door. "Sit down," she said.

Ian obeyed.

Kent sat in the chair Peter had vacated. From her pocket, she withdrew an envelope and handed it to Ian.

Inside the envelope were several printed pages. It took Ian a moment to figure out what he was reading. When comprehension hit, it was like a lead ball crashing against his chest. This was a partial transcript of the meeting he and his friends had held last week at

Tremont Electronics. The final page included a list of names and addresses: his own, Eric's, Tim's, and Sherry's.

"I did not come to arrest you," Kent said. "The transcript is only meant to discourage you from denying already-proven facts."

Ian crammed the pages back into the envelope and handed it to Lt. Kent. "If you're not here to arrest me, what do you want?"

"You're a religious believer," Kent said. "A Christian. A would-be Mormon. Why?"

The phrasing of the question jolted him. Outside of academic circles, he had never heard believers referred to as anything other than Garrett followers. To call them by their official or traditional names was to grant them too much legitimacy.

"Why?" Kent repeated.

Ian's throat was so dry he felt like he'd been gargling sand. "What do you mean?" he croaked.

"You are a historian," she said. "You know the lessons of the past. Why would you adopt religious superstitions that have long proven to be only a source of division and conflict?"

Ian loosened his tie with rubbery fingers and said nothing.

"Your treason is already irrefutably established," Kent said. "I am not asking you to incriminate yourself or anyone else. You have nothing to lose by answering my question."

"Why are you asking it?"

Her bone-white fingers crumpled the corner of the envelope. "I am—curious."

"Are you a traitor, or is this part of some police research project?"

Her already pale cheeks turned gray. After a heavy moment of silence, she slid the envelope in her pocket and said, "I am not here on police business. Answer my question."

"You're a traitor?"

"Answer my question."

Ian reached for the insulated cup on the corner of his desk and sipped cold water, drinking slowly to give himself time to think.

"What makes you so certain Jesus Christ exists?" Kent asked. "Did your parents teach you these things?"

"Are you kidding?"

"Your study of history, then?"

"Partly," he admitted.

"You wrote your doctoral dissertation on James Tremont's religious background."

"Yes."

"Were you corrupted by your research?"

"It was a factor."

"A significant factor, I imagine, since you are enamored of the same type of Christianity forced on President Tremont in his childhood."

Again, her words startled Ian. Few people were aware of the specific nature of Tremont's religious background. Ian hadn't heard it discussed until he was well into his graduate studies.

"How did you get hold of David Garrett's pamphlet?" Kent asked.

"Found it on campus."

"Where did you get the Book of Mormon?"

Ian said nothing. Was there any hope he could keep Laura Stewart out of this?

Kent's eyes were opaque, but tension showed in the brittle, white lines of her face. "You have a meeting tonight," she said. "At Tremont Electronics on Ingram Road."

"How exactly have you been monitoring us?"

"There is a voice transmitter concealed in the lounge where you hold your meetings."

"How long has it been there?"

"Since the beginning of October."

So she had eavesdropped on all three of their recent meetings. "How did you know where we were meeting?"

"It was not difficult to deduce."

"Tell me, please."

She shrugged. "Bus-card records showed that until your arrest, you had a regular pattern of weekend trips to Ingram Road. After your arrest, you stopped those trips. You also severed contact with Eric Vettori, with whom you had formerly had frequent association. Vettori's file showed he was unlikely to have ended the friendship due to disgust at your arrest or fear for his reputation. It seemed more credible that he was a participant in your treason and you were avoiding each other because you feared police attention.

"With Vettori's workplace on Ingram Road, it was possible you had been holding treasonous meetings at the electronics building. Many anarchists prefer to meet away from home to avoid the scrutiny of their Neighborhood Security Watch. I planted the transmitter on the assumption that you would resume meeting once you felt safe doing so."

"Why are you here?" Ian asked. "If you don't want to arrest us, what do you want?"

Sweat glistened at her hairline like miniature balls of ice. "I want to come to your meeting tonight."

"Why?"

"To observe. I will not interfere with your activities."

"That's not—easy to believe, Lieutenant."

"Give me time to convince you that I am not here under orders. Allow me to attend the meeting."

Ian lifted his hands. "Can I stop you? Come if you want, but it won't be much of a meeting."

"Then do not tell your friends who I am."

"What?"

"Introduce me however you like, but do not tell them I am with the police."

"You're crazy!"

"If you reveal my identity, your friends will panic. They may do something stupid and get themselves arrested."

"If you want to learn about us, why didn't you stay in your office and listen through your eavesdropping devices?"

"I am not here simply to gather data."

"You want to join us?"

Kent hesitated. Did her carefully stony expression admit a flicker of pain? "I—might."

"Why?" Ian asked, watching her closely.

"I have . . . questions."

"Questions?"

She tilted her head in a slight nod.

"Questions even the Tremont Police Service can't answer?"

Another curt nod.

"What could possibly corrupt a police officer to the point that she would let a Garrett follower go free and then try to join his treasonous discussion group?"

Kent's now-drawn expression reminded Ian of the way his mother had looked in her last weeks of life, as pain overwhelmed inadequate medication. "Your friends would never welcome a police officer," she said. "Please. Let me attend anonymously."

"You didn't answer my question."

She licked pale lips, but said nothing.

"Why should I trust you?" Ian found himself speaking gently. The pain in Kent's face made it impossible to be harsh.

"I protected you." Her voice was almost a whisper. "I released you when I shouldn't have. I lied on the record of your screening. Isn't that enough?"

"You also tortured me," Ian said.

Kent averted her eyes. Ian waited for her to offer some excuse to reconcile her brutal behavior with her claim of being a traitor, but she didn't speak.

"How do I know you didn't release me as part of some police plot?" Ian asked.

"What would we gain by releasing you?"

"The names of my friends. Information about my treason."

"Why would we waste our time tracking you when a memory stimulant drug would have given us all the information we required?"

A truth drug. Nausea spiraled in Ian's stomach. "If you have a drug like that, why didn't you use it on me the moment I was arrested?"

"The nature of Information Extraction makes it impractical for use on prisoners who may not be guilty of significant crimes. Had I followed correct procedure, I would have sent you for Information Extraction when I finished screening you, only after guilt was established." A bead of sweat slipped down her forehead and soaked into the black curve of her eyebrow. "You fear this is a trap. It's not. But if it were, there would be nothing you could do to protect your friends, regardless of what you tell them about me."

"If you really want to join us, you can't do it under false pretenses."

"If you tell your friends my identity now, there will be nothing for me to join. Your group will immediately disband."

She was right. Ian couldn't imagine Sherry, Tim, and Eric talking treason with a police officer.

"I am not asking you to keep silence indefinitely," Kent said. "I am only asking you to give your friends time to get used to me."

"Look, I really can't hide—"

"One meeting, then." She gripped the arms of the chair so tightly that her hands were white-knuckled claws. "Conceal my identity until after the meeting tonight."

"Lieutenant—"

"Please. After the meeting I will speak with you alone and answer whatever questions you wish to ask concerning my—motivations. Then you may reevaluate and conclude whether it would be wiser to tell your friends the truth immediately, or to wait."

"Why not just explain yourself now?"

"No . . . there's not time."

"Then explain at the meeting. To all of us."

"Explanations are not . . . easily given." Kent's voice cracked, revealing a glimpse of her desperation. She swallowed and drew a deep, slow breath. "I would prefer not to offer explanations in such a tense environment."

A tense environment. Ian pictured Eric subjecting an ashen-faced Lt. Kent to a relentless grilling about why she was there.

"Please," she said. "Your meeting will not provide me any new evidence against you or your friends."

True, Ian reasoned. She already knew their treason in full. "*You're crazy, or that lieutenant is crazy, or the police are playing some sick game*—" The words came to him again. "Are you armed?" Ian asked over the mental echo of Eric's disquieting suggestions.

"I did not bring any weapons."

Ian regarded her dubiously.

She rose to her feet, removing her long black coat, and handed the coat to him. She was wearing a white sweater that fit smoothly against her body and a pair of black slacks cut slim. She turned slowly so he could observe her from all angles. Unless she had the disassembled bits of a gun hidden in her socks, he couldn't see how she could have any weapons concealed on her. He searched the pockets of her coat and handed it back.

Taking her to the meeting couldn't make things worse for his friends, but once they found out he'd brought a police officer undercover . . . Ian grimaced at the thought of Eric's anger. But if he immediately introduced Kent as a police officer, there would be no welcome for her—only hostility and fear.

If she was telling the truth about protecting him, then he owed her a colossal debt. He had no proof that she *was* telling the truth, but neither did he have proof to the contrary, and he found it hard to believe that chalky, anguished face belonged to a police officer carrying out a routine assignment.

"All right," he conceded. "I'll give you one meeting, but afterward, you'd better be ready to explain yourself."

An indecipherable mix of relief and fear flashed on her face. "I will answer your questions. What will you—tell your friends about me?"

"Let's see." What could he tell them that would be true but wouldn't violate his agreement? "What's your first name?"

"Alisa," she murmured.

Alisa. Not what he would have guessed. The name seemed too gentle. "Very well, Alisa. I'll introduce you as someone interested in what we're doing and leave it at that. If you want to add anything, go ahead, but tell the truth or I'll correct you."

Blood was seeping back into her face, but she still appeared on the verge of collapse. "Will they accept such a sketchy introduction?"

"As long as you're with me, yes. Do you need to sit down for a few minutes before we leave? You don't look too well."

"I'm fine." Kent opened the door and headed for the stairs. Ian followed her.

Lt. Kent had a car parked behind the Ryce Building, an angular blue Honda. Ian climbed into the passenger seat and watched Kent out of the corner of his eye as she drove toward downtown. She held herself so stiffly that he thought if he touched her he might feel the lifeless chill of a statue, not living warmth. One thing was certain— she wasn't gloating over her success at getting him to take her to the meeting. She looked like she was battling a frantic urge to flee.

What made her willing to follow him into a nest of traitors?

At Tremont Electronics, Ian wiped his sweaty hands on his coat before unlocking the back door. He gestured Kent into a corridor lit only by an exit sign and reflections from the security lights in the parking lot. Kent stepped to the side, allowing Ian to pass in front of her and lead the way to the lounge.

"You sure you want to do this?" he asked.

"Proceed." It was a rasp of sound, the sort of noise Ian imagined Kent would make should he jam a gun into her ribs and announce he was going to kill her.

They were the first ones to arrive in the lounge; Eric wasn't due for another few minutes. Kent ran her hand along the underside of the cafeteria table and removed a silvery, button-sized object. The transmitter.

"Is there another of those in my apartment?" Ian asked.

Kent slipped the bug into her pocket. "Yes."

"And in my friends' apartments?"

"No."

At least his friends had escaped this intrusion. "I want you to come remove the transmitter. *Tonight.*"

"It's on the underside of the desk in your living room. Pull it off and unscrew the back. That will deactivate it." She hung her coat on a chair near the door and sat down, spine ruler-straight. "You won't tell your friends who I am?"

"I'll keep my word. Relax, all right? You look like you're facing a firing squad. We're not going to hurt you."

She swallowed, the tendons in her neck taut. "Your sister. She is not involved in any of your treasonous activities?"

Ian tensed. "No."

"Does she know of your devotion to your Book of Mormon?"

"No."

"Why haven't you told her?"

Ian didn't answer. He wasn't about to open up to Kent about the night he *had* tried to talk to Jill. Tried and failed miserably.

"Do you fear she would turn you in?" Kent asked.

"No. She'd never do that." Ian felt a burst of anger at himself. What was he doing, telling a police officer that Jill would place family above loyalty to the Council?

Heavy, rapid footsteps echoed off the stairs. Hardness formed over Kent's features like a mask.

Eric burst into the room and stopped in midstride.

"Hi, Eric," Ian said. "This is Alisa. She's interested in what we're doing, and she'll be joining us tonight."

"Uh—yeah," Eric said gruffly. "Thanks for the warning, Roshek. Nice to meet you, Alisa."

Kent nodded.

Eric shrugged off his jacket, his eyes glued to Lt. Kent. "You—uh—want something hot to drink?"

"No, thank you," Kent said quietly.

"You sure? It's freezing out tonight."

"I'm fine."

"Coke? Root beer?"

At the open admiration in Eric's expression, Ian took another look at Alisa Kent and had to concede that he would have found her strikingly attractive under other circumstances. Her satiny black hair was styled into the kind of twist that used to have Jill flinging her brush at the mirror when she was attempting something elegant for a formal occasion. Her dark eyes were mesmerizing, but right now they were cold and humorless; her skin was milky smooth, but too pale over gracefully sculpted cheekbones. Her full lips would have made for a beautiful smile, if Kent ever adopted that expression.

Eric removed a glass mug and a packet of apple powder from the cupboard. "A guy showed up at work today with a package of coffee." He filled his mug with steaming water. "Coffee! Can you believe it? The import tax alone must have cost him a week's salary. What a fool."

Tim trotted into the room, his weedy body lost inside an enormous green parka.

"You're early," Eric said. "You want people to see us all stampeding in here together?"

"Sorry. The buses were on time for once and—" Tim goggled at Lt. Kent.

"This is Alisa," Eric said. "Ian's friend."

"Um . . . wow. New recruits." Tim ran a hand over his chronically messy hair. "Hi."

Eric leaned against the counter and sipped his cider. "So, Alisa. You've done this sort of thing before?"

"No."

"First jaunt into treason?"

Kent said nothing. Eric opened his mouth to ask another question, but closed it at the subzero chill on Kent's face. Ian loosened his already loose tie and tried to look calm.

"How's Jill?" Tim asked. "She out with Lansbury's son again tonight?"

"'Fraid so."

"Can't you do something about that? I sure wouldn't want my sister all smoochy with a Lansbury."

"What can I do?"

"I thought you were her guardian. Ground her or something."

"She's twenty-two, Tim."

"Oh, yeah. Time flies."

Ian managed a smile. "The good news is that Daniel seems like a genuinely nice guy."

Tim looked dubious. "Marcus Lansbury's kid, a nice guy?"

"If you can overlook a mild case of arrogance," Ian said. "And he plays a decent game of chess."

"You play chess with him?" Eric asked.

"I did last night. He came to see Jill, but she was late getting back from her concert."

"So him and Jill are pretty serious?"

"She denies it, but yes."

"A Roshek and a Lansbury. What a pair." Eric snickered. "Has he got a sister you could marry?"

"No such luck. Jill said he's an only child."

The door swung open and Sherry entered, her freckled cheeks flushed from the cold. "Hi, everyone—oh—"

"Alisa," Eric made the introduction. "Ian's friend."

"It's about time we got another woman here." Sherry settled next to Lt. Kent. "Oh, I *love* your necklace!"

Kent looked startled. Her hand moved to her throat. "Thank you."

"I've been searching for something like that. You know, delicate, classy. The stuff in the stores is so clunky. Do you mind if I ask where you got it?"

A hint of pink colored Kent's cheekbones. "I—made it."

"You made it! Oh, you're a jewelry designer."

"No. It's just a hobby."

Ian leaned forward for a better view of the necklace he had hardly noticed Kent was wearing. Fine silver wires twined in an intricate, lacy pattern that curved just below the hollow of her throat.

"It's gorgeous," Sherry said. "Do you sell the jewelry you make?"

"No. I'm—new at it, just learning."

"Just learning! How long have you been doing it?"

"About a year." Kent's voice wasn't quite friendly, but it had lost much of its chill.

"I've been looking for the perfect necklace to go with this dress that I . . . well . . . I guess I'd better go ahead and make my announcement." Sherry spread a big smile around the room. "I'm engaged. Sean asked me on Tuesday."

"Congratulations!" Ian said.

"Thanks." Sherry avoided looking at Eric's stunned expression. "But I'm afraid I won't be coming here again. I can't even stay tonight. I hate to drop out—especially now that the group is growing—"

"Yeah, sure," Eric said. "You've been looking for an excuse to jump ship."

Sherry stiffened. "That's not true, Eric. I just feel that—well, it really wouldn't be fair to Sean."

"Afraid the twit might turn you in?" Eric asked.

"Sean wouldn't turn me in." Sherry's biting tone matched Eric's. "But if I'm going to be involved in underground meetings, he ought to know about it, and right now he's not ready. Besides, I'll only be in Tremont for a couple more weeks. Sean just got promoted to manager and he's been transferred to the office in Hamilton. We're moving."

"We'll miss you," Ian inserted before Eric could toss out another snide comment.

"I'll miss all of you too, but I'm excited to move to Hamilton. I hear the mountains are beautiful. And Sean is going to teach me to ski."

Eric curled his lip. "With that twit teaching you, you'll probably break your neck."

"Shut up, Eric," Tim muttered.

Pointedly turning away from Eric, Sherry opened a canvas grocery bag and pulled out a faded copy of *The Federalist Papers*.

"I thought I'd better bring this back tonight. I'm embarrassed to admit that I didn't even finish the parts you marked for me, Ian. It was interesting, but kind of hard to understand." She rose to pass the book to Ian. Lt. Kent held out a hand.

"May I?"

"Sure." Sherry gave her the book.

Kent turned the pages carefully. Ian clenched his hands in his pockets. Before lending the book to Sherry, he had clipped out the title page where Laura's grandfather had written his name, but he still worried that somehow, with the knifelike intuition of a police officer, Kent would be able to identify the former owner of the book just by reading the notes scrawled in the margins.

Sherry glanced at her watch. "I've got to run."

"What's the rush?" Eric asked caustically. "Got to go help Sean hang some posters for the Watch?"

"I'm meeting a group of school friends for a late dinner," Sherry snapped.

"Stop in and say good-bye before you move," Ian said, glaring Eric to silence.

"I'll try to do that. Thanks for everything." Sherry waved and hurried out of the lounge.

Silence smothered the room. Kent was still perusing *The Federalist Papers,* Eric was glowering, and Ian was trying to think of something to say that didn't involve Sherry's impending marriage, Eric's jealousy, or Lt. Kent.

Tim pulled the handful of magnets from his pocket. "Gain Alisa, lose Sherry," he said. "Did you bring the radio, Eric?"

"Hey—yeah, I did." Eric reached eagerly for the backpack under his chair. "We can catch the end of—"

A loud knock at the door made them all jump.

"Sherry?" Tim mouthed.

"She wouldn't knock," Eric whispered.

Ian's heart thumped into his throat. He darted an accusing glare at Lt. Kent, but her face was bloodless with fear. With a quick, sharp motion, she tossed the book to Ian. He shoved it into his coat pocket.

The door swung open and into the silence boomed a cheerful voice. "Anybody home?" The man who sauntered into the lounge had a solid, muscular body, longish blond hair, and a grin that reminded Ian of the way his football-hero cousin smiled whenever he spotted a blacklisted person he could abuse.

"Man, you all look like kids with your hands in the cookie jar." The man plunked down on the couch.

"Who are you?" Eric asked roughly.

"A friend. You can call me Seven." His broad smile displayed a chipped front tooth. "Sorry to sneak up on you, but it wasn't safe to warn you first. Someone might have heard us talking, and we couldn't risk that. You know what I mean."

Eric stood, muscles flexed for a fight. "I don't know what you're talking about."

"Ah, cool down. We know everything you've been up to. Secret meetings, banned books, illegal radio broadcasts, blah blah blah. Do I look like the police? I told you, I'm a friend."

"A friend," Tim repeated hoarsely.

"Righto. I'm part of a group fighting for freedom."

"Freedom fighters!" Eric almost shouted the words.

"Try not to yell, eh? We call ourselves the Liberty Cadre. Heard of us?"

"Sure we have, everyone has." Eric's voice shook with excitement. "On the news they're always whining about the Liberty Cadre, but we thought maybe it didn't exist, that it was a Council lie to scare people into thinking the anarchists were some big menace."

"We exist, all right. We have cells all over the nation—and in the U.S. And we're always on the lookout for people who love freedom like we do."

"How did you find us?" Ian could barely hear his own voice over his noisy heartbeat.

Seven shrugged musclar shoulders. "We're pros at spotting the right kind of people. You don't need to know the details now. Hey, that reminds me—" He leaned over and fumbled at the leg of the couch. "Guess we don't need this anymore . . . Where is it . . . ? Ah . . ." He held up the transmitter he had retrieved, nearly identical to the one Kent had taken from the table.

"You were eavesdropping on us?" Eric's face creased with anger.

"Sure we were. You think we'd come blundering in here without knowing exactly what you were up to? We have to be careful."

"Did you say you're in the U.S.?" Tim almost fell off the edge of his chair as he leaned toward Seven. "How do you sneak people across the border?"

"Get real. The border nets are nothing to the Cadre. We can get phony IDs and phony travel passes."

"You can go to the U.S. whenever you want?" Eric asked.

"We go when we need to. Tons of people there support us. How do you think we get our weapons?"

"An armed resistance!"

Seven chuckled at Eric's awestruck tone. "Sit down before you keel over. Did you think you're the only ones who've figured out Jimmy Tremont was a liar and our parents were morons to follow him? We've had enough."

Ian began mentally listing the atrocities publicized as the work of the Liberty Cadre. Of course, who said the Liberty Cadre had really committed those crimes? He glanced at Lt. Kent to see how she was taking this. She was staring straight ahead, jaw rigid, eyes smoking with a fury that seemed to heat black pupils into glowing coals. Was she angry at being caught off guard by this Liberty Cadre recruiter—or was it something else?

"You said you can forge IDs?" Tim's magnets lay in his palm in a forgotten lump.

"How else could we move people when the police get hot on their trails?" Seven asked. "We can move them to other cities, or if things really get hot, move them to the U.S. or Canada. Right now, if you and your friends get in trouble, you're stuck. With the Cadre, we can get you to safety."

Eric looked ready to break into a tap dance. "This is incredible!"

"The police have been trying to stamp us out for years, but we just get stronger. Those Council clowns are on the way out. We need your help, all of you."

"Are you nuts? Of course we'll help," Eric said. "This is what we've been waiting for! The chance to fight, to really make a difference—how big are you?"

"Beats me. Our leader didn't figure I needed to know the head count. We're big enough to cause trouble. Lots of trouble."

"What is your leadership structure?" Ian asked.

"We call our leader Zero. We don't know his name, but we know he has powerful connections all over the place. He keeps his identity secret so no one can tattle on him if they're arrested."

Eric nodded and sat down. "Smart."

"Is he alone responsible for your agenda?" Ian asked. "Or do your members work together to decide—"

"We're fighting a war, Roshek. Soldiers don't sit and yak about strategy. That's up to the general. Zero knows what he's doing."

"Do you have police contacts?" Tim asked breathlessly.

"Sure we do."

Kent shifted in her seat. She was looking at Seven and there was no mistaking the hatred in her gaze. Seven didn't seem to notice.

Eric grinned at Ian. "I've got to hand it to you, pal. You were right when you said wait, that the time to fight would come."

"Well—look, we've got to examine all the—" Ian began cautiously.

"Don't get cold feet now. The Liberty Cadre is a lot better than books and pamphlets and windbags like Spencer Brannigan," Eric said.

"Brannigan!" Seven exclaimed. "You're joking, right? You think anyone on the Council is going to help us?"

"Roshek thinks Brannigan's going to fix Health Services," Eric said. "And free the nation."

"I said his willingness to discuss problems in Health Services is a step forward," Ian clarified. "That's all."

"Yeah, we know about that speech where he blasted his own department." Seven rolled his eyes. "Reform. Big deal. That's like dumping a cup of bleach in your septic tank and telling the kids it's now a swimming pool. We don't need reform. We need revolution. Brannigan is worthless."

"So much for your hero, Ian," Eric said, but under Ian's steady gaze, his grin went sheepish. "Sorry, sorry, just kidding."

"If you're looking for a hero, Roshek, find someone else to admire," Seven said. "If we want change, we've got to fight for it. The Cadre is the heart of what will become a national uprising. We're tired of being stepped on. We're freedom fighters and we're going to win." He paused and grinned at Lt. Kent, finally acknowledging her angry gaze. "Something you'd like to say?"

Kent spoke in a voice so filled with enmity that it chilled Ian to the bone. "*Freedom* fighters? Why don't you tell them the truth, you bloodthirsty, anarchist butcher?"

CHAPTER 6

Ian felt like someone had emptied a bucket of ice water over his head. Eric and Tim gaped at Lt. Kent, speechless.

"Well, then." Seven's voice drifted lazily into the silence. "If it's truth we're after, maybe there are a few things you'd like to say, sweetie. It was rude of you not to introduce yourself, but I guess the Tremont Police Service doesn't worry about good manners."

"*What?*" Eric sprang to his feet. "Wait, who *is* she?"

"Maybe you ought to ask your buddy Professor Roshek," Seven said.

Ian opened his mouth, but no words came. What could he say? That yes, Alisa was a police officer, but she sympathized with traitors? Who was going to believe that now?

"Tongue-tied?" Seven asked. "Hey, I'll be glad to help you out. Eric, meet Lt. Alisa Kent, honored member of the Tremont Police Service, currently assigned to the Sedition and Treason Division. Youngest officer in the history of the division to reach the rank of lieutenant, enough commendations to crash the memory banks at the Central Identity Network, recently received a gold-class James Tremont Patriotic Service Award. Plenty of brains and plenty of ambition. Got your eye on the Council someday, eh, Lieutenant? Councilor over Internal Defense?"

The silence in the lounge was so complete that the water dripping from the rusty faucet rang like gravel against sheet metal.

Eyes glassy with disbelief, Eric took a step toward Ian. "But you . . . I thought . . . she's the one who—?" He stopped. "You're insane. Absolutely *crazy.*"

"I can explain—Eric—"

"You can explain, huh?" Eric's rage exploded. *"You sold us out. That's how you saved your neck when you were arrested."*

Anger burned Ian's face. *"No."*

"Relax, Vettori," Seven said. "Roshek didn't tattle. The lieutenant isn't here on official business. This is just some off-duty entertainment." His muscles rippled with the grace of a boa constrictor as he linked his fingers behind his neck. "Isn't that right, honey?"

Kent said nothing.

"Don't get shy," Seven said. "We're on the same side now."

"The same side?" Kent's tone dripped venom. "With you and your gang of assassins, bombers, and saboteurs? We'll never be on the same side—Mr. Siskell."

"Now, honey, it's reckless of you to go around blabbing people's secret identities. You ought to be more careful. We'll have to work with you before you're fit for the Cadre."

"Fit for the Cadre?" At the fury in Kent's voice, Tim shot a panicky look at Ian. Ian could only stare blankly back.

"We're your only friends now, sweetheart," Seven—Siskell—said. "Think what your boss—Hofstader, isn't it?—would do if he learned what you've been up to."

"Are you threatening me?"

"Oh, sweetie, don't get uptight! This isn't blackmail. It's an invitation. We want your help."

"I'm not interested in slaughtering innocent civilians."

Siskell's mouth slid into a greasy smile. "Yeah, you'd never hurt the innocent. Just out of curiosity, did you ever tell your friend Dr. Roshek how that university contraband sweep was arranged?"

"Tell me what?" Ian asked.

"That it was a setup, for starters."

"A setup!" Tim's eyes bulged. "Are you saying the police planted those pamphlets?"

"Think about it. Kent and her friends had to make sure there were enough 'anarchists' to catch. It would have been a sad day if all the searchers found in peoples backpacks were moldy peanut-butter sandwiches."

"They slipped contraband stuff into random bags?" Tim squeaked.

"Not random. They picked students who were known to be kind of . . . oh . . . outspoken or weird. They tracked them for a couple of weeks to get their schedules and their routes down—they wanted at least a couple of traitors to pass through each search station, see." Siskell's grin widened. "Oh, and they told the supervisors not to interfere if things got rough *and* they encouraged the searchers to make examples out of anyone caught—to rile up the crowd—which pretty well guaranteed that blood was going to splatter."

"You've got to be kidding," Eric said.

"Ask the lieutenant if it's true."

Kent said nothing. Ian thought of the auburn-haired girl, blood streaming down her face. She'd been innocent.

"Want to be free of a government that would pull that kind of stunt?" Siskell asked. "That's what the Cadre is fighting for."

"The Tremont Police Service does what is necessary to ensure national security." Kent spat the words at Siskell. "What does the Cadre offer? Chaos. Anarchy."

"Freedom," Siskell said. "But I guess you don't know what that word means. Or did your old friend Dave Garrett teach you a thing or two before you killed him?"

Kent's shoulders jerked, and for an instant it were as though the locked door that shielded her soul opened a crack, her face exposing a maelstrom of such scorching agony that Ian stared in shock. She leapt up and walked out of the lounge.

"Stop her," Tim moaned. "She'll tell the police—"

Eric lunged for the door.

"Let her go," Siskell said. "She won't turn you in."

Eric jerked around to face Siskell. "But she hates us! You heard her."

"She hates the Liberty Cadre," Ian clarified as he grasped at a scrap of understanding.

The door at the top of the stairs thumped shut, silencing Kent's footsteps.

"She feels guilty about what she's doing," Siskell said. "She's gone sour on the police, so she frees Roshek and inches toward your group. You're not doing any real damage, and she's curious. But the instant she meets up with a group that has power, she starts screaming 'anarchist.'"

Eric's legs were still bent, ready to launch him in pursuit of Lt. Kent. "What makes you think she *has* gone sour on the police?"

"She's not under orders. We made sure of that before we contacted you. If her pals learn she's been flirting with treason—" Siskell drew a finger across his throat. "But you played a dangerous game tonight, Roshek. How could you be sure you weren't setting your friends up in a trap?"

"She already knew everything about us," Ian said, burning with confusion. He explained how he had come to bring Lt. Kent to the meeting.

"This doesn't make sense." Tim withered in his chair like a deflated balloon. "How can she torture Ian and then turn around and join our meetings?"

"The poor girl's a tad confused." Siskell slapped a hand over his heart. "Tragic, the people who turn traitor. Even lifelong superpatriots like Alisa Kent. Junior Regional Security Watch Rep at 15, police lieutenant at 26, anarchist at 30."

"Regional Security Watch Rep?" Eric said. "I don't remember her speaking at our regional meetings."

"Oh, she didn't grow up in Tremont. She's from up north. Jameston."

Eric balled his fists. "So if she's a traitor but she's not with the Liberty Cadre, what *has* she been involved in?"

"Nothing, as far as we know, except for neglecting to chuck your pal Roshek into prison. Quit hovering there, Vettori, you're giving me the twitchies. We'll keep the reins on Kent. She can't hurt you."

"*She can't hurt us?* She's a police officer!"

"A police officer with a flaw." Siskell's chipped tooth caught the light as he grinned. "We'll make good use of her."

"She knew your name," Eric said uncertainly.

"Yeah, sad, eh? I work all underground now. More fun that way."

Tim looked dubious. "If the police know who you are, how can you sneak around Tremont without getting caught?"

Siskell waved his right forearm. "Phony ID, Tim. And I'm careful about where I go and when. I'm out mostly at night. Disguises—hair color, skin color, wigs, contacts—like I said, it's fun."

The gleeful malice in Siskell's voice reminded Ian of all the accusations Lt. Kent had aimed at the Liberty Cadre. "What type of operations *is* the Liberty Cadre involved in, Mr. . . . uh . . . Siskell? Are the things the news reports say about the Cadre true?"

"You think we can bring down the government without spilling some blood?"

"I'm just asking if—"

"Say enough prayers and read enough Garrett claptrap and the Council will roll over and die. Is that it?"

"There is a time for armed rebellion," Ian said clearly. "But there's a large difference between a just war and cold-blooded terrorism."

"Anything to bring down monsters like Ryce and Lansbury is a just war."

"You think attacking civilians in an effort to intimidate—"

"If you support the Council, you're not innocent. We're talking about people still stupid enough to believe that if we keep ourselves under Jimmy T's heel that he'll make us kings, people who would tear you apart, Roshek, if they knew what you were. New America is a big, ugly mistake, and we'll do what it takes to bring it down."

Eric's gaze drilled into Ian. "I don't think the Cadre has the manpower to directly confront the police—and the army," Eric said. "They have to do what they can with what they've got."

Siskell nodded. "If you want to join the fight for freedom, here's your chance. But if you'd rather cower at the sidelines with your police friend, or pray, go ahead. Not everyone has the guts to fight for what they believe."

* * *

Clouds blocked the few stars visible above Tremont, painting the sky a solid, dull black as Ian emerged from Tremont Electronics. He was the first to leave the meeting. After an hour-long discussion about the Liberty Cadre, in which every concern Ian voiced was either mocked or ignored, Siskell had exchanged a pointed glance with Eric, commented on how late it was, and suggested the meeting be adjourned. Eric had instantly suggested that Ian leave first.

In reality, it was only ten, and Ian suspected that if he were to wait and watch the door of the electronics building, it would be a long time before anyone else exited. He could march back into the meeting, but by this point, he was glad to be out of there. He was worried about what Lt. Kent was up to, sickened by Siskell's inability to show any link between the Liberty Cadre's violent activities and their goal of bringing freedom to New America, and stung by the way Eric had joined Siskell in contemptuously dismissing everything Ian said. Eric's anger over Lt. Kent accounted for his contempt, but it didn't account for his instant infatuation with the Cadre. Tim had also shown mindless enthusiasm for every word Siskell spoke, but that didn't surprise Ian—Tim took his cues from Eric. If Eric had regarded the Cadre dubiously, Tim would have done the same.

Why couldn't Eric see that a gang like the Liberty Cadre would never bring freedom, regardless of how clever they were at forging ID chips?

The bus stop was jammed with people, so Ian stood outside the enclosure, his shoulders bowed against the wind. Was it coincidence that Siskell had shown up the same week as Lt. Kent? Not likely. A traitorous police officer would be of much greater value to the Liberty Cadre than a few members of a dissident discussion group. But if it was Kent they hoped to recruit, they had failed—yet Siskell hadn't seemed remotely dismayed by her hostility.

"Did your old friend Dave Garrett teach you a thing or two before you killed him?"

From Lt. Kent's reaction, it was plain that Siskell had struck a vicious blow. Had his reference to David Garrett as an "old friend" been merely sarcastic, or had Kent known Garrett prior to his arrest?

Shivering, Ian burrowed his chin deeper in the collar of his coat. It had been his own guilty similarities to David Garrett that had brought a halt to his interrogation. And it was interesting that Alisa Kent hailed from Jameston. *If memory serves me right . . .* Ian stripped off his gloves, yanked his computer out of his pocket, and did a quick search of the archived police bulletins.

David Garrett's picture flashed on the screen, a black man with a calm, intelligent face and hair salted with gray. He had first appeared on the police bulletins fifteen years ago, wanted for the crime of treason. He was a resident of Jameston; last known location also Jameston.

Perhaps Siskell *had* meant his gibe literally.

Ian switched to the news archives and skimmed the list of articles available on David Garrett. They were all from this past summer, dealing with his arrest and execution. There were no articles from fifteen years ago detailing the events that had sent him on the run in the first place—a fact that had puzzled Ian when he was working on his dissertation and got interested in the first man intrepid enough to try to teach James Tremont's hated childhood religion within the borders of New America. The lack of archived news reports was odd; if Garrett's original crimes had been widely enough known that thereafter believers were nicknamed "Garrett followers," there must have been ample coverage of his crimes at the time. Why weren't there any articles in the archives? Had censors pulled them, belatedly afraid that even negative coverage of Garrett's beliefs might stir interest?

Ian opened an article dealing with Garrett's arrest that gave sketchy information about his past. He'd read all these articles when they were first published, but it wouldn't hurt to refresh his memory.

In Jameston, Garrett had been the leader of a small group of religious believers devoted to the propaganda of the U.S.–based Church of Jesus Christ of Latter-day Saints, an organization which had opposed James Tremont prior to Separation, and which was known worldwide for its aggressive recruiting policies, rigid control of members, and intrusions into matters of civil government. When a tip to the police exposed Garrett's treason, he fled to the United States. As to how Garrett had crossed the border, the article didn't say, nor did it mention what had become of the other believers in his Jameston group.

Garrett had come to Tremont this past summer and attempted to incite anarchy by distributing religious pamphlets and books. Under the direction of Lt. Alisa Kent of the Sedition and Treason Division, the article noted, the police had tracked Garrett down and arrested him.

Ian tucked his computer under his arm and shoved his numb hands into his pockets. If Kent had known David Garrett before his arrest, so what? If Garrett had been a fugitive for fifteen years, Kent would have been a teenager when he fled to the U.S. A police officer didn't turn traitor just because she had to arrest an acquaintance she hadn't seen since she was a kid.

Kent had promised to explain herself after the meeting. He doubted she felt like talking after Siskell's disruptive visit, but Ian didn't feel like slipping back into the ignorance and fear that had submerged him for weeks after his arrest. He'd kept his part of the bargain—Siskell's revealing her had been outside his control—and she owed him those explanations.

Plus, it wouldn't hurt to warn her of Siskell's remark about the Liberty Cadre's making "good use of her."

Would a police officer be listed in the directory? Ian typed in Kent's name and found an entry: 46 Randolph Street, North Tremont. He checked the address for other residents and was not surprised to find that Kent lived alone.

Grimly, he looked up the bus numbers to get from Ingram Road to Randolph Street.

* * *

Lt. Kent's car was parked haphazardly in the driveway of a tidy, white-shingled duplex. The porch lights weren't lit above either door of the duplex, but on Kent's side, light glowed around the edges of the blinds.

Ian hesitated at Kent's front door, thinking absently of how the people of Anti-Nephi-Lehi had bowed before an approaching army, praising God as they awaited death. He couldn't picture himself showing such courage in the face of raised swords. Just the thought of facing one enigmatic police officer was enough to turn his knees to soup.

He pressed the doorbell and waited.

No response.

He rang the bell again. Nothing.

One slat in the blinds was twisted, allowing Ian a narrow view into the living room. He peered through the crack to see if Lt. Kent was lurking there, waiting for him to depart.

No sign of Kent. Just a wooden end table and a pearl-gray armchair—Ian squinted at the armchair and felt needles prickle his skin. Smears of crimson stained the upholstery along the top of the chair.

Ian grabbed the doorknob. Not locked. He edged into the living room and quietly pushed the door closed behind him.

Silence. Ian listened for even the softest hint of anything happening, but heard only the whoosh of air through furnace ducts.

Splinters of glass glittered on the carpet near the armchair, mixed with shreds of glossy paper and small spatters of blood. Ian picked up a scrap of photographic paper that showed a bit of a granite column. He dropped the fragment and selected a scrap that showed part of the blue-glass façade of police headquarters—a photograph of downtown Tremont . . . A glint of gold drew his eye to one of the shards of glass. Part of the national seal. Other shards had words etched in the glass. *Alis . . . must be part of Kent's name . . . Outstanding Patr—*

Understanding came along with the memory of Siskell's mocking voice: *". . . recently received a gold-class James Tremont Patriotic Service Award."* This was the plaque from that ceremony, a photograph of the government district in downtown Tremont, sealed in beautifully etched glass and accented in gold. He had seen the less prestigious standard-class version of the award many times in Marta Cluff's office or as she brandished it at Watch meetings.

Where *was* Lt. Kent? Drops of red marked a grisly trail leading out of the living room. Fighting the impulse to leave, Ian followed the trail.

He found Kent in the kitchen, hunched on the floor, knees drawn up to her chest, head buried in her crossed arms. Her hands dangled over the floor. Ian couldn't see her palms, but the backs of her hands were streaked with blood. From the size of the red splotches staining the tile, it was obvious she had made no effort to treat the cuts inflicted by the award she had apparently smashed and ripped to pieces.

Ian licked dry lips, feeling both sickened and relieved. The blood on the floor made him shudder, but he doubted it was even close to representing dangerous blood loss. Despite Kent's lack of attention to the wounds, the bleeding had stopped, as no new drips fell from her fingers.

He took a cautious step toward Lt. Kent, nearly tripping over his own feet. Kent remained motionless, oblivious.

Oh, Father, help her. Help me. What can I do? Did Kent even know he was here, or did she no longer connect with reality at all?

"Lieutenant?" he said.

She didn't move.

He stood in front of her. "Alisa."

No response.

He leaned over and shook her shoulder. She flinched, lifting her head so suddenly that Ian jumped. Her face was gray, her eyes glazed.

"Lieutenant? It's Ian Roshek."

Kent's eyes came slowly into focus, but they were empty, like she had no idea who he was. She rotated one hand and stared at her palm. Blood coated the skin, obscuring the cuts and making it impossible for Ian to even guess how bad the damage was.

Slowly, she lowered her hand to the floor and looked up at Ian. Comprehension flickered. "What are you doing here?"

"I—came to talk to you."

Her hand twitched where it rested on the stained floor. The ashen flesh pulled taut over her cheekbones gave her a skeletal look.

"You need a doctor." Ian reached to help her up.

She shrank from him.

"Don't be an idiot," he said. "Are you going to drive yourself to the hospital?"

She lifted her hand a few inches, then laid it carefully back on the floor.

"You need help," he said.

No response.

"Look, is there anyone I could call for you? A—friend or family member?"

The haze cleared from her face like he had slapped her awake. *"Get out of here."* Her voice was low, but it transmitted a wave of anger so intense that it seemed to sear Ian's flesh. He flinched, but spoke again anyway.

"Lieutenant, you need help. Let me—"

"Get out. *Get out.* Or I will call headquarters and tell them what you are."

Weakness spread through Ian's body. He felt like his bones were turning to mud. "You'd get arrested yourself."

"I should have destroyed you with the rest of them," she whispered. "Get out."

Paralyzed, Ian stared at the hate in her eyes. There was nothing he could say to her. What about her injuries? He could drag her to the emergency room, but he couldn't control what she said once she got there. He didn't doubt she was ready to betray both of them.

"You are garbage." Kent buried her bloodstained hands beneath her arms. "Unworthy of thought, unworthy of life. *Get out.*"

Ian turned and stumbled out of Kent's house.

He was only vaguely aware of the bus ride that took him home. His mind convulsed with images of hands drenched in red, and black eyes venomous with hate. *"I should have destroyed you with the rest of them."* With the rest of whom? With the believers like David Garrett she'd sent to their deaths?

Alisa Kent was insane. The Liberty Cadre *had* to leave her alone. If they tried to blackmail her, she'd turn them all in and take the consequences.

He didn't know how to contact the Cadre, but Eric probably did. The instant Ian entered his apartment, he called Eric. No answer, at Eric's or at Tim's. Were they still jabbering with Siskell at the electronics building? Ian could go downtown and try to catch them there, but it was already nearly midnight. By the time he arrived, they would be gone.

Ian left messages, using code words Eric and Tim would recognize as a demand for a meeting. He thought of calling Sherry Mason and inviting her too—Sherry might prove an ally. Ian was certain she'd never support the Liberty Cadre. The underground discussion group had been more than enough for her, something she'd gotten involved with when she was dating Eric. But now that she wanted to pull out, Ian reasoned, it would be selfish to overwhelm her with a report on the chaotic happenings since her departure. Let her be happy as she and Sean prepared to move to Hamilton.

Ian knelt and ran his hand along the underside of the desk. His fingers brushed a small, cold bump.

Jill's laughter rippled from the hallway outside the apartment. If she was laughing, that meant she wasn't alone. Ian popped the transmitter loose and dove into his bedroom. He couldn't face Jill and Daniel Lansbury without both of them noticing that something was wrong, and Daniel wouldn't be shy about probing for the source of Ian's condition.

Ian collapsed on his bed and lay in the darkness, wondering if Alisa Kent was still crouched on her kitchen floor, her hands sticky with drying blood.

CHAPTER 7

Jocelyn Lansbury smiled at Jill with lips that had somehow remained perfectly lipsticked all through lunch. Jill was uncomfortably aware that her own lipstick had transferred itself to her napkin and the rim of her glass.

"Daniel tells us you'll be soloing with the Philharmonic in December," Jocelyn said.

"Yes." Jill pressed her fork into the pastry shell enclosing a small scoop of sorbet. A chunk of pastry broke off, scattering flecks over the side of her plate onto the table. Jill bit her lip.

"On what dates, dear?"

"The sixth and seventh." Jill took a bite of sorbet. Not too sweet, with a nutty flavor she couldn't identify. It didn't surprise her that she didn't recognize the taste. She hadn't been able to identify most of the dishes she had eaten this Saturday afternoon, beyond vague categories like *fish* or *green vegetable*.

"We'd love to come hear you play, if at all possible," Jocelyn said. "Marcus?"

"It's already on my calendar." Marcus Lansbury smiled briefly at Jill.

Jill blushed. Throughout the meal, she had hardly dared look at Councilor Lansbury. One of the most important men in the nation, and here *she* was, spilling crumbs on his tablecloth and trying not to gawk at the woodwork adorning the vaulted ceiling. "Oh, I'm sure there will be much better concerts this season."

Daniel squeezed Jill's arm. "Jill is incurably modest. Her conductor thinks she's one of the most brilliant young players since

Thomas Copton. He told her she should have been aiming for a solo career all along instead of hiding in ensembles."

Jill blushed hotter. "I'm sure he was joking." She forked another small piece of pastry. It disintegrated before she could raise it to her mouth.

"When you hear her play, you'll know he wasn't joking. All of Tremont will thank him for dragging her out from behind that music stand where she tries to hide."

"Is all your family musical?" Jocelyn asked.

"Not really. But my parents were wonderful about supporting me, even though—" Jill stopped, embarrassed that she had almost admitted what a strain her violin lessons had been on the family budget. "Even though they weren't very musical themselves," she amended.

"Does your brother have any talent that way?" Daniel asked.

"Who knows? He's never taken his nose out of his books long enough to find out."

Daniel laughed. Jocelyn smiled and dabbed her lips with her napkin. Jill noted Jocelyn's ivory hands and manicured nails and thought suddenly of her own mother's hands, nothing like Jocelyn's. It was impossible to imagine Jocelyn's smooth hands mopping floors and scrubbing sinks at the local high school after a long day of teaching, all to finance a daughter's music lessons.

"What does your brother do?" Jocelyn asked.

"He teaches history at the University of Tremont." Jill shifted her gaze to the arched windows and the emerald shimmer of Lake Serena. She wasn't sure why she felt uncomfortable discussing Ian in front of the Lansburys. Maybe she'd be uncomfortable discussing anything under Marcus Lansbury's gaze. His eyes were a clear gray like Daniel's, but sharp and cold.

Daniel's phone beeped. He unclipped it from his belt. "Excuse me." To Jill's dismay, he exited the dining room, leaving her alone with his parents.

Jocelyn sighed. "The pages always come during meals, don't they? When Marcus was running the Tremont Research Lab, I wanted to take a hammer and smash his phone. The first year we were married, I could count on one hand the number of meals we had where we weren't interrupted."

"I hope it's better now," Jill said, then felt silly. *How could Councilor Lansbury be less busy now?* she chastised herself.

Jocelyn laughed. She had a charming laugh, light and warm. "People still *want* to interrupt him, but now they can't get past his secretary."

Marcus chuckled and adjusted his wife's pearl necklace where the clasp had slipped to the side. This husbandly gesture eased some of Jill's tension. Why was she so intimidated by Councilor Lansbury? He wasn't that scary. He hadn't said much during lunch, but when he did speak, he was pleasant. And Jocelyn had been flawlessly gracious. So why did Jill still feel like an escapee from the nearest kindergarten?

Daniel returned. "Sorry about that."

"Nothing too urgent, I hope," Jocelyn said.

"More annoying than urgent. But I do need to head to the Annex."

"We'll see that Jill gets home," Marcus said.

"Oh, no." Jill spoke quickly. "I'm fine taking the bus."

"Don't be silly," Jocelyn said. "My driver—"

"It's all right, Mother. I can take her. I have time." Daniel plucked the last bite of pastry off his plate with his fingers. "I told the nurse I'd be there in an hour."

Marcus nudged his empty dessert plate aside. "Then sit down for a moment, Daniel. There's something I need to say."

Daniel sat down, a guarded expression on his face.

"I trust," Marcus said, "that Jill has had the good sense not to gossip with her friends about your relationship."

Embarrassment heated Jill's cheeks.

"For a young woman like yourself, I understand that it would be tempting to take pride in dating Daniel Lansbury . . . perhaps to flaunt your association."

Jill wanted to say she had never bragged to anyone about dating Daniel, but her mouth was so dry that the words got stuck. Under the table, Daniel gripped her hand.

"Jill would never brag, Dad," he said curtly. "And you know I've always been discreet."

"I would suggest, Daniel, that you be even more discreet than you have been. Minimize the amount of time you spend together in the public eye. If you want to attend her concerts, do so, but wait for her outside rather than meeting her in full view of her friends. If you want to drive her home, do so, but don't make a parade of walking her to the front door."

Daniel's face was stony. "People don't bother me when I'm out in public."

"The fact that they don't bother you doesn't mean they don't notice you."

"I'm not going to drop Jill off a mile from her apartment and let her walk home in the snow just to keep nosy neighbors from seeing us together."

"You don't have to go to that extreme," Marcus Lansbury said. "Park in the lot behind her building. Enter through the back door, take the freight elevator or the stairs to her floor."

"I don't have a key to the back door," Jill murmured.

Marcus Lansbury tossed a key onto the table in front of Jill. "You do now. Keep your relationship as private as possible. You will not regret that decision. It will make life easier for both of you."

Jocelyn rested a hand on her husband's arm. "Marcus, I'm sure Daniel and Jill have the sense to keep themselves out of the news."

"We do." Daniel picked up the key and rose to his feet, drawing Jill with him.

"Thank you for lunch," Jill said, unable to look either of Daniel's parents in the face. Daniel steered her out of the room before his parents could rise and accompany them to the door.

When they were in Daniel's car, he laughed ruefully. "Sorry about that. Dad can be incredibly blunt."

Jill smiled weakly. "Does he usually say things like that to the girls you bring home?"

Daniel paused. "He hasn't had many opportunities."

Meaning, Jill thought, that Councilor Lansbury *wasn't* in the habit of lecturing the women Daniel dated. She reeled at the thought that Councilor Lansbury had gone to the trouble of finding out where she lived and getting a key to the back door. At best, Daniel's father must view her as a starstruck kid, far too immature for Daniel; at worst, he must think she was a schemer who thought the Lansbury name could make her famous.

"I've never gossiped about you," she said.

"I know that." Daniel shoved his foot against the accelerator and the car shot down the driveway. "You don't even know how to brag. You should take lessons."

Jill rubbed her mother's ring, pressing the gold band into her skin. "Our apartment manager already knows all about you . . . Ms. Cluff."

"So?"

"I'm sure she's told the whole Watch board. She's always quizzing me about you—"

"Don't worry about it."

"Your father is worried. I don't think he . . . likes me much."

"Don't be silly. He's just trying to protect you. The more people who know about us, the more people who will bother you with questions." Daniel slowed as he approached a stop sign. "And besides, it can be a security risk. Anyone associated with the Lansburys makes an attractive target for the anarchists."

"Is that what he's worried about—the anarchists?"

Daniel peered intently at the empty intersection. "I'm sure it is. My Uncle Andrew got murdered when I was a kid, and my dad gets threats now and then. Naturally, my parents are cautious."

"I'm sorry about your uncle."

"Well, it was almost twenty years ago. The first known action of the Liberty Cadre."

"Oh, that's terrible." Jill wanted to believe that Councilor Lansbury was trying to protect her, but if it was the anarchist threat that worried him, why hadn't he said so? He obviously had no trouble being candid.

"Look at it this way." Daniel finally pressed his foot on the gas. "If he didn't like you, why would he be planning to come to your concert?"

"Maybe your mother charmed him into it."

Daniel smiled, but didn't refute the suggestion.

At Jill's apartment building, Daniel drove into the back parking lot instead of parking on the street as he usually did. "Doesn't hurt to be careful," he said. "Dad's right about that."

Jill nodded. She was sure Daniel's next words would be, "I'd better not walk you inside." And she'd agree, pretending she believed Councilor Lansbury really was concerned about her safety, pretending she didn't know that Daniel would call tomorrow to tell her it was a "busy time at work" and he didn't know when he'd be able to see her again.

But Daniel jumped out of the car and walked her toward the building, his arm around her shoulders. "I'll dive into a bush if anyone looks out their window," he whispered.

Jill laughed, feeling a little better.

Daniel unlocked the back door and handed her the key. "Mind if I leave you here? I need to get to work."

"I think I can find the stairs on my own," she said lightly.

"I'll call you tomorrow." A quick kiss, and Daniel headed toward his car. Jill closed the door, resisting the temptation to check her watch to see if Daniel really was up against his hour time limit or if he was just in a hurry to get away.

Ian wasn't home, to Jill's relief; he would have asked her about lunch at the Lansburys', and she didn't feel up to talking about it. But why was she letting Councilor Lansbury's words bother her so much? Daniel was an adult. He didn't need his parents' approval to date her.

But she couldn't imagine Daniel defying his father.

Jill changed into a sweater and jeans and automatically opened her violin case, but instead of lifting the violin, she plucked absently at the strings. What would her parents have thought of Daniel Lansbury? Her mother would have been nervous around Daniel until she got to know him, acutely conscious that he was the grandson of Jonathan Lansbury and the son of Marcus Lansbury. Her father would have viewed the relationship warily, like Ian had at first. But in the end, they would have liked Daniel.

She lifted her violin, then set it down again, anxiety winding inside her like a string on a peg. What time was it? Quarter past three . . . plenty of time before she had to be at the concert hall.

She grabbed her coat and headed out the door, glad again that Ian wasn't home. He'd ask where she was going, and she'd either have to lie or see that taut expression on his face, like he was stopping himself from saying something. Maybe just a comment that he was worried about her, that she visited there too often. Or—"*Jilly, do you really feel like they're just wiped out of existence? I mean, you visit their graves, you leave flowers. Do you feel like you're there honoring a . . . nothingness?"*

She dug her fingertips into her temples. Why did she keep dwelling on that ridiculous conversation? Ian had been out of his mind that night, overworked and exhausted.

He probably didn't even remember any of the crazy things he'd said.

Flecks of snow stung Jill's face as she crunched through dried leaves toward the cemetery gates.

The carnations she had left on Wednesday were brown and shriveling. She lifted the two wilted flowers off the grass in front of the headstone.

The grass was damp, but she sat down anyway and imagined herself spilling her worries about Daniel while her mother's hand stroked her hair. A warm hand, smelling of soap, skin dry around the knuckles, cuticles rough, nails clipped indifferently short.

* * *

On Saturday evening, Eric trudged into the lounge at Tremont Electronics, a scowl on his face.

"Hi," Ian said, trying to gauge whether Eric's scowl reflected more of last night's hostility or just his usual gruffness. "Thanks for coming."

"Tim won't be here," Eric said. "He's at work."

"I know. He called me."

Eric pulled off his gloves and tossed them on the cafeteria table. "Want something to drink?"

"No, thanks," Ian said, surprised and relieved at this overture of friendship. Twenty-four hours seemed to have done a good job of cooling Eric down.

Eric wandered to the vending machine. "It's stupid to be here. With just the two of us, why come all the way downtown?"

"Habit." Ian grinned wryly. "At least we know we won't be overheard."

Eric yanked the lid from a root beer and sat down at the table opposite Ian. "I guess you want to talk about the Cadre."

"Something like that," Ian said. "But first, I'm sorry about bringing Lt. Kent to the meeting without telling you who she was. It was a rotten decision."

"Lying to your friends out of some weird sense of obligation to a woman who tortured you." Eric snorted. "Sometimes I just don't get you."

"I'm really sorry."

Eric swigged his soda. "It all worked out anyway."

Ian was amazed. He had expected Eric to rage about his duplicity for weeks, and here he was dismissing it with a shrug. "Listen, uh . . . do you know how to get in touch with this guy Siskell?"

"You want to talk to him?"

"I need to talk to him, yes."

Eric grinned. "Good for you. I knew you had some brains in there. And yeah, I know how to contact him, but I promised I wouldn't tell anyone. I can pass on a message for you."

"I'd appreciate that."

"No problem." Eric scratched at the chipped tabletop with his thumbnail. "Look, Ian, I know we were a little rough on you last night. But the way you kept attacking Siskell instead of listening to what he was saying—"

"I listened."

"Whatever. But I think you got the wrong impression of what joining the Cadre would mean for you."

"Oh?"

"Yeah. After you left last night, Siskell was saying that if you don't want to fight, they aren't going to force a gun into your hand. There are other ways you can help."

"This isn't about fighting," Ian said. "Weren't you listening to me? You know I'm willing to fight when the time and circumstances are right."

"And when will that be?" Eric asked sourly. "When an angel yells 'charge'?" Before Ian could respond, Eric held up a hand. "All right, sorry, forget I said that. I'm just trying to tell you there are a lot of ways you can help. Let the Cadre get you out of Tremont. They could send you to the U.S. You could go join that church you're so passionate about."

A shock of hope rushed through Ian. For a moment, he couldn't speak—couldn't think—couldn't do anything but stare blankly at Eric.

Eric smirked. "Didn't think of that, did you, when you were griping about the Cadre last night?"

"You're crazy," Ian said. "The Cadre would never—"

"They can get you out of here. Think about it. The freedom to talk about your book whenever you want. Baptism and all that other religious stuff you say is so important."

"So just like that, the Cadre would slip me out of Tremont. Even though I don't want to join them."

"Offer to help them in ways you're comfortable with. Go to the U.S. and raise money for them."

"I don't want to raise money for them."

"Then think of something else. You could recruit a support network—"

"I don't want anything to do with them."

Eric drew back. "I thought you wanted to talk to Siskell."

"I do." Ian spoke harshly, angry at the yearning he couldn't quite stomp into submission. "But not about joining the Cadre. Last night after I left the meeting, I went to—"

"You were arrested a few months ago. You remember that?"

"It's hard to forget."

"You remember how that felt, being at the mercy of the police?"

"Will you give me a break?"

"Knowing you were headed for prison? Pal, if things don't change, that's all you've got to look forward to. Do you think you can hide forever? You're going to get in trouble again, and next time there won't be some wacko lieutenant to set you free."

"Eric—"

"You'll die in prison. Unless a group like the Cadre breaks the power of the Council."

"Listen to me—"

"They want to *free* us. They're *fighting* to free us. How can you be stupid enough to turn your back on them? This is what we've been waiting for!"

"*I don't want to argue about the Liberty Cadre right now,*" Ian snarled.

"Calm down," Eric said, plainly startled. "What's the matter with you?"

"Sorry." Ian's heart pounded crazily. What *was* the matter with him? If he lost his temper, he'd never convince Eric of anything. "Last night after I left the meeting, I went to see Lt. Kent."

"Why?" Irritation roughened Eric's voice.

"She looked extremely upset when she left the meeting. I was worried about what she might be up to."

"You walked out on a Cadre freedom fighter to go check up on a police officer?"

Ian's blood pressure began another climb. "I was kicked out, if you recall."

"That's because you were driving us nuts."

Ian drew a deep, slow breath. "Lt. Kent is furious at being pushed into contact with the Liberty Cadre. More than furious—she's crazy. If the Cadre tries to blackmail her, she'll turn us in."

Eric's thick brows rumpled low over his eyes, but he didn't look as alarmed as Ian had anticipated. "Did she send you to tell us that?"

"She didn't send me."

"She won't turn us in. She'd be committing suicide."

"I don't think she cares if she destroys herself. Last night—"

"If the Cadre thinks she's a threat, they'll take care of her."

"I don't think they understand—" Ian stopped as Eric's words sank in. "So they blackmail her," he guessed. "And if it looks like she's going to fall apart, they kill her."

"If they have to." Eric's matter-of-fact answer chilled Ian.

"You would condone her murder?"

"If she was threatening to turn us in, I'm sure not going to mourn her."

"What if they order *you* to kill her? Would you?"

Discomfort clouded Eric's face.

"That makes it a little different, doesn't it?" Ian said. "If you are ordered to slash Alisa Kent's throat—"

Eric slapped his hands against the table so viciously that his empty soda bottle bounced into the air. "Get your head out of the sand! For years we've been waiting for the chance to fight. Here it is, and all you can do is whine because God hasn't appeared to load your gun for you."

Knowing a response would only escalate the argument, Ian tried to keep his mouth shut, but frustration made short work of his self-control. "Just because the Liberty Cadre opposes the Council doesn't make what they're doing right, or even effective. You heard Siskell last night. He knows how to blow up random targets, but he doesn't have a clue where his fight is leading us."

"At least he's *fighting*. Not just reading and whining."

"Don't you see that a gang like the Liberty Cadre validates all the government's ranting? The Cadre blows up a civilian target and people think, hey, what do you know? The opponents of the Council *are* nothing but a batch of anarchists and murderers. So they hold out their hands for more government shackles because they think that's the only way to stay safe."

The veins bulged in Eric's neck. "Did your police honey feed you those lines?"

"The Liberty Cadre also alienates the United States and keeps them from supporting New America's dissidents, because as far as the U.S. can see, our 'freedom fighters' are the kind of terrorist thugs that cause the U.S. so much grief. That's what the Liberty Cadre is doing for us, Eric. They're isolating us from a nation that would otherwise want to help us, and they're strengthening the government's control. If their mystery leader 'Zero' doesn't realize that, then he's either a psychopath or an idiot."

Eric's face mottled red and purple. "You talk too much. You've always talked too much, and I'm sick of listening." He snatched up his gloves.

"Are you afraid to stay and talk this out?"

"Why should I stay? So you can quote dead prophets at me? Everything you say is useless."

"You know what your problem is? You're so thrilled to find a group 'doing something' that you won't take a good look at them because you're scared you'll see them for what they are."

"Yeah? And you won't take a good look at them because you're scared you might have to shut your books and get to work."

"Come on, Eric." Ian took a breath and attempted a friendly tone. "We've known each other since we were kids. You're not the kind of person who could condone—"

"Since we were kids, yeah. Since you were sitting in history class writing secret commentaries on the teacher's lectures, pointing out her lies and mistakes. That's all you've ever been good for. You can point out what's wrong, but you won't do anything to set it right."

Ian's temper snapped. "So rush into the Liberty Cadre with your eyes closed and go plant some bombs to blow up babies and school kids and pregnant women. That'll bring the Council to its knees."

Eric got up with fury on his face and balled his fists. Then he stomped out of the lounge and crashed the door shut behind him.

* * *

Ian trudged toward his apartment building, the wind cutting to the skin like his coat was made of gauze. He couldn't possibly have done a worse job of handling Eric. Arguing, letting anger get the better of him, provoking Eric, getting sidetracked from the reason he'd called Eric in the first place. *Well done, fool.*

The Liberty Cadre would do what it wanted with Lt. Kent. Ian couldn't stop them, and Eric didn't want to stop them.

"The Cadre could send you to the U.S. You could go join that church you're so passionate about."

Ian quickened his pace, furious with the way he'd hoped, just for an instant, that he might be able to justify joining hands with the Cadre—

The crash of steel cans hitting the sidewalk yanked Ian's attention back to his surroundings. Half a block in front of him, a woman in a yellow coat lay sprawled on the sidewalk. *She must have tripped—* No, Ian realized. She'd been pushed. Two teenage boys were vandalizing the contents of a spilled grocery bag, kicking cans into the gutter and smashing tomatoes and apples. That done, they trotted off.

Anger bit at Ian's already raw nerves. It was Angie Mallowan, blacklisted in August for what Marta Cluff termed "exploiting the neighbors." Angie had refused to stop hiring herself out to do repair work, a practice that cut into the wallets of the trio of incompetent grandsons Cluff usually brought in to unclog sinks and repair stoves.

Angie started to stand, then crumpled back to her knees, her yellow coat spread around her like the petals on a daffodil. *She's hurt,* Ian thought, watching her crawl to the gutter and paw through crumbled leaves to salvage a can. *How's she going to get home?*

Reluctant to catch up with Angie, Ian slowed his pace, wrestling with an overwhelming urge to walk past her like she was invisible. He couldn't risk helping a blacklisted woman, especially not Angie Mallowan. He'd already stepped onto thin ice where Angie was concerned because he'd spoken up for her at August's Watch meeting, saying Angie was a benefit, not a detriment, to the neighborhood and didn't deserve blacklisting.

Eric's warning rang in his skull. *"You're going to get in trouble again."* Marta Cluff was just the person to start that trouble. She'd been salivating for an excuse to blacklist him, and he had enough problems right now without bringing the Neighborhood Security Watch down on his head.

In the glow of the streetlight, Angie's face was pinched and pale. As Ian reached her, words studied in secret pierced his thoughts: *"If ye turn away the needy . . . ye are as hypocrites who do deny the faith."*

Feeling a frenzied impulse to dig the Book of Mormon out of his closet and start ripping out selected pages, Ian continued past Angie. He couldn't help her. Not tonight. It would be beyond idiocy to risk provoking Marta Cluff. He had enough problems.

Yeah, like your own cowardice. Like the fact that Eric was right—you can talk, but you're afraid to do anything. Do you think King Benjamin would have left an injured woman on an icy street because he was scared of some little gray-haired harpy?

Legs leaden with reluctance, Ian paused for a moment, then wheeled around and walked back toward Angie.

He picked up a bruised apple that had rolled along the sidewalk, handed it to Angie and hastily gathered up the rest of the groceries that looked salvageable. Angie's eyes bugged with astonishment as she accepted the groceries and loaded them into her canvas bag. Finally looking up into Ian's face, she gave a grunt of recognition.

"Roshek."

"Yeah, hi." Ian handed her a can of beans. "I think that's everything worth saving. Are you all right?"

"Do you *want* Cluff to hang you?"

"I'll help you up." Ian hooked his hand under Angie's elbow and hoisted her to her feet.

"My ankle," she mumbled. "I don't think I can walk."

Ian lifted the canvas bag out of her hand. "Put your arm around my neck."

"You're an idiot."

"You're in 374, aren't you? That's my building. I'll just help you inside."

"You shouldn't—" Angie's protest melted into a groan as she tried to rest her weight on her ankle.

"Come on," Ian said. "It's freezing out here."

He supported Angie as she limped into the building. To his relief, Marta Cluff's office door was closed and Cluff was nowhere in sight.

"I'm on the first floor," Angie said. "Number 108, down the hall there."

At 108, Angie removed her arm from Ian's shoulders and reached for her keys. Her hands were callused, with traces of grease embedded in her fingertips.

"Dr. Roshek! Ms. Mallowan!"

Slivers of ice pierced Ian's stomach.

"I am *appalled!*" Marta Cluff was scurrying toward them. "Absolutely sickened! Did you think you could sneak in here without being seen? I always monitor my security cameras. You, Dr. Roshek! Helping a blacklisted woman! It wasn't enough to praise her swindling schemes in front of the whole neighborhood, hmm?"

"Ms. Cluff—"

Cluff rounded on Angie. "And you, Angie Mallowan! Didn't patriotic counseling teach you anything? How could you let him help you?"

"I didn't want his help. He forced it on me."

"Some boys pushed her down," Ian said. "She hurt her ankle. She couldn't get inside on her own."

Cluff folded skinny arms against her cardigan. "She could have crawled."

"She's already injured. If she had suffered further injury by prolonged exposure to the cold, that would have placed an unnecessary burden on Health Services."

"Humph. You don't care a thing about burdening Health Services. You were just looking for another chance to spit at civilization."

"I'm sorry it came across that way," Ian said politely.

"You're a poor excuse for a citizen. Do you think you're safe from blacklisting now that your sister has such a famous boyfriend?"

Ian frowned in annoyance. "That thought never occurred to me."

Angie, looking relieved that she wasn't Cluff's primary target, hobbled into her apartment.

Cluff's mouth puckered into a sneer as she squinted up at Ian. "Little Jill in love. So sweet. Dr. Lansbury is such a fine man. Oh, I know they're still seeing each other, for all their creeping in and out the back door. Who do you think Councilor Lansbury's people came to for that key? He knew he could trust my discretion."

"I'm sure he could." If he remained polite, maybe the harpy would decide to leave him alone sooner.

"Jill is out with Dr. Lansbury tonight, isn't she?"

Ian shrugged, not wanting to provoke Cluff further, but irritated at her prying into Jill's private life.

"A fine man," Cluff said. "The son of Councilor Lansbury! You put on a good show for him, don't you?"

"I don't know what you mean."

"Pretending to be a decent citizen . . . Someone really should warn him about you. It's sad to imagine how our little Jill would feel if her brother ruined her chances with Daniel Lansbury. She'd hate you for that, wouldn't she?"

Fury hardened Ian's muscles to steel. "If you have a problem with me, deal with me. Leave Jill out of it."

"It's only fair to her, isn't it? A nice girl, but with a blind spot about her brother. It would be a kindness to force her to see the truth." Cluff jabbed her finger into Ian's ribs. "And I'm sure there are all *kinds* of things she could tell me about you . . . things the Watch ought to know about." Humming cheerfully, Cluff scampered toward her office.

* * *

Wind clawed at Scott Siskell as he crossed the deserted Tremont Park with Five at his side. It was a cold, bleak Monday evening.

Siskell zipped his coat to his chin and frowned as he watched his companion out of the corner of his eye. Five had probably planned such a miserable rendezvous on purpose.

Five sucked vigorously on the butterscotch candy in his mouth. "Anything new?"

Siskell pressed his stringy hair over his ears. "I'm getting frostbite."

"The *report*, Seven."

"All right, all right. The bugs I planted in Kent's house and coat lining aren't transmitting, so I guess she found them and—" He whacked his gloved palms together.

"We figured she'd scan for transmitters sooner or later."

"News from Roshek's bug. Roshek met with Vettori last night and tried to convince him we're bad bullies. He also wants us to leave Alisa Kent alone. He's afraid if we blackmail her, she'll be loony enough to turn them in."

"We already know she's unstable." Five stripped a curled brown leaf from an oak tree. "It's a concern, but not a critical one. If she does crack, we'll lose Eric Vettori and Tim Sandring, which at this point is no loss at all."

Siskell smirked. "I'll tell that to Eric."

"Any change in Vettori's and Sandring's interest in the Cadre?"

"Nope. They're so excited their heads are spinning. Vettori's, anyway. I kinda get the feeling that Timmy boy just does whatever Eric says."

"Zero wants to transfer them out of Tremont immediately," Five said. "He wants Vettori in Newbold Bay. Do you think they'll have a problem with that?"

"I doubt it. Vettori's parents are here, but his relationship with them is freezy. Sandring's family is in Kapworth. It won't hurt him any to leave Tremont, unless—does Zero want Sandring in Newbold Bay too? Because I think Tim's counting on following Eric wherever he goes."

"Zero wants Sandring in Paxton."

"Uh-oh. Timmy won't like that."

Five shrugged. "Tell him it's temporary. By the time he figures out it's not, it'll be too late. The transfers should be arranged by the end of the week." Five fished another butterscotch drop from his pocket.

"Zero wants us to meet with Ten, 7:00 P.M. tomorrow. There's been a change. Kent's to be the informant now. Zero says she's a better candidate than his former choice."

"Oh, I love it!" Siskell flashed a savage smile.

"First session will take place Friday evening."

"Man oh man, I can't wait."

"This isn't for your entertainment," Five snapped.

"Everything is for my entertainment, Five-o. Especially everything involving that cute police officer." Siskell snatched the candy from Five's fingers. "You eat too much sugar. Shrimpy guys like you need protein." He popped the candy into his own mouth.

* * *

"May I check my messages?" Jill hovered near the computer. "Richard is sending some changes for this weekend's concert."

"Make it fast." Ian was lounging on the couch, watching the evening news on the screen. "I want to see this next story."

Jill hit a key and scanned the list of messages. Ian fidgeted. Normally he wouldn't have cared about missing part of the news, but the reporter had announced that the next story would deal with changes in the Health Services Department. Ian was eager to see if Councilor Spencer Brannigan was following through on his vow to implement reforms.

"Thanks." Jill switched the screen back to the newscast and curled up in the armchair with her music folder in her lap.

The reporter began the story on Health Services. As Ian listened, he smiled in satisfaction. "Hey, Jilly, did you hear that?"

Jill was busy jotting something on a sheet of music. "Hear what?" she murmured.

"They're reinstating the Health Services Appeals Board."

Her head jerked up. "When?"

"It will begin hearing cases next summer."

Jill chewed her lip and resumed writing. "It wouldn't have helped her anyway," she said softly.

"It may not have helped Mom. But it will keep a lot of other people away from the Euthanasia Centers in the future—if the

Appeals Board functions as it should, completely independent of the rest of Health Services."

"I'm sure it will," Jill said quickly.

The phone rang. Jill leapt to the desk, glanced anxiously at the ID box, and snatched up the phone. "Hi, Daniel!"

"Move away from the screen, Jilly," Ian said, trying to ignore the cold prickle along his nerves at Jill's delight.

Jill smirked and stuck her tongue out at him, but withdrew into the kitchen, the handset held to her ear.

Ian turned up the volume on the news, telling himself he didn't want to risk eavesdropping on Jill's conversation. There was no reason to think Cluff would have followed through on her threat. She *liked* having Daniel Lansbury around—it reflected well on the neighborhood. Jill said she was constantly asking about Daniel . . .

But when Jill returned a few minutes later, her eyes were dull. Ian turned off the newscast. "What's wrong?" he asked gently.

Jill picked up her music folder and set it down again, meticulously aligning it with the edge of the desk. "Daniel canceled our date for Friday."

"Did . . . something come up at work?"

"No . . ." Jill lifted the pot of African violets and repositioned it closer to the monitor. "He said he . . . he thinks it's better if we don't see each other again."

Ian swallowed. He should have been relieved to have Daniel Lansbury out of Jill's life, but he'd never wanted to hurt Jill. And now, after she was in love with Daniel, he'd torn away her hopes and mangled them. He should have told Daniel up front what kind of a record he had so Daniel could have retreated before Jill got emotionally involved. *But you didn't have the guts, did you? You kept your head down, and now Jill's suffering for it.*

"Everything was fine when I saw him last night." Jill's voice cracked. "Why would he have asked me out for Friday if . . . But I knew his father didn't like me—"

Ian studied his sock-clad feet. "Did you ask him what was wrong?"

"No. It's obvious, isn't it? His family is so important, and I'm not . . . well . . ."

Ian thought fleetingly how disappointed Cluff would be that Daniel hadn't made a point of blaming Ian for the breakup. But if Daniel wasn't willing to tell the story, Ian would have to do it. He couldn't let Jill blame herself for Daniel's departure. "Jilly, this has nothing to do with you, or with Daniel's father not liking you. It's my fault Daniel doesn't want to see you anymore."

"What do you mean?"

"Ever since you started dating Daniel, I figured sooner or later he was going to learn you were related to a . . . questionable character."

"That's ridiculous!"

Bracing himself for the pain he'd see in Jill's eyes, he looked up at her. "Marta Cluff and I had a run-in Saturday night before you got home. While she was bawling me out, she mentioned you and Daniel."

"What did you argue about?" Jill's wet blue eyes were bewildered.

"Some kids pushed Angie Mallowan down and she hurt her ankle. I helped her to her apartment."

"Angie Mallowan! Oh, Ian, not again!"

"Do you think I should have left her unable to walk and freezing on the sidewalk?"

Jill averted her eyes and twisted her mother's gold ring. "What did Ms. Cluff say about Daniel?"

"That if he had any idea what kind of person I am—"

"What is *that* supposed to mean?" Tears trickled down her face, but her posture stiffened with defiance. "So you—you helped a blacklisted lady. Even the Watch says it's a waste of resources to injure blacklisted people to the point where they need medical care. You were trying to keep Angie from ending up in the hospital."

"It's not just that."

"And when you . . . got arrested . . . for helping that girl at the university, the police realized you didn't commit any crimes and they let you go. They didn't even let the Watch blacklist you."

"Jilly—"

"If people like Ms. Cluff and—Daniel Lansbury—are so rigid that they think a few innocent mistakes make a person bad—"

"They weren't mistakes." Ian stepped toward her. "I . . . look . . . there are some things I need to explain."

Naked panic showed in her eyes. "You don't have to explain anything! There's nothing to explain!"

"Come sit down." He touched her shoulder. "Please."

Jill backed away from him like he was wielding a butcher knife. "There's nothing wrong with you!" She ran down the hallway, and Ian stared after her as her bedroom door slammed shut.

* * *

"Come on, Lieutenant. Sleepy time . . . just rest that pretty head on your pillow . . ." Scott Siskell pressed a gloved finger to the receiver inserted in his ear. "Come on . . . we're dying of boredom here . . . poor Five is almost out of candy . . . All right, she triggered it. She's breathing the stuff now." Siskell heard a soft rustle of bedcovers through his earpiece, then quiet, steady breathing.

"She's out cold." In the darkness, Siskell groped along the carpet and snatched a black knit mask. Ten and Five did likewise. Siskell grabbed the projector case, Ten picked up her medical bag, and Five led the way out the back door of the unoccupied apartment adjoining Alisa Kent's home.

It took Siskell only a few seconds to pick the lock on Kent's back door. He swaggered through the darkened kitchen and down the hall toward Kent's bedroom, Ten following him. Five stopped in the living room.

Siskell flicked the wall switch. Light blazed over Kent's marble-white face. She didn't stir.

Ten placed her bag on the floor near the nightstand and folded the bedcovers down to Kent's waist.

"Ah, honey," Siskell said in disappointment, eyeing the high neckline of Alisa Kent's nightgown. "I was hoping for something a little more . . . Or actually a little *less*—"

"Shut up. I've got work to do." Ten's plump elbow nudged Siskell aside. "You know she'll only be unconscious for a few minutes."

Ten opened the medical bag and arranged her materials on the nightstand. Siskell watched with interest as Ten rolled up Kent's sleeve and rotated her arm so the inner surface of the arm faced upward.

"Ouch." Siskell winced at the sight of Kent's palm. "Looks like she gave a porcupine a back rub."

"It looks worse than it is. I read the report." Ten picked up a narrow strip of rubber. "She's lucky she didn't cut any tendons."

"Did the report say how she got herself so sliced up?"

Ten tightened the tourniquet around Kent's upper arm. "Do you think a police lieutenant would let a doctor write a report that made her look like a nut?"

"Man, it must be convenient to be able to bully people like she can."

"You want to join Colonel Edgefield's Tremont Police thugs so you can bully people? Zero might be interested to hear that." Ten tapped her finger on the crook of Kent's elbow. Veins swelled blue beneath Kent's pale skin.

"You know, Ten, that mask looks great on you. With your face hidden, you're almost pretty."

"Shut up." Ten slipped a tube tipped with a metal stylet into Kent's vein.

Five entered the room carrying a small table. Siskell opened the projector case and hefted the projector onto the table. Five clicked a switch on the projector and oriented it toward the space in front of Kent's bed.

Siskell opened his computer to review the outline for the session. After a moment of reading, he closed the computer. He already knew this stuff to the letter. "How much longer, Dr. Doom?"

"Almost there." Ten pulled the needle of a syringe out of a medication vial and injected the drug into the tube taped to Kent's arm.

Siskell slid the pillow from under Kent's head, rooted inside the pillowcase, and withdrew the walnut-sized device that had rendered Kent unconscious. He popped the empty capsule out of its slot, deactivated the monitor, and shoved both pieces into his pocket. "Let the fun begin," he said brightly.

"Fun," Ten repeated in disgust. "You think everything is a game." She picked up a second syringe and flushed the tubing. Kent sighed in her sleep and turned her head. "She'll be awake in a couple of minutes," Ten said. "Then you can begin."

Siskell grinned behind his mask. "Man, are we efficient." He patted Ten's fleshy shoulder. "Too bad Kent won't remember we were here. I'm sure she'd be impressed."

CHAPTER 8

Daniel Lansbury speared the last bite of mushroom omelet and avoided his father's penetrating gaze from across the breakfast table. He had tried all week to hide his unhappiness, but from the speculative look in his father's eyes and the concern in his mother's, Daniel knew he wasn't fooling his parents at all.

A sapphire-and-diamond bracelet glittered around Jocelyn Lansbury's wrist as she poured coffee into Marcus's cup. The sapphires reminded Daniel of the pendant he had given Jill a couple of weeks ago. A sapphire to match her eyes.

"More coffee, Daniel?" Jocelyn's tone was too gentle for such a mundane question, and Daniel sensed that a question unrelated to the meal was forthcoming.

He rose hastily to his feet. "No, thanks, Mother."

He retreated upstairs to his study. After a guilty moment of hesitation, he opened a desk drawer and retrieved the picture he had stashed there.

Absently running his thumbs along the embossed silver frame, he examined the picture. Jill was not a classic beauty. Her nose was too thin and long, her jaw too wide, her chin too pointed. The deep dimples in her cheeks were almost too cute. Shy and unsophisticated, quick to blush, easily flustered—was Jill Roshek really the caliber of woman who could stand at the side of the grandson of Jonathan Lansbury?

Daniel slapped Jill's picture onto the desk. What was he trying to prove to himself? Nothing about Jill's appearance or personality mattered anyway. Jill was out of his life, thanks to the behavior of her brother.

During the past week, he'd been too numbed by pain and too ashamed at ever getting involved with the Rosheks to think deeply about the things Marta Cluff told him when she'd accosted him last Saturday evening after he'd dropped Jill at her apartment. It had been easier just to sweep the whole mess aside and hope his feelings for Jill would fade quickly.

They weren't fading.

Daniel pictured Ian Roshek, feet propped on the arm of the couch, computer on his chest, lifting his eyes from whatever he was reading long enough to offer a friendly hello or farewell. It was disconcerting to think of him as Cluff described him: an antisocial man a heartbeat away from full-fledged anarchism. Shouldn't Daniel have been able to sense flaws in Ian's attitude—rudeness, stiffness, *something* to indicate that Ian was uncomfortable in the presence of a Lansbury? His father would doubtless have been able to spot something wrong with Ian.

At least Jill's citizenship was fine. Cluff had said as much, and Daniel couldn't imagine Jill ever challenging the Watch. If only there were a way to keep Ian's reputation from shadowing Jill . . . but that could only happen if Jill cut all ties with Ian, and Jill would never do that. She adored her brother.

Daniel mentally reviewed Cluff's report. The fact that Ian had spoken in defense of a woman recommended for blacklisting wasn't an issue. Ian was entitled to defend a candidate if he felt the evidence offered to support blacklisting was insufficient, and it was plain that Cluff was annoyed with Ian because he had publicly challenged her, not because his behavior in that instance had been out of line.

But to offer open assistance to the same woman after blacklisting had been formalized . . . That act was clearly defiant, a repudiation of the ruling of the neighborhood. And according to Cluff, Ian's voting record was spotty. Though he wasn't required to support blacklisting motions if he felt they were unjustified, a too-frequent refusal to vote usually indicated a lack of concern for national security. And getting arrested at that university contraband sweep! If Ian Roshek would protect a Garrett follower, what else would he do?

Strange that Daniel hadn't known about Ian's arrest. He'd met Jill on the same night as the contraband sweep, so the name Roshek should have leapt out at him from the news reports. But he didn't remember hearing anything about a professor getting arrested. Just students.

Daniel reached for his computer and checked the news archives. Nowhere was Ian Roshek's name mentioned in connection with the contraband sweep.

Puzzled, Daniel closed the computer. He didn't think Cluff was lying—even a petty, self-important busybody like Cluff wouldn't lie about something Daniel could so easily check—but it was interesting that the police hadn't released Ian's name to the media.

And Cluff had admitted—unwillingly—that she hadn't blacklisted Ian after his arrest because the police had instructed her not to do so. Daniel had never heard of the police limiting the Watch's authority like that. Apparently, Ian had made an excellent impression on the officer who'd screened him. Who had that been? Daniel racked his brain. Lt. Kent must have directed the sweep; she had probably questioned Ian herself. If she had taken steps to keep the teeth of the Watch out of his neck and the scandal of his arrest from the media, she must have been satisfied that he was a fundamentally solid citizen. Kent never doled out either unwarranted mercy or unwarranted punishment.

But Ian was obviously still struggling, or he wouldn't have helped that blacklisted woman last week. It would be interesting to study his file and get a more accurate picture of his problems. Maybe he wasn't nearly as bad off as Daniel thought.

A subtle, tingling hope made Daniel reach for Jill's picture. Had he let Marta Cluff's vengeful report manipulate him into thinking his only option was to avoid the Rosheks, when really there were other ways to handle this? Certainly Ian was well-intentioned. Maybe if he had some guidance—

A knock at the door startled Daniel. He crammed Jill's picture in the drawer, accidentally banging his knuckles on the edge of the desk. "Come in."

Marcus Lansbury entered. "May I speak with you, son?"

"I'm somewhat busy this morning—"

Marcus glanced pointedly at the empty desktop and closed computer. He settled into a leather chair across from Daniel. "How are you?"

"I'm fine."

"Your mother is worried about you."

"I don't know why." Daniel's heart sank. If Marcus was here to assuage Jocelyn's worries, he wouldn't quit until he had chipped away the last of Daniel's defenses and mined out every bit of information he wanted.

"You don't look well," Marcus said. "Is something wrong?"

"I'm fine."

"You're no longer dating Jill Roshek?"

Of course his father would know that, despite the fact that he'd never told him about his break with Jill. "That's right," he admitted.

"Her decision or yours?"

"Mine."

"Why did you end the relationship?"

Daniel didn't want to admit what had happened, but he knew it was useless to try to conceal it. "There are some problems with Jill's family."

"Her family?"

Tersely, Daniel repeated what Marta Cluff had told him.

His father's hands rested lightly on the arms of the chair, his back was regally straight, and his hair was silver-bright in the light from the window behind him. Daniel never could figure out how Marcus made every chair he sat in look like a throne.

"It's unfortunate that it took an outsider to bring this information to your attention," Marcus said.

Daniel examined the welt on his knuckles. "I didn't spend much time with Ian. And Jill never mentioned any of his problems."

"Why didn't you check on the Rosheks before you became serious about Jill? A woman so far outside your normal circle of associates—but that was part of her appeal, eh?"

"How was I supposed to check on them?"

"If you had asked me, I would have given you a full report, including information on Ian Roshek's problems."

"You checked on him?" Daniel didn't know why he was surprised.

"Of course."

"Then . . . that's why you made such a point about my not being seen in public with Jill?"

"Wise counsel."

Daniel suppressed a surge of irritation. "Why didn't you tell me Ian had problems?"

"I thought it would be more instructive for you to discover the truth on your own. You should have been perceptive enough to do that, Daniel."

Daniel gritted his teeth, imagining Marcus watching him in patronizing silence day after day, waiting for him to realize the character of the family he had befriended.

"In case you're wondering," Marcus said, "Jill's file is clean, except for one entry regarding an incident at the Euthanasia Center at the time of her mother's death. Has she told you about that?"

"No." Daniel wanted to ask what the incident was, but he didn't want to give his father the satisfaction of seeing him beg for information.

Marcus gave a small, glacial smile. "As for her brother, his record has never been exemplary, but his citizenship ratings were passable. It's only in the last few months that his behavior has taken a sharp dip into the antisocial."

Hope stirred within Daniel, stronger than before. So Ian's problems were a recent development. That would make it easier. "Well, he's not an anarchist," Daniel said.

"Give him time."

Irritation tightened Daniel's chest at the brusque way his father wrote Ian off. "Does it have to end that way?"

"It's a reasonable prediction."

"Only if no one wakes Ian up to what he's doing."

Marcus raised silver eyebrows. "He's been arrested already. He's had his warning."

Daniel straightened his shoulders, trying to shrug off the weight of humiliation. "I'm sure his arrest scared him, but fear fades. What it didn't do was *teach* him. He's an intelligent man. If he understood—"

"What are you suggesting?"

What *was* he suggesting? He hadn't even thought this idea through, and here he was presenting it to his father. Daniel knew that Marcus would reduce it to smoldering shreds, but he couldn't withdraw it now without looking even more foolish. "I'm a Detention Annex medical supervisor. I know how misperceptions can infiltrate a mind, twisting patriotism into treason."

"I'm glad you know your job."

Sweat from Daniel's palms smeared the polished desktop. "If I worked with Ian Roshek—informally—maybe I could help him correct his behavior before it's too late."

"You want to work with Ian. To counsel him, help him."

The calculating intensity in Marcus's eyes unnerved Daniel more than the disdain he had expected. "It will be an incredible waste if Ian ends up like you think he will," Daniel said.

"A waste?"

"He's a university professor, but if he gets blacklisted, what school would allow him in the classroom? He'll be fired, and even after he's worked his way back to full citizenship, he'll never teach again. And if he's arrested again, I doubt the police will have patience with him the second time around. He'll end up in prison. Look at the resources it took to educate him. Isn't it a waste if he uses that education to serve New America for only a few years?"

"I would call that a waste, yes."

Daniel wondered what his father was really thinking, but took courage from his words anyway. "Then wouldn't it be better to correct his course before it's too late?"

Marcus remained silent for a few moments. Then he said, "I presume you'd want to continue your relationship with Jill while you counsel Ian."

"Well—I hadn't really thought—"

"You've thought of little else."

Humiliated, Daniel said flatly, "Strengthening the nation doesn't always have to involve sacrifice."

Marcus laughed, surprising Daniel. "To take a man from the brink of treason and transform him into an upright citizen is a noble goal—no matter what your ulterior motives." Still no anger or contempt showed in his eyes—just razor-edged contemplation. "I presume you'd like to study Roshek's file so you can determine how best to counsel him."

"His . . . file would be helpful," Daniel conceded.

"I'll get you a copy." Marcus rose, his six-foot, four-inch frame looming over the desk. "Do you need anything else?"

Daniel floundered, relieved at his father's unexpected support, but unable to escape the uneasy sense that his world had just tilted beneath his feet. "I think the file is all I need for now. Dad, I'll be discreet. I would never risk—"

"As I'm sure you've noticed, I haven't permitted your relationship with Jill to receive any publicity. That will be the case until her brother is fully reformed—assuming you succeed. Consider, Daniel, that this may not turn out as well as you hope."

"I understand that."

"Then good luck." With a half-smile on his lips, Marcus exited the office.

* * *

Jill buttoned her coat and picked up the garment bag that contained her black concert dress.

"I'll be home around five." She spoke cheerfully as she lifted her violin case, but her smile was plastic. Ian knew she was trying not to care that instead of meeting Daniel Lansbury after the concert for a ride home, she would be shivering at a bus stop.

"I hope it goes well," Ian said.

"Thanks." Jill closed the door behind her as she left.

Ian leaned back on the couch and rubbed his eyes to ease the burning ache from lack of sleep. *"Hello. How are you? I'll be home at five. Good-bye."* That was as deep as their conversations got these days. Jill had spent the week avoiding him while trying to pretend everything was normal. She stayed in bed until he left for campus in the mornings. In the evenings, she hid out in the practice rooms at the concert hall, or so he assumed, since she returned home at bedtime with her eyes bloodshot and the callus on her neck chafed red from endless hours of practicing. He wished she'd confront him and rage at him for ruining her relationship with Daniel, but she wouldn't even admit she was upset.

"There's nothing wrong with you!" The memory of Jill's fierce denial pricked Ian with guilt. He longed to tell Jill the truth, but for whose benefit? She wasn't ready to listen and understand. Was he just selfishly desperate for someone to talk to? Neither Eric nor Tim would answer his calls or return his messages. How long would it be until Eric quit fuming and calmed down enough to discuss the Liberty Cadre objectively?

If Ian just had someone to confide in, someone who could withstand an avalanche of worries and offer good advice in return . . . Ian reached for the memory of amber eyes, warm fingers intertwined with his, chestnut hair polished by the sunlight reflecting off Lake Serena. He rarely thought about Laura anymore, but on this wintry Sunday afternoon, fatigue and loneliness brought the ache of might-have-beens. What would have happened if Laura hadn't transferred to the nursing program in Newbold Bay? What if she hadn't met Matt Travers?

Stop it. That was six years ago. What's the matter with you? And you know it wasn't just Matt Travers that came between you. You weren't as good a match as you tried to believe. Laura knew it. Why do you think she ran to Newbold Bay?

At least Ian could take comfort in the fact that there had been no word from Lt. Kent, or from anyone else in the Tremont Police Service. Maybe the Liberty Cadre had had the sense to leave Kent alone after all.

Ian's thoughts drifted back to Jill. Jill, still plastering her room with pictures of their father, who died in a car accident when Jill was thirteen, and their mother, euthanized due to cancer two years later. Still visiting their parents' graves at least weekly, still wearing their mother's wedding ring, still keeping their mother's clothes in boxes stacked in her closet.

Why couldn't he manage to tell her the truth that would make her happier than anything—that death was not the end, that their parents still existed, that they would live again? Every time he wanted to broach the subject, his courage failed at the memory of the way Jill had reacted last summer when he'd tried to talk to her about it—the confusion in her eyes, the fear masked beneath fake smiles and teasing accusations about incoherence due to "overwork." Then a panicked exit as she nearly ran from the room in her haste to get away from him. Just like she fled on Monday night when he tried to explain his defiance of the Watch.

Jill didn't *want* to know what he believed. She had already lost her parents. She couldn't endure listening to her brother confess to treason; to admit that he was a traitor was to admit that he could be snatched away from her in an instant.

And she was right—she could lose him at any time. He *was* going to get in trouble again, and next time, it might be trouble he couldn't get out of.

What would happen to him if he were arrested?

What would happen to Jill?

Did he know what he was doing? Or was he insane? Eric's gruff voice echoed in memory. *"Does that book kill brain cells?"*

He saw himself five months ago, caught between yearning and terror as he locked his bedroom door, closed his window against the June breeze, and read again the words that had already branded themselves into his mind: *"When ye shall receive these things, I would exhort you that ye would ask God, the Eternal Father, in the name of Christ, if these things are not true; and . . . he will manifest the truth of it unto you . . ."* How long had he sat there, rereading those words, afraid to ask, but unable to set the book aside?

And finally, sinking to his knees, determined to know.

And rising on legs that could barely hold him, his question answered with a certainty he had never imagined could exist.

He wasn't crazy.

Ian trotted into his bedroom and retrieved the box that held his stash of contraband. Carrying the Book of Mormon, he returned to the living room and flipped thoughtfully through the pages before settling on a favorite passage. *"And now, my sons, remember, remember that it is upon the rock of our Redeemer, who is Christ, the Son of God, that ye must build your foundation; that when the devil shall send forth his mighty winds, yea, his shafts in the whirlwind, yea, when all his hail and his mighty storm shall beat upon you, it shall have no power over you to drag you down—"*

So why did he feel like he was getting blown toward the edge of a cliff? Was his faith that frail?

The ringing of the doorbell spurred his heart to a gallop. He debated ignoring the bell. But what if it was Eric? He slipped the book behind the couch and went to open the door.

It was Daniel Lansbury. Wishing he'd followed his impulse to leave the door unanswered, Ian spoke coolly. "Jill has a matinee today. She won't be home until after five."

"I know. May I come in?"

"Uh—I guess so." Disconcerted, Ian stepped back to allow Daniel into the apartment. He didn't offer Daniel a seat, but Daniel draped his coat over the arm of the couch and sat down anyway. Ian's tongue went cottony as he imagined what would happen if Daniel peeked behind the couch and saw the book wedged there.

"Sit down," Daniel said. "I need to talk to you."

Ian swallowed, trying to moisten his mouth. "About what?"

"Sit down."

"Is it going to take that long?"

"Yes. Please—" Daniel waved a hand in the direction of the armchair.

"I'll stand, thanks."

"Suit yourself." Daniel leaned back and folded his arms. "I had an interesting meeting with your Watch president last Saturday night."

"I can guess what Cluff told you. And I know that's why you dumped Jill."

"That's what I'd like to discuss."

"What is there to say? You've decided we're not worthy of you. So be it. Thanks for stopping by."

"Relax, Ian. I'm not here to condemn you. I'd rather help you."

"Help me?"

"I've had a lot of experience studying the rationalizations that lead to treason. I do a lot of work for the police."

Strangling fingers grasped Ian's throat. Was Daniel accusing him of treason? No, not with that calm, analytical expression on his face. "I thought you worked at the Tremont Research Laboratory."

"I do. I'm also at the Detention Annex on a regular basis. Will you please sit down? This is important."

He sat. His legs no longer wanted to hold him up anyway.

"Let me tell you something, Ian. Very few of the traitors we care for at the Annex are anarchy-loving lunatics. Most are decent people who just slipped off the track somewhere."

"Thanks for the insight. But none of the things Ms. Cluff might have told you about me were—"

"Don't get defensive. I know you're not guilty of any crimes, but you're letting some misperceptions get the better of you. I've been studying your file, and recently you've shown some behavior patterns that are worrisome."

Ian hoped the sudden flush of blood in his neck wasn't noticeable. "You have access to citizen files?"

"I can get access, yes. From the reports in your file, it's plain that your concern for individuals makes it hard for you to understand the need for some of our more stringent security measures."

"Oh?" It was all he could manage at the moment.

"Ms. Cluff said you assisted a blacklisted woman. She also said you frequently don't support your Neighborhood Security Watch when it becomes necessary to blacklist a neighbor. I understand that blacklisting is unpleasant, but without the social sanctions administered by the Watch, the bad example of one person could corrupt an entire neighborhood. From a corrupt individual, to a corrupt neighborhood, to a corrupt city, to a corrupt nation, and everything James Tremont gave us crumbles into anarchy. Do you see what I'm saying?"

"Look, no matter how bad Cluff made it sound, nothing I did was outside the boundaries of the Watch rules. The woman I helped—"

"I'm not talking about breaking rules, Ian. I'm talking about your attitude. I'm saying you have some fundamental misperceptions that could *lead* you to break laws if you don't correct those misperceptions."

While Ian tried to think of a way to end this conversation immediately, Daniel forged onward. "Take the university contraband sweep in September. I know it must have been distressing, watching that girl caught with anarchist propaganda. But without lessons like that one, thousands of foolish kids could be sucked into reading and believing anarchist lies. The message sent by the patriotic anger of the students who dealt with the traitor resounded throughout the nation."

"Patriotic anger?" Ian knew he should keep his mouth shut, but the memory of the auburn-haired girl was too strong. "Daniel, those students were *laughing*."

Surprise and distaste flickered in Daniel's eyes, then disappeared behind his confident demeanor. "The students might have had an immature way of showing it, but they were reacting to the threat the girl posed to national security."

Never mind that the police framed her. Ian gritted his teeth to keep himself from saying something that would really get him in trouble.

"It takes harsh measures to keep chaos at bay," Daniel lectured. "You've got to learn to deny primitive instincts to help or protect a person when helping that individual would weaken the nation. The nation—the people as a whole—always comes first."

"I understand that," Ian said neutrally. What was Daniel up to?

"Intellectually, perhaps. But you've let your emotions overrule your mind too often lately. If something is unpleasant, you reject it—acting not out of rebellion, but out of misplaced compassion. Compassion has to be rigidly limited, or it becomes a destructive force."

Ian thought of Mormon's teachings on charity and wondered what he would make of the phrase "rigidly limited compassion."

Daniel pulled a memory card from his pocket. "This contains half a dozen case histories of people who started out much like you. All of them were troubled by the delusion that their own judgment was superior to the policies of their Neighborhood Security Watch. Eventually, they viewed themselves as above the edicts of the Council itself. Some of them eventually justified their rebellion through archaic superstitions and religious philosophies."

Ian couldn't speak.

"I'm sure you can figure out what happened," Daniel said. "Once they adopted such anarchist attitudes, they felt justified in committing a variety of crimes, including violent acts of terrorism."

"That's—unfortunate." How could he get Daniel to leave?

Daniel gave a slight, dry smile. "You think this doesn't apply to you, but it does. In fact, given your educational background and areas of specialization, I'd say you'd be particularly vulnerable to the impulse to justify rebellion by claiming it has the approval of some magical, supernatural being."

Sweat glued Ian's shirt to his back. "Thanks for the warning."

"I've offended you, but you need to hear this. You think you're immune to that type of delusion because you've studied the dangers of religious beliefs, but no one is immune. Religious delusions have an extremely infectious and contagious character. If your loyalty falters, Ian, you've got a lot of information in your mind that could provide fertile ground for treason."

Ian swallowed. "I understand what you're saying."

"But you don't believe me, and that's where you're putting yourself in danger. The more you think you're immune, the more vulnerable you are." Daniel tossed the card to Ian. "If you study these cases, it will help you see where your problems can lead. Take a week or so to look them over, and then we'll talk about them."

Ian tapped the card against his thigh. So Daniel Lansbury was determined to "help" him. First a reading assignment, then what? An escort to make sure he voted to ostracize the next neighbor brought up for blacklisting? He felt a grudging respect that Daniel cared enough about Jill to go to so much trouble in making the Roshek family fit associates for the Lansburys, but this situation needed to end immediately or it would become a disaster. Daniel was already probing at the borders of the truth. How long would it take a police-affiliated doctor to figure out that Ian Roshek was a traitor to the core?

"This is very generous of you," Ian said. "But I'd rather deal with these—issues—on my own."

Daniel smiled knowingly. "In other words, you don't want to deal with them at all."

"In other words, I appreciate the offer, but I don't need your help." Ian stood up. "Nice to see you again."

"I realize you're uncomfortable discussing this, but better here than at police headquarters. I wouldn't count on any reprieves if you get in trouble again. The police aren't going to give you a second chance. I'm sure Lt. Kent made that clear."

Ian hesitated out of fear of revealing too much, but couldn't help asking, "You . . . know Lt. Kent?"

"Of course. She's an excellent officer. One of the best. Study the case histories I gave you, and think about your own behavior. You'll see some frightening similarities."

Ian tossed the card back to Daniel.

Daniel's voice was soft, but his eyes were granite. "Ian, if you refuse to face your problems, then those problems are even more serious than I thought. I don't like resorting to threats, but if you won't cooperate with me, I can have you taken in for patriotic counseling."

Icy perspiration drenched Ian. He had never heard of anyone being sent to patriotic counseling without first being blacklisted, but he didn't doubt the son of Councilor Marcus Lansbury could arrange it. "You'd do that?"

"You need help. If you won't accept it from me, then I'll let patriotic counseling force it on you in a way you won't be able to resist. It would be handled discreetly. You wouldn't be blacklisted. The university could be told you were on a medical leave."

Never had Ian experienced such a powerful urge to smash someone's jaw. "Do you think your last name gives you authority over me? Get out of my apartment."

"Throw me out if you like, but if you do, you'll be in patriotic counseling within the week. Do you know much about patriotic counseling?"

Ian didn't reply. He knew only three facts about patriotic counseling: it always accompanied blacklisting, it was run jointly by the police and the Neighborhood Security Watch, and it began with a month in a compound somewhere near Tremont. Everything else he knew consisted of rumors. Hideous rumors.

"The problem that plagues all faltering citizens," Daniel said, "is the inability to see the end results of their behavior. Those results might not show up for years, even for generations, but they do inevitably come. The function of patriotic counseling is to help citizens connect their behavior with the inevitable ultimate results. For example, we were talking about people who place their own judgment above the Watch. At the beginning they think their behavior is harmless—but would they still feel that way if they realized they were readying the ground for the growth of superstitions, *and* if they'd suffered through the mayhem such superstitions have caused in the past?"

"Forget the explanations. They won't—"

Daniel interrupted him. "For the first week of patriotic counseling, a subject spends fourteen hours a day studying, in vivid detail, the ultimate results of his or her particular tendencies. At the end of that intellectual immersion, a memory stimulant drug is administered, transforming the information learned into a hallucinatory experience."

Ian didn't want to hear this. "This isn't going to—"

"Ever wonder what it would be like to get burned at the stake by people who are angry because you want to worship your imaginary god differently than they worship their imaginary god? Ever wonder what it would be like to get blown apart by terrorists who think they'll receive eternal rewards for leaving you with half your limbs on one side of the street and half on the other?" Daniel softened his voice. "Please don't make me put you through that. I can teach you the same lessons patriotic counseling would teach you, minus the suffering."

Ian stared at Daniel's pleasant, confident face. He couldn't think of anything to say.

"Study the case histories." Daniel stood up and extended the card. "Then we'll talk about them."

"I'm not going along with this," Ian said. *"I don't need help."*

Daniel set the card on top of the computer. "I understand that you're feeling angry and defensive right now. That's normal. But when you calm down, read the historics. I'm going to the concert hall now to wait for Jill. We have some things to talk about."

Ian felt a lift of relief. Jill wouldn't sit still to hear Daniel explain that her brother was a troubled citizen in need of guidance, and as for Daniel threatening him with patriotic counseling— "Yeah, go talk to her. Tell her what you've got planned for me." Once Jill threw Daniel out, Daniel would have no reason to be interested in Ian's patriotism, and that would be the end of this fiasco.

Daniel slipped his coat on. "Ian, do you think Jill *likes* watching you get in trouble?" Without waiting for an answer, he walked out of the apartment.

CHAPTER 9

Ian was in bed before Jill returned home Sunday night—his first hint that Daniel's meeting with Jill did not go as poorly as he'd hoped. Monday morning he got his second hint—a vase of crimson roses crowning the kitchen table. Ian hoped Jill had received the roses coolly and told Daniel she needed time to think, but he knew he was kidding himself. Articulate, clever Daniel had likely done a magnificent job of convincing Jill he needed to save her wayward brother. Beneath Jill's stubborn loyalty, Ian knew she was frightened for him, maybe frightened enough to clutch at Daniel Lansbury's offer of help.

Especially if it meant getting Daniel back in her life.

Ian crumpled into a chair and dumped wheat flakes into a bowl. The last thing he needed right now was Daniel breathing down his neck, but if he resisted Daniel's interference—

Ian snared a rosebud between his thumb and forefinger. While Daniel was showering Jill with roses, had he bothered to mention that he was threatening her brother with patriotic counseling?

Jill's bedroom door squeaked open. Ian released the rose and resumed eating.

Jill slipped into the kitchen. She smiled at him, but it was the false smile she always wore before solo performances. "Good morning," she said.

Ian grunted.

Jill opened the blinds on the kitchen window. "Better take your umbrella today."

Ian glanced at the sleet streaming down the glass and turned back to his soggy cereal.

"How are you doing?" Jill asked.

"According to Daniel Lansbury, I'm not doing very well at all."

"Ian . . ." Jill sat at the table, her face fixed in a calm, reasonable expression she had probably practiced in front of the mirror before coming to confront him. "Daniel just wants to help you."

"He's a helpful guy, all right. Did he tell you what he'll do to me if I don't obey his orders?"

"Please don't be upset. The only reason he even mentioned patriotic counseling is because he knew it was the only way to get you to listen."

Ian's hopes plunged. Daniel had already told her, and it hadn't fazed her.

"He doesn't want to hurt you," Jill said. "He wants to help you."

"This isn't about helping me. This is about hanging on to *you*. What are you thinking? Maybe Daniel is handsome and charming, but he's also arrogant, cold-blooded, and accustomed to getting everything he wants. If you have any sense, you'll get rid of him."

Jill's chin lifted. "You just want me to reject him so you don't have to admit that you—well, that you have problems."

"So now I have problems, huh? A few days ago you told me my 'problems' were innocent mistakes and Cluff and Daniel Lansbury were wrong."

Jill twisted her mother's ring on her finger. "I didn't realize how serious it was."

"So it's serious because Daniel Lansbury says it's serious. Now that you've talked to him, you can't think for yourself anymore."

Her cheeks reddened. "You never believe I can think for myself."

"The guy is manipulating you, Jilly."

"It's Jill, not Jilly," she snapped. "I'm not five years old."

"Do you support what Daniel is doing?"

"He's trying to help you. He's trying to keep you safe."

"So if he ships me off to patriotic counseling, you'll smile and wave good-bye?"

Tears filled her eyes, and Ian felt sick. Why was he lashing out at her like this? Jill truly thought Daniel was acting in her brother's interests. "I'm sorry," he said a bit more gently.

Jill mopped her eyes on the sleeve of her bathrobe. "It's all right. I understand why you're upset."

She *didn't* understand, and she could never understand unless he told her the truth about his treason. If he slapped the Book of Mormon on the table in front of her, saying, "*Here's my problem,*" what would happen? Jill would probably do what he wanted and break off her relationship with Daniel. Ian couldn't imagine that she'd risk having Daniel discover her brother's crimes.

And how would Daniel react to Jill's rejection? He would know Ian was behind the breakup, no matter what excuse Jill offered. Ian imagined Jill stammering out flimsy lies in response to Daniel's piercing questions. "*Ian told you to do this, didn't he? What did he say to you? Why are you so afraid?*" Daniel would either immediately send Ian to patriotic counseling or discern the source of Jill's fear and call the police.

"I know you're angry at Daniel," Jill said. "But please—all you have to do for now is read the case histories he gave you. That's not so hard, is it?"

"Jill—"

"Please. Just say you'll read them."

"This is ridiculous. I'm not going to let Daniel Lansbury—"

"You're always studying anyway." She smiled feebly. "What's a little extra reading?"

"Jilly—I mean *Jill.* I don't want to hurt you, but I can't pretend—"

"Please. Read the case histories."

Jill's blue eyes glistened with such pleading that Ian's resistance weakened. "I'll read them," he conceded. "But that's all I'm promising."

The relief in Jill's face made Ian want to hide his head in his hands. He pushed back from the table. "I'd better get to campus. Eight o'clock class."

* * *

The bus broke down halfway to campus. Rather than wait for a replacement, Ian walked the last mile to school while the wind whipped sleet into his face and tore his umbrella out of his hand. He arrived at the Ryce Building with his trouser legs soaked, his ears numb, and water streaming off his hair. He stopped in the restroom to towel and recomb his hair before he went to his office. At least the weather suited his mood.

He had been cruel to give Jill false hopes by promising to read the case histories, but now that he'd agreed to carry out Daniel's assignment, he couldn't bring himself to renege. And temporary cooperation would buy him some time while he figured out how to disentangle himself from Daniel's net.

A white envelope lay on the floor of his office. Curious, he picked it up. His name was penned on the envelope in an angular, efficient script. Why would someone shove a message under the door instead of just e-mailing it? He ripped the envelope open and unfolded a piece of paper.

It is necessary that I speak with you. Come alone to my house tomorrow, Tuesday, December 3, 7:00 P.M.
    A.K.

A.K. Alisa Kent. Ian's heart sank into his waterlogged shoes. What did she want? Had the Liberty Cadre tried to blackmail her? If they had, would she summon him to discuss it? Why would she want to talk to him at all unless it was in a police interrogation room?

Ian shoved the note into his pocket. Should he ignore Kent's summons? No. It wouldn't be wise to provoke her, he decided.

He spent an absentminded day on campus, carrying out his responsibilities while wishing he could go home and worry in peace. The instant he finished teaching, he returned to his office to collect his coat. He was hurrying toward the stairwell when a curt voice halted his escape.

"Dr. Roshek."

Ian looked over his shoulder to see the Education Regulatory Committee representative William Sheldon waddling along the corridor.

"Come into my office," Sheldon said.

* * *

Ian walked home, his temper worsening with each block. By the time he reached his apartment building, his nerves were ready to snap. How could Sheldon forbid him to help a struggling student on his own time?

Marta Cluff was polishing the table in the lobby with an acrid glass cleaner that stung Ian's sinuses. She cleared her throat at Ian as he stalked past. "A violation was noted in your record during the inspection on Saturday. A broken window!"

He continued toward the elevator. Cluff knew the window in his bedroom had been cracked by previous tenants. He'd discussed the window with her the first three times he'd been fined for it, but she had refused to cancel the fine—or fix the window.

Cluff raised her voice. "We do not tolerate tenants who vandalize this property!"

Ian tromped into the elevator. If he had to talk to Marta Cluff tonight, he'd have to wring her scrawny neck.

At his apartment, he was not surprised to see Daniel Lansbury. Everything else had gone wrong today; why should Daniel miss his cue? Again, Ian was struck forcefully by Daniel's resemblance to his powerful father. Dye the light brown hair silver, carve a few lines around the angular features, drape a few more pounds on Daniel's rangy frame and there was Councilor Marcus Lansbury, sitting on the couch next to Jill.

"Hi, Ian," Jill murmured. She had her black concert dress draped over her lap and a needle and thread in her hand.

Ian threw his coat in the closet without benefit of a hanger and turned to face Daniel and Jill.

"How are you doing?" Daniel's scrutiny made Ian feel like a diagram in a medical textbook.

"I'm tired," Ian said. "And I'm not in the mood for any 'help' from you."

Cheeks crimson, Jill focused intently on the hem she was mending.

"I didn't come here to talk to you," Daniel said mildly. "You haven't had time to read those case histories."

Ian felt a twinge of guilt at the sight of Jill's anguished face, but he ignored it and stalked out of the living room.

In his bedroom, he shed his work clothes and reached for his sweat suit. Maybe jogging a few miles would relieve some of the stress that felt like it was eating through the lining of his stomach. What he really needed was a basketball and a fierce round of one-on-one with Eric, but there was no chance of that today.

When he returned to the living room, he found Jill closing the front door. Daniel was gone.

"He didn't have to leave on my account," Ian said. "Not that I'm sorry he's gone."

"He didn't leave because of you." An unfamiliar edge sharpened Jill's voice. "He just stopped by for a few minutes on his break. He has to go back to work. Are you going to meet Eric?"

"No." Ian walked into the kitchen and snatched a chunk of cheese from the fridge and a sack of bread from the counter. With Daniel gone, his urge to exercise in the cold had evaporated.

Jill stood in the doorway, her arms curled around her like she was chilled. "Did something happen at work today?" she asked in a conciliatory tone as Ian slapped cheese sandwiches into a frying pan. "You looked so upset when you got home."

Ian nearly brushed the question aside. He didn't want his troubles at the university to reach the ears of Daniel Lansbury. But on second thought, what did it matter if Jill reported on him to Daniel? His conflict with Sheldon was only one more symptom of the same problem Daniel had already lectured him about. And it would be bleakly satisfying to unburden himself to Jill and see sympathy for Peter Critchlow in her eyes—not the distaste Daniel would want her to feel.

"Yeah, something happened. This afternoon I got collared by the history department rep from the Education Regulatory Committee."

Jill paled. "Why?"

"I've got a student, a freshman, who gets migraine headaches. He's had them off and on for years, but since he started at the university, they've started coming several times a week—blinding pain for hours a day. A doctor prescribed medication, but Review wouldn't authorize it—said the headaches were stress-induced and Peter can cure them with relaxation techniques. Relaxation! He's tried every technique in the book, but it's a little hard to relax when you're about to get tossed out of the university."

"Why would this get *you* in trouble?"

"With the headaches wiping him out, Peter's been struggling in his classes. I've been working with him, trying to help him."

"Why would the Committee get upset about that?"

"Sheldon doesn't like it that I've helped Peter with other classes besides mine—math, science. He said I was acting outside my responsibilities, undermining the approved system of academic tutoring and propping up a student who deserved to fail."

Jill pushed a blond curl behind her ear. "Why *doesn't* Peter go to the tutors?"

Ian sighed. "Jill, I don't know what it was like for you at the Conservatory, but at the university, the tutors are the friends and nephews and cousins of Committee members. There are a few good ones, but most of them either don't understand the material themselves or they'll sit cracking their gum while you struggle. It's a joke. Without my help, Peter won't make it through the year without getting an Academic Reprimand, and when he does get an AR, I guarantee he won't be able to bring his grades up high enough to make it through the probationary period."

"That's really too bad," she said quietly.

"He's a bright kid and he works as hard as he can. But Sheldon just sees him as an ideal chance to fill the department's recommended stats for ARs."

"Ian," Jill whispered.

"It's the truth." Ian slid a spatula under one of the sandwiches and flipped it over. "I called Health Services back in October to see if they'd change their minds about Peter's medication."

"Ian!"

"I thought maybe they didn't understand how these headaches are jeopardizing Peter's success at the university."

Jill looked sick to her stomach. "You could have really gotten in trouble."

Ian decided not to mention that Health Services *had* threatened to call the police if he didn't quit "harassing" them. He shrugged. "The kid needs help."

"You're not going to . . . well . . . do anything else foolish, are you?"

"Like meet with Peter Critchlow after Sheldon warned me not to? No. That would only make it worse for him. The only thing I can do is watch him self-destruct."

"I'm sorry. That poor boy. You must be very frustrated."

"I am." Ian softened at the compassion in her voice, feeling increasingly stupid for the way he had snapped at Daniel. "But frustration is no excuse for nastiness. I'm sorry I was rude. I'll behave next time." Being civil to Daniel wouldn't make things worse, and it would be easier on Jill.

Jill smiled thinly. "Daniel doesn't expect you to be polite to him right now. He said he doesn't care what names you call him as long as you cooperate."

Ian flipped the other sandwich. "Jill, I told you I'd read the case histories, and I will. But beyond that, Daniel is going to find himself confronting a lot more politeness than cooperation."

* * *

Snow flurries swirled in the sky and dusted Ian's hair as he walked toward Lt. Alisa Kent's duplex on Tuesday evening. His jaw was firm, his spine straight, and he had only one thought in mind.

Stay calm.

Regardless of whatever Kent wanted tonight, he would stay calm. To allow her to scare him was to yield her the upper hand, and tonight he was determined that she wasn't going to manipulate him.

Ian marched up the steps of Kent's duplex. Before he could ring the bell, the door swung open and Lt. Kent gestured him inside. Her expressionless face resembled stone more than flesh.

Ian couldn't help glancing at Kent's hands as he walked past her. The backs of her hands showed only the healing remnants of several shallow cuts. He wondered what the palms looked like.

Kent didn't offer him a seat, so he stood in the middle of the living room. On his previous visit, he'd been too shaken by the sight of blood and broken glass to get any feel for Alisa Kent's home, but now he observed the room with curiosity. It was immaculately clean and smelled of fresh paint. The furniture was upholstered in classic grays, reds, and blues, expertly coordinated with the landscape prints on the walls, the pearl-gray carpet, the silk flower arrangement, the pewter clock. The only item that looked like it had sneaked in behind the decorator's back was a bushy houseplant with shiny green runners trailing over the lamp table; it had a fat, complacent look, like an overindulged cat. The gleam of eyes peering from among the leaves made Ian blink hard; he did a double-take and realized the eyes were part of a ceramic leprechaun with skinny fingers hooked over the edge of the pot.

From her pocket, Kent withdrew a black, square device about the size of Ian's palm. She flicked a switch. "You are carrying a transmitter. Give it to me now."

"A transmitter! You mean you bugged me as well as my apartment?"

"I said give it to me."

"Why don't you tell me where it is first?" Ian had searched his apartment and the lounge at Tremont Electronics for more hidden bugs, but it hadn't occurred to him that he might be carrying one around with him.

The scanner wobbled in her hand and Ian realized she was trembling. She stepped closer and moved the scanner from shoulder height downward. At the level of his coat pockets, she paused and shifted the scanner left and right.

"Empty your right pocket," she said.

Ian pulled out his computer. "This is the only thing in there."

She took the computer, slid it out of its padded case, and handed the computer back to Ian.

"What are you doing?" he asked.

Kent ran her fingers over the case, then slipped her hand inside it. She probed at the inside of the case and withdrew her hand with a small, metal object pinched between two fingers.

Ian's mouth fell open.

Kent deactivated the transmitter and dropped it into her pocket. "You are a fool if you thought I would let you transmit this conversation to your Cadre friends."

"My *Cadre* friends?" Ian grabbed his computer case from Kent and stuck his hand inside it. His fingertips barely discerned a slit in the lining. Someone—Siskell?—had cut the lining and shoved a transmitter between the layers of fabric and padding. "Listen, Lieutenant, I didn't know anything about—"

"Have you joined the Liberty Cadre?"

"No."

"You will gather all your contraband literature and bring it to me."

"So you can read it, or burn it?"

"I will destroy it." Her eyes were bright and blank, as if the irises were chrome. "You are not to join the Liberty Cadre and you will cease all contact with your traitor friends."

"I never intended to join the Liberty Cadre."

"You come here carrying their transmitter and you think I'll believe you didn't intend to join them?"

"I told you, I didn't know the bug was there." Ian stowed the computer in his pocket. "If you'd stayed a little longer at that meeting, you'd know my opinion of the Cadre."

"You're all scum."

"Are they trying to blackmail you?"

"You have forty-eight hours to bring me your contraband litera-ture and to inform your friends that your association must end. You will make no attempts to corrupt other citizens. You will never again speak of your anarchist beliefs, and your behavior in all things will conform to accepted social patterns."

First Daniel Lansbury, now Alisa Kent. "What are you trying to do? Transform me into a patriot so you won't feel guilty over releasing me?"

"You have forty-eight hours."

"And if I won't cooperate? You can't arrest me without implicating yourself."

"I couldn't send you through the entire process of Information Extraction and sentencing, but I *could* have you arrested. I could subject you to another screening."

Ian's guts turned to ice. *Stay calm. Don't let her rattle you.* "You'd still have to let me go."

"Bear in mind that you are not the only one I could have arrested. I doubt you would enjoy seeing your sister taken to headquarters."

Murderous anger rushed over Ian. "If you dare hurt Jill—"

"Do not make it necessary. On Thursday evening you will bring me your books and give me your word that your treasonous activities will end."

It was all he could do to stop himself from grabbing Lt. Kent by the throat. "You'd take my word for it?" he asked acidly.

"Sometime within the next few months, I will have you brought in for a screening so I may learn if you are keeping your promise. If you have lied to me, then you are not the only one who will suffer."

Ian gripped one wrist with his other hand. *Stay calm. You won't help yourself or Jill by losing control.*

"Bring your book to me on Thursday evening." She walked toward the front door. "I will expect you at 7:00 P.M."

Book this time, Ian noted, not *books*. She claimed to want to confiscate all his illegal literature, but he had the feeling that only one book was truly the target of her anger. "So this is going to fix things," he said.

"I do not expect that these measures will uproot your devotion to your superstitions." She was talking too quickly, her words nearly crashing into each other. "But they will minimize the damage you can do." She pulled the door open. "Go."

Ian didn't move. He kept his gaze fixed on Lt. Kent, seeing the way the bones pressed through the skin of her face, the dark circles around her glassy eyes. "This isn't going to work, Alisa." He spoke quietly, deliberately using her first name rather than her police rank. She immediately clapped the door shut as if she feared a crowd of eavesdroppers were gathered on the porch.

"If you do not cooperate—" she began.

"No matter what you do to me, it won't make you feel better," Ian said. "It won't undo the fact that you released me in September, knowing I was a believer. And it won't undo the reason *why* you released me—whatever that was."

She broke eye contact with a twist of her head. "Get out of here."

He took a step toward her. "You arrested me at the university for allegedly protecting a traitor. You were making your way through an interrogation. Then, when you realized I shared the same religious beliefs as David Garrett, you tripped."

Her hand slid beneath her blazer. Ian steeled himself to look down the barrel of a gun, but after a moment Kent withdrew her hand, still empty. "I will not discuss this."

Ian drew a deep, steadying breath. "Let's talk about David Garrett."

Feverish redness suffused her cheeks. "What did the Cadre tell you?"

"They didn't tell me anything. Did you know Garrett in Jameston?"

"I have nothing to say to you."

"You knew him," Ian said. "And from the look on your face, he was someone you cared about."

"*No.* Get out of here, or you and your sister—"

"How did you know Garrett? You were only a teenager when he ran to the U.S."

"That's not your concern!"

Ian inched toward her. "How many people were involved in Garrett's religious meetings in Jameston fifteen years ago? I can't find any news reports that give the details of his original crimes."

Kent's gaze darted to the carpet, the walls, the door. Anywhere but toward Ian.

"Obviously you weren't involved yourself," Ian said. "But you knew Garrett and you must have known others in his group. Were friends of yours involved?"

"I will not discuss this!"

"Family?"

It was like plunging a knife in to the hilt and feeling hot blood gush over his hand. Kent recoiled, her eyes filled with the same agony Ian had witnessed before she fled the lounge at Tremont Electronics.

"Your *family?*" Ian said.

"Get out! Get out, *get out, get out!*" She yanked her gun from its holster, but Ian was already directly in front of her, and before she could aim the weapon, he grabbed her wrist and forced her hand into the air. He tore the gun from her fingers and threw it behind the couch.

Kent leapt toward the door, but Ian seized her arm.

"Don't panic. I just want to talk."

She wrenched her arm free. "I have nothing to say to you."

"Yes, you do."

Emotions were raw in her face—anguish, fury, shame. She backed away, cradling the fingers he had bruised in disarming her.

"Tell me about your family," Ian said gently.

"They are not worth discussing."

"They were involved with David Garrett's religious meetings in Jameston?"

"They were *scum*. Does that satisfy you?"

"Both your parents?"

"Yes."

"Brothers and sisters?"

"My sister." She was still breathing hard, but her voice was hollow.

"Do you have any other siblings?"

"No."

Her entire family, believers. "How could the child of Garrett followers become a police officer? Even if you weren't involved, their treason should have destroyed your reputation."

Kent ran her tongue over her lips. Her eyes stared through him.

Goosebumps prickled Ian's flesh. There *was* a way Alisa Kent's reputation could have survived that scandal not only unscathed, but enhanced.

"You turned them in, didn't you?" he said.

"They got what they deserved."

"And David Garrett?"

"David escaped. They didn't."

"How did you find out what they were up to?"

"They were foolish enough to hold a meeting in my family's home. Studying David's precious book."

"While *you* were there?"

She uttered a harsh, derisive laugh, but her expression was blank. "I was at a school dance. I returned home unexpectedly early."

"Where is your family now?"

"Dead."

"They were executed?"

"Yes."

Ian swallowed, but it didn't help his dry mouth. "Why weren't they sent to prison?"

"They were."

"They served time in prison first?"

"Yes."

"How long?"

"Fifteen years . . . my parents. Callie—my sister—was there for four years."

"What happened to Callie?"

"She died in prison. It was termed an 'accident.'"

"It wasn't an accident?"

"Prison guards are generally not fond of Garrett followers."

A chill spread through Ian's chest. He didn't want to know what had happened to Callie, though Alisa Kent would probably give him the specifics in emotionless detail if he asked for them. He should have been grateful that Kent was cooperating with his questions, but instead he felt fear rising at the emptiness in her face. What was she feeling? *Was* she feeling? "Then, if your parents spent fifteen years in prison—they were executed *this* year?"

"Yes. May. May eighteenth."

"Why did they spend so many years in prison before they were executed?"

Fury exploded through the blankness in her eyes like lava from an erupting volcano. "They were *fools!* Wouldn't recant—they deserved to die! *You* deserve to die, you anarchist liar!"

She lunged at him. Startled, Ian dodged to the side, nearly colliding with a chair. Kent veered to follow him, and he bent and threw himself toward her. Fists like balls of iron struck his shoulders, his chest, the side of his head as he caught her around the waist and tackled her to the ground.

She struggled out from under him, but Ian grabbed her shoulder and flipped her onto her stomach. Before she could push herself up, he sprang on top of her and used his weight to hold her down while he grabbed for her hands. *"Alisa—"*

She clawed blindly behind her in an effort to reach him. Ian caught her wrists and pinned them against her spine.

Kent writhed, tears pouring from eyes that were now black whirlpools of madness.

". . . traitors . . . worthless . . ." The words strangled in her throat, and for an instant she was silent. Then she gasped for air and sobs convulsed her body.

When her arms were limp in his grasp, he cautiously released her. Her hands slid to the ground at her sides and remained there.

Grimacing at the aches from the multiple bruises she had given him, Ian rose unsteadily to his feet and stepped out of striking range. Kent remained prone on the carpet, sobbing like a child.

Ian ran sweaty fingers through his hair, probing the lump where Kent's fist had connected with his skull. He wanted to just collapse into a chair and wait for his knees to stop shaking, but he couldn't leave Alisa Kent crying on the floor.

In the kitchen, he filled a glass with cold water and grabbed a clean dishtowel. Back in the living room, he placed the glass of water and the towel on a table and knelt at Kent's side. Touching her seemed about as intelligent as jabbing a grizzly bear with a stick, but he had to help her if possible. Gingerly, he rested his hand on her shoulder.

She didn't react. Braced to defend himself, Ian rolled Kent onto her back. She flopped like a cloth doll. Tears poured from beneath closed eyelids.

"Let's get you onto the couch." Ian slipped his arm beneath her shoulders and raised her off the ground. Her head tipped backward and her hands flew out, reaching for something to steady her. One hand caught the front of his shirt and the other clutched his arm in a grip that drove her nails into his flesh.

"Take it easy." He lifted her to her feet, but her legs wavered beneath her. With his arm around her waist, he helped her to the couch and tried to lower her onto the cushions. She clung to him like he was dangling her over a twenty-storey drop.

After a paralyzed moment of trepidation, Ian sat down with Alisa Kent and drew her into his arms. He expected her to shove him away, but she crumpled against his shoulder.

"They weren't supposed to die," she sobbed. "They weren't supposed to die."

CHAPTER 10

"They weren't supposed to die?" Ian repeated softly. "Did you think they'd just serve their sentences and return, free of their delusions?"

Jagged sobs were Alisa Kent's only reply. Ian couldn't see her face; her bowed head rested against his shoulder and he could see only tousled black hair spilling down the front of his shirt and rigid white fingers clinging to his arm.

"But after fifteen years in prison, they still wouldn't renounce their beliefs, and so they died," Ian finished for her. "Then David Garrett . . . he died too, still stubborn. That's why you let me go, isn't it? Their courage terrified you because you couldn't believe they could draw that much strength from a lie. You started to wonder if they might be right."

"No."

Ian put his finger under her chin and gently tilted her head back so he could look into her face. "What was your boss thinking when he assigned you to David Garrett's case? Was he *trying* to break you?"

Kent choked, face contorted as she fought to control herself.

Ian released her chin. She sank back against his shoulder, the warmth of her tears soaking his shirt.

Her panicky grip gradually relaxed, and her sobs faded to quiet, exhausted weeping. "No one deliberately assigned me to Garrett's case." She mumbled the words into Ian's chest. "The nature of his crimes and the area of his activity made him my responsibility."

Ian reached awkwardly for the dishtowel and laid it in her hands. "That's pretty monumental bad luck."

She pulled away from him and wiped her face with the towel. "Luck was not involved." Pain snagged her voice and she was sobbing again. "The choice was David's. He learned where I was assigned . . . he concentrated the distribution of his propaganda in that area."

"He wanted to confront you?"

"Fool . . . a *fool* . . . Should have stayed in the U.S. Even his *church* advised him not to come back—"

"They didn't want him to come?"

"They do not . . . encourage their members to spread their message in violation of law. Or at risk to their lives."

"Was it coincidence that his return came right on the heels of your parents' executions?"

She tore at the towel. "He knew their time had expired . . . he'd been monitoring Tremont broadcasts . . . saw their names . . ."

Tremont broadcasts. Ian always read the prison bulletins himself; he must have seen the Kents' names. But at the time they would have meant nothing to him. "Why did Garrett want to confront you?"

Her body twisted. "I don't want to *talk* about this."

"Who was David Garrett to you? You must have known him very well."

"A neighbor—my parents' best friend . . ."

"After he came to Tremont, before he was arrested . . . did he talk to you? Visit you?"

A wash of fury surged beneath the tears. "He came," she said savagely, "to surrender."

"To surrender! He surrendered to *you*?"

She nodded.

"That's not what the news said."

"The news reports were . . . inaccurate."

Ian was puzzled that Garrett would give himself up so easily, but then he swiftly realized the truth—Garrett had never intended his dispersal of contraband to be a long-term operation. The main reason he had come to Tremont was to confront Alisa Kent.

"What did Garrett say to you?" Ian asked.

"Please don't ask about this . . ."

"What did he say?"

"No." Her crying intensified into gasping sobs of panic. Ian guided her head back to his shoulder and stroked her hair like he

was soothing a child, smoothing rumpled, ebony strands with his fingertips.

When the worst of her sobbing had ebbed, he said quietly, "David Garrett wanted to help you, didn't he? He knew how your parents' executions would affect you. He cared enough to come . . . try to help you understand."

"He was . . . a *fool*."

"Before you found your family and David Garrett studying the Book of Mormon, did you have any idea what they were up to?"

Kent shook her head, a brief friction of damp hair against his shirt.

"You didn't suspect?" he asked.

"It was not . . . difficult for them to conceal what they were doing. I wasn't home much . . . I paid them little attention."

"Was it David Garrett who introduced them to the Book of Mormon?"

"They were . . . all deceived."

"And your parents taught your sister," Ian said. "But not you?"

She jerked away from him, bloodred fury contorting her face, eyes rabid with pain. "Callie was naive . . . they knew she'd believe anything they said—told *her* everything—told *her* . . ." She paused to swallow. "They never even tried to . . . they told *her*—" Kent crumpled under a new assault of tears. Ian drew her back into his arms and held her through sobs that shook her like they would snap her bones.

Exhaustion finally reduced Kent's sobbing to a feeble, labored gasp. Ian coaxed half a glass of water down her throat, but he didn't continue to speak to her. He'd done enough interrogating for the night.

Her head was heavy on his shoulder, her body increasingly limp as her tears eased to silence. Relieved that she was calm at last, Ian took awhile to realize that Kent was not just quiet, but unnaturally still. He touched her hand and found it ice cold.

"Alisa?"

She didn't answer. Ian tipped her head back. Her face was gray, her pupils dilated. She looked the way Jill had when news had come of their father's car accident.

"Alisa." What had his aunt done for Jill when she'd been sinking into shock? *Lay her down, keep her warm—?* Ian racked his brain, trying to remember the rest of it. *Loosen tight clothing—*

"Look, let's make you a little more comfortable." Hastily, Ian tugged off Kent's blazer, unbuckled her empty shoulder holster, unbuttoned her sleeves and the top button of her collar. She sat in apathetic silence, neither cooperating nor resisting.

"Lie down here—" No, the undersized couch was too short to accommodate her and the living room was uncomfortably chilly. "You need to be in bed," he concluded.

Kent didn't respond.

Ian wrapped his arm around her shoulders and guided her along the hallway, pushing doors open as he passed them. The first door led to an office, the second to a bathroom. On the third try, he found her bedroom. He ripped the bedcovers back and eased Kent onto the bed. Her head sank into the pillow. Her eyes closed.

Ian bent to remove Kent's shoes and a whirl of dizziness threw him off balance. He landed on his hands and knees, the room blurring around him.

The dizziness faded, leaving Ian queasy and bewildered. What was wrong with him? Maybe Kent wasn't the only one suffering a physical reaction to stress. Or maybe she'd clubbed him a lot harder than he'd realized.

He breathed deeply to clear his head, but the inhalation brought another swoop of dizziness. Digging his fingers into the carpet, he waited.

When the walls were solid and still, he rose carefully to his feet. This time the dizziness didn't return. Kent lay unmoving, apparently oblivious.

"Alisa?"

She didn't stir. She couldn't have fallen asleep so quickly. She must have fainted. Ian touched her throat, probing for the pulse beneath her ashen skin. Thoughts of calling the emergency line flitted through his brain, but he knew that was the last thing Kent would want.

He slid her shoes off and pulled the bedcovers over her shoulders. If she didn't regain consciousness within a few minutes, he *would* call an ambulance and risk the consequences.

* * *

Scott Siskell swore ferociously, hissing the obscenities through his chipped tooth. "She triggered it. She's sleeping like a baby—and that idiot Roshek is hovering over her like a worried daddy."

"Keep your voice down." Five paced angrily around the unoccupied apartment adjoining Alisa Kent's unit. "There's nothing we can do about it now."

"Sure there's something we can do about it." Siskell yanked the gun from under his jacket.

"Calm down," Ten said crossly. She was an egg-shaped shadow near the projector. "You know Zero doesn't want Roshek dead yet."

"This week, next week, who cares?" Siskell passed the gun from hand to hand. "Besides, Zero needs the last session finished tonight. Those bombs go off on Friday."

"We can't kill Roshek tonight," Five snapped. "Put your gun away."

Siskell swore as he shoved the gun back into its holster. The thought of spending another endless evening waiting for Kent to go to bed infuriated him. "Let's go in as soon as Roshek leaves."

"The capsule is already empty," Ten pointed out. "We can't go in there unless she's unconscious."

Ten's schoolteacher tone made Siskell want to crush her windpipe. "We wait until we're sure she's asleep," he growled. "Then we creep in there, zap her with a stun square, and do our work. She'll never know what hit her."

"What if she wakes up before we can zap her? Stun squares are unpredictable. Even if you knock her out, she might wake up before—"

"Will you shut up? I'm telling you, we could do it. And even if she knows we've been there, she won't know what we did to her. It won't mess anything up." Siskell looked over to where Five was pacing and sucking angrily on a maple drop. "Come on, Five, what do you say? Let's finish this tonight."

* * *

Nine minutes passed before Alisa Kent stirred. Fourteen minutes passed before she opened her eyes in response to Ian's voice, her expression so dazed that he doubted she could have told him her own name.

"Are you all right?" he asked in relief. "You fainted."

She started to sit up, but Ian rested his hand on her shoulder. "Lie still."

She sank back. A hint of pink had returned to her lips and to the swollen skin around her eyes. "May I have some water?" she whispered.

"I'll be right back." Ian hurried to the kitchen.

He returned to find Kent kneeling on the floor, hand scrabbling at the bedspread. Was she groping for a handhold so she could finish a stalled attempt to stand up?

"What are you doing? You need to stay in bed." Steadying her with a hand on her shoulder, Ian offered her the glass. She drank a few swallows.

He helped her back into the bed. "Now stay there, or you're going to pass out again."

"Please go," she whispered.

"I don't think so."

"Go. I retract what I . . . said earlier. I will not harm you . . . or your sister. Just go."

"I'll go," he said, "but only as far as the living room. Get some rest. When I'm sure you're all right, I'll head home. And I'll be back tomorrow night, but not to surrender any books. We have a lot to talk about."

New tears welled in her eyes. She turned away from him and drew the bedcovers up to her chin. "Leave me alone."

"Get some rest." Ian turned off the light on his way out the door.

An hour later, he yielded to the urge to check on Alisa Kent. Her door was ajar, so he could look in without disturbing her.

Light from the hallway cast a bright band across the carpet, stopping short of Kent's bed, but illuminating the room enough so Ian could see that her eyes were closed, her face soft with the vulnerability of deep sleep.

Ian tiptoed back down the hallway. As he passed Kent's study, a gleam of glass and gold caught his eye. Curious, he leaned into the room and flipped on the lights.

Oak shelves lined one wall of the study, filled from floor to ceiling with trophies, plaques, and framed certificates. Amazed, Ian stepped closer to examine the glittering evidence of Alisa Kent's achievements. He picked up a framed certificate declaring Alisa Kent the fifth-grade student of the year. Fifth grade? Shaking his head, he scanned the rest of the awards. Honor rolls, speech and debate contests, scholarships, high school valedictorian. Star-shaped trophies for Young Neighbor of the Year, three years running. A heavy wood-and-brass plaque honoring Kent as Northeast Regional Junior Security Representative. Pictures of Kent accepting her various awards—some snapshots, some professional photographs. Framed newspaper articles detailing her academic and citizenship awards.

Half a dozen trophies shaped like musical notes made Ian's eyes bulge. The Jameston Singers, first place in the Northeast Choral Competition. Second place. First place again. Alisa Kent *sang?* He picked up a photograph of the choir and found Kent on the back row, mouth curved in an arrogant smile, obsidian waves of hair flooding over her shoulders.

Awards from her college years. Athletic awards—volleyball, ski team, tennis team. Diplomas. A master's degree in political science, summa cum laude. *Interesting,* Ian thought. Did police officers usually go for advanced degrees before entering the police academy? Or had becoming a police officer not been Kent's original ambition?

Awards from the Tremont Police Service filled the last third of the shelves along with assorted patriotic awards she had received as an adult. The last item on the shelf was a photograph of Kent clad in a dress uniform, accepting her gold-class James Tremont Patriotic Service Award from Councilor Marcus Lansbury. The highest honor of all. There was no empty space on the shelf where the award could have fit. It must have hung in her living room until she smashed it and ripped it apart.

He turned away from the shelves, feeling slightly sick. Alisa Kent must be frantic to prove her self-worth if she felt compelled to surround herself with every award she'd won since childhood.

Against the opposite wall stood a worktable lit by a gooseneck lamp. Spools of gold and silver thread were lined up next to a plastic divider filled with beads. A tool case lay open and a half-finished necklace trailed silver wires across the table. Ian touched the necklace, admiring the intricate loops of wire accented with tiny, glittering crystals.

He opened the cupboard over the worktable and found dozens of hooks displaying finished pieces of jewelry, all of the quality that had Sherry Mason gushing compliments. Kent had told Sherry that she'd only been doing this for a year. She must have worked at it in every spare moment to produce this many pieces in so short a time.

Ian picked up one of the tools from the case. Initials were scratched into the handle: CK. He checked the top of the case and found a plastic ID tag: *Callie Kent, 270 Maplewood Dr., Jameston.* A chilly sensation slithered over his skin. *Alisa Kent's sister.*

"They told her." Kent had felt agonized jealousy at being shut out while Callie was drawn in—but how could she imagine that her parents would have dared entrust her with their beliefs, the girl with the conceited smile who ignored her family and collected patriotic awards like they were baseball cards?

When she'd betrayed them, had she acted partly out of fury that they had excluded her? Or out of genuinely outraged patriotism? Or out of the raging fear that her family's crimes, unreported, would destroy her ambitions?

Ian picked up a spool of gold thread, imagining Kent inter-twining gossamer threads for endless hours over the past year, her sister's tools in her hands, her back to the shelves crammed with public adulation, her mind darkening steadily with the fear of her parents' impending executions. Had she found comfort in taking up Callie's hobby, or had she been punishing herself, clawing at her guilt until it was raw and bleeding?

At eleven thirty, Ian checked on Alisa Kent again. She was still asleep, and chances were she'd stay that way for the rest of the night. She probably hadn't slept well for months, and now that she had finally succumbed to exhaustion, he doubted she would wake until morning.

He left her a note saying he'd return at seven o'clock tomorrow night, and slipped out the front door.

* * *

Behind Alisa Kent's closed eyelids, a headache pierced the blackness of unconsciousness. Whispers . . . leaves brushing together, drifting to the grass. Callie twirling a crimson maple leaf in her fingertips, humming to herself. Not humming. Talking. No—not Callie. Several voices.

A dream.

Alisa strained for consciousness. Light seared her eyes. A shadow lifted a bulky object onto a table. Another shadow thrust the needle of a hypodermic syringe into a vial.

Dreams. *Wake up.*

"Seven!" A shrill female voice startled Alisa. She sprang forward, but a gloved hand clamped around her throat and slammed her against her pillow.

"She sure wasn't out long. Hurry up, you fool!" The fingers dug viciously into her neck, choking her. Hands grabbed her arms and pinned them against the mattress.

"No, don't stun her again." A different voice, this one rough with fear. "It's too late. Just give her the shot."

Three intruders, clothed and masked in black. Alisa kicked at her assailants, her legs tangling in the bedcovers. She couldn't breathe.

"All right, it's done." The female voice again. The hand released Alisa's throat. She gasped for air as her thoughts shimmered away from reality.

CHAPTER 11

"Thanks for meeting me here." Daniel started the engine and backed out of his numbered parking slot. "I promise not to make you late for rehearsal."

"It doesn't start until three on Wednesdays," Jill said. "Lunch won't take that long."

"I've got to be back at the lab by two thirty anyway." Daniel drove out of the parking garage adjacent to the Tremont police complex. "I'm sorry I didn't have a chance to call you yesterday. I never had a minute free. You're playing the Mozart today, aren't you?"

"If I don't have a nervous breakdown first."

"You think Richard will be hard on you?"

"No, not at all. It's just . . . I wish I weren't soloing."

"You'll be fantastic." Daniel slowed for a traffic light. "How's your brother?"

The question she had been dreading. Jill focused on the statue of President Tremont towering on a granite pedestal in front of the Council Building. "Oh . . . he's all right."

"You don't sound very sure."

"Well, I think he's . . . worried about a lot of things."

"Did he talk to you about it?"

Jill picked at a hole in her glove.

"Jill, what did he say? The more I know, the more I can help him."

That was true, but she doubted Ian would be impressed by that argument. What would he think of her if he knew she took his confidences straight to Daniel?

But if she wanted Daniel to know how best to keep him safe . . . no more trouble with the police, no more trouble with the Watch . . . "Well—he told me about some problems he was having with the . . ." She chewed her lip. "With the Education Regulatory Committee."

"What kind of problems?" Daniel glanced at her. "I won't tell Ian you confided in me. Don't worry about that."

Jill blundered through Ian's story, trying to phrase it so it didn't sound like Ian had been overly critical of either Health Services or the Committee. It wasn't easy to soften Ian's words without distorting them, and by the time she finished, she knew her face was bright red.

Daniel was silent for only a few moments before saying kindly, "This type of trouble is exactly what I'd expect of Ian." His gloved fingers brushed Jill's cheek. "Once again, compassion for an individual makes it difficult for him to see the needs of the nation. He sees a suffering boy and can't comprehend why Health Services made the decision to use its resources elsewhere." Daniel frowned. "It takes perspective and maturity to realize that sometimes one person must be sacrificed for the good of the whole."

"And you'll help Ian gain that perspective."

"Yes." Daniel turned left on Ingram Road. "But it will take some work. Did Ian mention this student's name?"

"Oh—Peter. Peter . . ." Jill searched her memory. It had been an unusual last name that reminded her of squeaky hinges. "Peter Critchlow. Why?"

Daniel shrugged. "Did Ian say anything else?"

"No . . . no . . . that was all."

"You're a terrible liar," Daniel said with a fond smile.

Jill's cheeks burned so hot that she longed to roll down the window for a blast of cold air in her face. She didn't want to admit what Ian had said, but under Daniel's now-penetrating gaze, she didn't know how to conceal it. "He just said . . . he isn't sure he plans to cooperate with you."

Daniel laughed shortly. "I doubt he phrased it so diplomatically. Jill, don't get scared. I know Ian is stubborn. You don't get yourself in as much trouble as he has unless you've got a wide stubborn streak. It'll take time, patience, and probably a little bullying, but we'll straighten him out."

Jill nodded, but beneath her gratitude to Daniel flowed a stream of fear. What if Ian wouldn't cooperate, despite everything Daniel did? What if Ian's problems weren't something Daniel could fix? Sometimes the way Ian acted—the things he said . . .

She hastily tilted the conversation in a new direction. "I wish he'd get his nose out of his computer and find a girlfriend."

"Does he date much?"

"He asks someone out every now and then, but never for more than a date or two. I can't figure out who this perfect woman is that he's waiting for." She toyed with the chrome door latch. "He had a serious girlfriend awhile back. I think they were almost engaged. But she left Tremont to go to school, and while she was away, she met someone else."

"How long ago was this?"

"Oh . . . a long time. The year after our mother died. Six years ago. But I think it really hurt him. Maybe that's why he's so skittish about relationships now."

"Ah." Daniel grinned mischievously. "Well, after we've dealt with his other problems, we'll fix his social life."

"Oh, he'll *really* appreciate that." Jill laughed with Daniel, but inside, worry remained like a lump of ice.

Daniel parked at Pepper's Restaurant. "Italian all right?"

"Wonderful."

"I have something for you." He picked up a dress bag that lay across the backseat. "You could wear it for your solo debut this weekend."

Jill gasped. The sea-green fabric draped so gracefully that she wondered if it was silk. Seed pearls decorated the bodice of the gown. "Daniel! It's gorgeous!"

"I'm glad you like it. So are you going to invite me to the reception after the concert?"

Jill's heart flipped a somersault. "I thought you wouldn't want to come to such a public—"

Daniel waved her words aside. "It's a small party, right?"

"Just priority ticket holders."

"I'm a priority ticket holder. Mind if I come? I promise to use my good manners." He grinned. "Actually, I *have* to use my good manners—my parents will be there."

Jill's delight plunged into horror. "Your parents!"

"I *told* you Dad likes you."

Jill fingered the sleeve of the dress. Had she been wrong about Councilor Lansbury? If he was willing to be seen at the reception with her, she must have been wrong.

"Councilor Brannigan is coming as well, to the concert and the reception. He's heard me talk so much about you that he's dying to meet you."

"You're teasing!"

"Of course I'm not teasing. It'll be the best concert of the year. No one does Mozart's Fourth as well as you. Clear as crystal, light as a feather." Daniel returned the dress bag to the backseat. "Take the dress home and try it on. If it doesn't fit, let me know and I'll have it altered immediately. I'll go pick up our lunch. How does lobster ravioli sound?"

"Delicious," Jill said. She had no idea how lobster might taste.

"Back in a minute." Daniel exited the car.

Dazed, Jill watched Daniel stride toward the restaurant. Last week she'd been certain she would never see Daniel Lansbury again. Now, not only was their relationship stronger than ever, but Ian was getting the help he needed so he'd never get in trouble again. Everything would be wonderful.

As long as Ian cooperated with Daniel.

* * *

Irritable after a class where two hyperactive girls had repeatedly interrupted him to offer odd bits of trivia about James Tremont—did anyone really care about Tremont's shoe size?—Ian was so glad to be exiting the classroom that he paid no attention to the woman standing in the hallway until she fell into step beside him, hurrying to match his pace. He looked over and stopped in his tracks.

"Laura!"

A smile sparkled across her face. "Hi, Professor."

"I didn't know you were back in Tremont."

"We've only been back for a week or so." She stepped closer and rose up on her toes to kiss his cheek.

A flush crawled up his neck. He stepped back and tried to speak casually. "It's good to see you." Laura's chestnut-brown hair was twined in a long braid, and the autumn golds and reds of her scarf complemented the olive tint of her skin. Ian wished acutely that once—just *once*—he could look at Laura without noticing how beautiful she was.

"You free for a while?" she asked.

"Uh—yeah, I'm done teaching for the day."

"I know. I checked your schedule—how do you think I found you here? Come on, I'll buy you lunch."

He glanced involuntarily at the ring on Laura's left hand. "Uh—look, I was just going to grab something quick—"

"OK if I grab a sandwich along with you?" Her voice was light, but she had dropped the smile from her face. Ian got the message—this wasn't a social visit. He hoped Laura wasn't here to bring him any new contraband writings. After the sweep in September, the thought of Laura carrying illegal material around Tremont terrified him.

They bought sandwiches and walked down the wooded path that led to a park on the south end of campus. What would have been a beautiful stroll in June or October was a march through a dismal corridor of leafless branches in December, and Ian wasn't surprised that no one else was using either the path or the park. He gestured Laura toward one of the picnic tables.

"Grim day." Laura shivered as she eyed the steel-gray clouds. She turned up the collar of her red wool coat and tucked her scarf more securely around her neck. "Aren't you freezing?"

Ian looked at his tweed sports coat and realized his heavy coat was still hanging in his office. He *was* cold, but he hadn't noticed it until now. "I'm all right."

"Men." Laura unwrapped her sandwich. "No matter how old they are, they still need a mother to tell them to put on their coats."

"So are you glad to be back in Tremont?" Ian took a mechanical bite of ham and cheese.

"Very glad. Three months in Paxton was three months too long. Too small, and the training program was duller than dull. How have you been? You look tired."

"Thanks, nurse."

"Is everything all right?"

He'd been wishing for someone to confide in, and here was Laura Stewart Travers looking at him with concern in her amber eyes. Concern in her eyes and a wedding band on her finger. He wasn't going to dump his problems on Matt Travers's wife. "Things are fine," he said. Laura looked dubious, so he added quickly, "How's Matt?"

"Fine, he's fine. We found a great apartment. It's a lovely white frame house right across from the hospital on Wareham Street. We're in the basement and our apartment is tiny, but everything is *new*—no leaky pipes, no drafty windows. And we can walk to work in two minutes."

"It sounds great." Ian took another mouthful of sandwich. The bread was stale.

Laura nibbled at her own sandwich. She kept glancing around, and finally she said in a low voice, "I wanted to ask you—are you still studying that book I gave you?"

"You've given me a lot of books."

"I'm not talking about the political stuff from my grandfather's shed."

Ian looked out over the ragged grass, stubbornly green despite the chill. "I'm studying it, yes."

"You still believe it?"

"Yes. And it has what we've been searching for—the answers for how to get out of the mess we're in. The way to freedom. I wish you'd read it."

"Too deep for me. Why do you think I passed it on to you?" She laughed nervously. "But I came to warn you—" She looked around again. No one was in sight, but she dropped her voice to a whisper anyway.

"Matt has a lot of connections. He hears about what's going on in the Tremont Police, and some of the things he's said lately got me worrying about you."

Ian's stomach knotted around a lump of stale bread. "Why?"

"Ian, they're really coming down hard on religious believers."

Relief flickered through him. He had expected her to say something about Alisa Kent. "Is that new?"

"Not new, but worse. Especially for anyone associated with that Christian-Mormon book. You heard all about what happened to David Garrett?"

Ian thought of Alisa Kent sobbing on his shoulder. "Yeah."

"I guess Colonel Edgefield is really nervous about what kind of damage Garrett did this last time. He wasn't able to pass out very many of those books—he could only sneak a few of them into Tremont, and he didn't dare distribute electronic versions for fear of random scans—but the police are really paranoid about people reading them. Sedition and Treason is focusing a ton of resources on finding anyone who's been influenced by that book."

Ian wadded the wrapper around his half-eaten sandwich. "I'll be careful."

"That's not enough. You need to get rid of the book."

"No."

"Ian! Those old political books we found, even the ones on the banned list, would only get you a couple of years in prison. But that Mormon book—you'll be lucky if you even *make* it to prison. Matt's heard rumors that they're executing anyone who won't immediately renounce the book. Even if you do renounce it, the best you can hope for is to end up in a cell until you're an old man."

Dry branches rattled overhead and the wind cut into Ian's flesh. "I appreciate the warning."

"You're not listening, are you?"

"I am, Laura."

"Matt knows a lot about how the police operate. The interrogation technique they use—they call it 'Information Extraction'—"

Fear formed like ice crystals in Ian's blood.

"They have a drug they use, a stimulant that does crazy things to your brain. First you tell them anything they want to know. You have no control over what you say. And when it's over, you—it's like living in a nightmare. Some people get better, some don't." Laura squeezed his hand. "You don't want to get mixed up with the police. Get rid of that book. It's not worth it. I'm sorry I gave it to you."

"I'm not." He pulled his hand free.

"You know how they did that contraband sweep here a few months ago? That was because of David Garrett."

"Was it?" Ian said. "From what I've heard, it was all a setup. The police planted that literature on the people who were 'caught' with it."

Laura's eyes widened. *"You* heard that? From where?"

He shrugged. He didn't feel up to discussing the Liberty Cadre.

"You're right, the pamphlets were planted," Laura said. "But the point is that the police were trying to scare people who might come across Garrett's stuff. And that's only the first step. How long will it be until they start going door to door?"

"The book is hidden."

"How well?"

Not well enough to defeat a determined searcher. Ian looked away from Laura, knowing she had read the answer in his face.

"When it comes to survival, you've got to be practical." Laura checked her watch and rewrapped her sandwich. "I'd better go. I've got a meeting at the hospital this afternoon."

They stood up. "Thanks for coming to warn me," Ian said.

"I hope you listen. This is a dangerous time to be acting foolish."

"I understand."

"Sometimes I wonder how much of the real world you do understand."

"If God exists and speaks to us, and that book was written through His power," Ian said, "then which one of us doesn't understand the real world?"

A slight, rueful smile lifted the corners of her mouth. "Stay safe." She headed for the bus stop at the edge of the park. Ian watched her until the last glimpse of chestnut hair and red wool coat disappeared from sight.

His limbs were as cold and heavy as stone as he trudged up the hill toward his office. Why did Laura have to come today?

Warmth swept over his skin as he entered the Ryce Building, but the chill inside him remained untouched. *"They have a drug . . . that does crazy things to your brain . . . Some people get better, some don't . . . Get rid of that book."*

Fingers still half-numb, he unlocked his office door. If he could just hide in his office for a while, pray for the courage that was crumbling away—

Crumbling away? He'd never had that much courage to begin with, had never counted on having to stand alone while even Eric turned aside, while even Laura Travers chiseled away at his resolve.

He pushed the door open and his heart jolted. Alisa Kent was standing in his office.

Ian stepped inside and snapped the door shut. Kent's eyes were wild and she was breathing like she had been frantically pacing from wall to wall.

"Have you joined the Liberty Cadre?" Her question shot out like the hiss of an arrow. "Tell the truth. If you lie to me, you'll regret it."

"This is not a safe place to talk in the middle of the day." Ian tried to keep his voice calm. "Is your car parked behind the building?"

"Answer my—"

"I'll tell you anything you want to know, but not here." Ian opened the door. Kent stayed where she was, her black-gloved hand braced against the desk like it was the only thing keeping her upright.

"Come on." Ian gripped Kent's elbow and guided her out of the office, hoping she wasn't irrational enough to make a scene. A few students eyed Ian as he escorted Kent out of the building, but he saw curiosity in their gazes, not suspicion.

Kent unlocked her car, but before she could slide behind the wheel, Ian stuck out his arm to block her. "I'll drive. You don't look—uh—quite up to it."

He expected her to protest, but she handed him her keys without comment. Hoping his driving skills weren't so rusty as to make him a public menace, Ian drove carefully out of the parking lot and headed south.

"Stop anywhere. It doesn't matter." Kent's voice was like the edge of a knife.

"Take it easy. Let's get out of the center of campus." If she no longer cared about being overheard, was it because she had already decided to turn them in?

Ian steered into the deserted parking lot of a maintenance building located on the far edge of campus. Amid the wintry skeletons of oak and sumac trees, he parked behind the building and faced Alisa Kent.

"Now, tell me what—"

"Have you joined the Liberty Cadre?" The question lurched out, panicky now.

"I have not joined the Cadre."

"Don't *lie* to me."

"Alisa," he said quietly. "I told you last night I wasn't joining the Liberty Cadre. I find their attacks on civilians abhorrent, their recruiter Siskell an ignorant thug, and their leader Zero an idiot who hasn't figured out that his terrorist tactics only strengthen the status quo. What can I do to convince you that I'm not joining the Liberty Cadre? Do you want to arrest me, take me to headquarters, see what your little lie detectors have to say about my honesty? Is that what it would take?"

From the angry suspicion in her eyes, Ian feared she planned to take him up on his suggestion, but then she looked away, her shoulders slumping. "What time did you leave my house last night?"

"Around eleven thirty. Why?"

Her hand drifted to the neck of her black turtleneck sweater and tugged it higher on her throat. "Did you note anything unusual?"

"Like what?"

"People near my home . . . cars on the street . . . sounds or lights coming from the house that adjoins mine?"

"There wasn't anyone on the street. And I'm sure I would have noticed if there were lights on next door." The source of Kent's accusations abruptly became clear. "The Cadre came to you last night, didn't they? What did they want?"

She bent forward, her hands knotted in her lap.

"Alisa, what did they want? They're blackmailing you, aren't they?"

Kent said nothing.

"Fine, don't talk. Eric Vettori knows how to contact Siskell. I'll meet with Eric tonight and find out what's up. Give me your phone."

Kent surrendered it, not lifting her head.

Ian punched in the number of the phone Eric carried during working hours. He'd demand a meeting using the code words they had agreed on long ago should anyone need to alert the other members of the group to an emergency. Eric wouldn't dare ignore the emergency code.

"Tremont Electronics, Repair Service, Craig here."

Taken aback, Ian said, "May I talk to Eric Vettori?"

"Vettori's gone."

"He's not working today?"

"Nah, he quit."

"He quit!" Ian exclaimed. Alisa Kent gave him a sharp look. "Listen, do you know where Eric is working now?"

"No clue. He left real suddenly, didn't say much about it. I've got his route now. Can I help you?"

"No, thanks." Ian broke the connection. Why would Eric quit his job? He'd been thrilled to land that position. The pay and hours were the best he'd found.

"Your friend is no longer at Tremont Electronics?" Kent asked.

"I guess not." Ian raked his fingers through his hair. "He didn't say anything to me about changing jobs."

Kent pulled out her computer, stripped off her gloves, and typed rapidly into the keyboard. "Your friend is no longer in Tremont. He is registered in Newbold Bay."

"Newbold Bay!"

Kent typed something else and clicked the computer shut. "Your friend Sandring is gone too. He's in Paxton."

"Paxton? Wait a minute, this doesn't make sense. They wouldn't leave without telling me. How—"

"Clearly the Liberty Cadre arranged the moves." Kent spat the words out.

"What do you mean, the Cadre *arranged* them?"

"You idiot." Kent plucked her phone out of his hand. "Do you think it was coincidence that they both left Tremont at the same time? The Cadre evidently had need of them elsewhere."

"But they haven't joined—there hasn't been time—"

"Your friends didn't tell you they were joining the Liberty Cadre?"

Ian felt like he was stumbling through an underground cave with a burned-out flashlight in his hand. "I knew they were interested in the Cadre, but I thought they'd come to their senses. They *will* come to their senses—I've got to talk to them—"

"Even if your friends wanted to withdraw from the Cadre, they could not do so now, nor could they discuss the Cadre with you."

"Why not?"

"When they joined, the Cadre would have required them to swear an oath of secrecy and lifetime loyalty. If they violate that oath, the Cadre will kill them."

Horrified, Ian stared at Alisa Kent. Eric and Tim had bound themselves to the Liberty Cadre with unbreakable chains?

"Did you know so little of your friends that you couldn't anticipate their actions?" Kent asked.

"Look, you don't understand. Eric's not the kind of person who—he's impulsive, but—"

"From listening to him at your meetings, I'd say the Cadre is exactly what he's been looking for."

"No. *No.* He wants to fight, wants to take action, but not with the Cadre, not a terrorist gang. He could never condone—"

Kent began to laugh, a frenzied laugh that could cross into hysteria at any moment. "You are as big a fool as David Garrett was. Blind, trusting, stupidly optimistic."

"Take it easy, all right?"

She drew a stuttering breath, stifling the laughter. Her hand clutched her throat like the laughter had hurt.

Ian fought to submerge his shock over his friends' actions. Later he could be furious with Eric and Tim. Right now it was more important to help Alisa Kent. "What does the Cadre want with you?"

"I don't know." Her hand still gripped her throat.

"You don't know? What did they say?"

Kent lowered her hand into her lap and said nothing.

"Or is it irrelevant because you've already decided to turn us in?"

Fatigue sapped all expression from her face. Her head tipped against the seat and her hair fell back, exposing her neck. The purplish edge of a bruise peeked above her turtleneck sweater.

She hadn't had that bruise the night before. "Who gave you that bruise on your neck?"

Kent's hand flew upward and curved over the injury to hide it.

"Who was it? Siskell?"

She pressed waxen lips together.

Ian grasped Kent's wrist. Her arm stiffened, but she didn't resist as he drew her hand away from her throat.

He folded down the neck of her sweater, revealing a dark, oval bruise. On the right side of her neck, four smaller bruises formed an arc opposite the larger bruise on the left. The marks of a strangling hand.

"What did the Liberty Cadre do to you?" Ian asked.

Alisa Kent took a shaky breath and told her story in sporadic bursts, words propelled by desperation, alternating with silence poisoned by suspicion. It was clear she didn't trust him, but she obviously couldn't carry this burden alone, and he doubted there was anyone else she could turn to.

"I would have thought the episode a nightmare," Kent finished, "but for the physical evidence."

"Any marks besides the bruises on your neck?"

She slipped her coat off and pushed back the sleeves of her blazer. Both wrists were bruised—probably, Ian thought, from his own fingers as much as from those of her Cadre assailants.

Kent rolled her left sleeve up past the elbow. In the crook of the elbow, where blue veins passed beneath translucent skin, was a small red needle puncture. She spoke. "On my left shoulder blade there's a bruise typical of the mark left by a stun square."

"A stun square?"

"Like this." She reached under her blazer and withdrew what looked like a square of black plastic with a handle on one side. "The police use them to render uncooperative subjects unconscious."

"Oh. Right." Ian took the stun square and turned it over in his hand. Numerous metal nodes dotted the face of the stun square and an activator button nestled on the underside of the handle.

"I have no idea what the Cadre is doing," Kent said. "I have no idea what drug they administered. But I suspect this is not the first time they've done it."

Ian handed the stun square back. "You've had other experiences like this?"

"Not exactly. I don't recall the Liberty Cadre invading my home prior to this. But the way I felt this morning . . . over the past couple of weeks I've experienced that sensation on two other occasions."

"What do you mean? How did you feel this morning?"

She hesitated for so long that Ian thought she wasn't going to answer. He was about to rephrase the question and try again when she murmured, "Confused. Disoriented. Memories would emerge and slip away. One moment everything would seem clear, the next I couldn't even remember my name."

Ian's already icy blood dropped another few degrees. "How long did this confusion last?"

"I'm not sure. An hour . . . perhaps longer."

"And you've experienced that confusion on three occasions now?"

"Yes."

"You don't remember anything unusual from the nights preceding the first two episodes?"

"No. And last night, I recall nothing after the confrontation with the Cadre until I awoke at sunrise."

Laura's warning about the strange effects of the drug used in interrogations flashed into Ian's mind. "You—mentioned once that the police sometimes use a drug in interrogations. Could this be something like that—the Cadre getting information from you?"

"No. The aftereffects of the Broc memory stimulants are very different from what I experienced."

Memory stimulants. Whatever the Cadre had pumped into Kent's bloodstream had certainly affected her memory, but not in the sense of stimulating it. "What *are* the effects of those memory stimulants?"

Kent glanced at him, her eyes weary with pain. "If you want to know, ask your friend Lansbury. He's well acquainted with their use."

This response disconcerted Ian. The thought of Daniel Lansbury being an expert in those drugs was less than appealing. "Can you go to your boss and get some help protecting yourself? You're a Sedition and Treason officer. It wouldn't look suspicious that the Cadre is bothering you."

"It would be supremely foolish for me to go to Captain Hofstader."

"Are you afraid he'll figure out why the Cadre targeted you instead of some other officer?"

"I can't go to Hofstader!" she repeated fiercely.

"All right, calm down. Could you at least make it harder for the Cadre to reach you? Can you get a vacation or a leave from work? Can you get out of the city?"

Kent studied the empty loading dock. "I *am* on leave."

"You are? Since when?"

Her hands curled into fists, her fingers inadequate cover for the healing cuts on her palms. So apparently Alisa Kent's superiors were not completely oblivious to her deteriorating health.

"So you're on leave," Ian said. "That makes it easier. Leave Tremont."

"At best, a change of location will inconvenience the Cadre. It won't stop them."

"It's better than sitting at home waiting for them to come inject you with some unknown drug for some unknown purpose. And maybe the delay will give you time to figure out what they're doing and how to stop them."

Some of the anxiety eased from Kent's face. "Perhaps."

"You look ready to collapse." Ian twisted the key in the ignition. "I'm taking you home. I'll fix you something to eat, and you can rest. Later this afternoon, we can see about getting you out of the city."

Kent offered an occasional direction as Ian drove toward the north side of the city, but beyond that, she didn't speak.

Leaden clouds dulled the sky and shadowed the boxy wood-and-brick houses filling the suburbs of Tremont. In the bleak silence, Ian's thoughts returned to Eric. How could Eric leave Tremont without a word? Had his anger at Ian been that intense, or was he trying to dodge Ian's objections? It wasn't like Eric to avoid an argument, but maybe this time he didn't want to hear anything that might make him question his rapid decision.

Tim's departure was easier to understand. If Eric was going, Tim would go.

The oath his friends had taken, binding themselves to the Cadre— secret combinations. History repeating itself, from Kishkumen and Gadianton to James Tremont to Cadre leader Zero. Ian knew the defense Eric would make if Ian started talking of oath-bound secret societies and conspiracies. "*This is totally different, Roshek. We're fighting for freedom, not power.*"

A deep, glacial pain settled inside Ian. Eric on the basketball court, eyes electric with the excitement of competition, Eric shoving a fishing pole into Ian's hands and marching him into the mountains, Eric at the funerals of Ian's parents, compassion flowing from his gruff silence, Eric recruiting girlfriend Sherry and ex-roommate Tim to join the underground debates.

Was Kent right? Was the Cadre what Eric had always wanted?

No. Eric was infatuated with the first group he'd found that had the power to fight, but he'd never be at ease killing innocent people just to annoy the Council. Soon, his honeymoon with the Cadre would end. He'd want out.

But the Cadre would never let him go.

CHAPTER 12

"Would you like anything else?" Ian asked as Alisa Kent pushed her empty soup bowl aside.

"No. Thank you." Kent lifted tired, dark eyes and looked into his face. "You look ill," she said. "Are you all right?"

The question startled him. "I—yeah, I'm—" A sick wave of exhaustion erased his effort at a noncommittal response. "I just didn't expect that news about Eric."

"I'm sorry," Kent said quietly.

Her unexpected sympathy blunted the sharpest edges of his pain. Not knowing what to say, Ian picked up Kent's empty plate and bowl and set them in the sink.

"May I ask you something?" Kent said.

"Sure."

"Your maternal grandparents left the United States to follow James Tremont, bringing your mother and father with them."

"Yes," Ian said, relieved that the question hadn't been about Eric.

"They all agreed with Tremont that religion was a destructive force and that its elimination was necessary for a stable society."

"They agreed with Tremont that religious organizations and the institutions of free government stood in the way of the power they wanted," Ian said.

Her dark eyebrows arched. "As interpreted through your own prejudices."

"I've read my grandfather's journals. He was blunt about the fact that he expected a ruling position in the government they would establish after they murdered President Hayden and tore the United

States Constitution to shreds. Blunt about the fact that you couldn't completely control a people who looked beyond you for a source of morality and law."

"But he truly believed the elimination of religion would benefit society."

"He was zealous, all right."

"Your parents believed in the dangers of religion as well."

"Yeah, of course."

"They never questioned the convictions held by their parents—or rather, by your mother's parents?"

"Not where the banishment of religion was concerned."

"On other matters, then?"

Ian brushed his hand over the glistening white countertop, sweeping a single toast crumb into the sink. "Not directly."

"Indirectly, then?"

"Well, look at it this way. There was a . . . what's the best way to describe it? A sense of destiny and superiority that drove the generation that lifted James Tremont into power. They believed Separation was temporary and that soon millions of dissenters from the United States would join them. Then they'd be big enough and strong enough to assume leadership of a New America that stretched from coast to coast."

The intensity of Kent's gaze was unnerving. Ian had to make a conscious effort not to look away as he continued, "But by the time my parents were raising their own family, it was obvious that Tremont's glorious predictions were wrong—and that they were becoming prisoners of the people who had promised them power."

"Are you aware," Kent said, "that when you discuss your past you have a tendency to couch your statements in broad historical terms?"

Ian grinned feebly. "You're saying you didn't register for a history class?"

"I'm saying you are avoiding the issue. Every person of your parents' generation experienced those same political conditions, but the vast majority managed not to plant the seeds of treason in their children. Did your parents express disillusionment with the government?"

Ian poured the remaining soup into a mug and sat down at the table. "Probably no more than most other people in Tremont. There were occasional comments, whispered conversations, things left unsaid, questions I asked that they wouldn't answer. Did—you experience similar things with your parents?"

Kent averted her eyes, her shoulders tensing. "They showed little enthusiasm for the political situation. But they did not speak against the government in my presence."

"That's about how it was for me." Ian was tempted to ask Alisa Kent more questions about her family, but decided now was not the time. "My father did some grumbling under his breath, my mother was good at avoiding unpleasant subjects, but both of them remained in fundamental agreement with the philosophies underlying the establishment of New America." He added quietly, "They'd be horrified to know what their son has become."

"Then they cooperated in the information purges?"

"Yes." Ian cleared his throat. "I didn't get my books from them, if that's what you're asking."

"When did you first begin to question the things you'd been taught?"

Kent's keen gaze was eerily familiar from his interrogation, and Ian battled an urge to change the subject. He hadn't expected to spend the afternoon unearthing his past for her to examine. *Don't be such a coward. She's trying to make sense of something that intrigues and terrifies her. Do you want to help her or not?*

"Well—I guess it . . ." His voice trailed off. He sipped his soup and tried again. "When I was twelve, my mother was expecting a baby. She learned it had a heart defect—potentially repairable, but one that would require many surgeries, many hospital stays— extremely high expense. Health Services wouldn't authorize treatment. They declared the pregnancy nonviable. There was no possible way my parents could pay for treatment themselves, so they had the choice of aborting the baby or carrying it to term and having it die shortly after birth. My mother wanted to have the baby, but my father wouldn't let her go through that. So she had the abortion. It was . . . hard on her."

"Your parents told you the details of what was happening?"

"They—well—my mother was . . . she was normally very careful, but like I said, this was hard on her. She was too upset to worry about being discreet."

"What was your view of the matter?"

"I thought it was insane. Doctors *could* save the baby, but because treatment was too expensive they wanted to kill it instead? Was money worth more than life?"

"You did not accept that the nation's limited resources could not solve every problem?"

"I didn't accept that life had no intrinsic value."

"That's when you first started to question the things you'd been taught?"

Ian drummed his fingers on the table. "I suppose it was the first time I really thought about it. We were always learning in school how brilliant our society was, how we had freed ourselves from the corrupt traditions of the past. But after what my mother went through, I guess I was puzzled."

"Did you confide your concerns to your parents?"

"In roundabout ways."

"Your mother was a history teacher. Did she lead you in that direction to help answer your questions?"

"Yeah, she gave me books to read. The ones she used in lesson preparation."

"Did they help?"

"Considering that the authors were shameless cheerleaders for James Tremont and his New America, yes, it helped for a while. But once I started reading, I just kept going."

"When you were fifteen, you submitted a request to your Education Regulatory Committee for access to the university library."

"I'd run out of books to read at the public library," Ian said, unsettled by the fact that Kent had apparently memorized his file. "I'd already read everything they had on the history of New America and the history of the United States—which wasn't much, by the way. The university library had a much more extensive collection, and some of the books weren't as rigorously censored as the ones at the public library."

Kent shifted in her seat. "And the result of all your study?"

"That's not hard to guess, is it? The deeper I dug, the more I found contradictions, misinterpretations, and flat-out lies in the way history was taught in my school. Books that were published prior to Separation, or even in the years immediately following it, told very different stories than books published a decade or two later."

"Did you ask your mother about these inconsistencies?"

"She wouldn't have appreciated those kinds of questions."

Kent leaned forward, bracing her arms against the table. "Your study of history led to your interest in religion."

"Yeah, but it took awhile." Ian gulped the last of his lukewarm tomato soup. "At first, my reading seemed to confirm what I'd always been taught—that religions were primitive, trouble-causing superstitions. The Crusades . . . the Spanish Inquisition . . . the al-Qaeda terrorists—historically, it seemed people used God to justify anything. James Tremont *was* right about that. But what I saw going on in New America didn't seem much better, except Tremont had taken the place of God. The Council and the Tremont Police could use *his* name to justify anything. No wonder he'd banished religion. He didn't want God outranking him."

Kent's expression looked chiseled out of ice. She looked liked she was fighting not to react to his mockery of James Tremont like a police officer normally would, and Ian had the fleeting thought that he should have asked her to set her gun aside before he started talking. "I'm sorry," he said. "What I'm trying to say is that I was no longer convinced Tremont had it right. But it hadn't yet occurred to me that answers might lie in old superstitions. That was too radical a rejection of the things my parents had taught me."

"What answers were you looking for?" Kent asked.

Ian hesitated, thinking how to phrase it. "Truth," he said at last. "The best way to live. What we were capable of becoming. Happiness."

"At what point did you begin to think religion might hold your answers?"

Ian felt like Kent's gaze was pushing him backward. He broke eye contact, letting his gaze drift around the room. Neat vertical blinds covered the kitchen window, blocking out the gray remnants of the afternoon. Apples and oranges filled a small mesh basket on the windowsill, a colorful touch in a room otherwise devoted to sterile white and stainless steel.

"Are you uncomfortable with the question?" Kent asked.

"No." It was Alisa Kent herself, not her questions, that made him uneasy. But Ian doubted it would be helpful to tell her that.

"Near the end of my undergraduate work, I got my hands on some books—don't ask me from where—that included some of the philosophical and political writings that influenced the founders of the United States, along with documents and sources from early American history. This was the first time I'd been able to study intensively anything that presupposed the existence of God and divine law."

"These writings impressed you."

"They interested me."

"All of history interested you," Kent said icily. "I imagine this was different."

"All right, yes, it was different." Ian wished there weren't quite such an overtone of police officer in Kent's voice.

"Were the deaths of both your parents a spur to your interest in religious matters?"

"I suppose their deaths made me a little more anxious for answers."

"By the time your mother was euthanized, you were beginning your graduate studies." Kent spoke rapidly. "Among the books you requested from the Education Regulatory Committee were several works dealing with Christian beliefs."

"I needed sources for a couple of papers I was writing about the role of Christianity in the late twentieth-century U.S. "

"You were curious. You were mourning your parents. And you deliberately sought access to classified sources that discussed such religious beliefs as the immortal soul and life after death—including the Christian Bible."

"All right, yes," Ian said, his tension rising at the way Kent's questions were turning into accusations. "But grief wasn't my only motive."

"Eventually, you chose to analyze James Tremont's own religious background in your dissertation, which gave you access to scores of classified sources."

"Scores of James Tremont's personal writings, mainly."

"As well as writings that discussed the Mormon brand of Christianity."

"Writings that attacked and dissected Mormon Christianity. Secondhand sources were all the Committee would allow me."

"Despite repeated requests on your part for sources published by or favorable to Tremont's childhood church."

"I was trying to be objective instead of just getting everything filtered through James Tremont."

"Did you assume Tremont would lie?"

"In writing about a church he had once been part of but had rejected and attacked with the most vicious tactics imaginable, yeah, I questioned whether his analysis of that religion would be accurate."

Ice-cold silence.

Unable to endure the chilly atmosphere any longer, Ian said, "You know, this conversation would be a lot easier for me if it didn't feel so much like a police interrogation."

A startled look of dismay crossed Kent's face, and Ian instantly regretted his words. "I'm sorry. It's been a rotten day. That came out a lot harsher than I meant it to."

"You don't trust me. I understand that." Her voice was low. "But you have a courage and depth of conviction that I envy more than I can possibly say. I will never have your courage, but I would give anything to understand it."

Disarmed and abruptly consumed with inadequacy, Ian muttered, "Courage is not my specialty. I'm more of an expert in weak knees and sweaty palms."

"Your dissertation," Kent prompted, drawing the conversation back on track. "You mistrusted the resources available to you."

"I found them insufficient, but the Committee didn't agree. Since my stated intent was to examine how Tremont's religious background had opened his eyes to how religion weakens and corrupts society, they figured Tremont's own writings and some general information about his former church should be enough."

"And you gave the Committee what they wanted, presenting a negative portrait of Tremont's religious background."

"I'm not proud of it now. But at the time, I figured if I ever wanted to get my degree, I'd better give them what they expected."

"But you didn't agree with what you wrote."

"I wasn't sure what I agreed with. I hadn't discounted Christianity as a possible source of answers, but I didn't feel I'd found any answers yet either."

Kent brushed her hands over her face as though she could manually wipe away fear and exhaustion. "What was your impression of the Bible?"

"Oh, it fascinated me. But historically, different branches of Christianity had yanked the Bible in so many directions that I didn't see it as a source of definitive answers."

"But you wanted to believe it." She spoke softly, but threads of anxiety tightened around each word. "Having lost both your parents, you were naturally attracted to a belief in immortality."

"It's not that simple. Yes, it would have been nice to think I'd see my parents again, but I wasn't looking to comfort myself with fantasies. I didn't really believe *or* disbelieve the Bible. I felt there was something there, but I couldn't quite grasp it."

"When did you get hold of your Book of Mormon?"

"Last summer."

"Then it was part of the contraband recently brought into Tremont by David Garrett."

"I assume so. It was a new copy of the book, not something that had been gathering dust in someone's attic."

Her voice roughened. "How did it make its way to you?"

"I can't tell you that."

She gripped the edge of the table, her fingertips blanching white. "Did your source speak of connections with Garrett?"

"She never met him. She told me someone had passed the book on to her. I think it went through several people before it came to me." Ian noted the flush reddening Kent's cheekbones. "Alisa, it's too soon for this discussion. You're getting upset. We should wait—"

"*Please.* This is—not a matter I am adept at discussing, but I can't wait any longer for—" She swallowed, then swallowed again as though she couldn't moisten her mouth.

Ian nudged her water glass toward her. "Why don't you go lie down? When you're feeling better we can finish talking." He started to stand up, but Kent seized his wrist, a convulsive gesture that knocked her glass over.

Heart thudding, Ian edged to the side to avoid the dripping water. "Take it easy."

Her fingers cinched tighter. "If we had time, I would wait before pressing you on this matter. But I don't know what the Cadre is up to, and I don't know how much time we have left."

Ian tried to think of something reassuring to say, but realized with a rush of fear that Kent was right. Add the Cadre's meddling to all the other uncertain elements circling around them, and there was no guarantee they *would* have another chance to talk like this. "All right," he said evenly, refusing to allow the fear into his voice. Kent was frightened enough without his adding his own anxiety to the mix. "But you can let go of my arm. I promise I won't run away."

Kent loosened her grip just enough so he could work his hand free. "Someone gave you your book."

"Yes." He found a dishtowel and wiped up the spilled water.

Her hand was still stretched toward him as if she anticipated having to grab him again. "Had you wanted to read that particular book ever since you learned it was central to the beliefs of the church James Tremont hated?"

"I liked it because Tremont hated it?" Ian managed a wry smile. "There was a lot more to it than that." He touched her hand. "Relax. I'm not going anywhere."

Warily, she drew her arm back. "What had become of your concerns about the atrocities wrought in the name of God?"

"That was a key question that studying the Book of Mormon resolved for me. The more I studied, the more I understood that the destruction carried out in God's name came from those who *rejected* the laws of the God they claimed to follow. When people obeyed those laws, the result was peace and freedom. When they rejected or perverted those laws, the result was chaos and bloodshed."

"So you read your book." Her voice wobbled. "It appealed to you. But you had read many things that appealed to you without deciding that they held your answers."

"True. And I wanted to be sure." Ian watched her as he spoke, gauging her emotions. She looked apprehensive, but calmer, under control. "In the last chapter of the book, there is a promise. It says that after you read the book, if you ask God, sincerely wanting to know, He will tell you it's true."

"David Garrett . . . spoke of that promise."

"When he visited you?"

She nodded.

"What . . . else did he say?" This was the subject she had refused to discuss the night before.

Her shoulders drooped in a silent sigh and her face went paler, but she looked more tired than upset. "He . . . spoke of my parents. Their . . . their love for me. Their faith. His faith. I would prefer not to say more on the matter."

"All right." Ian didn't want to push Kent for details before she was emotionally ready to give them.

"You prayed concerning your book?" Kent asked.

"It took me awhile to work up the courage." Ian tossed the dish-towel into the sink.

"Did you fear that God would not answer your question?"

"I was more afraid that He *would*."

"I thought you wanted answers."

"I did. But when I realized I might have those answers in my hands, I got scared of what that knowledge would require of me. Believe it or not, I never *wanted* to end up in prison—or dead."

"But by this point, you'd already been engaged in illegal activities for years," Kent said, "studying a variety of illegally acquired literature, meeting with your traitor friends—"

"Yes, but I could still tailor my public behavior to keep me out of trouble. Sure, I wasn't in line for any patriotic-service awards, but I wasn't getting arrested either. But if I found out this book was true, that God was real, that He did give us laws to follow, I would be obligated to obey God. Even if His laws got me in trouble with, say, a police lieutenant who assumed only a traitor would protect another supposed traitor from getting torn to pieces. Does that make sense?"

She nodded slowly. "But you did seek your answer."

"Yes." Ian realized he was trembling. He hid his hands under the table, but too late—Kent's eyes followed the gesture.

"You received an answer?" she asked.

"Yes."

"What form did it take?"

"It's hard to explain it in words. I'd never experienced anything like it in my life. It was . . . *certainty*—" Ian's voice caught. He drew a deep, shaky breath. "Certainty. Burning conviction. Knowledge. I *knew* that book was true. I knew God was real, that He was listening to me. It was a peace and joy I can't describe."

Quiet shrouded the kitchen. Kent stared at him, an odd, frozen expression on her face. "Imagination," she whispered. "Wishful thinking."

"I know what I experienced," Ian said firmly.

"Such a subjective answer is no answer at all."

"And what would have been more definitive? Was God supposed to appear to me?" He smiled. "If I told you that happened, you'd dismiss it as a hallucination. Am I right?"

She moistened her lips and said nothing.

"Alisa, that book was written for *us*. The things we're experiencing are not new. This has all happened before—people turning against God, fighting to destroy freedom in order to feed their lust for power. Fighting against truth because it shows them for what they are."

Pain and anger flashed across her face, fading into sadness. "If your God exists, I have spent *my* life fighting against Him. There can be nothing in that book that would turn to my benefit."

"Have you read it?"

"No."

"The central message of the book is the gift of Jesus Christ, the Son of God—the sacrifice He made that lets us overcome mistakes, shortcomings, even acts of outright evil—and to *change*. There's nothing He wants more than to help us—to heal us." Warmth flooded Ian and words he had studied came easily to mind. "He said, 'Mine arm of mercy is extended towards you, and whosoever will come, him will I receive.' That's a pretty clear invitation, isn't it?"

Kent sat motionless. Her expression was bewildered, but beneath the bewilderment, hope glimmered like sunlight struggling through gray December clouds.

"You know I've told you the truth," Ian said. "This is what you've been looking for. The way to forgiveness."

Tears shimmered in her eyes. She rose to her feet and stumbled out of the kitchen.

Ian followed her. "Alisa—"

"Go now." Her voice was husky. "Go. I'm all right. I'll contact you later." She veered into her bedroom. Her door closed.

CHAPTER 13

Ian deliberated for only a few moments before he yielded to Alisa Kent's wishes and headed home. Kent seemed in control of herself, and she needed time to assimilate what he had told her. Tired but calm, Ian spent the rest of Wednesday afternoon in his room, studying the chapters in Third Nephi that surrounded the passage he had quoted to Alisa Kent, and thinking about the hope that had flickered in her eyes.

Wednesday evening, after much prayer and deliberation, he tucked the book into a cardboard envelope, took it to Alisa Kent's, and pushed it through the mail slot on her door. Somehow he sensed she would have an easier time accepting the book if she didn't have to take it directly from his hand.

When he returned home from campus on Thursday, he found an unsigned note on his dresser, penned in Kent's handwriting. She was leaving Tremont tomorrow morning to spend two weeks in a ski lodge maintained by the Tremont Police Service for the exclusive use of its officers. She would contact Ian upon returning from vacation.

Ian smiled grimly. A ski lodge filled with vacationing police officers. Let the Liberty Cadre try to bother Alisa Kent in *that* setting.

She didn't mention the book.

The phone rang. Peter Critchlow's name showed in the ID box, and Ian felt an instant weight of discouragement. He had talked to Peter briefly on Tuesday, and Peter had been desperate.

"Hello, Peter, this is Dr. Roshek."

"I've got great news!" Peter's voice boomed in Ian's ear.

Ian flicked the volume down a notch. "Great news?"

"I got a call from Health Services this afternoon. They approved my medication!"

"They approved it?"

"And they were so *polite*. I mean, they called me *'sir.'*"

"Sir!"

"I don't know why they changed their minds, and I'm not asking. But I'll be able to study now, and I plan to study *all* the time. I mean, the headaches won't be completely gone, but it'll be a lot better. I'm going to be a top student. I promise."

"I believe you."

"Thanks for all your help. I'm—" Peter lowered his voice to a mumble. "I'm sorry I got you in trouble with Dr. Sheldon."

"I'm frequently in trouble with Dr. Sheldon. It's not your fault."

"Well, I gotta go pick up my medicine. Thanks again. 'Bye."

"See you in class." Grinning, Ian hung up. He had heard of Health Services reversing decisions, but he had never heard of them being polite in the bargain.

Ian was sitting at the kitchen table, eating a chicken pie and editing a lecture, when he heard the front door open and the voices of Jill and Daniel Lansbury. Calmly, Ian continued eating. He hoped Daniel wasn't here to grill him about those case histories he hadn't read, but he wasn't going to try to avoid him.

Jill and Daniel lingered in the living room, chatting about Jill's upcoming concert. Ian had finished both his dinner and his editing before Daniel strode through the kitchen doorway. Jill followed him, offering Ian a hesitant "please don't eat us alive" sort of smile.

"How are you doing?" Daniel asked.

"Not bad," Ian said pleasantly. Hope brightened Jill's eyes.

"Have you had a chance to start looking over those case histories?"

"Not yet."

"Read them this week. Let's plan to discuss them a week from Saturday. Would you prefer to meet in the afternoon or the evening?"

Ian fixed a courteous expression on his face as he thought on how to respond. He'd already promised to read the case histories. He'd be foolish to provoke Daniel by refusing to discuss them, and he didn't want to needlessly upset Jill on the weekend of her solo debut.

"Afternoon or evening?" Daniel repeated. His friendly expression was mere silk draped over concrete.

"Afternoon is better," Ian said. He heard Jill draw an audible breath of relief.

"How about two o'clock next Saturday?"

"Fine."

"I'll pick you up. Considering the sensitive nature of some of the things we'll be discussing, I'm sure you'd prefer to meet somewhere without neighbors right through the walls."

"Uh—yeah."

"Before you start reading, do you have any questions for me?"

"No—" A sudden thought stopped the word halfway out of Ian's mouth. When he had asked Alisa Kent about the memory drug used by the police, she'd told him to ask Daniel Lansbury if he wanted information. At the time he hadn't taken the suggestion seriously, but what if he did ask Daniel? He'd prefer to know exactly what he was up against if—when—he was arrested again.

"You've got something on your mind," Daniel said. "What is it?"

Ian glanced at Jill, reluctant to bring up a subject that would worry her. "It's not really—"

"Why don't you walk me to my car?" Daniel correctly interpreted his hesitation. "Jill, I'll see you later."

"'Bye." Jill beamed at Ian as he followed Daniel out of the kitchen.

"Hope you don't mind the stairs," Daniel said.

"Not going down." Ian had forgotten that Jill and Daniel always took the stairs to avoid meeting neighbors in the elevator.

He trailed Daniel down five flights of stairs and out the back door. Realizing he didn't know what Daniel's car looked like, he scanned the parking lot for something expensively out of place. To his surprise, Daniel headed toward the far corner of the lot where an unremarkable green Toyota was parked. The car was new, but nothing that would attract excessive admiration—at least from the outside. Ian settled into the passenger seat and found himself encased in cream-colored leather and gleaming chrome, facing an instrument panel that looked high-tech enough to navigate to the moon.

Daniel started the engine and pressed a button. Instant heat enveloped them. "What's on your mind?"

"When I was . . . uh . . . arrested in September, the officer who talked to me mentioned a process called Information Extraction. I was wondering what that involves."

"Ah." Daniel relaxed against the leather headrest, the angles of his face dimly lit by the glow from the instrument panel. "I suppose it's only natural that would be on your mind after the things we talked about on Sunday. What did Lt. Kent tell you about it?"

Ian had to do a quick sorting to separate what Kent had told him at his interrogation from what she'd said later, and from what Laura Travers had told him. To his consternation, he realized that at his interrogation, Kent had only mentioned Information Extraction in the context of telling him where he was headed now that she'd found him guilty of reading anarchist literature. "Uh—she just said that if she found me guilty of any crimes, she'd send me for Information Extraction. She didn't give details."

"Ah." Daniel gave him a thoughtful look. "Please understand that I would never answer a question like this just to satisfy idle curiosity."

Ian squelched the impulse to say how much he wished his question *were* just idle curiosity.

"We don't discuss Information Extraction much outside the lab and the police complex," Daniel said. "I expect that anything I tell you will remain confidential."

"Of course."

"I wouldn't tell you anything at all, except I think it will be helpful in encouraging you to stay out of trouble."

"Uh—thanks." Ian tried not to roll his eyes.

"Now, you remember when I told you about the memory stimulant drugs used in patriotic counseling?"

"Yes."

"Information Extraction, or I-X, is a method of interrogation that makes use of the same drugs, but in a different way."

"How's that?"

"Let me give you some background," Daniel said, obviously warming to his lecture topic. "Twenty or so years ago while researching the mechanism of memory, a neurochemist named Patricia Broc developed a series of drugs that not only improved memory, but also dramatically overrode the ability to make rational decisions."

"Meaning?"

"Meaning, in the context of criminal interrogation, ask a question and the prisoner will answer, no matter how reluctant he would have been to answer that question when in full control of his faculties."

"How does that work?"

"I'll try to put it in terms you can understand." Daniel toyed with the steering wheel. "The Broc memory stimulants affect the brain's ability to foresee the consequences of behavior. A patient can clearly recall past events, but can't predict future ones, including the consequences of confession."

Ian thought of Laura's grim warnings. "Is the process—hard on the patient?"

"The interrogation itself is usually not unpleasant."

"Usually?"

"Well, Broc4—that's the formulation of the drug currently in use for I-X on healthy adults, as we use a less potent formulation for prisoners younger than sixteen—can occasionally cause problems during interrogation. Dangerous hypertension—that's high blood pressure— or abnormal heart rhythms, for example. Administration of the drug must be monitored by a doctor."

"Like you." Ian was careful to keep the distaste out of his voice. They even used these drugs on children?

"Yes, that's part of my job. But most problems come during what we call stage two. Once an interrogation is complete and the initial effects of the drug have worn off, the brain experiences a sharp withdrawal effect."

"Meaning?"

"Hallucinations. Remember what I told you about patriotic counseling."

Ian mulled that over. "Are the hallucinations following Information Extraction always horrible? Even without the prior conditioning they do in patriotic counseling?"

"Think about it. You've been arrested. Were you scared?"

"Daniel, that's a truly stupid question."

"Just answer it."

Ian sighed. "Yes, I was scared."

"You were worrying about what they were going to do to you."

"All right."

"You were reviewing every rumor you'd ever heard about what takes place at police headquarters and in the prison system."

"Uh . . . yes."

"That's typical. A prisoner's state of mind is one of fear and guilt—fear of pain, fear of imprisonment, fear of separation from family and friends, fear of death. Guilt over crimes committed, guilt over what loved ones will suffer because of those crimes. While blood levels of Broc4 are high, those fears are forgotten as the mind loses its ability to project the future. But once levels drop and stage two begins, those fears return and set the tone for hallucinatory episodes produced by imagination and overstimulated memory."

Despite the hot air blowing from the vents, Ian shivered. "So fears and regrets get mixed up with real memories?"

"Mixed, yes. Distorted and exaggerated into nightmarish hallucinations that seem completely real."

Daniel sounded so matter-of-fact that Ian lost the fight to hide his disgust. "Clever of the police to come up with a drug that gets patients to torture themselves. That must save a lot of man-hours."

Daniel shot him a razor-edged look of reproach. "The goal of I-X is to gather information. There's nothing the police would like more than for us at the lab to succeed in altering the Broc stimulants so interrogations could be conducted without the problematic aftereffects."

"How long do these hallucinations last?"

"It depends on how much Broc4 a patient receives. Typical recovery time in a healthy adult is two to three hours of stage two for every hour in stage one. Once active stage two ends, a patient will experience intermittent flashbacks for the next couple of weeks, requiring continual monitoring. Usually a patient is fully recovered within two weeks, but some may take a month or longer, and rarely there are severe complications."

"What kind of complications?"

"Occasionally, a patient doesn't emerge from stage two."

"What do you mean, 'doesn't emerge'?"

"Brain chemistry is permanently altered. The patient remains in a hallucinatory state, unresponsive to exterior stimuli."

"They *stay* that way?" Ian couldn't conceal his horror. "Don't you have drugs or something to control these hallucinations?"

"Antipsychotic drugs are a very temporary solution. To suppress the hallucinations, they have to be administered in such high dosages that the patient is nonfunctional. Furthermore, they tend to lose their effectiveness after a few weeks. They're useful if your goal is to allow a weakened patient to avoid the temporary stresses of stage two, but they can't control long-term Broc psychosis."

"So what happens to the people who get stuck in stage two? They live out their lives in some kind of permanent nightmare?"

Daniel finally looked slightly uncomfortable. "Broc psychosis is fatal. If the patient doesn't die from stresses on the heart, then neural disintegration will kill them within a couple of months. Usually a patient will be euthanized as soon as his condition is declared irreversible."

"You're telling me that an innocent person could go for Information Extraction and end up dying?"

"There aren't many innocent people who undergo I-X. The police screen most prisoners—like they did you—and only conduct an Information Extraction session if they discover evidence of serious crimes."

Ian paused. "How common is Broc psychosis?"

"It affects about two percent of the people exposed to Broc4, causing problems mainly in patients who've had repeated or prolonged exposure. We see only about half the problems that we saw with formula 3, by the way, so we're making progress."

Ian looked at Daniel lounging in his customized leather seat, sinewy fingers adjusting the temperature controls. Did he look so placid while he injected his patients with a drug he knew might kill them?

"The countless benefits the Broc memory stimulants yield to national security are worth the occasional problems," Daniel said. "Don't lose sight of that. I may have given you a skewed perspective by focusing on the problems, but, frankly, I'm trying to scare you."

"Thanks." Ian cleared his throat. "How . . . good is this Broc4 in getting information? Do people ever manage to conceal things or lie?"

"I've never heard of that happening. Prisoners will speak much more thoroughly and accurately than they would even if they were cooperating voluntarily. Remember, Broc4 is a memory stimulant. Stay out of trouble, Ian, and you'll never have to worry about any of this."

"Good advice." Ian fumbled for the door handle. *What does Jill see in this guy?*

"As I said before, I expect that you will keep this information confidential."

"Right." Ian climbed out of the car, as queasy as if he'd just driven fifty miles on corkscrew roads.

Ian opted for the stairs on the trip back to his apartment. Jill would be waiting, anxious to learn that all had gone well between Daniel and him. Five flights of stairs would give him time to manufacture a bland, unreadable smile.

Next week, he'd have to tell Jill that his talking to Daniel didn't mean he had any intention of buckling to Daniel's threats. But tonight—the night before Jill soloed with the Philharmonic—was not the time for that discussion. This weekend was Jill's time, her triumph, and Ian wasn't going to do anything to worry her.

Even if that meant acting like his conversation with Daniel had been a pleasure.

CHAPTER 14

Hands hot and stinging from vigorous applause, Ian wove through the crowd of musicians and instrument cases filling the basement of the Copton Concert Hall following Friday's concert. He reached the soloist's dressing room just as Jill emerged, her cheeks rosy and her eyes sapphire-bright.

"Nice job, Jilly," he said. "I didn't fall asleep once."

"Oh, you clod!" Jill flew at him in a whoosh of sea-green silk and hugged him so hard she nearly knocked him off his feet.

"Whoa, steady there!" Ian embraced her. "You really were wonderful. Mozart must have had you in mind when he wrote that little ditty."

Jill stumbled backward, laughing. "Thank you." She pressed her hands against her red cheeks. "Now that it's over, I can't stop shaking."

"It's over until tomorrow night when you have to play it again."

"Opening night is always hardest for me."

Ian stepped to the left to avoid getting flattened by a passing cello case and found himself facing a woman with elfin features and long red-brown hair. His heart jumped, then steadied. *It's Marie, you dork. Not Laura.*

"Hi, handsome," she said. "Where have you been hiding out?"

"Hi, Marie. How are you?"

"Could be better, could be worse." She tapped his knee with her violin case. "If you'd call me, things would definitely take a turn for the better."

"I'm a boring guy." Ian cast a beseeching look toward Jill, hoping she'd rescue him from her flirtatious stand partner, but Jill had been cornered by a tuxedoed man with a scraggly yellow mustache.

Resigned, Ian turned back to Marie Parker. "Jill was wonderful tonight, wasn't she?"

"Oh, of course. I can never figure out why she worries so much." Marie trailed her fingers through her hair. "But what are you up to these days? Still surgically attached to your computer, reading until those gorgeous hazel eyes of yours roll out of your head?"

"Yeah, that sums it up." Ian was profoundly relieved when Jill whirled to fling her arms around Marie. Why had he ever allowed Jill to coax him into taking Marie to a faculty picnic at Lake Serena last summer? *Never ask a woman on a date just because she resembles your old girlfriend,* Ian chided himself.

"She's always asking about you," Jill giggled as Marie walked off.

"Me and every other male within a ten-mile radius," Ian said. "Are you ready to go upstairs?"

Jill shuddered. "I think the concert was the easy part of tonight."

"How scary can a little reception be? All you have to do is smile and say 'thank you' to all the compliments."

"Councilor Lansbury is going to be there!" she hissed. "And Councilor Brannigan!"

Ian guided her into the elevator. "At least this is easier than meeting Councilor Lansbury for the first time, isn't it?"

"Thanks a lot for bringing that up again." The elevator opened and they stepped into a corridor carpeted in peacock blue. Crystal sconces glittered on the walls, interspersed with oil paintings of Tremont landmarks.

"Nice." Ian almost made a crack about finally finding out where his tax dollars went, but decided Jill wouldn't be amused.

A concert hall usher stood at the door of the reception room, monitoring an ID scanner. Two police officers stood nearby and two other officers stood at either end of the hallway. It hadn't occurred to Ian that the police would be there, but of course the presence of members of the Council would require security.

Ian swept his forearm past the scanner, received a nod of approval from the usher, and followed Jill into the reception room. The walls were mirrored, a chandelier shaped like an inverted waterfall swooped from the ceiling, and linen-draped buffet tables displayed more varieties of desserts than Ian had known existed.

"Jill, you were *brilliant.*" Daniel Lansbury drew Jill in for a brief, brotherly hug. Ian didn't doubt that once they were alone, Daniel would come up with a less brotherly way to show his appreciation for Jill's brilliance. The thought made Ian want to knock out a few of Daniel's teeth.

From all sides, women swathed in velvet and chiffon and men in tuxedos began moving toward Jill. Ian tried to step tactfully aside, but before he could retreat, Jill touched his arm.

"Stay with me," she whispered.

Gratified that Jill would want him close by when she already had Daniel to support her, Ian stayed with her, exchanging pleasantries with the dignitaries who came to congratulate Jill on her performance. He wasn't required to say much. Daniel Lansbury carried the weight of the conversations and did it with such charm that Ian grudgingly envied his social grace. How did Daniel make it look so easy?

Ian was sampling a raspberry chocolate cake and listening to Daniel flatter a diamond-encrusted group of women when a murmur buzzed through the room. Ian watched as Councilor Marcus Lansbury strode into the reception, his willowy blond wife at his side.

Conversations dwindled to respectful silence as Daniel's father approached Jill. Even though he had not yet spoken, the power of his presence crackled through the room like arcing electricity.

"Jill, your performance was remarkable." His voice was deeper than Daniel's, but with the same polished articulation.

"Beautiful." Jocelyn Lansbury clasped both of Jill's hands. In the background, conversations resumed their normal hum.

"Thank you." Jill glanced awkwardly at Ian, and Ian knew she was wondering if it would be presumptuous to introduce him.

"Dad, Mother, this is Jill's brother, Ian." Daniel made the introduction.

Amethysts clicked on Jocelyn Lansbury's bracelet as she extended a slender hand to Ian. "I'm delighted to meet you." She sounded so genuinely pleased that Ian felt handsomer, more intelligent, and better dressed than he'd been five seconds ago.

"The pleasure is mine, Ms. Lansbury." No wonder Daniel knew how to be charming, with such a role model.

"Dr. Roshek." Marcus Lansbury did not offer his hand to Ian, and the warmth in his expression disappeared like the sun moving behind clouds. Ian tensed. Had Daniel confided in his father about Jill's reprobate brother?

Jill nudged Ian's elbow, and he realized everyone was waiting for him to speak. "It's an honor to meet you, sir."

"Jill tells us you are a historian."

"Yes, sir." Out of the corner of his eye, Ian saw a man join the group, but he didn't dare turn to acknowledge the newcomer until Councilor Lansbury was finished with him.

"That is an important job." The chill in Marcus Lansbury's voice made Ian's mouth go dry. "It's the function of a historian to purge the mistakes and false traditions of the past from the philosophies of the present. I wonder if you understand the importance of that role."

Ian felt like his treason must be tattooed in his flesh for all to see. Jill's smile had turned phony, and Daniel was frowning into his champagne glass.

Jocelyn laughed lightly and touched a finger to Marcus's lips. "Don't lecture him, sweetheart. I'm sure Ian knows how vital his job is. That's probably why he chose it in the first place."

Marcus kissed Jocelyn's fingertips and intertwined his fingers with hers before his steel-gray eyes resumed boring into Ian.

"As an open window on the past through which all manner of sordid theories and events may be viewed, the teaching of history can create confusion. History must be judiciously taught, its lessons illuminated by the historian's determination to keep our children true to the legacy of James Tremont."

The man who had joined the group spoke. "But if that goal leads the historian to deliberately distort facts, is he teaching history or propaganda?"

Astonished, Ian turned to see a mild-looking man of medium height. His features were blunt, his receding brown hair peppered with gray.

"Don't be naive, Spencer." Marcus's voice could have sliced through granite. "The teaching of pure history is an impossibility. The events of the past are inevitably slanted through the historian's lens. It's the function of the Education Regulatory Committees to ensure that those lenses are properly ground."

"I'm not suggesting that propaganda doesn't have its place. I only suggest that we don't fool ourselves into thinking we can change the past by rewriting it in our textbooks."

Before Marcus could respond, Daniel leapt forward and grasped the newcomer's hand. "Councilor Brannigan, it's a pleasure to see you again."

"Daniel, you're looking well." Spencer Brannigan gripped Daniel's hand and smiled with obvious affection. Ian couldn't breathe. This was Spencer Brannigan, the newly appointed Councilor who spoke out against corruption in the Health Services System—and who, apparently, dared to challenge Marcus Lansbury.

"If you will excuse us." Marcus Lansbury escorted his wife away from the group. Ian's heart rate accelerated into triple digits as he watched Marcus go.

"Councilor, I'm pleased to introduce Jill Roshek," Daniel said "Jill, Councilor Spencer Brannigan."

"Jill, you are on your way to becoming a national treasure." Spencer Brannigan pressed Jill's hand between his palms. "How long have you been with the Philharmonic?"

"Only a year." Jill sounded flustered.

"You joined them at an excellent time. It's only in the last few years that they've become an orchestra we can really be proud of."

"Building up the arts is a slow process," Daniel said. He indicated Ian. "Councilor, this is Jill's brother, Ian Roshek."

"I apologize for interrupting your conversation." Brannigan held out his hand. "From the way Councilor Lansbury was badgering you, I assume you're a historian."

"I teach at the University of Tremont." Ian shook Brannigan's hand.

"Dad's in a severe mood tonight," Daniel observed. "Even for him."

"It was an exhausting day downtown. Perhaps that's the difficulty. Budget discussions can get fierce. Daniel, how is the lab treating you?"

"Same as usual."

"You're still on the Broc series."

"Yes."

"Making any progress?" Brannigan's smile twisted. "You certainly have the funds."

"Yes, the money's always there."

Brannigan plucked a chocolate-drizzled pastry from a tray offered by a passing server. "Well, don't work too hard. It's the unwieldy nature of the Broc stimulants that forces the police to limit their use to criminal interrogations. Were you to make them too safe, too easy to use . . ." Brannigan shook his head and rubbed his hand across his chin thoughtfully.

Ian looked at Jill. She wore an expression of polite interest, but her eyes were blank. Jill had no idea what Daniel and Councilor Brannigan were talking about.

"However, I know it's frustrating for the Broc team when—" A frown suddenly shadowed Brannigan's face. "Oh, dear. There's Nathan." Brannigan lifted his hand to acknowledge a man across the room.

Daniel waved a greeting as well, and the man walked toward them. He was stocky, with thick white hair and heavy-lidded, protuberant eyes. A twinge of recognition prompted Ian to observe the man more closely, but he couldn't think where they'd met before. Probably he was imagining things.

"Why don't you want to see Nate?" Daniel asked under his breath.

"We finalized the Health Services budget today. You tell me why I'm not eager to see him."

"Ah," Daniel said. "He won't be happy, I take it."

"He wants too much too fast," Brannigan murmured just before the man reached them. He raised his voice. "Good evening, Nathan."

"Spence—uh, Councilor, that is. Sorry. Got to get used to that. Good to see you." He shook Brannigan's hand, then Daniel's. "Lansbury, Becky just about bludgeoned me when I told her I talked to you yesterday but didn't invite you for dinner. Come over soon or I'm a dead man."

"I'd love to come. Tell Rebecca I'll call her."

"You'll bring this beautiful and talented lady, won't you?" The man squeezed Jill's hand. "Jill, I can't think when I've enjoyed a concert so much. I'm Nate Halbrook."

"Thank you, Mr. Halbrook." Jill's smile was slightly puzzled. Ian wondered if she too recognized Nathan Halbrook but couldn't place him in context.

"Nate is my brother-in-law," Brannigan said.

"Unfortunately for Councilor Brannigan." Halbrook turned his bulbous, slate-colored eyes toward Ian.

"I'm Ian Roshek, Jill's brother. Unfortunately for Jill."

Halbrook chuckled. He had a round, ruddy face that Ian thought would have been jolly but for the grim lines around his eyes.

"Where *is* Rebecca?" Brannigan asked.

"She had another commitment tonight. She hated to miss the concert, but told me to go without her." Halbrook's gaze fastened on Brannigan. "So how did it go today?"

"This is a party," Brannigan said. "We can save that discussion for later."

"So it's as I expected."

Brannigan rubbed his chin, looking tired. "Nate, I tried."

"So Broc and Preserval are still up to their eyeballs in dollar signs and the rest of Health Services—"

Brannigan cut him off. "We'll talk about it later."

Halbrook stabbed his fork into the meringue confection on his plate and directed a question at Ian and Jill. "Are you familiar with Preserval?"

"I read something about it in the news." Ian spoke casually, as though he didn't notice either the stoniness in Nathan Halbrook's voice or the warning look Spencer Brannigan was giving his brother-in-law. "Something about . . . uh . . . biostasis?"

"That's right." Daniel spoke before Halbrook could. "Preserval radically slows the body's biochemical processes."

"What does that mean?" Jill asked.

"An intravenous infusion of Preserval can bring a patient to the point where life signs are undetectable," Daniel said. "No heartbeat, no respiration, no nothing—but the body remains undamaged. The patient can be revived."

"Bringing people back from the dead!" declared Halbrook, widening his already-bulging eyes for emphasis.

"Not exactly," Daniel said. "If death has already occurred, Preserval can't reverse that. It doesn't regenerate cells. It keeps them from dying in the first place."

"I thought cells die in a few minutes without oxygen," Ian said. "How can you stay alive without breathing—and without a beating heart?"

"Preserval slows *all* biochemical processes, including those of decay," Daniel explained. "Cellular degeneration doesn't occur even when cells are temporarily deprived of food, oxygen, and waste-removal processes."

Ian was fascinated. "How long can this drug keep a person in stasis?"

"Not long, unfortunately. Even under ideal conditions, with Preserval administered at a controlled rate to a healthy patient, cells do begin to deteriorate after about eight hours. But researchers are working to extend its effectiveness—"

"To forever," Nathan Halbrook muttered darkly.

"Nathan." Brannigan's voice was soft, but the reproach in it was unmistakable.

"I apologize, Spencer. But it was leukemia today. Eight years old. Can you tell me why our priorities—"

"You're out of line," Brannigan said.

Halbrook heaved a sigh. "I know. I'm sorry."

"Things will change. But give us time."

Jill was studying the cheesecake on her plate like she was fascinated by mint leaves and curls of lemon zest. Ian understood her discomfiture. It was jarring to be among people who could speak about topics most people wouldn't dare mention. He glanced at Daniel and was surprised to see him regarding Nathan Halbrook with compassion.

Daniel noticed Ian's gaze upon him. "Nate is the director of the Tremont Euthanasia Center," Daniel said. "It's a difficult job, being continually confronted with all the diseases we still can't cure."

"It must be very frustrating," Ian said, memory drenching him. *The Tremont Euthanasia Center.* That was where they had encountered Nathan Halbrook. Jill's fingers clutched a handful of her skirt and she averted her gaze so she was no longer facing anyone in the group.

"You're coming to Merit Lake this summer, aren't you, Nate?" The warmth in Brannigan's voice eased the transition to a new topic. Ian lifted forkfuls of cake to his mouth, hardly tasting it as he grappled with painful memories, half listening to Brannigan, Halbrook, and Daniel discuss their vacation plans.

". . . and I told Sarah we couldn't possibly get to the cabin before June recess," Brannigan finished. "Oh—excuse me. I see Secretary Tomasi heading for the door, and I want to speak with her before she leaves."

"I'll have to take you both to our cabin this summer," Daniel said to Jill and Ian. "It's only a few miles from Councilor Brannigan's . . . Jill? What's the matter?"

"Nothing." Jill reached for the glass she had set on a nearby table. The goblet slipped from her fingers and spattered the carpet and Daniel's shoes with champagne as it hit the floor.

"Oh, no!" She grabbed her napkin and bent to blot up the mess. "I'm so sorry."

"Jill, don't clean it up. That's what the servers are for." Daniel signaled. Instantly a uniformed server was at their side, taking care of the spill. Jill stood, rotating her mother's ring on her finger, her cheeks scarlet.

"Here, sit down," Daniel said. "Are you sick?"

"I'm—I'm fine," Jill stammered. "I'm sorry."

"Anyone can drop a glass." Nathan Halbrook scanned Jill's face, and Ian sensed weary understanding. "Even someone with fingers as skilled as yours. My dear, have we met before? Is that the difficulty?"

Jill swallowed and looked at Ian.

"We've been in the Euth Center a couple of times," Ian said simply.

"I'm sorry, I don't recall you." Halbrook's face sagged, making him look like an aging bullfrog. "I make a point of not remembering the people I deal with."

"I'm sorry," Jill said. "I'm being very rude."

"My dear, you haven't done anything wrong. I apologize for catching you off guard." He looked around the room. "I'm going to go hunt up some more saturated fats at the dessert table since Becky's not here to keep me on my diet. Daniel, I'll have Becky call you."

"Thanks."

Halbrook lumbered away.

"Did you meet him when your mother was euthanized?" Daniel asked.

Jill nodded. "Where in the world did I put my dessert plate?"

"Your dad and Councilor Brannigan don't seem too fond of each other," Ian said, knowing Jill was desperate for a new topic of conversation.

"They have their differences." Daniel handed Jill her plate of lemon cheesecake and pulled out a chair for her.

"Why are they so at odds?" Ian asked.

"Councilor Brannigan has some ideas for reform that Dad considers risky. I've got to have some of that chocolate torte. Can I bring anyone anything?"

"No, thank you," Jill said.

Ian watched Daniel stride toward the dessert tables. Marcus Lansbury and Spencer Brannigan might dislike each other, but Daniel Lansbury and Spencer Brannigan were clearly on friendly terms. What did Daniel think of Brannigan's "risky" ideas?

Jill straightened the silver bud vase in the center of the table. "Mr. Halbrook left the room, and he looked upset," she whispered. "I think I offended him."

"Don't be silly."

"He said he was going to the dessert tables, but he left the room right after he talked with us."

"I'm sure it's not your fault he stepped out for a moment." Ian sat next to her. "I can't believe you remember him."

"I wasn't sure, until Daniel said he was from the Euth Center." Jill pushed a blond curl behind her ear. "But I remember his eyes. He has very distinctive eyes."

His eyes. Ian flashed on the memory of Nathan Halbrook leaning over a hysterical Jill, cradling her face in his hands so she couldn't look away, his voice firm but warm with compassion. And Jill, oblivious at first, but then responding, her gaze meeting Halbrook's, her struggling body relaxing in Ian's arms.

"I feel so stupid," Jill said. "He's Councilor Brannigan's brother-in-law, and I acted like a baby. Do you think I should go apologize?"

From the anxiety on Jill's face, Ian knew she would rather disintegrate into a pile of dust than go seek out Nathan Halbrook. "You already apologized, and besides, you didn't do anything to offend him."

Jill's eyes were still cloudy with concern.

"If it will make you feel better, I'll go talk to him," Ian offered. He didn't want Jill's worries about Nathan Halbrook to blight her evening. "You shouldn't leave the party."

"You don't have to do that," Jill said, brightening. "Unless you want to."

"It would be my pleasure. I'll go see if I can find him."

* * *

Daniel settled his lanky body into the chair next to Jill, his plate bearing a slice of dense, dark cake garnished with whipped cream and slivers of chocolate.

"Oh, that does look good," Jill said, less out of admiration for the cake than out of the desire to establish dessert as a safe topic of conversation. She still felt sick from recognizing Nathan Halbrook. All evening she'd been wishing her parents could have been here to listen to her play, and now seeing Halbrook was a bitter reminder that her wishes were worthless dreams. She'd never see her parents again.

"But what if death is temporary? A step on a longer path—"

Jill gouged her fingertips into her palms. *Stop thinking about that silly conversation.*

Daniel held out a forkful of cake. "Try a bite?"

Jill tasted it and feigned appreciation. "Very rich."

"Where did Ian go?"

Jill's smile wilted. Uncomfortably, she admitted where Ian had gone and why.

"You worry too much," Daniel said. "Nate is upset about some things that have nothing to do with you."

Jill traced her fork across the surface of her cheesecake, thinking of that brief, tense conversation between Nathan Halbrook and Councilor Brannigan.

Daniel sat back and resumed eating his torte, but he kept looking at the door, a crease deepening between his eyes. "I'd prefer Ian not spend a lot of time talking to Nate. Nate is not the sort of company Ian needs right now."

"Oh, no." Heat swept into Jill's cheeks. "I'm sorry."

"Stop apologizing, will you?" Daniel patted her shoulder. "I'm not chastising you. Nate is a great guy. But he has a difficult job, and in consequence he's not always as positive as he could be."

"Oh." Jill couldn't see how *anyone* who worked at the Euthanasia Center could manage to be positive.

Daniel spoke softly, his voice audible only to Jill. "In fact, he struggles with many of the same problems that trouble Ian—keeping the suffering of individuals in perspective, understanding the needs of the nation as a whole, recognizing that our resources can't fix everything."

Jill was startled. Councilor Brannigan's brother-in-law had problems like Ian's?

Daniel shifted to rise to his feet, and a knot formed in Jill's throat. If Daniel marched up like a reproachful father and snatched Ian away from Nathan Halbrook, Ian would probably be irritated enough to get stubborn when Daniel wanted to do things like discuss those case histories.

"I'm sure he'll be back in a moment," Jill said.

Daniel resumed eating his dessert. "Well, if Nate says anything inappropriate, I can always correct it later when I'm talking to Ian. Nate complains, but at least he has the sense to keep himself out of trouble, which is more than I can say for your brother."

* * *

Outside the reception room, the corridor was empty except for the officers at their posts and the usher at the door. Ian hesitated, debating which way to go, but when the eyes of the nearest officer narrowed at him in scrutiny, he decided he'd better not loiter. He strolled toward the restroom.

The restroom was deserted. He retraced his footsteps, pretending to ignore the officers as he passed the reception room, but feeling their alertness like icicles pricking his skin.

A gold-lettered sign told Ian he was heading for the west lounge. He rounded the corner and spotted Nathan Halbrook alone in the lounge, standing near the window, the angry set of his jaw stiffening the fleshy curves of his face. Halbrook turned and raised bushy eyebrows at Ian as he approached.

"Nice view." Ian gestured at the lights glittering on the surface of Lake Serena. "I hope you're out here to enjoy it and not because we drove you away. Jill's afraid she offended you."

"Oh, the poor child." Halbrook's face softened. "No, not at all. I'm sorry to have brought back unhappy memories. Someone close to you, I imagine?"

"Our mother," Ian said, appreciating Halbrook's gracious response. "Jill was fifteen. It was challenging for her."

Halbrook surveyed Ian, his gaze level. "So it was 'challenging' for Jill to see her mother taken to her death. 'Challenging.' I'll have to add that to my list of euphemisms." He turned back toward the window. "I presume it was so 'challenging' that Jill nearly got herself accused of interfering with the operations of the Euthanasia Center."

Halbrook's bluntness was as startling as a blast of freezing wind on a muggy August day. "Then you do remember us."

"No. But the most likely way for you to cross paths with the director would be to make a disturbance."

Ian blew the air out of his lungs. Clearly Nathan Halbrook was not a man who tiptoed around sensitive subjects. "We did get into some trouble. Jill had difficulty when the time came to—say good-bye."

"I've seen it countless times." Sadness chiseled deep furrows around Halbrook's eyes. "I smooth things over when I can, but it's not always possible to keep people from being arrested."

Ian watched the multicolored ripples of light on the lake and thought about Jill burying her face in her mother's neck, ignoring the Euth Center guard who had just told her it was time, ignoring her mother's gentle, then frantic efforts to disentangle herself before Jill got in trouble. Images and sensations Ian wished he could forget . . . his fingers bruising Jill's arms as he pried her loose, Jill's agonized sobs, the disgust on the guard's face.

"What was the reason for your mother's termination?" Halbrook asked.

"Ovarian cancer."

"Cancer." Halbrook spat the word out like he would propel it into the lake. "Another person we should have cured."

"We have a long way to go before we've conquered illness entirely."

"We'd conquer it a lot faster if we tried to cure difficult cases instead of shuffling them off to the Euth Centers." Halbrook lowered his voice. "Our doctors use outdated procedures and outdated equipment while we dump our money into projects like Preserval."

Ian had no idea what to say. He had never met anyone reckless enough to criticize Health Services to a stranger.

"Sorry," Halbrook said. "I'm ranting, aren't I?"

By now, it was plain why Nathan Halbrook remained Director of the Tremont Euthanasia Center instead of receiving a more prestigious job his family connections might warrant. Councilor Brannigan could probably keep the police from bothering Halbrook, but even a member of the Council couldn't take a man with a mouth like Halbrook's and put him in a visible political position.

"Why don't you like Preserval?" Ian asked cautiously.

"I suppose it has its uses. But they're pushing to make it more than it could ever be."

"Why are they so interested in that one drug?"

"They're trying to make it an elixir of immortality. If it can stop cellular degeneration for a few hours, why can't it stop it forever?"

"Who wants to live forever if you're just lying on a table in stasis?"

"They'd like to modify it so it stops the aging process while allowing for normal functioning."

"Very ambitious."

"Very unrealistic."

"If it's so unrealistic, why the funding?"

Halbrook's frog eyes slid half closed. "Rumor has it that President Ryce is afraid to die," he whispered. "Terrified of it. Preserval is her pet project."

Ian didn't speak. He couldn't risk even hinting at criticism of President Ryce with police officers just around the corner.

"Spencer's father is the one who opened the project." Halbrook kept his voice low. "Ten or twelve years ago."

"How does Councilor Brannigan feel about it?"

"He'd cut the funding if he could, but it's due to President Ryce's influence that he was appointed to the Council in the first place. If he offends her, he'll be cutting his own throat. Spencer has a lot of enemies, including Colonel Edgefield, who doesn't like the way Spencer wants to rein in the Tremont Police Service. Spencer has to be careful to keep the friends he has." Halbrook inspected Ian. "Well, well, well. All this griping from me and you haven't said a thing to shut me up. You *are* an odd one. Dan wasn't exaggerating."

Embarrassment flickered through Ian. "What did Daniel tell you?"

"That your patriotism and character could stand some improvement and he intends to improve them." Halbrook grinned. "Do you think I'd be rattling on like this if I thought you were one of those people who chats with the police hotline more than he talks to his wife? Even Spencer couldn't save my neck if I started complaining to people who didn't want to hear it."

"I didn't realize my flaws were the talk of Tremont," Ian said stiffly.

"They're not. Dan's not one to broadcast his business, but he's always confided in me. Hard for him to talk to his own father, as you can imagine. I've known him since he was ten years old, when he started taking piano lessons from my sister Caroline."

"Caroline was Councilor Brannigan's wife?"

"Yes. If you ask me, her death is the primary reason Spencer is so eager to reform Health Services. He feels—and he's right—that if our medical care was as good as it should be, Caroline would still be alive." Halbrook looked more closely at Ian. "Am I shocking you? You look like you've forgotten how to breathe."

"It's just strange to hear someone speak so—truthfully."

Halbrook laughed heartily. "Roshek, you're going to be good for Dan."

"Me?"

"Oh, he needs a friend his own age who isn't afraid to be candid. Most people are so twittery over the fact that his grandpa was James Tremont's best buddy that they treat him like he's above all humanity. He needs someone to shove him off that Lansbury perch."

Ian flattened his palms against the cold glass of the window. He took a deep breath. "How hard can I shove before Daniel . . . loses patience with me?"

"Sends you to patriotic counseling, you mean? You'd have to push him off his feet, out the door, and into a ditch to get him to do that. Don't get me wrong—he's not bluffing. He'll do it if he thinks it's the only way to help you. But he'll give you plenty of leeway, because he doesn't *want* to do it."

"I'd think it wouldn't bother him at all," Ian said acidly.

"Why do you say that?"

"Well . . ." What *did* make him think Daniel could put him through that kind of pain without any compunctions? He couldn't think of any reason beyond the fact that Daniel was a Lansbury.

"Because of his father?" Halbrook guessed.

Sheepishly, Ian nodded.

"He gets that all the time. People assume he's Marcus Junior. And the funny thing is, *he* thinks he's Marcus Junior. He's spent his life trying to match his father's footsteps, and believe me, he feels that pressure, but he comes up short on the ruthless genes. For example, just the other day, he was talking to Health Services, getting them to reverse their decision about some college kid they had denied medication."

"He *what?*"

"Surprised, aren't you?"

So *that* was why Health Services had changed their mind about Peter Critchlow. Jill must have told Peter's story to Daniel, and Daniel had gone to Health Services. "I didn't think Daniel would approve of challenging Health Services."

"He wouldn't approve if *you* tried a stunt like that. But he's different. He's part of the crew that makes the rules. Dating Jill is the first time I've seen him pull back from his father—pursuing a girl who isn't the daughter or granddaughter of one of his dad's colleagues. And now he's dirtying his hands trying to purify your family name . . . I can't figure out why his father didn't cut *that* one off before it started. Maybe he thinks Daniel will get Jill out of his system more quickly this way." Halbrook clapped a meaty hand on Ian's shoulder. "Come on, kid. Let's go back to the party and talk to your sister. I don't want her to waste any more time worrying that she's offended me. She couldn't do that if she tried."

But as they neared the reception, no sounds of conversation came from inside the room. Ian could hear a single voice speaking in the cadence of a presentation or a report.

"I didn't know there was going to be a program." Halbrook tugged at his bow tie. "I might have thought twice about coming."

A woman in a salmon-pink dress rushed out of the reception room, her face gray. Halbrook jumped out of her path to avoid a collision.

"That's a newscast," Ian said. "It must be a special report."

They hurried into the room. All the guests stood motionless, dessert dishes and champagne glasses abandoned. One wall panel had been rolled back to reveal a television screen, busy with images of a round, silvery building nearly obscured by billowing smoke.

"*. . . additional personnel are en route from all over the nation to assist in rescue operations . . .*"

Ian threaded his way to Jill's side. "What is it?" he whispered.

"An anarchist attack," Jill said.

A hammer slammed into Ian's chest. *The Liberty Cadre?* The screen showed rescue workers loading a child onto a stretcher. Blood poured from the child's forehead.

"What happened?" Ian choked the words out.

Daniel's face was taut with rage. "The anarchists bombed the Newbold Bay Community Center."

Newbold Bay . . . the Cadre had moved Eric to Newbold Bay . . .

"They were holding the National Junior Security Watch convention this weekend." Tears splotched the front of Jill's silk dress. "That building was full of *children.*"

Smoke thinned, exposing caved-in concrete and twisted steel girders.

"*. . . most vicious anarchist attack since the founding of New America. In a communiqué sent to Tremont, the Liberty Cadre stated: 'We will spill the blood of our children before we allow the Council to mold them into brainless slaves . . .'*"

Ian lurched toward the door.

"Ian," Jill cried.

Stomach contracting with uncontrollable horror, Ian staggered down the corridor and slammed open the door of the restroom. He splashed water over his face, but the water did nothing to ease the nausea. He swung around and fell to his knees in front of the toilet.

When the retching stopped, he wiped his mouth with the back of his hand and tried to stand on legs that refused to hold him. How could Eric be part of this? He *couldn't*, it wasn't possible—it *was* possible, it was inescapable—

A strong hand gripped his arm, steadying him. "Ian."

Ian yanked his arm away from Daniel and stumbled to the sink. "Leave me alone."

"I'm here to help you."

"Help me, then, go ahead, good luck." Ian wiped his hands on his suit coat and brushed past Daniel. Jill was hovering in the hallway, her eyes huge azure circles in a porcelain-white face.

"Ian, are you all right? You look—"

Ian ignored her.

"Wait! Where are you going?"

He had no idea where he was going. He just had to get out of the concert hall, away from the news report that pierced his eardrums like slivers of glass.

He knew all along that the Liberty Cadre targeted civilians. He knew Eric had gone to Newbold Bay to do the Cadre's bidding—Eric, with his electronics expertise and his mindless eagerness to take "action." He *knew*, yet he had done nothing to hinder the Cadre's operations.

If he had stopped Eric, maybe those children in Newbold Bay would still be alive.

* * *

Waves slapped against the shore. Ian hunched on a granite boulder and stared at the dim outlines of the monument dedicating the lake to Serena Tremont. Thoughts spun through his skull—he was freezing, he should go home, Jill would be worried. But he sat and stared at the monument, his initiative charred to cold, dead ash.

The glare of headlights reflected off the monument. Ian twisted his head and saw a car pulling into the parking area above the beach. Probably Daniel Lansbury coming to herd him home and tuck him into bed with a mug of hot milk laced with patriotism. Let Daniel do his best; it wouldn't change anything. It wouldn't restore breath to small, vulnerable lungs; it wouldn't restore limbs to health and wholeness.

Above the wash of the waves, Ian heard a car door slam. He braced his elbows on his knees, vaguely aware that he could feel neither his hands nor his feet. The beam of a flashlight flicked over him, then clicked to blackness.

"Come with me." The voice was Alisa Kent's.

Unable to muster surprise, Ian tried to stand. His knees crumpled like paper.

"Come. You'll freeze out here."

Ian made it to his feet and followed Kent to her car. He slid into the seat, numb hands reaching toward the hot air blowing from the vents.

"You are ill," Kent said. "Do you need a doctor?"

"Huh? No. How'd you find me?"

"Your sister said you left the concert hall a few minutes before I arrived. Your bus card showed no activity, so I assumed you were within walking distance."

"You talked to Jill and Daniel?"

"Dr. Lansbury was busy speaking with his parents. He didn't see me. I'll take you home." She drove out of the parking area.

Ian's brain couldn't seem to catch up with what was happening. "But you were on vacation. Ski lodge."

"The Liberty Cadre prefers that I remain in Tremont."

"The Cadre—what—"

"This morning I received a message from the lodge confirming 'my' request for cancellation of the reservation. I also received a message—this one in an envelope on my kitchen table—informing me that if I leave Tremont, you will forfeit your life."

"Me! That's ridiculous. You can't take that seriously. Get out of Tremont, go now—"

"The Cadre is not in the habit of making empty threats. They murdered dozens, perhaps hundreds of children tonight. Do you think they would hesitate to kill you?"

"You *can't stay here*—"

"In seventy-two hours, I will surrender to Captain Hofstader, the head of the Sedition and Treason Division."

Ian gaped at her. Her face was a sickly patch of white. "You're turning yourself in?"

"As matters stand, I am at the mercy of the Cadre. That is a situation I will no longer tolerate. I am surrendering, and you are going to the United States."

"What are you talking about?"

"I can tell you how to get to the U.S., on condition that you do not warn Vettori and Sandring that arrest is imminent."

Eric—the Cadre—Pain, slashing fury, and confusion tumbled in his mind. "What do you mean? Cross the border?"

"Due to a recent increase in unauthorized border crossings, changes are currently being made in the border nets and the computer system that monitors them. Until the work is completed, the nets will be inoperative."

"Inoperative!"

"Both the ground sensors and the automated aerial patrols are inactive at the moment. Work started two days ago and is scheduled to conclude on Tuesday."

"Unauthorized crossings—you mean from people like David Garrett—"

"David Garrett is one instance. There were many."

"But—if you knew the border nets were down, why didn't you take advantage of that to get away from the Cadre?"

"I only learned of the repairs when I went into headquarters tonight after the attack. Naturally, the work has been kept secret, but the entire police service was informed tonight because of the complications it might pose in apprehending the Cadre attackers."

"The Cadre knew the nets would be down, didn't they? They chose tonight so if anything went wrong—"

"You will drive my car to within a few miles of the border. Then you will abandon the car and cross on foot. Be very careful, as manned patrols have been radically increased."

Ian stared dumbly out the windshield as Kent drove into the city. Streetlights and traffic lights were random, incomprehensible blotches; buildings were meaningless hulks. Walk across the border—even if he could do that without getting shot, what of the wasteland strip, the swath of unoccupied territory the Tremont-Corlan Treaty had established between the U.S. and New America? How could he hike a hundred miles in bone-freezing cold—

"I will assemble survival gear from police storage." Kent seemed to read his thoughts. "You and your sister will have the supplies you need to cross the wasteland strip."

Jill. "If we reach the U.S. border—will they let us in?"

"You will fare better if you surrender to their border patrol rather than trying to cross unnoticed. They will detain you so they may determine your motives for fleeing New America. They fear terrorist incursions, and particularly after tonight they will be cautious. But in time you will be able to convince them that you are not a threat. You will not be ill-treated or returned to Tremont."

"Are there many people who—"

"Be silent and let me finish." Agitation worked its way to the surface of her voice. "If you would like to alert any non-Cadre friends of this opportunity to flee, do so, but I can provide survival gear only for you and your sister."

Ian thought instantly of Laura Travers. He'd tell Laura and Matt.

"Do not mention anything concerning me to the people you speak with," Kent said. "Though your friends may not be affiliated with the Cadre, they may ignorantly pass your message to people who are, and if the Cadre finds out what I am planning—"

"You're not really going to turn yourself in!"

"Do not waste your time trying to contact your friend Sherry Mason," Kent continued as if she hadn't heard him. "I've already checked on her, and she is in the hospital in Hamilton with back injuries sustained in a skiing accident. Even if she knew arrest was imminent, she could not do anything with that knowledge."

"Oh, Sherry," Ian groaned. "But there must be some way—"

"To remove her from a doctor's care would endanger her life. There is nothing you can do for her. Your focus should be on protecting yourself and your sister. And if you are tempted to leave your sister in Tremont because of the dangers involved in crossing the border or because she doesn't want to leave Dr. Lansbury, bear in mind that Lansbury cannot and will not protect her, no matter what his feelings for her. He would never knowingly protect a traitor."

"Jill isn't a traitor," Ian protested.

"Chances are she knows enough about you to warrant a prison sentence for concealing your treason. As the protector of a Garrett follower, things would not . . . go well for her."

Ian clenched his teeth to stop them from chattering. He'd take Jill to the United States if it meant dragging her by the hair.

"I will need time to assemble your survival supplies." Kent drove into the parking lot behind his building. "Take Saturday to rest and prepare. I suggest you leave Tremont on Sunday after dark."

Leave Tremont . . . He was leaving Tremont . . . but Alisa Kent—"What about you?"

"I will give you a twenty-four-hour head start before I surrender. Since the police can't pursue you into the wasteland strip, that should give you more than enough time to get out of range."

Ian didn't remember reaching for Kent, but he suddenly found his hand gripping her shoulder. "Come to the U.S. with us. You don't have to turn yourself in to escape the Cadre—"

"This is not just about the Cadre. I'm not running."

"Do you think you have to stay here to answer for—"

She shook off his hand with a savage motion. "I have made my decision."

"Alisa—"

"You are exhausted. I suggest you get some rest."

"Alisa—"

She opened the glove box and removed a cardboard envelope that she pushed into his hand. "You will want your book."

His sense of being caught in a whirlwind intensified. "Alisa, listen to me—"

She leaned across him and opened the passenger door. "Go."

"You can't turn yourself in."

"I'll call you tomorrow night. Go."

Numbly obedient, he stepped out of the car. "Alisa—" he tried again.

"I read it," she said quietly.

"You read—" But the door slammed shut before his clumsy fingers could catch it. He stood gripping the book in its envelope, watching her drive away.

CHAPTER 15

"Laura, at least think about it, and talk to Matt. It's the best chance you'll ever have."

Laura poured orange juice into Ian's glass. "Ian, we don't *want* to go. Our families are here. Tremont is our home."

"It's dangerous for you here."

"And it wouldn't be dangerous in the U.S.? We'd probably get shot by some teenage gang member. Or mugged on the subway."

"No one's claiming the U.S. is a paradise. But at least—"

"Would you like toast? Or pancakes?" Laura offered pleasantly.

"Thanks, no. I didn't expect you to feed me breakfast."

"If you show up at 7:00 A.M. on a Saturday, then you *should* expect breakfast."

"Sorry. I know it's early, but this is urgent. Please go wake Matt so you can discuss—"

"Forget it," she interrupted. "He was at work until two. Besides, I already know what he'll say, and I agree with it. If everyone who cares about freedom leaves Tremont, things will never change here." Quickly she held out a hand. "I don't mean you shouldn't go. I think it's the right choice for you."

"Laura . . ." Ian tried to think how to warn her without mentioning Alisa Kent's name. "Laura, when I leave Tremont, the police will label me a traitor and start searching for my friends to find out what I was up to before I left. They'll find you."

"It's been years since we dated. And I'm not listed in your file."

He was startled. "How do you know what's in my file?"

"I told you, Matt has friends. Go to the U.S., and good luck. But Matt and I will stay. Don't worry about me. I'll be fine."

* * *

Ian ladled potato soup out of a saucepan, splashing nearly as much on the countertop as he got into his bowl. He reached for a dishcloth to wipe up the spill and his hand brushed the hot pan.

"Ow!" He yanked his hand back, knocking a box of crackers into the sink. Irritably, he retrieved the crackers. After a sleepless night, this morning's futile conversation with Laura, and two unsuccessful attempts to visit Alisa Kent, his skull was filled with fog. Now, at eight o'clock Saturday night, he hadn't so much as decided which direction to head when they left Tremont tomorrow night.

While he ate his soup, he tried for the dozenth time to study a map of New America and plan his escape route. The closest border was forty-two miles southwest of Tremont. Should he cross there? Which parts of the border would be the most heavily manned? How close to the border should he drive before abandoning the car?

And what about Alisa Kent? She had phoned him today to say she would bring the car tomorrow morning. When she came to deliver it, he'd do everything in his power to convince her that submitting to the same evil that had taken the lives of Garrett and her family was not the way to answer for the things she had done.

"I read it." In two days, she had read the Book of Mormon. But what had she thought of it?

Crumbs stuck to Ian's sweaty fingers as he mashed a cracker and sprinkled it into his soup. He couldn't leave Kent here. As a traitorous police officer, she'd certainly be executed.

The doorbell rang. Hoping it was Alisa Kent, Ian sprinted into the living room and yanked the door open. It was Daniel Lansbury.

"Hi, Daniel," he said shortly. "Come in."

Exhaustion shadowed the skin under Daniel's eyes. "How are you doing?" he asked Ian.

"Not bad. Jill's in the shower, but she should be out in a few minutes. I guess you know her concert was canceled tonight."

"Yes." Daniel removed his coat as he walked through the door. "I'm heading home for a few hours of sleep myself, but I thought I'd stop here first and make sure you're all right."

"You shouldn't have bothered."

Daniel settled on the couch and stretched his long legs over the carpet. "Have you gotten any rest?"

"Yeah, a little bit." Remembering Nathan Halbrook's words, Ian found it increasingly difficult to meet Daniel's gaze. Had he ever given Daniel a chance, or had he simply passed judgment before he ever met him, condemning him as the son of Marcus Lansbury? As to Daniel's intrusive efforts to fix his patriotism, to Daniel's mind, this was probably the greatest kindness he could offer. How could Ian condemn Daniel for wanting to help him stay out of trouble? Or for falling in love with Jill? And Peter Critchlow—Daniel had cared enough about Peter's situation to take the time to intercede for a stranger.

"You look exhausted," Daniel said. "Why don't you sit down and relax?"

"Thanks," Ian said, then realized he'd just thanked Daniel for inviting him to sit down in his own living room.

He dropped into the armchair. When Ian left Tremont, Daniel Lansbury would be struck a double blow—the pain of losing Jill compounded by the humiliation of having befriended a Garrett follower. Even the name of Lansbury would be stretched thin to cover that kind of scandal. Ian studied the fraying threads on the arm of the chair and wrestled an urge to apologize to Daniel for what was about to happen.

To Ian's relief, the bathroom door squeaked open and Jill's light footsteps padded toward the living room. Daniel rose to his feet.

"Hi, Jilly," Ian said as she stuck her head into the living room. "You have company."

Jill's eyes lit up. Her damp blond hair curled around her face, and one hand clasped the collar of her bathrobe. "I didn't think you'd get off work tonight."

"I'm on call if they need someone with high security clearance." Daniel smiled wearily. "But I don't think that's likely to happen tonight. All arrests so far have been routine. How are you doing?"

"I'm fine. Let me get dressed." Jill disappeared back down the hall.

* * *

"You want more *information?*" Nineteen's pasty face crinkled in a sneer. "*That's* the urgent reason you wanted to meet with me tonight?"

"This is important." Eric yanked at the lumpy cushion behind his back. He hated this room in the back of the safe house, with its flea-bitten furniture and pink wallpaper so bright it blistered his eyeballs.

"You want a list of upcoming Cadre operations so you can blab every detail to the police if you're arrested?"

"I didn't say I wanted a list. I just want to know about the operations I'm part of." Eric's tongue felt like those dried apple slices his mother used to force-feed them every winter. "You put me to work wiring timers, but you don't even tell me where they're going?"

Nineteen straightened his yellow polka-dot tie. "You feel bad for those kiddie Watch robots that got blasted? Is that your problem?"

Something twisted inside Eric like a jagged piece of metal. "I didn't say that."

"Information goes out on a need-to-know basis. They made that clear to you at initiation." Nineteen pursed his lips in a mock pout. "I know that's hard to remember. But try."

The little snot. "If I'm involved in an operation, then I *need to know* what I'm working on," Eric said, mimicking Nineteen's condescending tone.

Nineteen leaned forward, closing in on Eric until Eric could smell his toothpaste. "You're new to this, so I'll cut you some slack. But you knew when you joined that you'd only get the information Zero wants you to have. You swore to obey orders. Now, after your first operation, you come sniveling and complaining. That's not too impressive."

Eric felt like the blood vessels in his face were going to rupture. "Maybe you're just too stupid to understand that the Cadre would function a lot better if—"

"Excuse me?" Nineteen cupped his hand around his ear. "I don't think I heard that right. It sounds like you think you can tell Zero how to run the Cadre."

"That's not what I meant."

"Good." Nineteen stood up. "Because if you ever come whining to me again, I'm reporting you. Got it?"

Eric opened his mouth, then clamped it shut. He didn't want this worm to go slithering to the Cadre leadership with twisted stories that would make Eric look bad.

"I said, *got it?*"

"Got it," Eric muttered.

"You got any complaints about last night's operation?"

"No."

"Glad to hear it. For a minute there, I thought you didn't support us." Nineteen sauntered toward the door. "That'd be too bad. Zero hates ungrateful whiners." He strutted out into the twilight.

Eric paced angrily around the safe house, waiting the required twenty minutes before following Nineteen's exit. When the time was up, he headed directly for the nearest bar. He needed a drink, something to cool him down. His gut burned like it was filled with boiling acid.

Two hours later, Eric was still huddled over a table in the corner of the bar, an empty beer glass clamped in his hand. He wasn't sure which number beer it was, but he'd been annoyed at the reproachful look the server gave him when she set it down. What business of hers was it how much he drank? It would take more liquor than this bar had in stock to douse the anger that made him want to track Nineteen down and stomp him into pulp.

Eric slashed his hand through the air to attract the attention of the server. She pivoted creakily toward him, moving like she had arthritic knees to match her floppy neck muscles.

"Gimme another one. Same." Eric held up his glass.

"You're drunk. No more booze. You want to order some food?"

"Your greasy burgers . . . are 'nuff to make anyone puke."

"Then go home so someone else can have your table. You've been here for hours." She shuffled off. Eric lurched to his feet and shoved his chair back so hard that it banged into the ugly ocean mural on the wall. If he had to return to his smelly wet-dog apartment, he'd ram his foot through the wall. He'd walk for a while instead, work off some of the anger.

The damp darkness seemed to cling to his skin. He'd joined the Cadre to fight for freedom, not to get bullied by a worm. *I don't care about those kids. Kids always die in wars.* But Nineteen should have told him their target. Eric didn't think he should have to wait with the rest of the nation to see what his handiwork blasted to rubble.

It was just another target, Eric tried to reason with himself. A wildly successful operation. No one could doubt now that the Cadre was a formidable threat to the Council's power.

But why kids?

Eric gritted his teeth. The Liberty Cadre was New America's only hope. So they *weren't* perfect. So Nineteen was a worm. He wouldn't have to listen to Nineteen for long. As soon as the Cadre realized Eric's worth, he'd be telling Nineteen what to do.

The sidewalk was crowded now, but no one seemed to be going anywhere. Eric cursed as he stumbled around clumps of people. Acrid air seared his throat. He knew he was near the Community Center, but he wasn't going to look up. He knew how it looked. He hadn't come this way on purpose—had he? He was just wandering, letting off steam.

But he should have gone another direction. It was too loud here. Machinery growled; voices shouted orders. Some lady howled like a sick animal. Why was she standing there with her nose shoved through the chain-link fence that surrounded the rubble? Waste of time.

Kids.

Eric slammed his fist against the fence, and the metal links shivered noisily. Several bystanders jumped back from the fence. Eric kept walking, punching the fence. Everyone was staring at him with stupid, startled eyes. They ought to all go home, he thought angrily.

Pain like fire exploded in his foot. He'd knocked his toe against a shoe-box-sized piece of concrete. He lifted the chunk off the sidewalk and heaved it against the fence, then staggered back as the concrete thunked to the ground and shattered. *Stupid fence. What is it here for, anyway? Do the police think people will swarm the rubble? There's nothing here worth looting.*

Just crumpled steel and dead kids. Kids.

Eric picked up one of the concrete fragments and slung it at the dent the first chunk had made in the fence. Inside the perimeter, the lawn was crowded with ambulances, cranes, bulldozers, and rescue workers with skeletal faces and bloody hands.

Pain ripped through him. He should have forced Nineteen to tell him where those bombs were going. Should have squeezed him until the truth popped out of that ugly mouth. Eric had pictured a bridge, a police station, a government office—

"Ian, I didn't know . . ." Was he speaking those words or just thinking them? Head spinning, Eric limped off the curb and swayed across the street. He shouldn't have drunk so much, he realized. *Might attract attention.* Cadre members had to be inconspicuous. Hadn't the Worm warned him of that in their first meeting?

He had to talk to Ian. Had to explain. Of course he couldn't talk openly about the bombing, but somehow he'd get the message across that if Nineteen had only *told* him, he never would have agreed—

Ian wouldn't hate him. He hadn't even hated that police officer who'd tortured him. He'd have some kind of advice, some kind of help, something from his book. Eric would go home and call Ian. Which street was this? He squinted at the street sign. The letters ran together.

The wail of a siren tore the dusty air. *Ambulance. When are they going to give up? No one could still be alive in that wreckage.*

Kids.

The siren stopped so abruptly that the silence thudded on Eric's eardrums. He blinked at flashing blue lights. *Not an ambulance. Police car.* It was parked at the curb in front of him. The doors swung open, and two officers leapt out.

"Hold it!" The command sailed around Eric's skull, surfing waves of alcoholic fuzziness. The officers were bearing down on him.

The police had figured it out. They knew he put those timers together. They knew he helped murder those kids. He couldn't let them take him.

Eric ran.

* * *

As soon as Jill returned to the living room, Ian excused himself and retreated to his bedroom. This would be the last time Jill would ever see Daniel Lansbury, and Ian wanted to give them this time alone. He would have left the apartment altogether, but he was too distracted to think where to go and too tired to roam aimlessly around Tremont just to give Jill some privacy.

Struggling to direct his thoughts into a productive channel, Ian surveyed his room. What should he take with him to the United States? He wouldn't want to carry much beyond the survival supplies Alisa Kent would provide, but he'd take a few family photographs, and of course his Book of Mormon—

No. There was no need to risk carrying the book with him. He could easily and openly acquire another copy once he reached the U.S.

That was a remarkable, dizzying thought.

Ian dragged the box of old textbooks out of his closet, popped up the floorboard and retrieved his box of contraband. He removed the books and papers one by one, flipping through crisp pamphlets and yellowed pages. For a long time he sat with the Book of Mormon in his hands, imagining what it would be like to openly discuss it, to openly declare his faith, to freely associate with people who shared that faith. To be baptized. To receive the gift of the Holy Ghost in his life.

He shook himself and laid the book on the stack of literature he had piled on his bed. Time to get organized. He still hadn't even decided where to cross the border.

Tomorrow morning, he'd tell Jill they were leaving Tremont after sunset. He'd have to allow her enough time to process a tidal wave of information—the nature of his treason, Eric's Liberty Cadre membership, Lt. Alisa Kent's assistance, and most of all, what would happen to Jill should she remain in Tremont.

Would she ever forgive him for what he was doing to her?

Yes. Because freed of the fear of punishment, she would finally be willing to listen to the truth he longed to share with her. The knowledge that she could be with her parents again would be worth more to her than all she had left behind in Tremont. Including Daniel Lansbury.

The ringing of the phone jolted Ian. *Alisa Kent?*

"Ian." Jill knocked at the door. "Phone for you."

"Thanks." Ian opened the door a crack, careful to block the doorway so Jill wouldn't see the books on his bed.

Jill handed him the handset, her eyes sparkling. "It's a girrrrrl," she whispered, drawing out the word like she had when she was a giggly thirteen-year-old.

"Thanks." Ian smiled at her, but swiftly shut his bedroom door. "Hello?"

"This is Alisa Kent. A difficulty has arisen." Her voice was whispery. "It will require a change in schedule."

"What's wrong?"

"Eric Vettori has been arrested in Newbold Bay."

Fear shot through Ian's body. "When?"

"About twenty minutes ago. He was arrested near the Community Center, or what remains of it. Apparently he was intoxicated, vandalizing the fence enclosing the site. When officers approached him, he attempted to flee. Such resistance will raise suspicions that he has much to hide. His recent move from Tremont is another red flag."

"How soon will they question him?"

"They are backed up right now, but Vettori has been rated priority one, so they won't bother screening him. They've given him medication to speed the breakdown of alcohol in his bloodstream and as soon as the medical supervisor gives clearance, they'll take him for Information Extraction. An hour . . . perhaps more, perhaps less. If you want any chance of making it to the border before Vettori gives the police your name, then leave *now.*"

"Your car—"

"Is parked in front of your building. The keys are on the seat, and your supplies are in the trunk, packed in two backpacks. All necessities are included—food, shelter, medical and hygiene supplies. I recommend that you add only a change of clothing."

"Where are *you?*"

"That's not your concern."

"Alisa! Where are you? Why didn't you come up to my apartment? Why didn't you tell me you were here? Come back. Come with us."

"I have told you my plans. I will not revise them."

In the background, Ian heard the hiss of a bus braking. "Come with us. *Come with us!* Just tell me where you are; I'll come get you—"

"Good-bye, Ian. And . . . thank you."

"Alisa, *no!* Don't do this—"

"May your God sustain you." Kent broke the connection.

"Don't do this, please don't do this." Ian jammed his finger against the button to reconnect the call. Kent's voice mail picked up. He disconnected and tried again. Same result.

Ian threw the phone to the floor. Kent wasn't going to answer. There was nothing he could do to change her mind. All he could do was grab Jill and run.

Ian rushed out of his bedroom and found Daniel and Jill at the kitchen table, bowls of soup in front of them. Daniel rose instantly to his feet. "What's wrong?"

Ian paused. He didn't want to raise Daniel's suspicions about the phone call, but how could he convince him to leave without doing that? He struggled to keep his voice under control. "Jill, I need to talk to you about a family matter. Daniel, I'm sorry, but I'd like you to leave."

Jill's brow creased with anxiety. "What happened?"

Ian ignored her and gestured at the door, his mind throbbing with the deafening thud of seconds ticking away. "I'm sorry, Daniel."

Daniel studied Ian's face in an unsubtle assessment of his mental state. "If there's a problem, maybe I can help."

"Thanks, but there's nothing you can do. Like I said, it's a family matter. Private." Ian walked to the couch and snatched Daniel's coat.

Jill and Daniel came slowly out of the kitchen, Jill clutching Daniel's hand.

"I'm sorry," Ian said again as he shoved the coat at Daniel.

"That woman who called you," Jill said. "What—"

"Later," Ian interrupted, so harshly that Jill flinched.

"Ian, this past week—and particularly last night—has been very stressful and exhausting for you," Daniel said. "You're not in a strong position to cope with any new problems."

"I'm all right—I swear I'm all right. It's not a new problem. This is just something that our family needs to deal with. There's nothing you can do to help."

"I can help with quite a bit," Daniel said. "You might be surprised."

"I appreciate the offer." Ian opened the door. "But let me talk to Jill first."

After a pause, Daniel said, "All right, Ian. I can respect that." He touched Jill's cheek. "Call me as soon as you can. Don't worry about waking me up or interrupting me at work. If I can't answer your call right away, I'll call you the instant I'm free."

Jill nodded. Her eyes were glistening, and she was again gripping Daniel's hand. Ian felt his stomach fold over. "Good night, Daniel," he said firmly.

Daniel kissed Jill lightly on the lips and straightened up. He slid his arms into his coat, moving like he had no intention of finishing before summer.

Ian wondered what would happen if he physically threw Daniel out of the apartment. "Sorry about this," he repeated. "If I need help, I'll call you."

"See that he does, Jill."

"I will."

Daniel gave Ian one last speculative look and walked out the door. Ian locked it behind him and spun around to confront a white-faced Jill.

"What's happened?" Jill asked. "What's wrong?"

Ian scanned Jill's clothing—a red corduroy dress, white tights, shabby brown loafers. She couldn't hike across the wasteland strip dressed like that.

"Go change into clothes good for walking in winter weather. Jeans, boots, your heaviest sweater. A couple of layers of socks."

"Ian! It's ten o'clock at night! Where are we going?"

"I'll explain everything later. Go change your clothes." When Jill didn't move, Ian grabbed her arm and propelled her toward her bedroom. In his own room, he pulled on a hooded sweatshirt and exchanged his shoes for boots. He shoved an extra set of clothes into his backpack and, as an afterthought, snatched his father's old pocket-knife. There was probably a better knife included with Kent's survival supplies, but an extra one might be useful. He tucked the knife in his pocket.

Jill was still in her room and Ian heard the scrape of a drawer opening. He dove down the hall to pound on her door. "Hurry up."

"Come in already."

Ian flung the door open. Jill was huddled on the floor, lacing her boots.

"Bring a change of clothes," he said. "Something warm."

"Why do I need extra clothes?"

"Later. Just *hurry.*"

"You don't have to yell." Tears trickled from her eyes as she stood and pulled another drawer open. Ian shot a look around the room. Jill would want the picture of their parents that she kept at her bedside and her framed snapshot of Daniel Lansbury. She'd also want the sapphire pendant Daniel had given her. Ian made a hasty circuit of the room, grabbing the pictures and jewelry.

"What are you doing?" Jill gasped.

"You've got thirty seconds to get what you need. Then we leave."

Beneath the tears, Jill's eyes were blue flames. "I'm not going anywhere until you explain what's happening. What is this 'family matter'? Who was that woman who called you?"

"Please just trust me."

"How can I trust you when you're acting crazy?"

Ian opened her closet and snagged the first sweater and slacks his fingers touched. He crammed the clothing into his backpack and slung it over his shoulder.

"I'm not going." Jill trailed him into the living room. "I'm not going until you explain."

Ian grabbed coats, hats, and gloves. "There's no time."

"What do you mean, there's no time? You're not making sense. You're sick." Jill knocked over the African violet as she reached for a phone that wasn't there. "I'm calling—where did you put the phone?"

Ian draped Jill's coat around her shoulders. "Let's go."

"I told you, I won't—"

The truth erupted from Ian. "I'm a religious believer, Jill. Like David Garrett. In less than an hour, the police will be after us. Do you want to be arrested, tortured, sent to prison? That's what will happen to you if we stay here."

Jill's lips blanched white. "That's crazy. You're not a traitor. You're confused; you're just upset over that anarchist attack. Daniel said—"

Ian seized Jill's arm and hauled her out of the apartment toward the stairwell. He raced down flight after flight, forcing Jill to match his pace.

"Stop," Jill panted. "*Please stop.* You're hurting me."

He didn't loosen his grip. "I'm sorry." He burst out of the stairwell and raced across the lobby.

"Please." Jill was crying as they reached Alisa Kent's car parked at the curb. "Ian, you're sick."

Ian yanked the door open and pushed Jill into the passenger seat. She cowered against her door as Ian sped along Maddox Road.

"Whose . . . car is this?" She slid her coat off her shoulders and hugged it in her lap.

"It belongs to a police officer named Alisa Kent. She knows I'm a believer, but for reasons of her own, she's offered us a way to escape Tremont."

"Escape Tremont!"

"We're going to the U.S. The border nets are down."

"You're talking *nonsense*. The border nets are never down. Let's call Daniel. He'll help you."

"Didn't you hear anything I said?" They were nearing the university. A row of flagpoles lining the top of the stadium reminded Ian of waiting gallows. He glanced in the rearview mirror, almost certain he'd see the silver gleam of a patrol car. The instant Eric confessed, the police would start looking for Kent's car. The sooner he could abandon the car, the better, but first he'd have to pass through downtown, get on the southbound freeway—

"Don't you see you're imagining things?" Jill was making a futile effort to sound soothing. "A police officer would never help a traitor escape. The border nets never shut down."

Ian's muscles knotted as he was forced to brake behind a bus. "I've tried to tell you the truth before, but you never wanted to listen."

"I know the truth!" Her soothing tone crumbled under a rush of tears. "You're the one who's confused."

"Jill, listen to me. Last summer I got hold of a book, an incredible book—"

"*Stop* this."

He growled in frustration and lapsed into silence. Once they were out of downtown, he could divert enough attention from the road to offer better explanations. By the time they reached the border, he hoped Jill would be over her initial panic and into the pliable numbness of shock.

"We've got to call Daniel," Jill whispered, shuffling the coat in her lap. "Please let him help you."

"I'm sorry." Ian balled his fists, waiting as students boarded the bus at a pace that would have made snails look swift. "Come *on*, people, hurry up," he muttered.

A smothering wave of coat suddenly engulfed his head. Startled, he swiped at the coat as he heard Jill's door swing open.

"Jilly, no!" He clawed for her arm, but she was already out of the car.

Ian flung his door open, but froze when a horn blared behind him. If he left the car blocking this narrow street, it would be impounded.

"No no *no!*" A flash of blond curls was his last glimpse of Jill as she darted behind the Jensen Building.

Ian stomped on the accelerator. There was a phone booth near the bike racks south of the Jensen Building; Jill would probably stop there to call Daniel.

Ian screeched into the nearest parking lot, leapt from the car, and raced to the Jensen Building.

His heart plunged. A girl with cropped red hair was using the Jensen Building phone. If Jill had found this phone busy, where would she have gone next? Along the main sidewalk toward the well-lighted student-activities building?

In the lounge of the activities building, dozens of students clustered on couches and chairs watching the latest report on the Newbold Bay bombing. Ian raced past the students, seeking the bank of phones near the snack bar.

They were deserted.

"Excuse me!" Ian sprang into the path of a student janitor. "I'm looking for my sister, I think she just ran through here. Blond curly hair, green sweater."

The boy gave his broom a shove. "Haven't seen her."

Ian wanted to scream with frustration. There were additional phones upstairs—would Jill have gone there for more privacy? He flew across the lounge and up the stairs.

No Jill.

Furious with himself at the wasted time, Ian retraced his path. Back at the Jensen Building, he threw his gaze in all directions as he tried to read Jill's mind. Had she gone south toward the stadium? West toward the administration building?

The girl with the red hair was still using the Jensen Building booth. Ian hurried up to her. "Excuse me."

"I'm almost finished."

"I don't need the phone. I'm looking for my sister, I think she ran past here a few minutes ago. Curly blond hair, green sweater. Did you see her?"

"Yeah, she ran past." The girl tucked the phone more tightly against her ear. "What? I wasn't talking to you. Anyway, then Shannon said that Kev wouldn't—"

"Excuse me. Could you tell me which direction my sister was heading? It's important."

The girl scowled at him. "That way, I think." She pointed toward the administration building. Ian whirled and raced in that direction.

Frigid air knifed his lungs as he circled the buildings on the west side of campus. Again, no Jill.

He looked at his watch. More than half an hour had passed since Lt. Kent had warned him to get out of Tremont. How could he have let Jill slip away only two miles from—

"You idiot!" Ian said to himself. "You *idiot.*" He sprinted toward the parking lot where he had left Kent's car. Jill wouldn't have stayed on campus to call Daniel. She would have gone *home.*

* * *

Jill's tears fell in blinding sheets as she collapsed onto the couch. She had managed not to cry in the taxi, but as soon as she entered her apartment building, the tears had started to flow. Ian was crazy. None of what he said was true. What was she going to do?

Jill pressed her face against the upholstery, fighting to control herself. She couldn't call Daniel while she was crying like this. First she'd go wash her face and get a drink of water.

"He'll be all right," she whispered. "He'll be all right."

Her legs quivered as she walked toward the bathroom. Ian's door gaped open. A stack of books and papers was on his bed.

Books. Hardbound and paperback books, most with faded spines and yellowed edges. She hadn't realized Ian owned old books like these. They must be on loan from the university archives.

"Last summer I got hold of a book, an incredible book—"

She lurched forward and landed on her knees at Ian's bedside. The book on top of the stack looked newer than the others, the cover smooth and bright. She snatched the book and swiped tears from her eyes so she could read the title.

The Book of Mormon: Another Testament of Jesus Christ.

Horrified, she dropped the book. It was contraband. Religious literature. She scrabbled through the rest of the books and papers. Were they all contraband? She didn't recognize most of the titles; they looked like political and historical writings. But just the fact that Ian had kept them hidden—and what about the pamphlets? She unfolded a shiny white paper and scanned the first few sentences.

More religious propaganda.

Ian *was* a traitor. She couldn't call Daniel. Daniel would have no choice but to turn Ian over to the police.

Jill swept the writings into her arms. She'd hide the literature in a canvas grocery bag. Weighted with rocks, the bag would sink to the bottom of Lake Serena.

* * *

As his apartment building came into view, terror knocked the air from Ian's lungs. Two police cars were parked in front of the building and four officers were treading purposefully toward the lobby doors.

"No," Ian whispered. "Please, not yet."

He wrenched Kent's car into the parking lot of the townhouses across the street. *Is Jill in the apartment? Or did I guess wrong?* Maybe she was still hiding on campus, finally aware of her peril, afraid to call Daniel, afraid to come home.

Ian sprang from the car and grabbed the two survival backpacks from the trunk. If Eric had already confessed, then Ian would never be able to drive Kent's car across Tremont without being stopped. He'd have to find another way to the border, but that was a worry for later. Right now he needed to find Jill.

Ian hid the backpacks behind a row of bushes. No one would notice them there, at least not until daylight. Maybe—*Oh, Father, please help us*—maybe he and Jill would have the chance to retrieve them. He crept toward the street and stopped behind the massive trunk of a maple, counting windows in his apartment building to figure out if his own apartment was lighted.

Muscles twitched in his legs as he fought the compulsion to go tearing across the street to search for Jill. Police officers were already in his apartment. All he could do was wait and pray that they would exit the building without Jill. *Help her, please help her, she's never hurt anyone—*

The minutes scraped by. His throat was dry, parched by every freezing breath of air. Was someone walking through the lobby of the building? He could see movement, but he was too far away to identify the people behind the glass doors. *Please protect her.*

The doors flared open and two officers marched out. Between the officers stumbled a small blond woman.

"*Jill.*" The rawness of his throat strangled the cry into a whisper.

CHAPTER 16

Daniel whisked his ID chip past the elevator scanner. The authorization light flashed green and the elevator vaulted him toward the tenth floor of police headquarters. He'd been annoyed when Captain Hofstader had first summoned him to oversee an Information Extraction session—was there a conspiracy against his getting any sleep?—but now that he was here, his curiosity was high. Hofstader wanted to do the session in a private room off his office, not in the I-X wing of the Detention Annex. Such secrecy could only mean Hofstader had arrested someone who possessed critical information about the Liberty Cadre, and he didn't want word of the arrest to get out until I-X was complete.

It frustrated Daniel that he hadn't had a chance to check on the Rosheks before coming to work. No matter what was wrong, he was sure Ian would need help coping with it. Daniel had tried to call Jill, but she hadn't answered. As soon as this I-X was complete, he'd call her again, regardless of how late it was.

The elevator doors opened, revealing the lean, flinty face of Lt. Blake Peale. *Terrific.* His favorite officer.

"Took you long enough," Peale said. "Follow me."

Daniel suppressed his irritation at Peale's brusque greeting. Peale was always rude, and this was no time to get distracted by personal dislike.

Hofstader's office was deserted. Peale approached a door on the back wall of the office and waved his forearm past the ID scanner. A lock retracted and Peale shoved the door open, revealing a dead-end corridor bleached bright by a track of lights running along the center of the ceiling. Two black metal doors were set on each side of the corridor.

Captain Hofstader emerged from the second room on the right. His skin was colorless, his bristly sideburns dark with sweat.

"Peale, check on the teams and make sure everything's ready."

"Yes, sir." Peale marched into the room Hofstader had exited.

"You'll have to do all the prep," Hofstader said to Daniel. "Until we know exactly what we're dealing with, I don't want any of the medics involved."

"Yes, sir."

Hofstader's voice was a growl of thunder. "Your patient is Lt. Alisa Kent."

"Lt. Kent!" Daniel exclaimed.

"She was implicated in the confession of a Cadre member arrested in Newbold Bay. He's not sure if she's Cadre. They may have negotiated a deal with her that he didn't know about. But she's definitely a Garrett sympathizer."

Daniel raised his eyebrows. The Cadre *and* Garrett? That was a strange combination.

The sight of a highly respected police lieutenant lying strapped to the prisoner's chair in the middle of an interrogation room sent a high-voltage surge through Daniel, but his shock faded almost instantly. Up until a few months ago, Kent had been the last person Daniel would have pegged as an anarchist, but now that he thought about it, it had been obvious for a while that something was wrong with her. Rumor had ascribed her wan appearance and abrupt, unexplained medical leave to burnout, but apparently excessive devotion to the Tremont Police Service had not been the root of Kent's decline.

Daniel picked up the blank medical chart that lay on the counter, slipped it into its port, and downloaded the medical summary from Kent's file. He skimmed the information and set the chart aside, satisfied that Kent had no medical conditions that might pose problems for the administration of Broc4.

Kent's eyes were closed, her eyelashes a slash of black on a face so pale that her skin almost blended into her white blouse. Daniel regarded Kent's clothing with disapproval. A long-sleeved, high-necked blouse was less than ideal for a medical procedure that carried the risk of an unexpected emergency, but apparently Hofstader hadn't wanted to waste time getting her into a prisoner's uniform. At least they'd had the foresight to unbutton her sleeves before strapping her wrists down.

How can she breathe in such a high, tight collar? Daniel unbuttoned the cloth around her neck and saw that her flesh was marked with bruises. A quarrel with her anarchist friends? And what of the numerous partly healed lacerations that marred her palms? Kent was going to be an interesting study.

She lay motionless as Daniel rolled up her sleeve and disinfected the skin on her shoulder. Her flesh was cold, but her muscles were relaxed and her expression wasn't one Daniel had ever seen on a prisoner's face before. Calm? No . . . she didn't look calm. Fear was there, unmistakably. But there was no resistance. *Submissive.* That was the word he wanted. She looked as though she were enduring these procedures by her own choice, not because she had been dragged here in handcuffs.

She didn't flinch as he injected the subcutaneous monitor. With a flick of his finger, he activated the screens. The monitor was operating properly, and all her vital signs looked good. Now for the line that would provide a route for the Broc4 and any other drugs that became necessary during the session.

Captain Hofstader entered the room as Daniel was hooking the IV tubing to the catheter that now snaked from Kent's arm.

"Ready?" Hofstader asked.

"Yes, sir." Daniel taped the plastic tubing to Kent's arm.

Hofstader gave the order. "Administer the Broc4."

Daniel used his ID to unlock the drawer containing vials of Broc4. He drew fifty milligrams into a syringe and emptied it into Kent's IV port.

Kent's fingers curled into fists.

Hofstader glanced at Lt. Peale, who had seated himself at the computer station near Kent's feet. Peale scratched his blond crew cut and nodded. "Four teams standing by. And there's been another arrest. He scanned the screen in front of him. "Woman by the name of Sherry Mason. She's under guard at the hospital in Hamilton. Member of Eric Vettori's talk group. Vettori says she wasn't a Cadre member. She's got spinal injuries. The med supervisor in Hamilton is determining whether she's strong enough for I-X."

"If they learn that she *did* have Cadre ties, then I want immediate notification."

"I'll let them know, sir."

Hofstader lumbered to Lt. Kent's side. "Is she ready?"

"Go ahead, sir," Daniel said.

Hofstader didn't sit in the interrogator's chair. Instead, he leaned over the reclining figure of Lt. Kent. "Lt. Kent. State your full name and occupation."

Kent gazed up at him, her eyes bright with the characteristic sheen of the Broc series. "Alisa Michelle Kent. Lieutenant with the Tremont Police Service."

"Are you a traitor to the government and people of New America?"

"Yes."

"Are you part of an anarchist organization?"

"Yes."

Hofstader's broad shoulders tensed. "What organization?"

"The Liberty Cadre."

Astonishment, fury, and triumph warred on Hofstader's face, and his hand clamped around Kent's arm. Daniel wondered if Hofstader thought she might break free of the straps, kick down the locked door, and flee headquarters before she could answer his questions in full.

"Who is your leader?" Hofstader asked.

"Zero."

Hofstader frowned. "Do you know his real name?"

"No."

"Do you know how to find him?"

"No."

"Do you know how to contact him?"

"Through Scott Siskell."

"Siskell was your contact?"

"Yes."

"Do you know how to find Siskell?"

"No."

"How did you contact Siskell?"

"I sent coded messages to John Conklin."

"You used a phone registered under a fake ID?"

"Yes."

"Under what name?"

"Karen Macy."

Peale spoke up. "They found the phone in Kent's bedroom closet." He hit a button on his keyboard. "Word just came from the team searching her house."

Hofstader nodded. "Kent, give me the names of all other Liberty Cadre members you know of—who haven't already been arrested or killed."

"Timothy Sandring," Kent said.

"Police in Newbold Bay got his name from Vettori," Peale interjected. "He's in Paxton. They're still looking for him."

"Kent, do you know how to locate Sandring?"

"No."

"Do you know the names of any other Cadre members who are still at large?"

Kent winced as though something had stung her.

Hofstader repeated his question. "Lt. Kent. Do you know of any other Cadre members who are still at large?"

She squirmed and averted her head. Daniel checked the screen in front of him that displayed the level of Broc4 in her bloodstream. "Try the question again," he said.

Hofstader grasped the top of Kent's skull and swiveled her head around so she was facing him again. "Do you know the names of any other Cadre members who are still at large?"

Kent went limp. "No."

"Did you have contact with any other Cadre members?"

"Yes."

"Did you refer to the others only by number?"

"Yes."

Hofstader grunted in frustration. "Did you ever see the faces of any Cadre members besides Scott Siskell, Eric Vettori, and Timothy Sandring?"

"No."

"Did you ever meet Zero?"

"Once."

Hofstader's eyes lit with interest. "Describe him."

"Five nine or ten, average build, light skin, hair on the back of his hands light brown mixed with gray, nails trimmed and clean, no scars or calluses, gold wedding band on his left hand, platinum-and-diamond signet ring on his right hand. Dressed in a black turtleneck sweater, black trousers, black knit mask that covered his head and face."

Hofstader swore under his breath. "You never saw his face at all?"

"No."

"Describe his voice."

"He spoke in a whisper."

"Did he have any distinctive speech patterns or mannerisms?"

"He periodically rubbed his chin with his hand while we spoke."

"Anything else?"

"No."

"The signet ring he was wearing—describe it in detail."

"Half-inch-wide platinum band, oval top engraved with the national seal, emerald-cut diamonds on either side of the seal."

"The national seal," Hofstader muttered, glancing at Peale. Daniel's skin prickled.

"Odd ring for Zero to wear," Peale said. "Sounds like some type of commemorative jewelry."

"Captain," Daniel said.

"What is it?"

"That ring sounds like a Tremont signet."

"A what?"

"A copy of the ring President Tremont wore. Ten or so years ago, they issued them to high-ranking executive officials."

Peale's upper lip arched in a sneer.

"How widely were they distributed?" Hofstader asked.

"They went to the President and members of the Council. I think they also went to Council Assistants. I don't know if they went to anyone else."

"Check on it, Peale."

Peale typed rapidly. "Let's see. They were distributed eight years ago . . . went exclusively to the people Lansbury just listed . . . fifty-two rings made and distributed . . . none have ever been reported lost or stolen."

Zero . . . a member of the Council or a Council Assistant? Daniel wanted to discard the idea as ridiculous, but he knew enough about the Liberty Cadre to realize Zero had to be someone in a position of power. Not a Councilor—that was absurd—but perhaps one of the Assistants had become corrupt.

Peale hit a button and the printer spewed out a sheet of paper.

"Here's a picture of it." Peale handed the paper to Hofstader.

Hofstader held the picture in front of Kent's face. "Does this look like Zero's ring?"

"Yes," she said.

"Odd that Zero would wear it, knowing it could help identify him," Peale pointed out.

"He may have forgotten he had it on," Hofstader replied. "Even Zero can get cocky and careless. Or the ring could be a forgery, a false lead." He dropped into the chair at Kent's side. "Kent, when did you meet with Zero?"

"This year, January 14th."

"Where?"

"A room approximately ten feet by ten feet with cinderblock walls, a water-stained ceiling, a green vinyl floor, an army cot, two folding chairs, no windows."

"Where was this room located?"

"Somewhere in Tremont."

"Do you have any idea where in Tremont?"

"No."

"Were you unconscious when they took you there?"

Kent's mouth started to form a yes, but the word changed into a gasp. Her hands twitched and went rigid, the fingers curved.

Daniel frowned at the monitor. Kent's pulse rate had shot upward.

"What's wrong?" Hofstader snapped.

"I don't know," Daniel said. "Lt. Kent, are you in pain?"

Kent didn't seem to hear him. She was looking past him to the left, like someone was standing next to his chair.

"Alisa?" Daniel said. "Can you hear me?"

There was no response. Watching Kent's face for any changes, Daniel reached over and pinched her arm. Her expression didn't flicker.

"Lansbury?" Hofstader said.

"Well, if this were a third or fourth session, I'd guess we were seeing premature stage two."

"What does that—"

Kent's body jerked, and she screamed. Before Daniel could react, the pain cleared from her face, leaving only the bright blankness of a prisoner ready for further questions.

"Alisa, can you hear me?" Daniel asked.

"Yes." She was slightly out of breath, but her voice was brisk, revealing no trace of distress.

"What's going on?" Hofstader asked.

Daniel shook his head. "I've never seen it in a first I-X, but it definitely looks like premature stage two."

"What's that?"

"She's already starting to hallucinate. This type of problem can result from extensive recent exposure to the Broc series, but there was nothing in Kent's medical record—"

Hofstader shifted his weight impatiently. "Can't you take care of it?"

"I'll give her another thirty milligrams. That should keep her solidly in stage one, even if for some reason she has an unusually high tolerance." Daniel drew up the additional dose of Broc4 and injected it into Kent's IV port. "She should be all right now," he said after a few moments of watching his screen.

"Lt. Kent." Hofstader sounded like he might be on the verge of trying to extract answers with blows from his fists. "Were you involved in the bombing at Newbold Bay?"

"Yes."

"What was your role?"

"I helped plan it. I suggested the target."

"Sir." Peale spoke. "I suggest we get the names of Kent's other anarchist friends before we get the details on her Cadre activities. Then those arrests can go forward while we investigate the Cadre."

Hofstader looked startled, then nodded grimly. "Kent, give me the names of any other criminals you know of who are still at large."

"Ian Roshek," Kent said.

A sickening jolt shook Daniel, like he'd walked full-speed into a wall.

"Another member of Eric Vettori's seditious talk group here in Tremont," Peale reported, tapping keys on his computer. "Longtime traitor, now a religious believer sucked in by Garrett's propaganda.

He's still a fugitive, but they just brought his sister in. Garzo has her on L2."

Hofstader nodded. "Kent, do you know how to locate Ian Roshek?"

"He is driving my car toward the border."

Daniel stared blindly at the monitors.

"There's already a bulletin out for the car," Peale said. "It wasn't found at her residence."

"Kent, which direction is Roshek heading toward the border?"

"I don't know."

"What are the names of your other anarchist friends?"

"There are no more."

Daniel tried to swallow, but his throat was glued shut. Jill had been arrested. Ian was an anarchist, on the run. The report in Ian's file—written by Lt. Kent—must have been a lie.

A religious believer.

A Garrett follower.

Distantly, Daniel heard Hofstader probing Lt. Kent's knowledge of the Newbold Bay bombing, but Daniel could no longer focus his attention on her confession. Had Jill known of her brother's treason? Had she been involved?

The officer interrogating her would learn of Daniel Lansbury's connection to the Rosheks. Once the officer relayed that information to Captain Hofstader, what would Hofstader do?

And what would his father do?

Daniel gripped the vial of Broc4 in clammy fingers as he pictured Marcus Lansbury learning that his son was the friend of a traitor.

* * *

Wind lashed through downtown Tremont, driving the few remaining pedestrians into the shelter of the bus stops. Alone, Ian skidded over the sidewalk, his face numb, his feet carved of ice.

Jill was a prisoner, Alisa Kent was a prisoner, and soon he'd be in custody as well. There would be no escape to the United States. Kent's car was useless to him now, and he couldn't walk the forty miles to the border without being apprehended, especially not if he made himself conspicuous by carrying a backpack loaded with survival supplies. The police were already looking for him. And as soon as his name was broadcast in the police bulletins, everyone in Tremont would be looking for him.

He had to warn Laura Travers of his imminent arrest. Laura would have to be willing to leave Tremont now, knowing that when the police interrogated Ian, her name would come out. But until the police caught up with Ian, they wouldn't be searching for Laura. She and Matt could make it to safety. He had failed Jill, failed Alisa Kent. But maybe he could save Laura.

Legs and lungs aching from the panicky hour of walking that had brought him across town, he trudged down the stairs of the white frame house opposite the hospital and jabbed the bell to Laura's basement apartment.

The door opened and Laura's amber eyes widened. She pulled him into the apartment and shut the door.

"Are you in trouble?"

"Big trouble," he confirmed.

"What happened?"

"Long story. But I'm not going to make it to the border. The police are after me, and once they get me, they'll be coming for you. You and Matt need to get out of Tremont *now*."

"Matt's at work. He'll be home in a couple of hours."

"Call him. Tell him it's an emergency and he has to come home now. Do you have a car? I have survival supplies you can use—"

"Come sit down. You're shaking."

"*There's no time.* You've got to—"

"Not so loud. There are neighbors right through the ceiling."

"Listen to me. You've got to call Matt—"

"Calm down. We're not in immediate danger—unless someone followed you here."

"No one followed me. I don't *think* anyone followed me. But—"

"Sit down and tell me what happened."

Ian seized her shoulders. She was just like Jill, refusing to believe she was in danger. "Laura, *listen to me*—"

"Hush." She pressed her hand over his wind-chapped lips. "I told you Matt has connections with the police. They'll warn us if the police get interested in us."

He swatted her hand away. "Still, it's not safe for you—"

"Sit down." She tugged him toward the couch.

"*No*—there's not time for—"

"Ian, you're shaking. You can hardly stand up. Sit and catch your breath. We have time. Trust me."

With the couch directly in front of him, Ian could no longer convince his knees to hold him up. He crumpled onto the cushions.

Laura sat next to him. "Tell me what happened."

Ian tried to think where to begin, but all that rose from his mind was a frothy mess of panic. Jill in the hands of the police, Jill and Alisa Kent. *Oh, Father in Heaven, help them, please help them—how did I let this happen?*

"Ian." Laura grasped his hands. "Calm down. We can help you."

He laughed wildly. "Can Matt's friends free two prisoners?"

"Just tell me what happened."

"I have a friend who—joined the Liberty Cadre."

Laura caught her breath. "When did this happen?"

"Just a couple of weeks ago." Ian sketched out the story of Eric, the Liberty Cadre, Lt. Kent, and the events that had sent him on the run tonight. When he spoke of Jill's arrest, each word seemed to slash him like a knife. "It's my fault—if I hadn't been so unbelievably *stupid*, I could have kept her in the car until—"

"It's not your fault she ran away from you." Laura toyed pensively with a lock of her chestnut hair. "Your mistake was trying to take her in the first place."

Ian stared at Laura. "You think I should have left her behind?"

"You should have known she wouldn't come." Laura's eyes were wet, but the tears looked somehow cold, like water beginning to freeze. "When it comes to survival, you've got to be practical."

"How can you—"

"If you hadn't tried to take Jill with you, you could have made it to the U.S. Instead, you're in a lot of trouble."

"Your friends—Matt's friends in the police—could they do anything to help Jill and—"

"Are you crazy? They can't interfere in a major investigation. They're sources of information, not magicians."

Ian's hope died to blackness.

"You'll be safe here tonight," Laura said. "When Matt gets home we'll figure out how to get you to the U.S. Meanwhile, I'll bring you something hot to drink. You're still shivering."

Ian accepted the steaming mug that Laura offered him. Hot milk, golden brown with the sweetness of caramel. "I forgot about this," he said, attempting a smile.

"Laura's specialty for winter evenings."

The ceramic mug warmed his tingling fingers and the hot milk soothed his raw throat. "I still think you should go to the U.S. Matt's police contacts can't guarantee your safety."

"We'll be fine."

"Laura, the border nets will probably never be down like this again."

"Quit nagging."

Ian drained the last of the milk and accepted Laura's offer of a refill. Halfway through the second mug, the first wisps of sleepiness lightly brushed his consciousness, then thickened into an unnatural weight that had his head wobbling like his brain had turned to lead. What was wrong with him? He couldn't sleep now—they had to talk to Matt—

"Lie down, Ian." Laura's face wavered out of focus as she took the mug from his hand.

"No—I just need some fresh air—" He thought he was standing, but the ground kept lurching upward. The carpet was spongy beneath his fingers.

"Laura." He tried to push himself up. The floor tilted again.

"It's all right." Her hands were under his arms, surprisingly strong, helping him onto the couch. "You just need to rest."

"What did you—you put something in that milk—"

"You need to rest."

"Laura—" but his tongue was deadened, blurring the words he wanted to say. His head drooped back against the couch and this time he couldn't lift it.

CHAPTER 17

Head bowed, Daniel Lansbury trudged into the lobby of the Executive Council Building. Far overhead, circular windows were admitting the first light of a foggy gray dawn. The lobby was deserted except for two security guards behind a reception desk and another two hulking near the elevators that led up to the Council offices.

In the chill morning silence, Daniel's shoes echoed off the marble floor like a drumroll announcing his arrival. *Here comes a fool.* He stopped at the reception desk, scanned his ID, and stated his destination. At the elevators, he scanned his ID a second time, and the guards permitted him to board.

The summons had come at daybreak while Daniel was resting in one of the on-call rooms in a hopeless effort to get some sleep. His father wanted to talk to him at his office, immediately.

Without being told, Daniel knew what must have transpired to bring the news of his idiocy to his father's ears. The officer interrogating Jill had learned of Daniel's connection to the Rosheks. He had passed that information to Captain Hofstader, who, shocked at such a report but afraid to meddle with the Lansbury family, had immediately turned the matter over to Colonel Edgefield, head of the Tremont Police Service. Edgefield, not daring to authorize action against the son of the Councilor over Internal Defense, had scrambled to Marcus Lansbury to ask his advice. And Daniel knew precisely what his father had told Colonel Edgefield.

"Let me handle it."

Daniel pressed his hands over his face. He should have spoken to Captain Hofstader last night and admitted his connection to the Rosheks, but he hadn't been able to find an opportunity to speak to Hofstader alone. Immediately after gathering the most crucial information on Kent's crimes, Hofstader had gone to give an initial report to Colonel Edgefield, leaving Lt. Peale to gather the remaining details. As Peale's harsh voice questioned Kent about her interaction with Ian Roshek and his traitor friends, Daniel had plunged deeper into self-hatred. Why hadn't he immediately recognized the nature of Ian's problems?

Had Jill known the truth? Kent hadn't named Jill as a traitor, but Jill must have known something of her brother's treason. Garrett followers usually harbored a compulsion to spread their poison. It was too much to hope that Ian had spared Jill.

The elevator doors opened and Daniel's empty stomach churned with acid. Today he took no pleasure in the thoughts that usually warmed him when he strolled along this hallway with its cherrywood paneling and gold leaf molding—thoughts of occupying a suite of offices along this corridor and serving on the Council as his grandfather, his uncle, and his father had done. After his conduct with the Rosheks, he'd be lucky if he wasn't occupying a prison cell instead.

His arm felt as heavy and unwieldy as a sandbag as he lifted it toward the ID scanner that guarded his father's door. The scanner chimed and a green light indicated that Marcus had unlocked the door.

Marcus Lansbury waited behind his massive desk, his eyes dark hollows carved into rock. "Come in and close the door."

Daniel obeyed.

"You have a great deal of explaining to do," Marcus said.

"Dad, I didn't know. How could I have known? When I set out to work with Ian Roshek, I was proceeding on the assumption that Lt. Kent's report of his screening was accurate."

"You excuse your blindness on the basis of one phony report?"

"It skewed my judgment. If Kent could fool everyone from Colonel Edgefield on down, how was I supposed to know she was a liar?"

"That's a poor excuse. Is it possible you did realize Dr. Roshek was a traitor, but you ignored that knowledge because of your feelings for Jill?"

"*No.*" Daniel was adamant.

Marcus's leather chair creaked as he leaned back and pierced Daniel with a look. "I believe in your innocence because I know your character. But the police are not so easy to convince."

Daniel took a breath. "Are they—are you going to let them arrest me?"

"You've been an idiot. Do you know how my enemies would drool over the fact that my son's girlfriend is a traitor?"

Dismay kicked Daniel in the stomach. So Jill *was* guilty. Before he could stop it, a question escaped his lips. "What did she do?"

"Do the details matter?" Marcus asked coldly. "An anarchist is an anarchist."

Daniel clenched his jaw and stared past his father to the window that formed the entire back wall of the office.

"It's understandable that you'd be curious about her," Marcus said. "Considering your feelings for her."

"I have no feelings for a traitor." But his questions roared like flames. He *had* to know what Jill had done, what lies she had told him, how much she had hidden behind that sweet smile. But he wouldn't ask.

Marcus sighed. "Sit down, Daniel."

Daniel sat awkwardly in one of the chairs that faced his father's desk.

"If you wish, I'll tell you the results of Jill Roshek's I-X," Marcus said. "Perhaps this will convince you that the pain you feel over her loss is a waste of emotion."

Shame seared Daniel's face.

Marcus slid his computer monitor closer, and pressed a button. "Up until last night, Jill was not involved in any illegal activities, nor was she aware that her brother regularly attended seditious meetings, had long been involved in the study of contraband literature, and had recently fallen prey to the religious propaganda brought to Tremont by David Garrett. However, Jill did know that Ian had some superstitious ideas and antisocial tendencies, and she did harbor fears that his peculiarities might cross the line into treason."

Marcus glanced at his screen. "Last night, Ian Roshek told his sister the truth about his crimes and tried to force her to flee with him to the United States. Confused, Jill eluded her brother and returned to her apartment, where she discovered Ian's stash of contraband books—including that foul book espoused by Garrett." Marcus's mouth curved in an icy smile, and his gaze now pierced

Daniel. "Instead of notifying the police, she decided to destroy her brother's books so the police wouldn't find them. She was arrested with the books in her hands."

Daniel closed his eyes, struggling to keep the anguish from showing on his face.

"You see why the police have questions about your loyalty," Marcus said. "Considering the nature of your associates, they would be remiss if they did not suspect you."

Daniel said nothing. What could he offer? *I didn't know.* It sounded weaker each time he spoke it.

"It has been suggested that you submit to a screening."

Daniel's eyes flew open. Then he looked down in resignation. "I'll cooperate, of course."

"I'm glad you choose to be reasonable. However, there will be no screening. I don't need the scandal of my son being dragged in for questioning. Oliver Edgefield is sensible enough to realize that you were ignorant of the Rosheks' treason."

A ripple of relief passed through Daniel. At least he would be spared the humiliation of being grilled by the police.

Marcus wandered to the window. Police headquarters normally dominated the view, but now Daniel could only see vague blue glimmers through the fog.

"It will be prudent to bury this unfortunate matter," Marcus said. "I've seen to it that Jill Roshek's arrest was not publicized and that Ian Roshek is not listed in the police bulletins. Hofstader's teams will find Dr. Roshek easily enough without his treason being broadcast over the news. Only the officers immediately involved with Jill Roshek's and Alisa Kent's cases know of your connection to the Rosheks, and they're under strict orders to keep that information confidential."

Daniel felt no surprise at how completely Marcus had the situation under control. "Does Captain Hofstader still want me to serve as medical supervisor for Alisa Kent?"

"Oliver has informed Captain Hofstader that there is no need to make changes in your assignment. Removing you from the case would only draw attention to you and result in gossip. Stay and do your duty. Do you understand?"

"Yes, sir."

"In the midst of the excitement surrounding Kent's arrest, it won't be difficult to bury your fragment of this scandal. Kent could be the most important Cadre member ever arrested. Edgefield may finally have the key to destroying their organization."

Daniel tried to rouse a feeling of triumph, but couldn't lift it past the pain. "Will Colonel Edgefield tell the media of Lt. Kent's arrest, or will he keep it silent to avoid embarrassment for the police?"

"Kent's treason will be trumpeted throughout the nation. The nation will rejoice to see a key figure in the Newbold Bay bombing brought to justice, and the reputation of the Tremont Police Service will only be enhanced by their willingness to root out and publicly punish an anarchist in their own ranks." Marcus straightened an onyx cuff link. "You should be honored to be playing a role in Alisa Kent's downfall. I trust you'll play that role well and not allow your mind to wander from your responsibilities. From what Oliver told me, last night's I-X was somewhat less than perfectly executed."

"That's not because I was distracted, Dad." Daniel kept his voice low to hide his anger. "Kent had a bizarrely high level of tolerance for Broc4. I was pushing the dosage up beyond safe levels, and she still kept slipping into premature stage two."

"How do you explain that?"

"I don't know. Tests all turned up normal, her medical record offers no clues, and I've never seen that kind of problem in a patient who hasn't had recent exposure to the Broc series."

"Clearly prior exposure isn't the root of Lt. Kent's problem," Marcus said briskly. "You're probably dealing with a genetic susceptibility."

"Maybe."

"She's still in stage two?"

"Yes. And probably will be for several more hours."

"You're concerned about Broc psychosis, I assume."

"I'm monitoring her." Daniel tried not to sound defensive. Did his father think he was so rattled over Jill's arrest that he had become incompetent?

"It wouldn't necessarily be a bad thing for Kent to develop Broc psychosis once Hofstader is finished with her," Marcus said softly. "It's appropriate that she should suffer—as should anyone who jeopardizes national security. I trust you still agree with that?"

Though furious that his father would ask such a question of him, Daniel still couldn't stop his mind from skidding to thoughts of Jill trapped in the nightmare of I-X recovery. "Of course I agree with it."

"Does it bother you that Jill Roshek is suffering?"

"She earned it," Daniel said tonelessly.

"You realize she'll go to prison. I wouldn't be surprised if she receives fifteen or even twenty years."

Daniel couldn't hide his shock. "Twenty years!"

"Consider the circumstances. If she had turned her brother in even as belatedly as a few days ago, it would have exposed Lt. Kent's treachery and prevented the bombing at Newbold Bay. I'd say she earned her twenty years, and more."

Daniel clutched the arms of his chair. Jill entombed in a concrete cell, her face gaunt and pale. A Garrett sympathizer, she'd be kept in isolation, rarely seeing other prisoners and never speaking to them. Jill at the mercy of the prison guards—

"Son." Marcus's voice was suddenly gentle and Daniel looked at his father in surprise. "It *would* be possible for me to tell Oliver Edgefield to urge the sentencing committee toward leniency. Would you like me to do that?"

Before Daniel had time to think, the words poured from his mouth. "Dad, please. Jill acted out of ignorance and weakness, not malice. That's obvious. She probably doesn't even know much about Garrett or what he stood for. She only wanted to protect her brother, the only family she has left—" Daniel stopped, chilled by the glint in his father's eyes.

"You're quick to make excuses for a traitor," Marcus said. "Quick to beg mercy for one who deserves the harshest of punishments."

Shame weighed on Daniel until he felt his spine would buckle. Marcus had never intended to help Jill. His offer had been a test.

"I expected better things from you, Daniel. You are of the blood of those who have the right and duty to rule. Your grandfather stood at James Tremont's side at the founding of New America. Your uncle gave his life for this nation. And what do you do with that heritage? You fall in love with a weak, foolish girl who throws her loyalty aside the first time it's tested. You befriend a man who would ally himself with James Tremont's most relentless enemies."

"Dad, I never thought—"

"I may rethink the suggestion that you undergo a screening. Perhaps it would be beneficial in helping you identify your shortcomings."

Sweat trickled down Daniel's sides. "Dad," he protested feebly.

"You've disappointed me." In contrast to the words, there was a dark satisfaction in his father's eyes that puzzled Daniel.

"Get back to the Annex and do your duty," Marcus said. "And see that you keep your childish distress to yourself. Do you understand?"

"Yes, sir," Daniel whispered.

* * *

The heavy clothes Ian had chosen to protect himself against the cold of the wasteland strip were now relegated to protecting him from the chill in Laura's apartment. With Laura and Matt at work, the thermostat had automatically lowered the temperature as if the apartment were unoccupied. To complete the impression of nobody home, the blinds were closed and the lights off. In the false twilight, Ian sat on the couch, huddled inside his coat.

When he had slogged his way to consciousness around ten that morning, he'd been confronted by a wiry man with tawny eyes the same shade as his hair. So this was Matt Travers. Matt had reeled off a list of instructions: no noise, no lights, no running water, and above all, do not leave the apartment. Ian had promised strict compliance. The last thing he wanted was to cause problems for Laura and Matt.

Matt had evaded Ian's questions about how the Traverses and their friends planned to deal with the situation, saying only that everything would be taken care of. Normally Ian would have pressed harder, but thanks to whatever drug Laura had slipped him last night, it was all he could do to knit syllables into words. Matt had left for work at eleven, telling Ian that Laura would be home at six that night.

Ian groaned softly. He still couldn't believe Laura had pulled such a sneaky trick. Granted, there was no way he would have slept last night without chemical aid, but he didn't think that was a choice Laura should have made for him. It sickened him to think of how he had snoozed the night away while Jill and Alisa Kent—

Ian jammed his knuckles against his stinging eyes. How could he have been so careless as to let Jill run away from him? Why had he directed all his attention to watching for patrol cars and none to watching Jill? Why hadn't he realized how frightened she was, how ready to run? He should have kept hold of her arm— should have tied her up and locked her in the trunk, if that's what it took—

And even after she fled the car, he still could have found her in time if he hadn't compounded his stupidity by running all over campus like a fool.

Anguish and fury swelled inside him, building to agonizing pressure. What was Jill suffering right now? Had the police screened her, like they had him? Had they put her through Information Extraction? If they had, what had she endured thanks to their vicious memory drug? Fears mixed with real experiences . . . experiences like the deaths of her parents?

Was the worst over for her by now, or was she one of the minority who would never recover from Information Extraction?

No. It won't happen to her. Daniel had said that problems occurred mainly in people who had a lot of exposure to the memory stimulant drug. That wouldn't be Jill. It would take only a few questions for the police to conclude that she knew nothing significant.

But what about Alisa Kent? Her interrogation would be longer, but even she wouldn't have many crimes to confess. But the recovery process—Kent's guilt over her family and David Garrett already tortured her every lucid moment. What kind of hallucinations would her mind create when her guilt and pain were distorted by imagination? Her sister's death at the hands of prison guards . . . her parents' executions . . .

Ian lurched to his feet. If he kept thinking like this, he'd drive himself insane. He couldn't help Jill; he couldn't help Alisa Kent. *Think of Laura. Think what will happen to her if you blow your second chance at escape and get her and Matt arrested. You've made enough mistakes.*

Ian stood uncertainly, almost afraid to move for fear the neighbors would hear him, but knowing he could no longer sit motionless while anguish clawed his guts to ribbons. He had to find something to distract him until Laura came home from work.

The sight of the computer on the desk made his throat constrict. He could read the morning news.

The first page of the newspaper flashed on the screen and adrenaline stung Ian's nerves. Alisa Kent's picture was directly beneath the headline: *Mastermind Behind Newbold Bombing Arrested in Tremont.*

"What?" Ian skimmed through the article. Alisa Kent had been the Cadre's police informant for three years? She was the one who suggested bombing the National Junior Security Watch Convention at the Newbold Bay Community Center?

Certain his sanity had escaped him, Ian read the article again. The only information that meshed with what he had expected were the statements that Kent was linked with a follower of executed religious anarchist David Garrett, and that Kent's arrest had followed the arrest of a Cadre member in Newbold Bay, Eric Vettori, who had confessed to helping assemble the bombs that destroyed the Community Center.

Ian skimmed the rest of the news, searching for information on Jill's arrest and on his status as a fugitive. There was nothing. His name wasn't mentioned in connection with Alisa Kent or Eric, and he wasn't listed in the police bulletins. These omissions bewildered him until he realized the obvious answer. Who had the power to keep the Rosheks' names out of the news, and a motive for doing so? Daniel Lansbury's father.

But what of the announcement that Alisa Kent was a member of the Liberty Cadre? Ian returned to page one, where Kent's picture dominated the screen. It was an old picture; her hair was chin-length and she was wearing a gray police uniform. He studied the picture as though Kent's opaque black eyes and unsmiling mouth could give him the answer. *Had* she been a Cadre member all along? Had her evident hatred for the Cadre stemmed from her desire to withdraw from their gang and their refusal to let her go? Or had she feigned her hatred so no one would suspect her involvement with them?

Was he a big enough fool to have missed the truth entirely?

Ian felt like he was wading through knee-deep mud as he moved back to the couch. If Kent had been a Cadre member for three years, then she would have been a hardened anarchist long before she interrogated him after that university contraband sweep. He couldn't believe that. He had witnessed too much of her pain as she took her first toddling steps into treason.

But if the police—via the media—were lying, then why? Colonel Edgefield could take a bow for capturing a Cadre anarchist, but at the same time he'd have to hang his head in shame that the anarchist was one of his own people. The Council? Had they spread this lie out of an arrogant need to pretend that the Cadre threat was under control? The nation would be deceived, but the Cadre would recognize the Council as pathetically weak for claiming false victory. Ian couldn't imagine President Ryce and her colleagues putting themselves in that position.

A phony news release didn't seem to benefit anyone. If the police really *believed* Alisa Kent was a Cadre member, then it was the Cadre itself that would benefit as the police entangled themselves in false information. But the police had interrogated Kent. They would have to know exactly what crimes she had committed, thanks to their superaccurate memory drug.

Wait. In his mind, Ian heard Alisa Kent describing her confrontation with the Cadre that had left her with a bruised neck, a needle puncture in her arm, and no awareness of what took place once an unknown drug began circulating in her system. Then, the following morning, disorientation to the point of amnesia.

"One moment everything seemed clear, the next I couldn't even remember my name."

Disrupted memory.

Ian began to pace, avoiding the tiled kitchen area so his boots would make no sound. Had the Liberty Cadre managed to conduct some sort of mental conditioning or hypnosis, inducing Kent to give a false confession during Information Extraction? Ian had no idea if such a thing were possible. Daniel Lansbury would know, but Ian couldn't exactly call him and ask.

If the Cadre had planted a false confession in Kent's mind, what else had they put there? False leads for the police? Phony information about Cadre operations and members? How could they prevent Kent from telling the truth once Information Extraction was over? Maybe they didn't have to worry about that. She could deny her confession all she wanted, but who would listen?

He had to talk to Laura. Matt's police connections might be able to induce their bosses to take a second look at Alisa Kent's testimony.

It was twenty past twelve. Laura would be home in five hours and forty minutes.

It was going to be a long wait.

* * *

Half a day had passed since Daniel's meeting with his father, but humiliation still scorched him as he approached the monitoring station on the high-security level at the Detention Annex.

"Hey, Dr. Lansbury." Burly security medic Vance Ashworth waved a hand in greeting. He popped a chart out of its slot and handed it to Daniel. "It's a shaky three, but you said to call you as soon as there were any breaks."

Daniel scanned Lt. Kent's chart to see if anything had been added since he had last reviewed it from his office computer. "She was nonresponsive again when you checked her ten minutes ago?"

"She doesn't stay responsive for long." Vance shrugged his weightlifter's shoulders. "The reversions are coming fast and furious. Like I said, it's a shaky three. More like a two and a half." He chuckled. "I gotta admit, we were hoping she wouldn't come out of two at all—serve her right. I can't believe *she's* an anarchist. But I always thought she was weird—"

Daniel's phone rang. He unclipped it from his belt. "Lansbury."

"Peale here. I want another I-X with Kent right away."

Daniel grimaced. Peale apparently hadn't wasted any time in acting on the report that Alisa Kent was emerging from stage two. "Just a moment, Lieutenant." He clicked Kent's chart back into its slot and walked away from the monitoring station so he could carry on the conversation in semiprivacy.

"Another session is impossible right now," Daniel said. "Kent's recovery from last night's session was extremely prolonged—"

"I'm not interested in medical hand-wringing. We've got an investigation to conduct, and we've waited too long already."

"Kent was in stage two *five times* as long as she was in stage one. You know anything over a three-to-one ratio signals trouble. We can't—"

"Quit stalling and go get her ready."

Daniel's temper gnawed at his self-control. "I cannot administer Broc4 to a patient who's having reversions every few minutes. That's a sure recipe for Broc psychosis—if Kent's heart can even withstand the amount of Broc4 it would take to push her into stage one. I strongly advise that you wait at least forty-eight hours before you question her again."

"Forty-eight hours!" Peale's disgust was clear. "I knew you'd drag your heels on this."

"I'm working to keep Kent functional for police purposes," Daniel said coldly. "If you object, talk to Captain Hofstader."

Peale hung up without replying.

Daniel stalked back to the monitoring station and retrieved Alisa Kent's chart. "Ashworth, come with me. Let's go have a look at Kent."

As Daniel entered the I-X recovery wing, his phone rang.

"Hofstader says four hours," Peale said. "Then we question her, ready or not."

* * *

"Don't you hear how paranoid you sound?" Laura wadded her dinner napkin. "Didn't it occur to you that Lt. Kent probably lied to you about not being a member of the Liberty Cadre?"

"She's not with the Cadre," Ian said. "I'm sure of that. I know this sounds crazy, but over the last couple of weeks the Liberty Cadre did *something* to Alisa Kent, and now there's this announcement—"

"She *told* you the Cadre injected her with some kind of drug. She *told* you she was having problems with her memory. You don't have any evidence beyond the word of a woman who is probably insane."

Ian swallowed a forkful of carrots. "I'm not asking you to believe my theory. All I'm asking is that you relay it to Matt's police friends and see if they can get their bosses to take a second look at Lt. Kent."

"Whose side are you on, anyway?" The anger in Laura's voice surprised Ian. "I thought you wanted things to be different. I thought you wanted freedom. Now you're telling me we should help the police?"

"This isn't about helping the police. It's about stopping the Liberty Cadre."

"Why do you want to do that? If the Liberty Cadre is framing Kent, they probably have a good reason for it."

"A good reason! As good a reason as they had for murdering children?"

"They made a strong statement in Newbold Bay, a declaration of war against the government's efforts to brainwash our children. They're a group the Council can't ignore."

Horror needled Ian's spine. "You've changed, Laura."

"You're so narrow-minded." Laura walked to the sink and dumped her uneaten plate of stew down the drain. "All you can see is the ideals you find in books. You can't see what's *necessary.*"

Suddenly queasy, Ian shoved his plate aside. Laura stood with her back to him, light glancing off the chestnut braid twirled into a knot at the nape of her neck.

"Laura," Ian said. "Matt's police connections—would one of them be called 'Zero'?"

"Don't jump to conclusions." Laura began rinsing dishes. "I just think you're being naive. And whatever is happening with Lt. Kent is not your problem. Or mine." She shoved a pan into the sink with a crash.

Confused, Ian watched Laura angrily rinsing dishes. Never in a lifetime would he have believed that Laura Travers could condone terrorist butchery.

But he had seen Laura only a handful of times in the last six years. What did he know about her current life? Very little. What did he know about Matt Travers? Almost nothing.

Last night when Laura doped his drink, had she done that to keep him insensible while she and Matt discussed things she didn't want him to hear? She knew he despised the Liberty Cadre. He'd made that clear when he was telling her about Eric. She knew he'd never accept any help the Cadre offered.

Not that the Cadre would help him. Would they send some of their operatives to shepherd him—an enemy who was trying to interfere with their manipulation of Alisa Kent—over the border? Not a chance. The only "help" they would give him would be a bullet in the head.

But Laura couldn't be involved with the Liberty Cadre.

Could she?

Laura had always been restless for change, but she had never been cruel.

But Eric Vettori hadn't been cruel either.

"Laura," Ian said. "Look at me."

She glanced over her shoulder, then returned her attention to the dishes. "I'm sorry. I shouldn't be barking at you. You've had a rough time. And we've always seen things a little differently."

"Laura. Turn around and look at me."

She dried her hands and turned to face him. Her face was drawn, her eyes shiny. "What is it?"

"Are you involved with the Liberty Cadre?"

"Will you relax?" She tried to smile. "I told you I wasn't."

Ian wanted to believe her, but uneasiness still crawled over him like icy-footed insects. Slowly, he rose to his feet.

"Look, I appreciate all your help. But I think it's time for me to go."

"Don't be ridiculous! Where would you go? You can't wander through Tremont on your own. You'll be arrested for sure."

"Where did you put my coat?"

"*Ian.* You can't leave. It's not safe."

"My coat, please."

"Let me call Matt." Laura was starting to sound frantic. "He can come home on his break and we can talk about this."

"Are you planning to drug me before the conversation begins?"

"I'm sorry about that. I thought it would be the best thing for you to get some rest—"

Ian glanced around the living room and kitchen area, looking for a closet. He couldn't leave without his coat. His coat and his old pocketknife were the only survival supplies he had left, unless the backpacks he'd stashed behind those bushes hadn't been discovered yet.

Laura swooped to his side. "I'm sorry. I didn't realize this Alisa Kent was so important to you. I guess it wouldn't hurt to have Matt talk to his friends. Maybe they can find out what's going on with her."

Ian regarded Laura dubiously. "I thought you didn't want to help the police."

"I don't want to let them frame your girlfriend either." Laura pressed his hand, her fingers clammy from the dishwater. "I'm sorry I upset you. Please, finish your dinner. Matt can come home on his break and we'll tell him about—"

The front door swung open, making them both jump. Ian expected Matt Travers to walk in, but it wasn't Matt. A husky man with a square jaw and a cocky grin shut the door behind him and peeled off a ski cap to reveal close-clipped brown hair. The short brown hair wasn't familiar, but the face with its cocky smile was. Siskell, the Liberty Cadre recruiter.

Siskell ambled toward Ian, his chipped tooth showing in a smirk. "In a little trouble, Roshek?"

"Nothing I need your help with." Ian looked down at Laura's bowed head. "You lied to me."

"Relax, Professor," Siskell said. "I'm here as a friend. I heard you want to get to the U.S. No problem. Be happy to help you."

"No, thanks."

"Don't be stupid. You know you can't get across the border on your own."

"Do you really expect me to believe you're taking me to the U.S.?"

"Hey, I just want to help." Siskell brought a gun out of his pocket. "Let's go. We can't be sure how much longer the border nets will be down."

CHAPTER 18

Daniel swept his ID past the scanner controlling the door to Information Extraction room 6. The door clicked open, allowing Alisa Kent's terrified sobs to spill into the corridor.

". . . can't . . . please . . . *it's wrong* . . ."

"You shoulda thought of that before you killed those kids," Vance Ashworth said. "Bet you're sorry now."

Kent arched her body, fighting the restraining straps with more energy than Daniel thought she had left. ". . . *wrong* . . . it's wrong—"

Vance looked up as Daniel entered the room. "She's all set." He scrawled the last of his report onto Kent's chart and passed it to Daniel. "She only had one reversion in the last half hour, and she's oriented as to person, place and time. But she's pretty hazy on why she's here. Keeps rambling about how she's not a Cadre anarchist, that she didn't kill those kids. That's a good one, huh?"

"Interesting." Daniel had never heard anyone retract a Broc-induced confession. "Thank you, Vance. You can go."

Vance swaggered toward the door. He winked at Officer Rae Pulansky, who was seated at the computer station. "See ya, Pulansky. Is that a new haircut? Cute."

Blushing, Pulansky smoothed her mouse-brown hair. "'Bye, Ashworth."

"Listen—*listen* to me." Kent's sobs stuttered into words. "Cadre . . . they—"

"Lt. Peale is on his way, Dr. Lansbury," Pulansky said.

"Thanks." Daniel was relieved to hear Pulansky speak in the same deferential tone she had always used with him. "Is Captain Hofstader coming?"

"No. He's assigned Lt. Peale to manage the details of this investigation."

Daniel studied Kent's chart. It was going to take a colossal amount of Broc4 to push her into stage one, but he didn't want to give her one molecule more than necessary. "Do you have any idea how long the session will be?"

"Very brief, I think."

"*Please.*" Kent's eyes were swollen, crimson slits. Matted black hair stuck to her neck and blood crusted on lips that she had bitten until the flesh resembled raw hamburger. ". . . need to . . . talk to . . . Captain Hofstader—"

Peale entered, pushing a projector on a metal cart.

"She ready?" he barked at Daniel.

Daniel plunged a needle into a vial of Broc4. "We were waiting for you."

"Drug her and let's go."

"*No!*" Kent writhed as Daniel reached for the IV port. "No— *don't! Please*—it's wrong, it's a *lie*—" Daniel's thumb depressed the plunger, and Kent's words disintegrated into hysterical sobbing.

"You'd better keep her in hand, Lansbury." Peale positioned the cart to the left of the door. "I don't want any delays."

Daniel ignored him. If Peale wanted a smooth I-X, he should have waited until Kent had more fully recovered from the first session.

Peale leaned over the projector, but the strident beeping of the cardiac monitor brought his head around. "What's the problem?"

Daniel silenced the monitor. "Her heart is beating too fast. It's not dangerous—yet."

"Why is she still bawling? Didn't you give her enough juice?"

"I gave her as much as she can tolerate," Daniel said steadily. "She'll calm down in a moment." Already the Broc4 had blanked the terror from Kent's eyes and her sobs were becoming mechanical.

Peale muttered something under his breath that Daniel chose not to hear, then swung toward Pulansky. "You ready?"

"Yes, Lieutenant."

Peale stomped to Kent's side. "Kent, state your full name and occupation."

Spastic trembling shook her body. "Alisa . . . Alisa Michelle Kent. Lieutenant with the . . . with the . . . Tremont . . . Police Service."

Peale scowled at Daniel. "She doesn't sound right."

"She sounds like anyone would after ten hours of stage two. I advise you to ask your most important questions first, and *quickly.*"

"Lights, two percent," Peale said. The room darkened. "Projector, Program 1."

A black-masked and black-clothed figure appeared in front of the projector. The figure strode toward Alisa Kent and returned to stand in front of the projector.

"Does this figure look like Zero?" Peale asked.

"No."

"Why not?"

"The shoulders are too broad." Kent's voice was a dry scrape of sound. "The hands are too big. He didn't walk like that."

"What's wrong with his walk?"

"Too aggressive. Too fast."

"He was more graceful? More casual?"

"Yes."

"Program 2," Peale said. A modified Zero appeared, strolled toward Kent, retreated.

"Could this new image be Zero?"

"No."

"Why not?"

"Too stocky."

"Program 3." Peale proceeded through nine more representations of Zero. Seven times Kent rejected the image. Twice she indicated that the image did resemble Zero. Daniel watched the parade of black-masked figures, unable to stop himself from analyzing the body types and postures and working to match them with the names of Council Assistants.

"Program 1A." A Zero figure appeared sitting in a folding chair, his hands moving in the unconscious gestures of someone engaged in conversation. His right hand stroked his masked chin; a few moments later he repeated the gesture.

"Kent, is there anything wrong with this representation of Zero?"

"Yes."

"What is it?"

"He always stroked his chin with his left hand."

Peale's mouth bent in a smile. "Lights, one hundred percent." The overhead light panels flared. "That's all, Lansbury. We may want to question her again soon, so keep her ready."

Daniel extended Kent's chart toward Peale. "She needs rest."

Contempt and incredulity narrowed Peale's eyes. "You've got to be kidding."

"You're going to kill her."

"She doesn't deserve rest."

"It's your investigation. But I'll note in Kent's chart that you refused the counsel of the medical supervisor, even when I explained that your decision posed a clear danger to Kent's usefulness to the police. If she dies or slips into Broc psychosis before you're done with her, it's on your head."

"What's your problem, Lansbury? You feeling a little tender toward anarchist scum since you found out your girlfriend is one of them?"

Fury surged through Daniel like molten steel.

"My problem," he said savagely, "is your stupidity. If I can't give Kent the care she needs, I can't keep her functional. If you'd like a different medical supervisor on this case, submit the request to Captain Hofstader."

"What I'd like," Peale said, "is you—right there." He pointed to where Lt. Kent lay strapped to the prisoner's chair.

Daniel shoved Kent's chart at Peale, barely restraining the urge to jam it into his gut. "Authorize sedation or forget ever questioning Kent again."

Peale's gaze was poisonous as he took the chart out of Daniel's hands. "If you're guilty of anything, I'll bring you down. And not even Daddy will be able to protect you." He scribbled his name on Kent's chart. "There's your authorization, if you're so set on being the gentle friend of traitors. Come on, Pulansky. We've got work to do. Some of us are still in the business of fighting anarchists." Peale tossed the chart to Daniel and exited the room with Pulansky in tow.

* * *

Laura's fingernails gouged Ian's elbow. "The gun isn't necessary," she whispered.

"Sorry," Siskell said genially. "I'm just convincing Roshek that we're in a hurry. Move it, Professor."

"Wait," Laura said. "He needs his coat. It's freezing out there."

"Sure, yeah, get the man his coat."

Laura hurried down the hallway and returned with Ian's coat. Her face was chalky.

"Thanks for everything, Laura," Ian said coldly.

"He's—he's here to help you."

"You don't believe that."

Laura's eyes shone with tears. She took a tentative step toward Siskell. "What are you going to do to him?"

"Don't worry, sweetheart. We'll take him to the U.S. That's what he wants, isn't it?"

"You won't hurt him?"

"Not if he cooperates."

"You *swear* you won't hurt him?"

"On my mother's grave, babe. The gun's just to make sure he doesn't do anything stupid and get us all arrested. See, Roshek's a dunce when it comes to keeping himself safe, so we have to babysit. Let's go, Professor."

With a gun aimed at his heart, what choice did he have? Ian put his coat on and gave Laura's stricken face one last look. She opened her mouth to speak, but then turned away in silence.

Ian walked out of the apartment, Siskell at his heels. Fog dimmed the streetlights and a car idled at the curb. The bus stop across the street was filled with people. Should he attract their attention? The commotion might make trouble for the Cadre—

Siskell pressed up close behind Ian and jabbed the gun against his spine. "Into the car. Backseat."

Ian opened the car door and slid inside. Siskell followed.

"Go," Siskell said to the driver, of whom Ian could see only a strip of dark hair beneath the back of a baseball cap. The car accelerated.

Siskell grinned at Ian. "Pretty girl. Bet her husband wouldn't like her getting all weepy over you. You're lucky I rescued you before he got home."

"Where are we going?" Ian tried to keep his voice steady.

"Somewhere safe."

"Like a grave in the backyard of your headquarters?"

Siskell whistled through his chipped tooth. "Oh, man, you really have gone nutty. We're all your friends."

"Yeah? Then put the gun away."

"Can't. If we let you go, you'll blunder into a squad of police officers and *wham*, you'll be joining your girlfriend at the Detention Annex."

"Tough break for you, losing a valuable contact like Alisa Kent."

"Yeah, we're all crying buckets."

"I'll bet. Alisa Kent never did a thing for the Cadre. What did you do to her to set her up like that?"

"You idiot punk. Lt. Kent has been one of us for three years. Didn't she tell you?" Siskell heaved a sigh. "Man oh man, but we're in trouble now. Kent's out there spilling our secrets to her police buddies!"

"What secrets?"

"You think I'm going to tell you *that?*"

"I'm amazed you pulled it off," Ian said, sensing that flattery might open Siskell's mouth. "It couldn't have been easy tampering with Kent's confession."

"Yeah, not bad, eh?"

"Not bad, but not that useful either. How much good is it really going to do the Cadre to have Lt. Kent confess to being the Newbold Bay bomber?"

"You're missing the point," Siskell said with satisfaction.

"What is the point, then?"

Siskell smirked and shifted his grip on the gun. He was clearly bursting to brag. "The point," he stage-whispered, "is that Kent knows enough to take the police to Zero himself."

"*Seven*," the driver snapped.

"Oh, ease up. Dr. Roshek will be happy to hear that such a bloodthirsty villain is about to get what he deserves. Let's cheer up his last moments."

Last moments. So much for the playacting about going to the U.S.

"You're frowning, Roshek. I thought you'd be happy. Oh, I forgot. You think this guy is some kind of hero—"

"Shut up, Seven."

"All right, all right. Eat your candy and don't be so crabby."

They had passed out of the city center and were speeding along a narrow road crowded on both sides with walls of leafless trees. No streetlights illuminated the misty darkness, and no other cars were in sight. Ian slid his hand into his pocket and closed his fingers over his pocketknife. "Who *is* Zero?" he asked to distract Siskell.

"Oh, well, that's classified. You should have asked your sweetie Alisa."

Kent's information couldn't possibly implicate the real Zero, Ian realized. The Cadre wouldn't allow any of their real secrets to reach the ears of Colonel Edgefield. If they wanted to rid themselves of a hated leader, they'd do so with a bullet.

"You're setting someone up with phony information channeled through Lt. Kent." Ian hunched forward so his bulky coat would conceal the movement of his hand as he worked to ease the largest blade of the knife open. "That's right, isn't it?"

"Now *that's* just a crazy theory," Siskell said complacently.

Ian's fingertips finally managed to pinch the edge of the blade and coax it open. It was short and dull. At best, it could serve as a distraction to give him a chance at the gun. "What do you hope to achieve by framing someone as Zero?"

"A good laugh."

"Shut *up*, Seven."

The barrel of the gun tilted to the right as Siskell leaned forward and whacked the driver on the shoulder. "Will you relax? It wouldn't hurt you to have a little fun—"

Ian drove the blade into Siskell's gun hand, knocking it against the front seat. Siskell screamed. The knife fell to the floor as Ian grabbed at the gun and tried to wrench it from Siskell's bleeding hand. Siskell clamped his other hand around the gun, and the barrel swung toward the ceiling, the seat, and the driver as Ian and Siskell wrestled over it.

The driver slammed on the brakes and sprang from the car to open the back door. Siskell rammed his shoulder into Ian's chest, throwing both of them out of the car.

Ian hit the pavement with Siskell on top of him. He gasped for air as he rolled, knocking Siskell off him. The driver leapt toward them, but jumped back as the gun, clenched in four blood-slick hands, swung in his direction. Ian expected a bullet from the driver, but apparently he was unarmed or he was afraid of hitting Siskell.

Suddenly Siskell reversed his push on the gun and slammed his hands downward, crushing Ian's knuckles against the road. Ian's fingers started to slip as again Siskell forced the barrel of the gun in his direction.

Siskell's jacket had fallen open, and in the glow from the car's interior light, Ian saw a black square clipped to Siskell's belt. A stun square.

Ian suddenly released the gun. Caught off guard, Siskell fell forward, smacking the gun against the ground. Ian snatched the stun square, pressed the activator button, and slapped the square against Siskell's chest. The stun square buzzed. Siskell collapsed.

Ian grabbed the gun from Siskell's hand just as the driver's boot landed on Ian's wrist, grinding his arm into the road. The driver bent to snatch the gun, and Ian swung his body in a wild arc, crashing his legs into the driver. The driver hurtled forward; his head slammed into the edge of the open car door. Ian grabbed the gun and threw himself into the driver's seat of the idling car. He shifted the car into gear and stomped on the accelerator, both doors flapping open. The rearview mirror offered a glimpse of the driver sitting dazedly in the road next to Siskell's motionless hulk as Ian sped away.

After several miles of mindless driving, Ian calmed down enough to stop the car and close the doors. Where was he? He wasn't familiar with this deserted, winding road, where branches almost formed a canopy overhead. He checked the dashboard, hoping for directions, but the car didn't have a navigation system.

The narrow road finally emerged from the trees, widening as it approached an intersection. A sign pointed toward southbound national freeway 2.

The road that leads to the border.

Crazy hope swam through his brain. He now had a car the police weren't searching for. He could drive to Maddox Road and see if the backpacks were behind those bushes. He could escape Tremont.

He glanced at the gun he had tossed on the passenger seat. He even had the means to defend himself.

But what of the things Siskell had bragged about? The Liberty Cadre *had* tampered with Alisa Kent's memory. They were using her to feed false information to the police regarding the identity of Zero. Why were they doing this? Who would the Cadre want to see falsely accused of anarchist activities?

Ian pressed harder on the accelerator. He didn't know what the Cadre was up to, and he couldn't stop them anyway. If he tried to warn the police that Kent's confession was false, they'd arrest him, but they wouldn't listen to him. Kent herself would have better luck convincing them that something was wrong.

He tried to mentally map out the best route to Maddox Road, but had trouble paying attention to anything but the sick sensation compressing his chest. The police wouldn't listen to Alisa Kent denying her own guilt. It would take outside evidence before they'd even begin to think something was wrong with her confession. Would he run away and leave her to be punished as the Newbold Bay bomber? Leave some innocent person to be framed as Zero?

"You can't do anything about it," Ian said aloud. It was idiotic to invite arrest, torture, imprisonment, all in a futile attempt to tell the police they were being duped.

So you let the Liberty Cadre win. You send them off to kill more children. You let other people suffer for your cowardice.

The way you did Jill.

Branches whipped the side of the car. Heart hammering, Ian steered back into the center of the lane. *Forget the Cadre. You can't stop them. The police would never listen to you.*

But if he could find someone with influence and credibility who was willing to carry the story to the police—someone like Daniel Lansbury—

Ian touched the cold metal of the gun. He couldn't make Daniel believe his story. But he could make him sit still long enough to listen to it.

Would Daniel be at home or at work right now? Probably at work, pumping memory drugs into the multitude of people arrested in connection with the bombing. Daniel's car would be in the parking garage a couple of blocks from the Tremont police complex. Jill had bragged that Daniel had a reserved space there. He'd meet

Daniel and tell him everything he knew about the Liberty Cadre's plotting.

Then he'd head straight for the border, leaving Daniel to carry the report to the police.

* * *

Ian hid behind a concrete pillar three parking slots to the right of Daniel's green Toyota. His escape car was parked behind a closed furniture store half a mile away.

He had called Daniel, disguised his voice, and identified himself as a worker at the garage. Emergency repairs of a ventilation fan made it necessary for Daniel to move his car as soon as possible. Daniel had responded with annoyance, but agreed to move his car within the hour. Ian hoped he'd get here before someone noticed Ian lurking behind the pillar and called the police. At least his navy blue coat didn't show the blood that had dripped from Siskell's hand as they'd wrestled over the gun.

Time dragged, giving Ian too much opportunity to think about Laura's betrayal. He was willing to believe that until Siskell pulled a gun, Laura had convinced herself the Cadre really would help him. But the anguish in her face as Siskell ordered him out the door—at that point, she had known Siskell was going to kill him. Yet she hadn't interfered, hadn't tried to distract or delay Siskell. She'd just turned away and let Siskell herd him toward his death.

Would Eric have done the same thing?

From behind the pillar, Ian watched the elevator bringing passengers from the underground shuttle that linked the parking garage to the Tremont police complex. He was on the verge of either heart failure or mental breakdown by the time Daniel Lansbury emerged. Daniel's bony shoulders slumped, and stress had added ten years' worth of lines to his face. Ian fought a last-ditch battle against the temptation to remain hidden—to let Daniel move his car and return to the Detention Annex none the wiser. It would be so much easier.

Yeah, easier. Tell that to the people who will be the Cadre's next victims. Ian waited until Daniel opened the car door. As Daniel bent to slide inside the car, Ian darted from behind the pillar, yanked open the passenger door, and plunked into the seat.

Daniel froze, his key halfway to the ignition.

Ian slammed his door. "I need to talk to you. I have some information about Lt. Alisa Kent and the Liberty Cadre."

Daniel's gaze flicked toward the phone on the dashboard. Before Daniel could speak, Ian reached over and punched the button to cancel the voice-activated system. "Not yet. First hear me out."

"I have nothing to say to you."

"Just listen. The Liberty Cadre is feeding the police false information through Lt. Kent. She's not part of the Cadre, and anything she's said about them during Information Extraction is garbage."

"What are you talking about?"

"Alisa Kent is not with the Liberty Cadre," Ian repeated. "They set her up. Last night when she was arrested—you were on call, weren't you? You told Jill you were on call for top-security cases. Were you there when they questioned Lt. Kent?"

"I was there," Daniel said. "And I can tell you that Alisa Kent is unquestionably a member of the Liberty Cadre. If she told you otherwise, then she lied, and you were naive to believe her."

"She's denied her confession, hasn't she? When she isn't drugged, I mean. She's told you she's not with the Cadre."

For an instant, Daniel looked startled. Then his expression iced over and he pulled the phone off his belt.

"*Wait*," Ian said.

"I'm calling the police."

Seeing no alternative, Ian drew the gun out of his pocket. "Put the phone away."

Daniel's mouth went slack, then closed into a hard line of anger.

"Put the phone away." What was Ian going to do if Daniel refused to be intimidated and called the police?

Daniel clipped the phone back onto his belt. "What do you want?"

"Only to talk to you." Ian tried to moisten his lips, but his tongue was a blob of cotton. "Drive out of the garage. This isn't the best place to chat."

"Whose blood is on your fingers?"

Ian glanced at his hands. Reddish-brown smears formed a gruesome contrast with his winter-pale skin. "Drive out of the garage and I'll explain."

"Where are we going?"

"Just for a drive. Once I'm done talking, I'll get out of your car. You'll never hear from me again."

Daniel scrutinized Ian, plainly measuring how likely he was to pull the trigger if thwarted. At last, he shifted the car into reverse.

Ian settled back against his seat, hands so slippery with sweat that he wondered if he could keep his grip on the gun. He was no better than Siskell. The fact that he wasn't willing to hurt Daniel was irrelevant; Daniel didn't know he was bluffing.

"Once you're out of the parking garage, turn right," Ian said, trying to ignore the growing feeling of self-contempt. "Then left on Ingram Road."

His expression carved of stone, Daniel made the turns as ordered.

While Daniel drove, Ian related the story of Alisa Kent's passage into treason and how she got mixed up with the Liberty Cadre. Daniel listened in scornful silence, but when Ian began talking about Kent's middle-of-the-night confrontation with the Cadre and her bewilderment as to what they were doing to her, Daniel shot him a sharp, troubled look. Ian felt a seed of hope sprouting. Was he getting through to Daniel?

Ian finished by describing his confrontation with Siskell. "From Siskell's bragging, it sounds like the Cadre is using Lt. Kent to frame someone as their leader Zero. I don't know who or why, but I know they're playing the police for fools."

Daniel sped into the parking lot of a busy grocery store, steered into a space next to a bakery truck, and braked so viciously that Ian nearly collided with the dashboard. "I don't know what your game is, but I won't play."

Ian's gut tied itself into another knot. People were all over the parking lot, entering or leaving the store. He should order Daniel to drive out of here, but he was weary of acting the part of the kidnapper.

"Why would I be here if this story is false?" Ian kept the gun low. On this misty evening, he hoped it was unlikely anyone could see through the car windows clearly enough to notice the weapon. "And you don't have to take my word for anything. You're an expert in Information Extraction. Can't you tell if the Cadre tampered with Lt. Kent's testimony? Aren't there tests you could run?"

"I've already lost enough credibility, thanks to you. And now I'm supposed to run tests on your say-so?"

"You'd rather let the Cadre win than risk looking foolish?"

"You stick a gun in my ribs and expect me to believe you're working against the Liberty Cadre? Tell me, Garrett follower, did God order you to come shoot me?"

Desperation surged through Ian. He was certain Daniel had seen some validity in the story, but Daniel was unwilling to break through layers of hostility to examine it objectively.

"Get out of the car," Daniel spat. "You rotten little coward."

Ian couldn't move. The gun seemed melded to his palm, and his fingers cramped around it like they would never straighten out again. *Rotten little coward.* That's what he was, consumed by the compulsion to leap from the car and escape Tremont. "I'm asking you to take an objective look at the evidence. That's all."

"I've seen plenty of evidence. It all tells me you're a liar who spreads trouble wherever he goes and a coward who leaves others to pay for his crimes. You destroyed Jill. Her only crime was trying to protect *you*."

Oh, Jilly. Despising himself, Ian averted his eyes from the wrath in Daniel's face. If he ran away now, it wouldn't be because it was impossible to convince Daniel Lansbury of what the Cadre was doing. It was because he cared more about saving his own neck than he did about saving hundreds of innocent lives. Because he *was* a coward.

A faithless coward.

"Get out of the car," Daniel said. "I'm not passing your ridiculous story on to Captain Hofstader."

"Then I'll talk to Hofstader myself." Ian's muscles were as stiff as chilled clay, but he managed to open his fingers.

The gun fell and landed with a soft thump near Daniel's feet.

CHAPTER 19

The astonishment on Daniel's face tightened to suspicion. He picked up the gun. "You're surrendering?"

Ian stared out the windshield and waited for Daniel to call the police.

"You really believe all this nonsense about a Liberty Cadre conspiracy, don't you?" Daniel said.

"I've already told you why I believe it. But you're the one in a position to verify it."

Daniel aimed the gun at Ian. There was nothing awkward or uncertain in his pose. He looked like he knew exactly how to handle Siskell's weapon. "You'd rather surrender than let the Cadre trick the police. Why?"

"I don't want another Newbold Bay."

"*You* don't want another Newbold Bay? I didn't see you doing anything to stop the first one. Your friend was the guy wiring timers."

This last weight of guilt settled on Ian with nauseating force. *I'm sorry. Oh, Father, help me; I'm sorry.*

"You claim Lt. Kent told you the Cadre came to her three times. When did these episodes occur?"

"She didn't give me dates," Ian said, relieved that Daniel would abandon his cynicism long enough to ask that question. "She just said it was over the past couple of weeks. But I know the last incident—the one where she woke up while the Cadre was there—took place . . . let's see. She talked to me about it on Wednesday, this past Wednesday. So Tuesday night. December third."

"She remembers nothing after the Cadre administered their drug?"

"Nothing until she woke up in the morning."

"She said she experienced severe confusion upon awakening?"

Ian strained to recall Kent's exact words. "She said she was disoriented to the point of amnesia . . . couldn't even remember her name for a while. Her memory would return and then she'd go blank again."

Daniel's forehead creased in a distracted frown. Then he jammed the barrel of the gun into Ian's stomach, pinning him against the passenger door.

"If you make a fool of me again, I swear I'll see to it that they execute you."

It was like being skewered by a white-hot blade. Ian's hands twitched toward the gun to push it away, but the hate in Daniel's eyes stopped him. Daniel craved an excuse to shoot him.

Daniel withdrew the gun. Ian crumpled forward.

"I want your hands where I can see them," Daniel said. "Put them on the dashboard."

Ian stretched trembling hands toward the dashboard. Daniel touched the button to activate the car phone. "Dad, private line."

In a few moments, Marcus Lansbury's voice boomed from the speaker. "What is it, Daniel?"

"I need to talk to you, immediately, in person."

"What about?"

"I've received some new information concerning the Liberty Cadre and Lt. Alisa Kent."

Hope numbed the edges of Ian's pain to where he could breathe again.

"Why are you reporting this to me and not Captain Hofstader?" Marcus asked.

"The information is—not something the police would expect to hear. They might be unwilling to—"

"Very well, you're afraid they won't listen to you. What is your source?"

Daniel wrapped his left hand around his right as though to steady the gun preparatory to firing. "Ian Roshek," he said stiffly. "He's with me now. He's surrendering."

Ian braced himself for a scathing response from Daniel's father.

"He's surrendering?" Marcus Lansbury's voice was calm. "That's the first sensible choice he's made in a long time."

"I realize he's not a credible source." Daniel's voice went from stiff to brittle. "But he's not with the Liberty Cadre, and—"

"You don't need to defend yourself. If you judge that Dr. Roshek's information has merit, then it's worth investigating. I presume the police are on their way to arrest him?"

Daniel's shoulders relaxed. "I haven't called them yet. I wanted to consult with you first."

"Then don't call them. I'd like to hear Dr. Roshek's information firsthand, after which I'll contact Colonel Edgefield personally. As you noted, the police are sometimes ill-equipped to adjust to the unexpected. I'd prefer not to pass this matter into their hands until I'm thoroughly acquainted with the situation."

Ian managed to sit up straight despite the pain spiking through his gut. Councilor Lansbury wanted to *talk* to him?

"What do you want me to do?" Daniel asked.

"Where are you?"

"In the parking lot of the Ingram Road Foodshop, in my car. I have a gun. Ian Roshek's gun."

"Ah. If Dr. Roshek makes any attempt at escape, you will shoot to kill. Is that clear?"

"Yes, sir."

"Stay where you are. I'll send security to escort you and Dr. Roshek to the house."

Twenty minutes later, a white sedan pulled up, and a beefy man in a suit and tie stepped out and climbed into the back of Daniel's car.

"I'll take the gun, Dr. Lansbury," the security man said. Daniel passed the gun over the seat.

The man passed a set of handcuffs to Daniel. "Cuff Roshek's hands behind his back."

Ian slouched against the dashboard and put his hands behind him so Daniel could fasten the handcuffs.

"Drive us to the house," the man said. "Roshek, I've got a gun trained on you."

Daniel headed east toward Lake Serena. The nearer they came to the lake, the thicker the fog grew, until billows of mist closed around the car. Daniel turned off the main road into a neighborhood where

Ian could see only the gated ends of driveways. The presumably spacious homes at the ends of the driveways were only misty patches of security lights.

Daniel slowed the car. One of the gates swung open, and they turned onto a curving driveway. Ian squinted into the fog and discerned the fuzzy outlines of a mansion fronted by white columns. Daniel circled to the back of the house and pulled into the second of six garages.

An anemic-looking man in a neat pin-striped suit was waiting in the garage. "Your father is in his study," he said to Daniel. "Mr. Jameson," he said, looking at the guard, "Councilor Lansbury would like you to escort Dr. Roshek to the study as well."

"Yes, sir." The security man hauled Ian out of the car. Still unable to draw a deep breath without setting his stomach muscles ablaze, Ian trotted alongside the guard as cooperatively as he could.

In his study, Marcus Lansbury sat behind an immense mahogany desk. His chair was high-backed burgundy leather, as majestically oversized as the desk. *The king holds court*, Ian thought, knees rubbery as the security guard brought him to stand before Marcus Lansbury.

"Roshek's gun, sir." Security man Jameson extended the weapon. Marcus stowed it in a desk drawer and gestured at a chair facing his desk. Jameson pushed Ian into the chair.

"Daniel—" Marcus nodded at the chair next to Ian's. Daniel sat down.

"Mr. Jameson, you may leave," Marcus said. "Remain in the hall outside."

"Yes, sir." The security man exited the study. The man in the pinstripes had followed them in, and now took an unobtrusive seat on the couch near a sculpted marble fireplace.

"Now, Dr. Roshek," Marcus said. "What is this information regarding the Liberty Cadre and Lt. Alisa Kent?"

Ian told Marcus Lansbury the same things he'd told Daniel. Marcus listened in silence, his expression unreadable. When Ian finished, Marcus made no comment, but turned his knife-blade eyes on his son.

"What makes you think this story has credence?"

"It's been obvious from the beginning that Alisa Kent's case is unusual," Daniel said. "I've searched the Annex records and I can't find a single instance—not *one*—of premature stage two in a first I-X.

Kent reacted to Broc4 like someone who's been swimming in it—or swimming in a chemically related drug."

"You think she was exposed to a drug that altered her experience under Broc4?"

"I'm saying it's possible. There are a number of Broc derivatives on which little study has been done—"

"But you don't yet have any conclusive evidence that the Cadre tampered with Lt. Kent's confession. Is that correct?"

Daniel peered down at his white knuckles. Ian had never imagined that confident, arrogant Daniel could appear so unsure of himself. "Right now it's just a theory. But if something was done to her, we should be able to determine that."

"Has Lt. Kent retracted her confession?"

"She's . . . tried. Before this afternoon's I-X, she was rambling something about lies and the Cadre and how she needed to talk to Captain Hofstader. And the medic who was caring for her mentioned that she kept denying involvement in the Newbold Bay bombing."

"But none of you believed her."

"Dad, besides the fact that she had confessed to being a Cadre terrorist and a Garrett sympathizer, she was so exhausted that she was incoherent. Of course we didn't listen to anything she said."

Marcus shifted his gaze back to Ian. "Where is the car you took from Siskell and his associate?"

Grateful that Marcus Lansbury hadn't immediately dismissed the entire story, Ian said, "It's behind that big furniture store on Ingram Road. Terry's."

"Why did you leave it there?"

"I was—planning to go back for it." Ian leaned forward to relieve some of the pressure on his shackled hands. His wrist throbbed where the Cadre driver's boot had bruised it.

"You intended to drive to the border?"

It was strange how remote those plans seemed now. "Yes."

"Why did you surrender?"

Ian glanced at Daniel. Daniel was studying him, a guarded expression on his face. "It was the only way to get Daniel to listen to me. The only way to stop the Liberty Cadre."

Marcus's gaze pierced him like needles. "In all his boasting, did Siskell give you any hint as to whom they're framing as their leader?"

"No. He never—" Ian stopped, remembering something. Siskell *had* made one cryptic comment about the Cadre's target. *"Oh, I forgot. You think this guy is some kind of hero."* What did that mean?

"Well?" Marcus prompted.

"The only thing he said was something about my thinking the guy they're framing was a hero, which doesn't make sense."

"So Mr. Siskell thought you admired the person they had chosen as their target." Marcus paused. "It's rumored that Zero must be in a high government position. Is there anyone in power that a traitor like you might admire?"

Admire . . . a hero . . . "If you're looking for a hero, find someone else to admire." The lounge at Tremont Electronics appeared in Ian's memory. The meeting Siskell had attended. Siskell's jeering dismissal of the newly appointed member of the Council . . . "Spencer Brannigan," Ian whispered.

Marcus smiled at Ian like he'd just passed some sort of test. "Ah. Spencer Brannigan."

"Councilor Brannigan!" Daniel exclaimed. "That's the silliest—" He fell abruptly silent.

"Yes, Daniel?" Marcus said.

"I don't know . . . I was just thinking of the information Kent gave us about Zero."

"Yes?"

"She never saw his face, but what physical description she did provide would fit Councilor Brannigan perfectly. Height, weight, coloring, body type . . . even the way he walks. And the ring . . . the Tremont signet. Councilor Brannigan usually wears it."

"Why do you think the anarchists would want to destroy Spencer Brannigan? Of all the Council, Spencer is the most . . . what's a polite way to say it?"

"Dad—"

"The most naive about what is required for a strong, stable government. The first to suggest foolish and dangerous alterations in the way New America is governed. The most likely to endear himself to people who clutch at the foolish traditions of the past. Why didn't the anarchists target someone like me, who fights for strength and security?"

"I imagine they would have liked to target you," Daniel said, an edge to his voice. "But they knew they couldn't get away with framing you as Zero because no one would believe it, no matter how much evidence they invented."

Marcus rose to his feet. "But you think people would believe it about Spencer Brannigan?"

"Like you said, there are those who think Councilor Brannigan is too radical and too eager for change."

"True." Marcus pivoted toward the painting of Jonathan Lansbury that hung on the wall behind his desk. The portrait of his father held his attention for a moment before he turned toward Ian and Daniel.

"You've posed some interesting theories, gentlemen. But I don't think Colonel Edgefield needs to hear them."

Ian felt like the gun had been rammed into his stomach a second time. "You don't think there's even a remote possibility this could be true?"

"This nation doesn't need a Spencer Brannigan. He would have us repeat the same mistakes that brought the United States to chaos and made Separation necessary in the first place. When Brannigan is exposed as an anarchist, his ideas will die—as they must die if James Tremont's New America is to survive."

Ian stared in horror at Marcus Lansbury's confident smile. "You would allow the Liberty Cadre to manipulate the police and frame an innocent man just because you personally disagree with Councilor Brannigan's politics?"

"We're not talking about my personal feelings. We're talking about the safety of an entire nation."

Daniel spoke. "*Dad.* We're talking about anarchists. Think of Newbold Bay! Think of Uncle Andrew!"

"Don't lecture me, Daniel," Marcus Lansbury said sharply.

"I just don't see—"

"Let me tell you what's going to happen over the next few weeks," Marcus said. "The police will gather evidence sufficient to convince them that Spencer Brannigan is the head of the Liberty Cadre. Hearing that his arrest is imminent, Brannigan will commit suicide. His so-called reforms will go up in smoke. Any government leader who has ever spoken a kind word for his programs will be stained by the taint of anarchism. President Ryce will be exposed for the corrupt and weak leader that she is. After all, she was the one responsible for bringing Spencer Brannigan onto the Council. She'll have no choice but to resign."

"How can you—" Daniel began, but Marcus overrode him.

"A new president will be selected by the Council," Marcus said. "The Liberty Cadre will no longer exist. Scattered religious psychotics—such as you, Dr. Roshek—will be driven into extinction. Within a few years, we'll break through our borders, rid the continent of the rotting remnants of the failed United States government, and establish New America as James Tremont envisioned it—coast to coast. A beautiful vision, worth the cost of bringing it to reality."

Marcus Lansbury's words flooded over Ian, washing away all his thoughts except one horrible realization. "You knew all along that the Cadre was using Lt. Kent to frame Councilor Brannigan."

"That's correct."

Daniel stared from Ian to his father. "You *knew*? Then why haven't you stopped the Cadre?"

Marcus Lansbury smiled. "The Liberty Cadre is merely a tool, wielded solely for the purpose of strengthening national security."

"A tool," Ian said, "wielded by . . . by *you?*"

"That is correct."

"*You* are Zero?"

Daniel sprang to his feet. "Ian!"

Marcus laughed. "He's correct, Daniel. I am Zero."

CHAPTER 20

Daniel staggered like a blow had knocked him off balance. "How can you joke about this?"

"I'm not joking," Marcus said. "I didn't plan to tell you so soon, but circumstances have made it necessary."

Shock had crushed the air from Ian's lungs and he could hardly get breath to speak. "The Liberty Cadre was—it was never what it appeared to be at all."

"That's correct." Marcus gestured toward the man in the pin-striped suit. "Mr. Kinnock, please ask Mr. Jameson to return to my office."

The man immediately rose from the couch and went toward the door.

"Your people thought they were fighting a revolution," Ian said hoarsely. "Instead you were using terrorism to catapult yourself to power."

Marcus gave him a look of contempt. "Everything I've done has been for the sake of national security."

"National security? You killed your own brother!"

"*Ian*—" Daniel began, but Ian kept talking. "The assassination of Andrew Lansbury—that's the first time anyone heard from the Cadre. Is that how it started? You murdered your brother so you could steal his power?"

Security man Jameson entered with Kinnock.

"*Dad,*" Daniel said desperately.

Marcus moved toward Daniel. "Mr. Jameson, you and Mr. Kinnock may remove Dr. Roshek, but first render him unconscious. I want as little disturbance as possible."

Ian started to his feet but sank back at the sight of Jameson's gun. Jameson unhooked a stun square from his belt.

"No—wait, this is ridiculous—" Daniel tried to step into Jameson's path, but Marcus caught his arm and pulled him back. Jameson slapped the stun square against Ian's shoulder, and a skull-rattling buzz blanked out Ian's consciousness.

* * *

"I don't understand." Daniel's knees shook like they would buckle. "I don't understand," he repeated.

"Be patient, son."

"What are you going to do to him?"

"The fate of a traitor shouldn't concern you," Marcus said icily, and through his shock, Daniel felt the familiar twinge of shame.

Kinnock hooked his hands under Ian's arms and helped Jameson hoist him out of the chair. "Sir, where shall we take him?" Kinnock asked.

"The storage room beneath my garage. Tie him up and gag him. Mr. Jameson, stand guard. When the fog over the lake thins, we'll take care of him."

The words pounded senselessly against Daniel's ears. This couldn't be happening.

Jameson and Kinnock carried Ian Roshek from the room. Marcus prodded Daniel toward the chair nearest the fireplace.

"Do you need some water?" Marcus asked. "Or something stronger?"

"No. Dad, this is crazy. You can't possibly be involved with the Liberty Cadre."

Marcus nudged him into the chair. "People have short memories, Daniel. That was your grandfather's greatest worry—that as time passed, our people would grow careless and sloppy. They'd forget why James Tremont brought them together, and slide back into the corrupt traditions that riddle the rest of this continent."

"But—what—"

"When danger is acute, people remain vigilant and united, willing to do whatever is necessary to protect themselves. But in times of peace, they grow complacent, and chafe at what they see as unnecessary restrictions—not realizing that those restrictions are what allow them their peace."

"But—Uncle Andrew—"

Marcus relaxed into a velvet-upholstered wing chair facing Daniel. "Andrew was a man of limited vision and ability, able to see only *today*. He was appointed to the position of Councilor over Internal Defense because he was Jonathan Lansbury's oldest child, not because he merited that position."

"But you—you couldn't possibly have—"

Marcus spoke calmly. "It was the most difficult thing I ever did, but it was necessary."

"Your own *brother?*"

"Should I have protected my brother at the cost of endangering the nation? Andrew was a weak link, inadequate for such a vital position. Do you think James Tremont would have wanted the nation he founded put at risk because of one weak man?"

"You killed Uncle Andrew."

"Not personally. I found people suited to the job. People who could see the advantages of placing me on the Council."

"But the Liberty Cadre—"

"There was no Cadre yet. There were only a few of us, sworn to support each other in the cause of removing a man who threatened the nation's security. But after Andrew's death was publicly blamed on 'anarchists,' I realized I was overlooking a vital opportunity. What better way to keep people devoted to maintaining national security than to give them a taste of what would happen if we got careless?"

"You *created* the Liberty Cadre," Daniel said. "*You.*"

"It was necessary. But to make the group useful, I needed to move beyond my core of supporters, to recruit people who didn't have the capacity to understand what I was doing."

Daniel stretched cold fingers toward the fire, but the flames seemed to give no heat. He was asleep; he was dreaming.

"Since the most insidious threat to peace would be a resurgence of religion, my first intention was to create an organization founded on religious rhetoric," Marcus continued. "It would have been an effective way of reminding the nation of the inherently anarchic character of groups that place allegiance to a nonexistent god above allegiance to the state."

"You wanted to create a *religious* group?"

"Yes, but that turned out to be more problematic than I had anticipated. It takes time, Daniel, to create religious fanatics, and I found that even the scum I was recruiting weren't degenerate enough to commit crimes in the name of a fictional god. They preferred to do their work under the nebulous banner of freedom—of 'liberty.' It didn't matter particularly; anarchy is anarchy, no matter what clothes it wears—following your own selfish desires or—" He paused. "Or following your own selfish desires projected onto an imaginary god. And I found that the vicious nature of the Cadre's crimes was enough to taint anarchists of every breed, including Garrett followers like your friend Dr. Roshek."

Your friend. Daniel flushed.

"Within a year, I had a handful of recruits for the Liberty Cadre, and those recruits soon brought others into the group. We sent a statement to the police claiming responsibility for Andrew's death, and declaring our intention to destroy the government of New America and give power back to the people."

"But—the police have arrested many Cadre members and none of them has ever said the smallest thing implicating you—"

Marcus chuckled. "I worked only through my core supporters—the ones who were with me for Andrew's death, the only ones who knew what the Cadre was really about. None of the garbage I recruited ever saw my face or knew my name."

Daniel felt he was sliding down toward madness, flailing to catch himself but unable to find a handhold. "But—the things the Cadre did—Newbold Bay—"

"Harsh measures are required when danger is at hand," Marcus said flatly. "Prior to Separation, those brave men and women who worked to reform the United States government used many harsh measures to undermine the corrosive influence of religious organizations and to keep us safe from our enemies. Do you object to the way Senator Tremont and your grandfather worked to break the U.S. government apart so they could build it up as it needed to be? The assassination of President Hayden—was that gentle and pretty?"

"They did what was necessary," Daniel said automatically.

"And so did I." Marcus's face warmed with pleasure. "Ah, but the Liberty Cadre *was* effective! Even Oliver Edgefield could never have created such an efficient way to eradicate support for anarchists. Who could have sympathy for a gang of assassins and mass murderers? What rational citizen would step out of line in the smallest degree when any rebellious behavior made it look like he supported the Liberty Cadre? The Cadre was destroying the revolution they hoped to foment, and they were too intoxicated with their 'successes' to realize it."

The grandfather clock began to chime the ten o'clock hour. Daniel started, reminded that he ought to be at the Detention Annex adding his own efforts to the random nerve-stimulation therapy he had ordered for Alisa Kent. *Lt. Kent.* "How did you alter Lt. Kent's testimony under I-X?"

"Through a conditioning process involving BrocD14. Are you familiar with that drug at all?"

"I know it's a derivative of the Broc memory stimulants . . . it produces periods of amnesia. The lab shelved it long ago because it didn't serve police purposes. I've never worked with it."

"Ah. I experimented with D14 during my time at the lab. I found that it turns the brain into a blank canvas where any sort of picture may be painted. Once the drug wears off, the subject has no memory of the time spent under its influence. But under the neurochemical state produced by its cousin drugs—the Broc memory stimulants— conditioning done under D14 will surface."

"I've never—this isn't recorded anywhere, is it?"

"No. I suspected—accurately—that I might like to make private use of D14, so I edited the results of my tests in the record." One corner of his mouth curved upward. "Using Alisa Kent to transmit information to the police was not my original plan, of course, since her treason only came to my attention a matter of weeks ago. But she's perfect in the role. A genuine traitor who fancied herself an enemy of the Liberty Cadre! Of all people, a Sedition and Treason officer should have seen the paradox in such a course. I found it poetic that she should confess to Cadre membership."

Daniel frowned. "How did you find out she was a traitor?"

"Through a report from one of my operatives concerning Ian Roshek—though I've had my eye on Kent for several years now. I researched every police officer, searching for weak links."

"But she was such an excellent officer!"

"Perhaps too good. Too dedicated. A candidate for burnout or worse. And in light of her family history, I wondered if she might be vulnerable to corruption." Marcus stroked his fingers along the arms of his chair. "I found it strange that a few years ago Kent petitioned Colonel Edgefield to have all publicly available information concerning her family placed on classified status."

"What kind of information?"

"Oh, there were numerous news reports concerning her family's arrest and the honors she received for turning them in. She told Oliver she felt tainted by her background and didn't want this information available to any curious citizen who happened to search the news archives."

"What's strange about that? They were Garrett followers! Who wouldn't want to keep that hidden?"

"Think about it, Daniel. In light of her quick action in bringing her family to justice, her background shouldn't have been a shameful secret, but proof of her patriotism. Did she have unhealthy motives in wanting to hide the past? Pain over the loss of her worthless family? Guilt over her actions? Either could indicate the seeds of treason. Unfortunately, those seeds *were* present and they grew. A sad case."

Daniel couldn't think of anything to say.

"I know this must be difficult for you," Marcus said. "But you do understand what I've told you. I am not leading an anarchist rebellion. Nothing could be further from the truth."

"But—Councilor Brannigan! You'll kill him?"

Ice glazed Marcus's eyes. "Spencer Brannigan is a dangerous man."

"He wants to fix problems in the government—not overthrow it!"

"Are you naive enough to believe whatever Brannigan tells you? 'Fix problems' . . . Are you aware that he speaks of such things as restrictions on police powers, limiting the Council via a new written constitution, and friendly relations with the United States?"

"I—well—"

"No, you didn't know. And even if you did, you're too inexperienced to understand the implications of Brannigan's 'reforms.' As a patriot and a statesman—as the son of Jonathan Lansbury—I can't sit idly by and let destruction come."

Daniel couldn't control the trembling in his voice. "When will you kill him?"

"Soon. We don't want his suicide too far removed from his imminent arrest. Hofstader's bloodhounds are busy trailing the clues Lt. Kent gave them, and already they are sniffing around Spencer Brannigan. They're proceeding cautiously, of course, since they're dealing with a member of the Council. But within a day or two they'll have enough evidence to arrest him. Colonel Edgefield will tell me when they're ready to move on Brannigan. My operatives will ensure that he's dead before the police can take him."

"Is Colonel Edgefield part of the Liberty Cadre?"

"Oliver doesn't have that much imagination. He's useful, but ignorantly so."

"Why didn't you tell *me* what you were doing?"

"I considered drawing you into the circle, but I questioned whether you had the maturity to handle it." Marcus's eyes bored into Daniel. "As we've seen, your judgment is not always sound."

Everything within Daniel felt tangled in knots. "You knew all along that Ian Roshek was a Garrett follower. Why did you allow me to associate with the Rosheks when—"

"You love Jill," Marcus said bluntly.

Daniel looked at the carpet. "Dad—"

"I'm not testing you. I'm stating a fact. You love Jill Roshek, despite the poor decisions she's made. You are distressed that she will receive a long prison sentence. I don't admire your feelings, but I understand them." Marcus waited for Daniel to look at him before continuing. "I'm not averse to helping Jill—if you are willing to help me."

Daniel's mouth went sand-dry. "What do you mean?"

"We'd planned to tip the police ourselves about Kent's Cadre involvement and keep reins on the timetable and any Annex personnel who dealt with Kent. But thanks to Eric Vettori's untimely arrest, things didn't go so smoothly." The light from brass floor lamps created shadows on Marcus's face, inking his eyes black.

"I wasn't overly concerned because I'd been told Kent knew nothing of the conditioning sessions that altered her testimony." Anger contorted his face. "Since Kent *is* aware of when and how we worked on her, I'd prefer that she not have any opportunity to give that report to Clayton Hofstader. I have contacts in the Annex, but to move personnel in order to give them access to Kent might raise suspicions. You are already her medical supervisor. You have free access to her."

Daniel's breath stalled like hands had closed around his throat. "You want me to kill her?"

"No, no. Her sudden death might raise questions. I only want you to accelerate what would likely be a natural course."

"What do you mean?"

"She's still in stage two following this afternoon's I-X. Correct?"

"Yes. I gave her five hours of sleep, then ordered random nerve stimulation. That's been going on for about two hours now."

"No breaks?"

"A few short ones. Three minutes or less."

"So the prognosis is still uncertain."

"Uncertain, but any breaks are a good sign. She's doing better than I expected."

"Ah. Tell me what would happen if you were to inject her with Broc4 at this time."

Daniel wiped his sweaty face with his sleeve. "For a person in Alisa Kent's condition, I'd say any Broc4 in the next twenty-four hours would almost certainly induce irreversible Broc psychosis."

"Ah."

Daniel felt dizzy. "You want me to—to deliberately—?"

"I want you to insure that it happens. Broc psychosis is wonderful justice for an officer turned traitor. And let's hope she lives a good long while in that condition."

Daniel fumbled at the collar of his uniform. "You'd encourage Colonel Edgefield to keep her alive even after it becomes clear that her condition is permanent?"

"Why should we offer the merciful release of the Euthanasia Center to an officer who betrayed her trust? Let Kent suffer through a few weeks or months of Broc psychosis until her neurons disintegrate or her heart gives out. Her fate will effectively deter her colleagues from dabbling with treason."

"Dad. Dad, *please.*"

"It's necessary, as the Liberty Cadre was necessary." Marcus softened his tone. "It all comes together for the safety and peace of our people. Do you understand?"

Daniel let his head fall forward in a mindless nod.

"I'm asking a very small favor from you, Daniel. If you assist me, I'll speak to Oliver Edgefield on Jill's behalf. I have the power to recommend a light punishment for Jill—or even freedom. Of course, I also have the power to recommend twenty years in prison . . . or a life sentence . . . or execution."

"Execution!"

"Why not? She's proved herself a threat to the nation. We're better off without her."

Daniel's throat constricted with suffocating pressure.

"I'm sorry to push you like this," Marcus said. "But I don't want Kent able to raise doubts about her confession."

"But no one will believe her!"

"Probably not. But I prefer not to take that risk, especially since I now have a simple route to silencing her."

A simple route, Daniel thought bitterly. And what made him so pliable? Jill. An ugly thought entered Daniel's mind. Was this why his father hadn't objected to his continuing his relationship with her? Marcus must have seen an opportunity to gain a stranglehold on his son.

"I want you to take care of Lt. Kent tonight," Marcus said.

"I—I can't get hold of Broc4 without accounting for it," Daniel stammered. "You know that."

"Of course. I'll send a vial with you to the Annex."

"You have it here?"

"I need it now and then," Marcus said.

Daniel's phone rang. "Lansbury," he answered, forcing calm into his voice.

"Dr. Lansbury, this is Rhoda Schweitzer at the Annex. Our little sweetheart is making progress. The monitor just marked a twelve-minute break."

"Thanks, Rhoda. Drop it to eighty/ten and stay with her. I'll be there soon."

"Will do."

Daniel cut the connection.

"Progress?" Marcus asked.

"A twelve-minute break."

"Go now." Marcus rose from his chair. "I don't want her to progress any further, or it may raise questions when she relapses."

Daniel stood up. Marcus rested his hand, hard and steady, on Daniel's shoulder. "I did what your grandfather would have done. What James Tremont himself would have done. The people who died at the hands of the Liberty Cadre sacrificed their lives for peace and security."

Andrew Lansbury. The children in Newbold Bay. "It's just a lot to assimilate all at once," Daniel said.

"I know. Given time, you'll understand completely, but for now you must trust me." Marcus's fingers tightened on Daniel's shoulder. "And I'm sure you'd never be so foolish as to try to take what I've told you to the police."

Daniel swallowed. Go to the police? Tell them his father . . . his *father* . . . was Zero?

"Understand this, Daniel." Marcus's voice was gentle, but his eyes were discs of iron. "Your reputation is already shaky because of your association with the Rosheks. One call from me to Colonel Edgefield would instantly discredit anything you might tell him. You'd be dismissed as a man in the middle of a mental breakdown. And within the hour, you'd find yourself a heavily drugged inmate of the psychiatric wing at Tremont Regional Hospital. Is that clear?"

A thousand ice-cold knives grazed Daniel's skin. "I wouldn't go to the police."

Marcus's face relaxed into a paternal smile, and he released Daniel's shoulder. "You are my son. You know what's necessary for the safety of New America. And I guarantee that one day you will hold a seat on the Council. Now let me get you that Broc4."

* * *

"Oh, dear." Rhoda Schweitzer clucked her tongue at Daniel as he entered the treatment room. "You look like death. We should have left Kent on automatic and let you get some rest."

Smiling was about as comfortable as bending his knees backward, but Daniel faked a pleasant expression for Rhoda's benefit. "I doubt Captain Hofstader would be impressed if I left Kent to the care of a machine."

"I'd like to leave Kent to the care of maggots." The malice in Rhoda's eyes clashed with her grandmotherly face as she looked at Alisa Kent strapped to the treatment table. Kent's neck was twisted to the side, tendons straining through ashen skin, limbs jerking. Perspiration soaked her prisoner's uniform. Daniel adjusted the clamp on the intravenous line to increase the flow of fluid into Kent's arm, then wondered why he'd bothered. As soon as he gave her the Broc4, dehydration would be the least of her problems.

Rhoda handed the chart to Daniel. "She's gone now, as you can see, but I'm sorry to say she's making significant progress. Two more breaks—one for 4.3 minutes and the other for 5.8 minutes. It's a shame that nerve stimulation is working on Kent. Every time I look at her, I see the bodies of those children being dug out of—"

"You can go now, Rhoda. I know you're busy."

"Thanks." Rhoda pinched Kent's cheek, digging her nails in. "Sweet dreams, honey."

The door shut behind Rhoda. Daniel settled onto the stool near the monitor, dropped Kent's chart onto the counter, and buried his head in his hands. On the drive to the Detention Annex, he had operated without thinking, his body going through a familiar routine while his mind remained blank. But now that he was here, the reality was bursting through his shock.

His father was the head of the Liberty Cadre. Spencer Brannigan was marked for death. And Alisa Kent—Daniel reached into the pocket of his lab coat and withdrew the vial of Broc4 that his father had given him.

One small, painless act, and Jill would be safe. If he refused his father's request, Jill would suffer—maybe even die—and still Marcus Lansbury's plans would roll forward. Alisa Kent was not a serious danger to him.

Why had his father sent him here? To eliminate a minor threat? Or to test his loyalty? When he carried out Zero's order, he would join Zero's cause.

One small act and he was part of the Liberty Cadre.

But the Liberty Cadre didn't even really exist.

Alisa Kent moaned and Daniel lifted his head to look at her. His eyes moved from the welt Rhoda had pinched into her cheek to the purple blotches on her neck, bruises inflicted by the crushing fingers of a Cadre attacker.

Kent writhed, pulling against the straps like she was reaching for something she thought was in front of her. Tears streamed over flesh already burned raw by hours of weeping. Without even checking the monitor, Daniel knew she wasn't fighting to escape the pain generated in random patterns by the two dozen black discs that dotted her body; the nerve stimulators were cycling on and off at eighty-percent power, and if she could feel their effects, she wouldn't just be squirming.

Rhoda was expecting him to take manual control, coordinating the effects of the nerve stimulators with his own verbal efforts to coax Alisa Kent into responding, but he couldn't bring himself to go through such a charade when he was about to render his efforts useless. He'd rather carry out his father's orders and be done with it.

He'd inject Lt. Kent with Broc4 and stay with her until the immediate physiological effects of the injection had passed and she was solidly in stage two. Then he'd tell Rhoda that Kent didn't seem to be making progress and that she should call him if there was any improvement.

There wouldn't be any improvement. His father would be pleased. Jill would be safe. And Councilor Brannigan—

Was Spencer Brannigan a threat to national security?

Don't think about him. Think about Jill. Daniel stripped the protective cover off a needle.

A hoarse cry from Alisa Kent made him drop the syringe. The monitor showed a flickering green light. A break. The computer automatically dropped stimulator intensity to ten percent, and Kent's cries subsided into gasps. She was responsive now, and would be for several more minutes. Should he wait until she was insensible before continuing? No. Just because she could feel the discs stimulating her nerves didn't mean she was oriented enough to realize what Dr. Lansbury was doing to her. Even if she did understand, what could she do about it?

Daniel retrieved the fallen syringe and discarded it in the disposal bin.

Kent's left arm jerked, then her right leg. Nine seconds of quiet, then her entire body twitched. By the time Daniel had a fresh syringe in hand and was again reaching for the vial of Broc4, Kent's tears had turned into ragged, pleading sobs of pain and exhaustion.

Daniel tried to ignore her, but he tensed with each jolt from the stimulators. What was the matter with him? This was treatment, not torture, one of the few treatments with any effect on incipient Broc psychosis. And at any rate, ten percent was no worse than being jabbed with a thick needle. But Kent's weeping made Daniel feel like he was fracturing her bones one by one.

Disgusted with himself, Daniel flipped the power switch off. Why begrudge Kent a few seconds of rest before he hurtled her into what could prove to be weeks of torment?

Think of Jill. His hands shook so badly that he almost stabbed himself as he plunged the needle into the vial of Broc4.

Jill . . . a seat on the Council . . .

Daniel swallowed against the sensation of hands squeezing his throat. He tore open an alcohol wipe and swabbed an injection port on Kent's IV line. There was only one rational choice he could make. So what if Alisa Kent suffered? She *was* a traitor. If she had remained loyal, she would never have placed herself in circumstances where Marcus Lansbury could use her.

Self-contempt stiffened Daniel's jaw. If he had stayed away from the Rosheks, he never would have placed himself in circumstances where Marcus Lansbury could use *him*.

Kent swung her head toward him. Her eyes were a mess of tears and dilated blood vessels, but she was straining to focus. Daniel fought the urge to retreat from her. *Hurry. Just finish it.*

He slid the needle through the injection port, but hesitated, staring at the full syringe in his hand. A gentle push on the plunger would empty the Broc4 into Kent's bloodstream.

Kent's lips quivered and a croaking noise rasped from her throat. What was she trying to say? To ask him what drug he was administering? To beg him to believe she was not the Newbold bomber? It would never occur to her that he already knew the truth and didn't intend to act on it. She would trust that Daniel Lansbury wanted to stop the Liberty Cadre.

Ian Roshek had likewise trusted him.

Daniel's thumb trembled on the plunger of the syringe. Because he had taken Ian to his father, the Cadre's plans were sweeping forward. By dawn Ian's corpse would lie at the bottom of Lake Serena.

"The people who died at the hands of the Liberty Cadre sacrificed their lives for peace and security."

Or had they sacrificed their lives for Marcus Lansbury's ambition?

The beginnings of the Cadre—Andrew Lansbury murdered so Marcus could step into his position. Had Andrew truly been incompetent? Or had his father merely grown impatient at the realization that it would be years before he could hope for his own seat on the Council? And even then, he'd never have rivaled the power his brother held as Councilor over Internal Defense.

Sweat soaked Daniel's hands. His father, so arrogantly sure that everything he did was motivated by pure patriotism. So arrogantly sure of his right to rule.

So sure of his power over his son, so sure the rewards he offered were irresistible, so sure he had cut off all Daniel's options. So in control.

Like always.

Daniel wavered under a rush of revulsion so powerful it left him dizzy. He was dooming Alisa Kent to a prolonged, torturous death. He was condoning the murder of Spencer Brannigan. Ultimately, he was condoning the bombing at Newbold Bay, Andrew Lansbury's death, and hundreds of other Cadre casualties. Did he really believe those acts to be necessary for the safety of New America?

Or was he cooperating with his father because he didn't have half the courage of a Garrett follower who had been willing to sacrifice everything just to get Daniel to help him stop a murderous anarchist group?

Slowly, Daniel drew the needle out of the port without injecting the Broc4.

CHAPTER 21

Ian's hands were numb, his arms cramped, and his legs so stiff that he doubted he could walk even if ordered to do so at gunpoint. It felt like hours since he'd awakened, slumped against a metal pole in this cold, pitch-black room, hands shackled behind the pole, ropes sawing into his ankles, mouth taped securely shut. Was he still at the Lansburys'?

What was Daniel doing now? Taking a blood oath to initiate himself into the Cadre? Ian doubted that Daniel's horror at learning his father was the head of the Liberty Cadre could long withstand Marcus Lansbury's persuasions and explanations.

Zero. Marcus Lansbury is Zero. It made such perfect sense. All along, Ian had assumed Zero was a fool for not realizing that his operations were only strengthening the status quo. Now it turned out that Zero was getting exactly the results he wanted. What would Eric Vettori think if he knew?

Strange how sorry he felt for Eric now. Eric and his hotheaded passion to "do something."

Shivering, Ian tried to flex his fingers, but stopped when pain sizzled up his arms. Fury at his own helplessness had led him to struggle until the handcuffs had scraped the skin from his wrists. Now he wished he'd had the sense to hold still. He rested his head against the pole, praying for the thousandth time that something would stop Marcus Lansbury before Spencer Brannigan was dead, Alisa Kent was irrevocably branded a child-slaughtering terrorist, and Marcus Lansbury ascended to the presidency.

The click of the door startled Ian's heart into a frantic drumbeat. Lights flared. Ian squeezed his eyes shut and opened them to see Daniel Lansbury leaning over him.

"You can do exactly as I tell you, or you can stay here and die," Daniel whispered. "What's your choice? Will you cooperate?"

Lightheaded with hope, Ian nodded. Daniel drew a knife from his pocket and sliced through the rope binding Ian's ankles. "I should have let Dad murder you," he muttered. "It's better than you deserve."

With the gag still over his mouth, Ian could only accept that comment in silence. Daniel moved behind him and unlocked the handcuffs. Ian's freed arms felt buoyant as he flexed the stiffness out of his shoulders.

Daniel stepped in front of him. Remembering his promise to cooperate, Ian allowed Daniel to snap the handcuffs back onto his swollen wrists. At least his hands were locked in front of him this time. Ian tried to remove the gag, but his numb fingers couldn't locate the edge of the tape. Daniel leaned down and ripped the gag loose.

"Thanks," Ian gasped.

Daniel hauled him upright. Ian stumbled on pincushion feet as Daniel propelled him past shelves of boxes into a brightly lit passageway. Jameson was sprawled on the floor, eyes closed.

Daniel shoved Ian past the unconscious guard, through a doorway at the end of the passageway, and up a flight of stairs. At the top of the stairs, a door led into the garage, where Daniel's car was parked. The man in the pin-striped suit lay crumpled on the ground.

Ian collapsed into the passenger seat of Daniel's car. "What did you do to those guys?"

"Drugged them. They'll be asleep for maybe ten more minutes." Daniel accelerated along the driveway. The fog had thinned and wind shook the trees.

"Are we going to the police?" Ian watched with relief as the gate at the end of the driveway swung open.

"They wouldn't listen." Daniel mopped sweat off his face with an angry swipe of his arm. "We have to go directly to Councilor Brannigan and get him to contact President Ryce. She's the only one with enough power to stop Dad. I'd go to Ryce myself, but I wouldn't be able to get access to her. Trying would only get us arrested."

"How did you manage to—" Ian stifled the question. Daniel appeared to be on the brink of losing control; this was no time to quiz him about how he had outwitted his father. "Have you told Councilor Brannigan we're coming?"

"Do you have any idea how irrational this story is going to sound? We need to speak to him in person, and even then I'll be lucky if he doesn't think I'm crazy. An insane story . . . a Garrett follower as my only witness . . . at least I've *got* a witness—" Daniel barked a wild, bitter laugh.

"How far is it?"

"Two or three miles. And once we get there, keep your mouth shut unless I tell you to speak."

Daniel drove along the lakeshore and finally turned onto a narrow, secluded road. The road led down a forested hill to a gate, and Ian realized they were not on a road, but a driveway. At the bottom of the hill, blurred by thinning ribbons of mist, was a home with tall, triangular windows and dark-wood siding.

Daniel stopped at the gate next to a control box and rolled down his window. Ian expected him to scan his ID, but instead he honked the horn repeatedly, hurtling blasts of sound into the midnight sky.

"Dr. Lansbury!" An alert bass voice spoke from the intercom. "What's the problem?"

"Open the gate," Daniel said. "I can't scan my ID. I'll explain to Councilor Brannigan."

"What's the nature of your business?"

"I need to discuss that with Councilor Brannigan."

"It's late. The Councilor is in bed."

"Wake him up. This is critical."

"Who's with you?"

"His name is Ian Roshek. He's wanted by the police and will be in custody before the night is over. Before that happens, it's urgent that we speak with Councilor Brannigan on a matter vital to his safety. Don't notify the police yet. We'll explain our reasons to Councilor Brannigan, and I guarantee he'll support them."

Long silence. "Just a moment, Dr. Lansbury."

Daniel drummed his fingers on the steering wheel. Ian's anxiety skyrocketed. He feared that even Daniel's lifelong friendship with

Spencer Brannigan wouldn't be enough to get them in the door under these bizarre circumstances.

The bass voice spoke. "We'll open the gate. Drive down and park in front of the house. *Do not get out of your car.* We'll meet you at your car."

"Agreed," Daniel said. Ian closed his eyes in a silent prayer of thanks.

The gate slid open and Daniel drove down the hill to Brannigan's house. Two figures waited on the porch—a huge, olive-skinned man and a raw-boned, blond man with hair cut straight across his forehead. They wore dark suits and ties, and Ian concluded they must be members of the same government security service as Marcus Lansbury's guard Jameson. The blond man opened Daniel's door while the larger man ushered Ian out of the car.

"Keep that gate closed, no matter what." Daniel spoke rapidly. "Don't let *anyone* in, not even the police. Councilor Brannigan's life is at stake."

"All right, Dr. Lansbury. Come inside, please." The security man's soothing, overpolite tone clearly registered his opinion of Daniel's sanity. Ian suppressed a wince. If Brannigan regarded Daniel with the same degree of doubt, they were sunk.

Inside the house, Brannigan stood waiting in an arched doorway that led into a living room. Only the puffiness under his eyes indicated he had been yanked out of sleep. He was fully dressed and his gray-streaked hair was neatly combed. He directed one brisk look at Ian before approaching Daniel and clasping his hand.

"What in the name of James Tremont is going on here?" Brannigan asked.

Daniel opened his mouth, but no words emerged. He pulled his hand out of Brannigan's grasp and stepped backward, face suddenly rigid with anguish. Panic shot through Ian. Daniel looked like he was going to bolt out the door, his father's secrets unspoken.

"All right, we'll take it slowly," Brannigan said. "Let's go sit down. Mr. Perris, come with us. Mr. Martinez, take Dr. Roshek to—"

"No." Daniel's voice cracked. "Bring him with us. He may be able to answer some questions I can't."

Brannigan led them into the living room. Security man Martinez shoved Ian onto a couch and moved a few steps away, stopping in front of a marble pedestal table displaying a vase of chrysanthemums.

His gaze locked on Ian, monitoring every twitch. The blond guard, Perris, stood in the doorway, angled so he could see into the living room and out into the entrance hall.

Ignoring Spencer Brannigan's urgings to sit down, Daniel launched into an explanation. Brannigan listened, a mixture of shock and incredulity in his eyes. When at last Daniel paused, Brannigan said, "Daniel, this is insane. Your *father* is the leader of the Liberty Cadre? Your *father* is plotting to kill me?"

"You're telling me it's insane? I never would have believed it if I hadn't heard it from his own mouth. You've got to contact President Ryce and convince her to stop Dad. It's no good going directly to the police. Colonel Edgefield won't help us."

"So Colonel Edgefield is part of this . . . Liberty Cadre conspiracy?" The dubious note in Brannigan's voice made Ian grit his teeth. He leaned forward on the couch, winning himself a warning look from Martinez.

"Not directly involved." Daniel was struggling without success to keep his voice level. "But Colonel Edgefield won't dare move against Dad unless the evidence is incontestable."

"I see." Brannigan stood silent for a moment, stroking his chin. "Daniel, you are very agitated. You would do well to sit down."

Security guard Perris reached abruptly for the phone clipped to his belt. Ian watched askance as Perris read whatever was displayed on the screen. Perris's eyes narrowed and he glanced at Daniel Lansbury.

Daniel remained standing and spoke urgently. "Councilor, you've got to act *now*. Call President Ryce!"

"Daniel . . . please listen to me. You've been under a tremendous amount of stress. Jill Roshek's arrest—"

"This has nothing to do with that!"

"—*and* you've been associating with some questionable influences." Brannigan flung a stony look at Ian. "Let's sit down and take this slowly."

"There's not time to take it slowly! How long do you think it will take Dad to figure out I came to you?"

"Daniel . . ."

Ian couldn't keep quiet any longer. "Councilor, Daniel's not telling you some crazy theory he stitched together from mismatched pieces of evidence. We heard this from Marcus Lansbury himself."

Brannigan frowned at him, but said nothing.

"You know Daniel," Ian said. "And you know Councilor Lansbury. I'd say it's a lot easier to believe Councilor Lansbury found a creative way to further his ambitions than to believe Daniel has lost his wits so completely that he'd make up a story like *this*."

Security man Perris walked over to Martinez and whispered in his ear.

"The Council would need proof," Brannigan said.

"It won't be hard to find the physical proof that the Cadre tampered with Alisa Kent's testimony," Daniel said.

Brannigan's dubious frown returned. "This is absurd. Your father is certainly a ruthless and ambitious man, but I can't believe that—"

"Do you think I'd make up something this ludicrous?"

"I don't doubt that you believe what you're saying. But considering the strain you're under, I wonder if you could have misinterpreted—"

"There was nothing to misinterpret! Dad was very clear."

Ian wanted to grab Brannigan by the shirt and shake him. "Sir, you know Daniel is not a liar, so either he's right or he's insane. Are you willing to gamble your life on the assumption that Daniel has lost his mind?"

Brannigan searched Daniel's face. "No," he said at last. "No, I don't want to take that gamble. You are under great strain, Daniel, but I hope it would take more than that to render you delusional. Sit down. I'll go call President Ryce. It will be up to her as to how to proceed."

The insect buzz of a stun square startled Ian, and a thud shook the floor. Security man Martinez lay crumpled on the carpet, his body a motionless heap of blue suit a yard away from Ian's feet. Perris stood next to his unconscious colleague, gun in one hand, stun square in the other. The gun was pointed at Spencer Brannigan.

"Stay where you are, Councilor. And don't bother triggering a security alert. I already deactivated the system. Dr. Lansbury, drop your phone to the floor."

"Paul?" Brannigan whispered.

Perris swished his hand in an impatient gesture, his eyes cold. Daniel tossed his phone to the carpet.

Ian's tongue was parched, his limbs useless mush. *Of course.* This was how Marcus Lansbury had ensured that the Liberty Cadre would be able to murder Spencer Brannigan at the proper moment. One of Brannigan's own security men was a Cadre member.

"It wasn't supposed to happen this way," Perris said, "but it looks like Zero has changed his mind."

Brannigan moistened pale lips. "What about Daniel?" he asked coolly. "Would Councilor Lansbury order the death of his own son?"

"I don't know anything about Councilor Lansbury or where Dr. Lansbury got this crazy idea that he's Zero." Perris aimed the gun at Daniel. "But it sounds like Zero has some special plans for you. Sit down and stay out of my way, or I'll just explain I had no choice but to shoot you."

Daniel drew an angry breath and squared his shoulders, but Brannigan snapped, "Sit down, Daniel. There's no sense in you getting yourself killed."

"I'm not going to let—"

"*Sit down.* There's nothing you can do."

Daniel sat on the edge of the nearest chair. His face was gray.

Ian clenched his hands in his lap, the handcuffs searing his wrists. They had come this far only to sit helpless as Marcus Lansbury claimed his victory. Unless— "It's no good, Perris. Even if you kill Councilor Brannigan, Councilor Lansbury will still be connected with this mess."

Perris shrugged. "I don't know what you're talking about. I carry out my orders and Zero does the rest."

"Zero, whose name you now know," Ian said. "He can't afford that. Once you finish this assignment, his next victim will be *you.*"

Perris's jutting cheekbones flushed red. "You're wrong. There's no *way* Councilor Lansbury is Zero!"

"How else could Daniel have known the Cadre was planning to assassinate Councilor Brannigan?"

"I don't know! It doesn't matter."

"My father used you," Daniel said. "And if he thinks you could expose him, he'll kill you."

"If your father is Zero, then I'm Jim Tremont's Great-Aunt Susie."

"You're just tools to him," Ian tried again.

"You're crazy."

Ian tasted salty sweat as it slid down his upper lip. "*You're* crazy if you don't listen. Your life is riding on this. Councilor Lansbury *is* Zero and everything he's told you is a lie. You heard Daniel's report."

Perris began to look uncertain. "But Lansbury isn't—he can't be—" He shifted his grip on the gun.

"I can get you out of here, Paul," Brannigan said. "Take me as a hostage to ensure your safety. But first let me notify President Ryce about Councilor Lansbury. Think about it—if Zero is *not* Marcus Lansbury, what does the Liberty Cadre lose by implicating him? But if he *is* and you let me warn President Ryce, then he won't be able to touch you. You'll have a fair chance at escape."

"Yeah, right."

"I could get you to the United States."

Perris let the muzzle of the gun drop slightly. "How?"

"Fly you there," Brannigan said. "I'll order my pilot to take us both to the U.S. The police won't try to stop us."

"Uh-huh. And then we get shot down by the U.S. Air Force."

"Not with me on board."

"So they wait until we're on the ground and then they arrest me and ship me back to Tremont. Or shoot me. And you'd be useless as a hostage once we're on U.S. soil. They aren't going to shelter a Cadre man just to save the life of a New American Councilor."

"Then enter the U.S. on foot," Brannigan said. "I'll get you over the Tremont border with enough supplies to get you through the wasteland strip. If you're resourceful enough to work for the Cadre, you're resourceful enough to cross into the U.S. without getting caught."

Perris stood paralyzed.

"Think about what you're doing," Brannigan said. "Zero lied to you. You're not fighting for freedom. You might as well be wearing a police badge. Save your own life and let me get you out of here."

Perris shook his head and lifted the barrel of the gun to aim at Brannigan's heart. "You're lying. You're all crazy. Zero knows what he is doing. I'll take my chances with the Cadre before I'll gamble on your help. Sorry, Councilor." His finger began to close on the trigger.

"*No!*" Ian shouted the word without thinking as he hurled himself toward the Cadre assassin. Perris swung the gun in his direction and fired. Pain tore through Ian's chest. He tripped over the fallen

Martinez and crashed into Perris's legs, knocking Perris against the pedestal table.

Perris and the table toppled backward, Perris kicking to free his foot from beneath Ian's arm. He rolled away from the table, scrambling to stand, aiming but firing wildly as his foot slipped on the vase that lay in a pile of wet chrysanthemums. The crack of gunfire rattled Ian's eardrums once, twice, half a dozen times. Perris lurched backward, his gun falling from his hand.

Ian twisted his neck and saw Daniel Lansbury crouching over Martinez, a gun in his hand—Martinez's weapon, snatched from the holster of the unconscious security guard while Perris had been entangled with Ian and the table.

Daniel rushed to pick up Perris's weapon. Ian struggled to rise from the floor. The weight of his body pinned his shackled hands beneath him, and he couldn't seem to push himself up. Hot blood was soaking his shirt, but he didn't feel any pain except where the handcuffs dug into raw wrists. *Strange . . .*

An urgent jumble of voices . . . the thump of running footsteps . . . the slam of a door. A man wearing flannel pajamas sped past. Security guard Martinez wobbled to his feet.

Sirens wailed—soft, then earsplitting. The clatter of an approaching helicopter shook the room. Dizzily, Ian tried to roll onto his side. Brannigan was standing near the couch, speaking urgently into a phone. Why didn't Daniel get Brannigan out of here? He was still in danger—

Hands grabbed Ian and eased him onto his back. Daniel was kneeling next to him.

"Get Brannigan out of here," Ian gasped. "Your father might be—"

"The police are already on their way, and Councilor Brannigan is talking with President Ryce right now."

The grating pressure of the handcuffs was gone, his coat was open, fabric was tearing under Daniel's hands. "Daniel, *no* . . . you're wasting time . . . get Brannigan out of here before your father sends someone else—"

"Dad's people are already here. Councilor Brannigan's staff intercepted them, and they're under guard out by the gate." Something pressed against Ian's chest. Daniel's fingers were smeared with blood.

Ian had a hazy impression of blue and gray uniforms, hands prodding him, lifting him, the bang of a door, the growl of an engine, glaring lights. The pain came at last—excruciating, overwhelming, spiraling him into nothingness.

CHAPTER 22

It looked *almost* like the hospital room where they'd kept him ever since he'd come out of surgery. There were the same monitors and tubes and flashing red numbers, and Ian blearily decided it must be an illusion that the walls had closed in and turned gray and the painted door had been stripped to bare steel. Standing near the door was a young woman in a police uniform. Bobbed brown hair, a solemn, quiet face. He'd seen her a couple of times, but her name was lost in a haze of pain and drugs.

A tall figure in blue was leaning over him, peeling back the bandages on his chest. Hoping to drift back to sleep, Ian let his eyes close, but a dull sense of recognition nudged him back toward alertness. He blinked his eyes into focus.

"Daniel," he mumbled. "You work at the hospital?"

"You're at the Detention Annex now." Daniel refastened the bandages. "They brought you here last night."

"Oh." Ian made a feeble effort to locate that memory and found only blankness. "Guess I wasn't . . . paying attention."

"They sedated you for the transfer." Daniel picked up Ian's chart.

Wanting a better look at his surroundings, Ian tried to push himself up on his elbows, but pain left him grinding the enamel off his teeth. He sank back.

"Teresa just gave you your pain medication," Daniel said. "You'll be feeling it in a moment."

"Thanks," Ian gasped. *Teresa . . . oh yeah, the nurse from the hospital, the older one with the military bearing and an air of authority like she commands a battleship in her spare time.* What was she doing at the Detention Annex? And why was Daniel Lansbury caring for him? They wouldn't have assigned Daniel—

"How did you get stuck with me as a patient?"

"Colonel Edgefield is limiting the number of people who come into contact with prisoners who have classified information about the Liberty Cadre. I'm your medical supervisor. The only other people you'll see here are the same two nurses who cared for you at the hospital and a couple of police officers."

"Why the paranoia? They—know I won't talk."

"They know you won't talk when you can control what comes out of your mouth. But when you're so medicated that you don't know what you're saying, or when you're hallucinating—" He shrugged. "They have to be careful."

Ian tried to swallow. His lips were cracked, his throat lined with sandpaper. "How—how is Jill?"

"She's on the medium-security floor. I haven't seen her."

"Have you heard anything?"

"She's all right. She's recovering well."

Relief doused a few of the hot coals filling Ian's chest. "What will happen to her?"

Daniel jotted something on Ian's chart. "No sentences have been issued yet."

Since Daniel didn't seem averse to answering questions, Ian cautiously ventured another one. "Alisa Kent?"

"Recovering slowly."

Ian wanted to ask how much the Liberty Cadre's tampering with Kent's mind had affected her recovery from Information Extraction, but he didn't dare mention the Cadre with a police officer standing sentinel at the door. His ignorance about the aftermath of the confrontation at Brannigan's maddened him. Had Marcus Lansbury been captured? Had the Cadre been destroyed?

The door swung open and a man with a blond crew cut and a narrow, rock-hard face marched into the room. Ian tensed at the sight of the man who had warned him that if he spoke to anyone about the Liberty Cadre, Jill would suffer. Even through the blur of pain and medication, he remembered that warning with stark clarity.

"Everything on schedule?" Lt. Peale asked.

"The session can go forward tomorrow morning," Daniel said.

"On time! What do you know?" Lt. Peale mocked.

Daniel's mouth tightened, but he said nothing.

"Just thought Roshek might like to see today's news." Peale dropped a folded printout on the bed next to Ian. Eagerly, Ian reached for it, but Daniel swiped it away.

"Later," Daniel snapped, startling Ian.

A hard smile on his lips, Peale took the paper out of Daniel's hand and returned it to Ian. "Don't be such a mother hen, Lansbury."

"This is not a good time to upset—"

"Don't fuss. We've still got a day before the I-X."

Puzzled at the hostility arcing between the two men, Ian awkwardly unfolded the paper.

And new pain spread outward from his chest like liquid fire.

"Exciting to be headline news, isn't it?" Peale said. "Bet you scummy Garrett martyr types just dream of this kind of thing."

"Is this a joke?"

"Depends on your sense of humor." Peale leaned close to his ear. "Did it ever occur to you that if Garrett's god exists, He doesn't like you very much?"

Daniel ripped the paper out of Ian's hands. "He needs rest."

"Oh, sorry. Am I upsetting your friend?"

"It's Captain Whitney you'll be upsetting if you do anything to delay the I-X."

"That won't happen. Roshek's got twenty-four hours to settle down. This will just give him plenty to think about afterwards."

"He's not going to be thinking about anything afterwards. He doesn't have the strength to endure stage two; we'll have to keep him medicated until he's through it." Daniel held the newspaper out to Peale.

"Keep it," Peale said. "You might find it entertaining."

Daniel's voice was solid ice. "No, thanks."

"Little touchy, aren't you? What would you rather have them print? The truth?"

Daniel blanched white with fury.

"See you tomorrow." Peale strode out of the room.

"Give that back, Daniel." Ian reached for the newspaper, but Daniel rolled it and shoved it into the pocket of his lab coat.

"You've read enough."

"Not enough to make sense of it." Ian pushed himself up on his elbows, ignoring the pain and the nauseating swish of dizziness. "I'm Zero's *henchman*? I killed your parents? I tried to kill Spencer Brannigan?"

Daniel pressed him back onto the pillow. "Stay quiet."

Anger shook Ian in waves, and his heart pumped so fast he felt he couldn't draw in enough oxygen to keep it beating. He hadn't expected the Council to announce that Marcus Lansbury was Zero. He'd hoped, but hadn't expected it. But this—to end up center stage in a production of lies— He closed his eyes, fighting to calm himself.

He heard Daniel talking to someone, the door opening, the murmur of a female voice. A hand touched his arm. He opened one eye and saw Daniel sliding a needle into his IV port.

"What—is that?"

"It's going to help you get some rest."

"I—don't want it."

"Did I ask you what you wanted?"

"What . . . does the news say about Jill?"

"She's not involved."

Relief shimmered alongside the sedative spreading through his body. "They're . . . planning to kill me, aren't they? A public execution—"

"Get some rest, Ian."

"Why did they . . . go to so much trouble . . . to save my life?" He struggled to stay conscious.

"When they brought you to the hospital, they weren't sure what information you had about the Cadre and David Garrett's movement. They needed to question you."

"Stupid . . . they already know what I know . . . what about Alisa Kent? She's . . . still the Newbold Bay bomber?" His words were thick; he could barely understand them himself.

"Get some rest."

"Just *tell* me . . ." But strength was gone; even his anger rippled thin and cool.

He slept.

CHAPTER 23

Lt. Blake Peale lingered in his office, keeping the door ajar so he could see into the corridor. He wanted to enjoy the expression on Daniel Lansbury's face when Lansbury left Captain Whitney's office.

It would be a pleasure to see Lansbury's arrogance shattered at last. In the month since the Council and a select few police officers had learned that Marcus Lansbury was the head of the Liberty Cadre, Daniel Lansbury had still acted as though he were above the reach of the police. Unassailable in his loyalty. Untouchable! And Colonel Edgefield had fed Lansbury's delusions by keeping him in his high-security position at the Detention Annex.

Peale hoped things would improve now that Edgefield had finally been forced to resign and Colonel Glenna McLaughlin had been elevated to Edgefield's post. Peale was disappointed that McLaughlin hadn't immediately relieved Daniel Lansbury of his responsibilities, but he understood the reason behind her lack of action. At this late date, McLaughlin probably didn't want to expose any new personnel to prisoners who knew the truth about the Liberty Cadre.

Peale conceded that Daniel Lansbury had proven dedicated to the destruction of the Cadre, first figuring out a way to reverse the conditioning process that allowed the Cadre to falsify I-X testimony, then overseeing the interrogation and recovery of Cadre prisoners. Outwardly, he'd done his job. But inwardly, he was rotten. The evidence was so plain. His father, the head of the Liberty Cadre! His girlfriend, a traitor. His friend, a Garrett follower. Then there was the way he treated his patients—vigorously intervening to ward off Broc psychosis in Alisa Kent, keeping

Ian Roshek so drugged up following I-X that Roshek hardly suffered at all.

Smiling, Peale buffed his silver badge with his sleeve. Jill Roshek's refusal to cooperate with Colonel McLaughlin had provided the perfect opportunity for Peale to expose Lansbury's inner decay. Captain Whitney, who had taken the disgraced Hofstader's place as the head of the Sedition and Treason Division, approved his suggestion and relayed it to Colonel McLaughlin, who also gave it the nod and presented it to the Council. Of course, Peale wasn't naive enough to think McLaughlin had mentioned him by name. But Peale had certainly done well for his career.

Half an hour passed before Daniel Lansbury emerged from Captain Whitney's office. His bony face was pale, his eyes glassy.

Chuckling under his breath, Peale waited until Daniel Lansbury boarded the elevator. Then he went to visit Whitney.

"Come in, Blake." Whitney reached for a steaming coffee mug.

"How'd he take it?"

Whitney grunted. "Not well. He begged for the chance to reason with her. I said he could try. Pulansky's taking him over there now."

Peale frowned. "What if he talks her into it?"

"What if he does? Have you forgotten that Colonel McLaughlin *wants* that denunciation?"

"No, sir."

"If Lansbury refuses to carry out his assignment, you can take him down. But if he proves loyal, I expect you to back off."

"Yes, sir." Peale wasn't worried. The only thing Daniel Lansbury was going to prove was that his veins ran with the blood of a traitor.

* * *

The beep of the lock startled Jill Roshek out of her dismal daydreaming. Quickly, she sat up and faced the door.

The sight of her visitor jarred her with the momentary fear that the hallucinations had returned. Unable to breathe, she stared at him.

Daniel Lansbury stepped into the cell. Someone in the hall pushed the door shut behind him.

"Hello, Jill," he said. "How are you feeling?"

"I'm all right." Blood burned her cheeks. She slid back against the wall and folded her arms around her knees. Daniel looked different. Older.

"You've lost too much weight." He sounded nervous.

"I'm all right."

Daniel crossed the cell, moving hesitantly like he was afraid to approach her. He sat on the end of the cot. "Captain Whitney told me you've been informed of Ian's crimes."

Jill pushed tangled hair behind her ear. "Yes."

"He also told me you were invited to make a speech at the execution in exchange for a reduced sentence, but you refused."

"That's—that's right."

"I hope you'll reconsider, Jill. If you refuse to give that speech, they'll take it to mean that you support what Ian did."

"I know."

"Jill . . . if you support him, that makes you an anarchist as well. Do you understand that?"

"Yes."

"If you won't denounce him—"

"I know all that," she interrupted harshly.

"All they want you to say is that you reject what he stood for. It's just a public way of distancing yourself from him, a way to reaffirm your own patriotism."

"That's not all it is." She rubbed the skin on her right ring finger. The police had taken her mother's ring along with everything else, but she still reached for it when she got anxious. "They want me to lie about him."

"What makes you think they want you to lie?"

It was difficult to get the words out in front of Daniel Lansbury. He'd be appalled to hear her criticize the Tremont Police Service. But what did it matter anyway? He couldn't possibly think worse of her than he did now. "They want me to say Ian was a murderer, a leader of the anarchists that killed the children in Newbold Bay."

Daniel didn't look her in the eyes as he spoke. "How do you know he wasn't? You have no idea what he was up to."

"He'd never hurt anyone."

"He hurt *you.*" Daniel's voice sharpened. "He's the reason you're in here."

"That's not true. I'm in here for what *I* did. I could have turned him over to the police. It was my own choice not to."

"It still comes back to Ian's crimes."

"I don't care."

"You *know* he's a criminal. You *know* he's an anarchist."

"I know he's a religious believer. I know he studied contraband literature. But that's only part of what Colonel McLaughlin wants me to say."

"What difference does it make? An anarchist is an anarchist. Are you more loyal to your traitor brother than to your country?"

Tears welled in her eyes. She blinked, hoping the tears would disappear before Daniel noticed them. "I won't lie about him."

"Jill—"

"He'd rather die than hurt anyone else."

Daniel's face was stony, and Jill wondered if he was fighting to hide the contempt he felt for her. "Ian will die no matter what you do. It's foolish for you to die as well."

The tears overflowed. "I'd rather die than get up there and say that he—that he—"

"Think about what Ian would want. Don't you think he'd rather have you cooperate with the police than die because you won't say a few meaningless words?"

Meaningless words. Daniel was as good as admitting that the accusations Colonel McLaughlin had leveled at Ian were lies. "He'd die before he'd get up there and lie about *me,*" she said.

Daniel reached for her hand. At the touch of his fingers, she felt limp with desperation.

"Please think about it," he said. "You've got a few more days to decide."

She drew a shaky breath. "I've already decided." Daniel could probably feel how badly she was shaking, but she couldn't gather the willpower to pull her hand away. She wanted to cling to him, cry on his shoulder, beg him to help her.

"It's just a speech." Daniel released her hand. "Just words."

"I won't get up there and tell people he's some kind of . . . monster who deserves to die."

"He *does* deserve to die! You know that for yourself." The savagery in Daniel's voice shocked Jill. "He told you he was a religious believer. You saw his book—David Garrett's propaganda. He allied himself with the enemies of James Tremont and tried to influence others to do the same. Isn't that enough?"

"How did he get caught?"

"What do you mean?"

"When he was arrested. How did he get caught? He was going to the United States. He had a car; he said that woman, that officer—Alisa Kent—had given him a way to escape. Why didn't he make it?"

"Jill, that's completely irrelevant."

"He didn't even try to leave, did he?" Tears streamed off her jaw, dotting her prisoner's uniform. "Because I ran away from him. He stayed to find me."

"Jill, *please.*" The misery in Daniel's eyes made her mouth fall open. Daniel *did* still care.

"Can't you help us?" she pleaded. "Can't you do something—ask your father to help—?"

Daniel closed his eyes. "I can't help you unless you cooperate with Colonel McLaughlin."

A sob swelled in her throat. She pressed her face to her knees, struggling to control herself.

For a long moment, Daniel was silent. Then he stood and walked over to rap on the cell door. The door opened, then banged shut.

* * *

"It's good to see you, Daniel." Spencer Brannigan's welcoming smile looked dulled by fatigue as he gestured Daniel into the house. "I've been worried about you."

"I'm sorry I haven't answered your messages. I've been busy."

"I understand." Brannigan squeezed his shoulder, a silent acknowledgment that he knew it wasn't simply lack of time that had kept Daniel away. Daniel had dreaded coming tonight. But Brannigan was the only one who could help him now.

"Nate Halbrook was over here a few nights ago," Brannigan said. "He was asking about you."

Daniel had been ignoring Nate's messages too. "Yes . . . I need to call him." He eyed the living room as they passed the arched doorway. The bloodstained carpet was now spotless ivory, the bullet-pocked wall an unmarred expanse of new paint. Despite the lack of visible damage, Daniel was relieved that Brannigan bypassed the room and led him to another room, decorated in emerald green and soft white. Caroline's music room. Daniel touched the polished lid of the grand piano, thinking of the hours spent here in childhood music lessons and wishing Caroline could be here now with that determined sparkle in her eyes, that motherly protectiveness, that witty sense of humor.

"Have a seat," Brannigan said. "What would you like to drink?"

"Just water, thanks."

"Are you on call?"

"Yes."

"When are they going to let you rest?"

"I don't want to rest. And I couldn't take time off even if I did want to."

"Yes, it's been chaotic downtown. The Council has been reviewing the reports." Brannigan poured mineral water into a glass and offered it to Daniel. "Three officers of the Tremont Police Service and a Detention Annex doctor exposed as Cadre members, along with a dozen people in other government departments. Thirty-nine Cadre members accounted for nationwide, either arrested or dead, out of a grand total of forty-six members—if Todd Kinnock knows what he's talking about."

Daniel absently traced his finger through the condensation on the side of his glass. Todd Kinnock, his father's quietly efficient secretary, now exposed as "One," Zero's top man. Kinnock *thought* he'd been completely in Marcus Lansbury's confidence, and the police seemed convinced that Kinnock's information was complete, but Daniel had his doubts. His father was too careful to confide everything in one person.

Brannigan settled in an armchair. His gaze was kind, but penetrating. "How are you doing?"

Daniel shrugged.

"Both your parents gone . . . I suppose it's not much comfort to you that your mother wasn't actively involved with the Cadre."

"She's involved now. She's on the run with Zero." Daniel avoided Brannigan's eyes. He didn't like thinking about his mother. It hurt too much to wonder if she hated him now, sharing the rage and contempt his father must feel for him.

"The Council has done an efficient job of publicizing a humiliating disaster as a triumph," Brannigan said. "Your father has been transformed from anarchist to martyr, and Ian Roshek and Alisa Kent are conveniently in place to represent the defeated Liberty Cadre."

Daniel stared into his glass. The water rippled as a tremor shook his hand. "I'm surprised the Council didn't vote to name Ian Roshek as Zero himself."

"Believe me, there are those who would have liked to present Dr. Roshek as Zero. But unfortunately, Roshek lacked the connections that would have made him a credible Zero. Alisa Kent was a more believable candidate, but she had already been publicized as a Cadre police informant, and it would have been awkward to change her role. The Council will have to be content with the story that the never-to-be-named Zero died in a shoot-out with the police—much as they would have liked to cast the chief villain as the star in a public execution."

"They'll still have their public execution." Daniel tried to make the words dispassionate, but anger coiled around them.

"Yes," Brannigan said. "They'll have their execution. I'm sorry, Daniel."

Daniel set his glass aside, accidentally knocking over a photo of Caroline. He fumbled to right the frame. "They told you."

"Of course they told us. Colonel McLaughlin sought Council sanction before she approved the assignment. A public show of vengeance. As far as the nation knows, Ian Roshek killed your parents. Thus you'll represent the nation in destroying Roshek, Newbold Bay bomber Alisa Kent, and, symbolically, the Liberty Cadre itself. As long as we need an executioner, why not throw in a loyalty test for you as well?"

Pain wrenched Daniel's chest. "Why do they have to drag Jill into this?"

"They're a bit edgy about this deception they're trumpeting. Colonel McLaughlin suggested that Jill be offered the chance to denounce her brother at his execution in exchange for a reduced sentence. Jill's fervent denunciation of Ian Roshek as an anarchist assassin would shore up the police fictions."

"She won't do it," Daniel said.

"Yes, I know. And Jill's stubborn loyalty to her brother is all the excuse Colonel McLaughlin needed to order her execution as well. They won't have their dramatic denunciation, but they will be able to tie off a loose end." Anguish darkened Brannigan's eyes. "Plus it gives them that tidy opportunity to test *your* loyalty. If, for the sake of the nation, you can execute the woman you loved, then you *are* a solid patriot and should be allowed to continue your life without police interference. If you balk, you'll have destroyed yourself—and they'll execute her anyway. Either way, they'll have solved the problem of how to deal with Zero's son."

"Can you do something to help her? They're planning to execute her in secret. They could just as easily let her live. The nation won't know the difference."

"Don't you think I've tried? I fought all of this in the Council, but the vote went against me. Yesterday I spent an hour in private conference with President Ryce, and I'll tell you, Daniel, in confidence, that Ryce would like to help, but she won't. She was shaken when she learned your father regarded her as weak and corrupt, and she won't veto a Council ruling if it means doing anything that might be construed as merciful toward traitors."

Despair weighted Daniel. "What do I do now?"

"If you refuse to perform the executions, or any one of them, that will be interpreted as an act of treason. I'm sorry to speak so bluntly, but facts are facts."

Treason. The word seemed to echo off the vaulted ceiling.

"You would be executed," Brannigan added baldly. "Considering the classified knowledge you hold, Colonel McLaughlin would never risk sending you to prison."

Coldness trickled through Daniel.

"You'd be executed and Jill would still die. Your death wouldn't save her."

Daniel smiled bitterly. Wasn't that the same argument he had tried to use on Jill this afternoon?

"This is an ugly, ugly situation," Brannigan said. "But the Council has ruled, and we are required to accept their decision." His voice softened. "Don't lose hope. As the execution nears, Jill may well change her mind."

"She won't." Not Jill, not the woman so fiercely, blindly loyal to Ian that she had refused to recognize his treason even when he'd done everything short of quoting Garrett's propaganda to her face.

"How is Ian Roshek taking all this?" Brannigan asked after a moment.

"No one's told him what's happening with Jill. And I've been ordered not to tell him either."

"Odd. I'd have thought they would enjoy throwing it in his face. And as to his upcoming debut as a Cadre assassin?"

"Furious at first. Now he seems calm. Resigned. He doesn't talk about it."

"If it were me," Brannigan said, "I think I'd have a lot to say."

"I'm sure there's a lot he'd like to say, but the police warned him that if he discussed the Cadre outside of interrogation, Jill would pay for it."

Brannigan winced. He picked up a white porcelain rose and rotated it in his hands. "I read your report on Roshek."

"You did?"

"A very thorough report. Very objective. And very devoid of the disparaging psychological catchphrases normally used to describe religious believers." Brannigan ran his fingers over the rose petals and examined the fragile leaves before setting the rose aside. "You spent a great deal of time talking to him about his beliefs, didn't you?"

Daniel's face reddened. "I'm not sure what you're implying, Councilor. As Ian Roshek's medical supervisor, analyzing the philosophy that he used to justify his crimes is part of my job."

"But admiring him and his Mormon philosophy is not."

"*Councilor.*" Daniel was outraged.

"The police and the Council are questioning your loyalty. Are they justified?"

"How can they question my loyalty? I gave them my father!"

"Alisa Kent made a similar sacrifice," Brannigan pointed out.

"And she was honored for it. Why am I being treated like a criminal?"

"I suppose you *would* have been honored for turning your father in, except that we were so embarrassed to learn that Marcus Lansbury was Zero that we weren't inclined to praise the person who brought the truth to our attention. And—I'm sorry, Daniel—there were also the facts that you spent the months prior to Zero's exposure falling in love with a traitor and befriending a Garrett follower."

Daniel was so angry that the words he wanted to speak stuck in his throat like splinters of wood.

"I'm speaking bluntly for your benefit," Brannigan said. "*Are* the police and the Council justified in questioning your loyalty?"

"*No.*"

"Then you're ready and willing to perform the executions?"

Daniel's anger died in a cold rush of confusion.

"I'm sorry," Brannigan said. "Perhaps I've spoken too harshly. There aren't many people whose patriotism could meet the challenge we've set for you. Let me just ask you this: is it only *Jill's* impending execution that bothers you?"

The question should have infuriated Daniel, but he felt only emptiness.

"You watched Ian Roshek give up his chance for freedom to come back and fight the Liberty Cadre," Brannigan said. "You saw him willing to die in order to save my life. He's a traitor and you shouldn't admire him, but you do."

Daniel couldn't muster the energy to defend himself. Maybe Brannigan was right. Maybe he wasn't. Daniel didn't want to think about it.

"Don't you think I understand your feelings?" Brannigan said. "I'm sickened by how the Council has voted to handle this matter. Sickened—enraged—and helpless." His mouth thinned. "I'd appreciate it if you don't repeat what I just said. I don't want to give my enemies more excuses to accuse me of anarchist sympathies."

"I love Jill." It was like unlocking heavy chains to admit that truth aloud—truth he had denied to himself since the moment of Jill's arrest. "I thought if I didn't have to execute Jill, then I could do the others, but after talking to Jill this afternoon, and you now, I don't know what I think. Maybe I deserve what's happening to me."

"It's easy to be loyal to the Council until their decisions bring pain to you personally. When pain comes, you find out if your loyalty has any roots."

Daniel could hear his father's voice, cold and furious, censuring him for turning against his heritage. For shaming his family.

His father. Zero. The man who had murdered his own brother to gain his seat on the Council.

Brannigan's eyes were tired, filled with sadness. "Would you like my advice?"

"Please," Daniel whispered.

"Go ahead with the executions. It will hurt you, but it won't make a difference to the prisoners—not for long. Your feelings in the matter—your love for Jill, your reluctant admiration for Ian Roshek, your sympathy for Alisa Kent—"

"I never said I sympathized with—"

"Well, do you?"

Daniel paused, then sighed, a miserable smile on his lips. Why deny it? He had already tacitly admitted to far worse failings. "I guess I do. Hers is a painful story."

"I agree. But you've already done everything you can to help these people. The life on the line now is *yours*. Remember that, ultimately, it will make no difference to the Rosheks and to Alisa Kent who carries out the duties of executioner."

Daniel tried to consider the truth of Brannigan's statement, but his mind was deadened.

"Propaganda aside, things in New America are not perfect," Brannigan said. "James Tremont was far from perfect. His successors are not perfect. But we *do* have order. We have peace. And even when the Council makes some missteps, as I believe they've done this time, we're obligated to support them."

Daniel nodded mechanically.

"We can fix what's wrong in the system, but it's a slow, painstaking process." Brannigan stretched his hand toward Daniel. "I *need* you, Daniel. The nation needs you. You know I'm working for reforms that will keep us from being at the mercy of greedy people who cloak their ambition beneath so-called devotion to 'Tremont's legacy.' With your father discredited—and not present to deride every word I speak—talk of a written constitution has become more serious. Things will change, but it will take time. You can play a role in bringing about that change. Show your inflexible loyalty at the executions and you'll have all the support you need to eventually gain a seat on the Council. Don't sacrifice yourself for nothing. Live, and help us."

Brannigan's voice merged eerily with Daniel's memory of the voice of Marcus Lansbury. Offering rewards, stating a price.

Living with the memory of Jill looking up at him while he slipped that deadly needle into her arm.

Sweeping through his numbness came the same revulsion he'd felt while standing over Alisa Kent with a syringe of Broc4 in his hand, struggling to convince himself that murdering her through the slow, agonizing disintegration of her mind was an act of patriotic necessity.

His father's words: *"It's necessary, as the Liberty Cadre was necessary."*

As Ian's death was necessary, as Jill's death was necessary.

I can't do this. The thought came with a conviction he hadn't expected, and a peaceful feeling seemed to wipe out his confusion.

"You're exhausted," Brannigan said. "Stay here tonight and get some sleep. I'll call the Detention Annex personally and see to it that someone covers your responsibilities. They've asked too much of you."

"I'm fine." He did feel fine, better than he'd felt in weeks, with a warm sense of calm that unsnarled the knots in his chest. He'd made his decision. He wasn't going to perform the executions—any of them.

From the way Brannigan was looking at him, Daniel knew he had sensed a change, but Brannigan misinterpreted it. "It will be terrible for you. I know that." Brannigan's voice was gravelly with pain. "This whole situation is maddening. Absurd. An execution turned into a theatrical production, complete with actors in the starring roles—people being executed mainly for fictional crimes."

Daniel's mouth curled in a macabre smile. *A theatrical production.* Well, they'd have to find someone else to cast as the executioner. What would McLaughlin tell the media to excuse his disappearance? An accident? A gun in the hand of some Cadre straggler?

What would it be like to die? Was Ian Roshek right? Was there an immortal soul, a part of him that would continue to live after his body was in the ground?

It was strangely easy to believe that now.

"I'm sorry," Brannigan said. "I can't tell you how sorry I am. If there were anything I could do to take this out of your hands—"

"I know. Thank you for talking to President Ryce. But they've got their script—" he stopped.

A theatrical production. The words filled Daniel's mind like sunlight.

"Daniel?"

Daniel tried to moisten his lips, but his mouth had dried to paper. "Nothing. I'm all right."

"You're ill," Brannigan said. "I'll show you to a room."

"I'm fine. Thank you, Councilor. I appreciate your advice."

"Stay here tonight. You shouldn't be alone."

"I'm fine. You're right; it's foolish to sacrifice myself for nothing. At least I can ensure that the executions are smooth and painless. Done with dignity."

Relief loosened some of the anxiety in Brannigan's face, but he still looked doubtful as he escorted Daniel to the door. "Call me tomorrow."

"I will. Thank you." Daniel hurried down the flagstone steps toward his car, conscious of Brannigan's uneasy gaze following him.

Daniel sped away from Brannigan's. Half an hour later, he arrived at Nathan Halbrook's.

CHAPTER 24

As soon as the officers finished strapping her to the Euth Center gurney, Jill closed her eyes. It would be easier to stay calm if she couldn't see her surroundings, and especially if she didn't have to look anyone in the face.

She filled her mind with the memory that had comforted her over the past weeks—Ian's words about death being temporary, about their parents still existing. She knew now that he'd been talking about his religious beliefs, ideas that were probably contained in that book he'd kept hidden. It was treasonous to hope the things Ian believed were true, but she didn't care. She was already condemned to death.

A click—the swish of the door opening—the rhythm of shoes on tile. Who was entering the room? The executioner? She sealed her eyes more securely shut and pictured her mother, the creases at the corners of her eyes when she smiled. The bristly warmth of her father's cheek when she kissed him good night.

Maybe soon she'd be with them.

Was there really a God? How could there be?

But Ian had believed.

Chilly fingers touched her arm, and something squeezed her arm above the elbow. She flinched at the sting of a needle entering her vein.

"You made a stupid decision, Jill." Lt. Peale's voice grated like rocks scraping on concrete. "A beautiful young woman with a promising musical career ahead of you, and you chucked it all away. If you'd cooperated with us, you wouldn't have been even thirty years old when you finished your prison sentence."

Jill bit the inside of her lip.

"You'd love to denounce your brother now, wouldn't you? You'd say anything we wanted."

She shook her head.

"Too late anyway. You made your choice. Oh—you might want to say hello to your executioner. I think you know Dr. Lansbury?"

Jill's eyes flew open. Standing above her, his fingers connecting the tube in her arm to a tube extending from the termination machine, was Daniel Lansbury.

"Daniel!" she cried. *"Daniel."*

He didn't even look at her.

* * *

As Lt. Peale and Officer Pulansky escorted Ian from his cell on the evening of his execution, they kept such a crushing grip on his arms that he was tempted to tell them to relax. In view of the weakness that lingered from his injuries, the thought of escape was laughable. Even if they had removed the handcuffs and leg irons, thrown the doors open, and given him a head start, he probably couldn't have made it more than five steps before collapsing.

Ian hoped the trip to the Tremont Euthanasia Center would allow him to see Alisa Kent, but she was not in the van with him. Had Colonel McLaughlin decided to transport the prisoners separately to keep them from speaking to each other on forbidden topics? She should know by now that he wouldn't risk Jill's safety by discussing the Cadre with anyone.

The van sped toward the Euthanasia Center, and Ian's worries about Jill burgeoned. Why wouldn't anyone tell him what was happening to her? Daniel Lansbury had volunteered information on the fates of all the other people involved in this catastrophe: Eric Vettori, Tim Sandring, Sherry Mason, and Laura and Matt Travers had all been arrested and shipped to the most isolated of prisons. Cadre thug Siskell was dead, murdered by another Cadre member. Todd Kinnock had been quietly executed. Marcus Lansbury was missing, but Daniel had hinted that the police were not searching for him with any genuine enthusiasm. A large-scale manhunt was impossible when only a handful of officers even knew Marcus was still alive, and if they did bring him in, they'd face the problematic task of keeping his arrest and execution secret. Ian wondered if Marcus might have fled to the United States.

But as to Jill, Daniel either didn't know or wouldn't tell what had been decided for her.

The van stopped. Pulansky opened the doors and Peale shoved Ian into an underground garage. A row of white Euth Center vehicles, a scattering of patrol cars, and several glossy black limousines were the only other vehicles parked there. Ian's escorts ushered him through a steel door into a brown-tiled corridor. At the end of the corridor, they passed through a set of double doors into a room scorched by clusters of lights.

The room was two stories high. On the ground level, two gurneys were set up about five feet apart. Next to each gurney stood what looked like a white cabinet on wheels. Ian scrutinized the cabinets—termination machines, containing the chemicals that would administer death, and the monitors that would tell the executioner when the job was done.

Somehow, he had expected them to look more ominous.

A windowed gallery ringed the second story of the room, jammed with government officials and representatives from the National, Regional, and Neighborhood Security Watches. Only a dozen or so people were seated on the ground floor within earshot of the prisoners. Ian scanned the group, recognizing Colonel McLaughlin and Patrick Haines, the man who had taken Marcus Lansbury's place as Councilor over Internal Defense. The sight of Spencer Brannigan brought a jab of despair. Even Brannigan was supporting this travesty. At least Brannigan looked grim and pale, distinctly not happy to be there.

Standing near the wall was the familiar, lanky figure of Daniel Lansbury. Why hadn't Daniel mentioned that he would personally witness the executions?

The treading of boots announced the arrival of the second condemned prisoner and her escorts. Pain twisted inside Ian at the sight of Alisa Kent. Her tan prisoner's uniform sagged over her gaunt body, and her arms seemed white twigs ready to snap under the weight of the manacles encircling her wrists. Her gaze met Ian's—

dazed, apprehensive. He smiled a wry greeting. To his surprise, her mouth curved in a tentative response.

At a nod from Colonel McLaughlin, Peale and Pulansky yanked Ian toward one of the gurneys so roughly that Ian stumbled. With the chains binding his ankles, he had trouble regaining his footing and ended up being dragged the last few steps.

With an effort, Ian kept his expression blank. He knew they were trying to provoke him to anger, or more dramatically yet, to resistance. Calmly, he waited as Pulansky unlocked his restraints. He moved to climb onto the gurney, and Peale spoke, his voice a low hiss.

"Too bad you won't be able to watch your sister's execution."

Ian's fingers gouged the padded edge of the gurney. *"What?"*

"I'm sure you would have gotten a kick out of seeing her die, but the timing didn't work out."

"You're going to kill her? *Why?* I never violated your orders. I never talked."

"So?"

"What's her crime? She didn't do anything worthy of death."

"She's scum," Peale said complacently. "Like her brother."

"It's not for any crime, is it? What did you make up for *her?*"

"Lie down." Grinning, Peale shoved Ian against the side of the gurney.

Ian's newly freed hand grabbed Peale's arm. "She doesn't know the truth. She's no threat."

Peale knocked Ian's hand away and Pulansky grabbed his arm. Ian jerked away from Pulansky, elbowing Peale aside so he could see to where Councilor Haines and Colonel McLaughlin were seated.

"Please—Councilor—Colonel—Jill Roshek doesn't deserve to die." Ian struggled as Peale and Pulanksy turned him away. "Jill doesn't *know* anything; it's pointless to—"

McLaughlin made a slight gesture in Ian's direction. The two officers who had escorted Alisa Kent charged toward him.

"*Please.* You've got your showpiece execution; have mercy and let Jill live. She doesn't—" Multiple hands hauled Ian backward and slammed him onto the gurney. Straps bit into his wrists, his upper arms, his ankles. He strained to look past the officers to where Haines and McLaughlin watched in impassive silence.

"*Please,*" he gasped, winded by the pain in his chest. "Don't kill her, don't turn this into a sordid joke. She—" Hands pinned his head to the gurney.

"Anarchists do like to rant, don't they?" Lt. Peale fastened a wide strip of tape over Ian's mouth. "We thought we might need a gag for you."

The other officers moved away, leaving Peale at Ian's side. Peale leaned over and spoke so only Ian could hear him. "Bravo, Roshek. Thanks for the entertainment. Just so you know, the spectators in the gallery enjoyed the fight, but they couldn't hear a word you were saying. The nation *will* hear your ranting—after it's edited. You'll be shouting curses and threats at the Council on national television."

Rage hammered at every cell in Ian's body.

"Oh. And your sister's already dead. Lansbury executed her two days ago. Now he can finish off you and Kent."

Peale swaggered over to where the officers were fastening Alisa Kent to the second gurney. Daniel Lansbury approached Ian, his expression granite.

Ian averted his face. If he looked at Daniel, he'd end up struggling like a maniac, wanting only to rip the gag loose so he could shout his fury.

Daniel had killed Jill for what he knew was a lie.

Daniel's fingers were colder than ice on Ian's arm, and the prick of the needle hurt like the stab of a knife. Ian tried to slow his breathing, tried to stop himself from trembling. *Jill's already dead. You can't help her; you can't change things. She's with your parents now. Do you think she's sad about that?*

Calmer, Ian watched as Daniel walked to the gurney where Alisa Kent lay. The termination machine blocked Ian's view of Kent; he could see only her legs and one thin, pale hand. If he could just speak to her—

Tiredness spread over him, weakening his muscles, tugging at his eyelids. He'd have his chance to speak to Alisa Kent. And to Jill.

A slight ache marked the spot where the tube penetrated his skin and he could sense the coolness of fluid dripping into his arm. Saline? The poison wouldn't come until President Ryce had delivered a speech from her office at the Council Building.

"*. . . The spirits of all men, as soon as they are departed from this mortal body . . . are taken home to that God who gave them life . . .*"

Daniel Lansbury stepped away from Alisa Kent. A trumpet fanfare blared and Amanda Ryce's brusque voice echoed in the execution room. Ian shut her words out of his mind and returned to words of comfort:

"The Son reigneth, and hath power over the dead; therefore, he bringeth to pass the resurrection—" Ian's thoughts smeared like paint, and his body seemed to sink into the gurney. Had Daniel given him a sedative? No . . . they'd want him alert and terrified until the last moment. Was he going into shock?

Ian squirmed, limbs barely responsive, numb to the straps binding them. Ryce's voice blurred into murky ripples of sound, sweeping away his resistance. He rode the currents, relaxing in the wash of meaningless syllables.

A crash of applause skimmed Ian's awareness, and then silence filled his ears like water. *Speech must be over . . .* Dimly, he saw Daniel rise from a stool at the head of the gurneys and walk toward Alisa Kent's termination machine.

A beep pierced the quiet.

Alisa . . . Ian watched through blurred eyes as Kent's hand quivered . . . relaxed. Another beep, long and sharp.

Alisa.

Behind the soundproof glass above him, Ian glimpsed an eruption of movement. Applause . . . celebration . . . the bomber of Newbold Bay was dead.

Slowly, Ian turned his heavy head toward Colonel McLaughlin and her colleagues. Stiff, blank faces. Stiff, dutiful applause.

McLaughlin lifted her hand, and Daniel approached Ian's termination machine.

Daniel's bony fingers . . . inexorable . . . steady. Touching the controls.

Ian let his weighted eyelids slide shut. *Oh, God, forgive my shortcomings. I did my best.*

For an endless moment, he felt nothing. Then blackness sparkled across his mind, carrying him into oblivion.

CHAPTER 25

It was interesting, Daniel thought, how resolutely the witnesses leaving the execution room avoided looking toward the sheet-covered bodies of Ian Roshek and Alisa Kent.

At Daniel's elbow stood Nathan Halbrook, maintaining a mien of professional solemnity. When the room was empty except for a couple of police officers, Halbrook said briskly, "Clean up time. Take Roshek, if you don't mind, Dr. Lansbury, and I'll take Kent."

Daniel switched off the power to Ian's termination machine and folded back the sheet covering him. The black line of tape over Ian's mouth was a sharp contrast to his slack, bloodless flesh. Daniel peeled the gag loose and wadded the tape, his fingers shaky with anger.

"Hoping for some last words, Lansbury?"

Daniel jumped. He hadn't heard Peale approach.

"Twitchy?" Peale said. "I'd think you'd be a pro at killing people by now."

Daniel was glad that Peale's medical knowledge only ran as deep as half-forgotten first aid training from the police academy. He threw the tape into the disposal bin and faced Peale in silence. Peale's mocking smile flattened. Daniel knew Peale still hated him, but was afraid to push too hard against the man who had so thoroughly earned the Council's respect.

"Councilor Haines is waiting for you in the hall," Peale said as Daniel reached to disconnect the tube that linked Ian to the termination machine. "He said to let the Euth Center staff finish up here."

Daniel's heartbeat accelerated. Over the top of the termination machine, he exchanged a glance with Halbrook.

"We'll take care of everything, Dr. Lansbury." Halbrook deftly slipped the tube from Alisa Kent's limp arm. "You've done your duty."

Daniel draped the sheet back over Ian and followed Peale out of the execution room. Thirty-two minutes had passed since he had declared Alisa Kent dead. Twenty-one minutes for Ian Roshek. According to the simulations, he should have a comfortable four-hour cushion. He hoped Haines wouldn't take up much of that four hours. Daniel's thoughts veered into an awkward prayer. *God, if Ian's right, if You're real, help him. Help all of us.*

Councilor Haines, Spencer Brannigan, and several uniformed police officers stood near the doors that led to the underground garage. Fear writhed inside Daniel as he approached the silent group. Was Haines going to tell him he was under arrest?

Smiling, Haines offered his hand to Daniel. "Well done, Dr. Lansbury."

Able to breathe again, Daniel grasped Haines's hand. "Thank you, sir."

"I would consider it an honor if you'd attend the celebration at the Council Building tonight. As my guest."

"Sir—thank you. I . . ." Daniel's voice trailed off. President Ryce would be at the gathering, many of the Council and Council Assistants, perhaps Colonel McLaughlin. For Haines to invite Daniel was tantamount to announcing that he was backing Daniel Lansbury for a position in the highest levels of government. To refuse would be inexcusable. But how long would the party last? Cocktails, dinner— could he plead exhaustion and slip out early? . . . *too close . . . cutting it too close . . .*

"Patrick, I must protest." Spencer Brannigan's hand closed on Daniel's elbow. "Dr. Lansbury is honored and overwhelmed by your invitation—too honored to respond candidly. He's been through an extended emotional trauma. He's exhausted, and I'd guess the last thing he wants at the moment is a party. Let the nation celebrate. Daniel needs rest. I'll take him home."

Haines pierced Daniel with a look. He must have seen enough signs of exhaustion to convince him that Brannigan was right, for he nodded. "If that's what Dr. Lansbury wants."

"Thank you for the invitation, sir," Daniel said. "But I think I'll take Councilor Brannigan's advice."

Haines nodded again and moved toward the doors.

Muscles liquid with gratitude, Daniel stumbled as Brannigan propelled him toward the door. "You don't need to take me home, Councilor. I've got my car."

"Give me your keys. I'll have the car delivered to your house."

"I'm not too tired to drive."

"Give me your keys." Brannigan's voice was steely. Nervously, Daniel dug his keys out of his pocket and handed them to Brannigan. It didn't matter if he didn't have his car for a while. He could use one of the other vehicles at the house if he needed to head to Nate's before Brannigan's staff returned his car.

Brannigan pushed through the doors into the parking garage. His security man, Martinez, drove up in the limousine Brannigan used on state occasions. He jumped out of the car and swung the door open for Daniel and Brannigan.

The comfortable leather-and-wood interior of the car looked inexplicably like a prison, and Daniel felt that if he stepped inside he'd be trapped. "Councilor, thank you, but this isn't necessary—"

"Get in the car."

Trembling now, Daniel sank onto the leather upholstery. Brannigan followed, seating himself opposite Daniel. Martinez popped the door shut.

Traffic on Ingram Road was clogged with people heading to various celebrations. Afraid to look at Brannigan, Daniel watched the excited faces of passing revelers.

"The arrogant hypocrisy of the Lansburys," Brannigan said. "Outwardly, you are patriotism personified, but when you want something, you'll undermine everything you claim to support."

Ice prickled Daniel's nerves. "I don't know what you mean."

"I didn't agree with it either, Daniel. I protested through every channel legally open to me. But when I lost, I upheld the Council decision."

"I upheld their decision. I followed their orders."

"Then you wouldn't mind if I called Colonel McLaughlin and suggested she send officers to attend the cremations of Ian Roshek and Alisa Kent?"

Daniel swallowed against a swirl of nausea. "What are you suggesting?"

"You tell me. Maybe you'd like to explain why both your victims experienced a steady, marked decline in heart rate, blood pressure, and respirations beginning the instant you started what was supposedly only a saline drip."

Daniel's heart slammed into his ribs. How could Brannigan know that? The vital signs hadn't been displayed on the video screens until the start of the execution sequence—

Brannigan *hadn't* known. He'd been fishing. Daniel fumbled to recover, hoping his face hadn't shown too much. "If you're asking why their vital signs were weak at the start of the execution sequence, they were probably frightened. Heading into shock."

"Then maybe you'd like to explain why in the last few weeks a doctor who is on the Broc team—and who has been so busy at the Detention Annex that he shouldn't have had time for any extra-curricular research at all—suddenly developed a frenzied interest in reading everything he could find about a drug called Preserval."

"Wait—that's not—"

"You're no computer expert. You had no idea how to erase the trail you left through the Preserval records. You just assumed no one would check on you. And you were nearly right—it wouldn't occur to Colonel McLaughlin or Captain Whitney that anything you did at the lab could have a bearing on the upcoming execution. Not many people know anything about Preserval beyond a few sketchy press releases, and the police are just as ignorant as the rest of the population."

"You're misinterpreting—"

"I suppose it's partly my fault, talking about the executions as a theatrical production. That's what gave you the idea, wasn't it? I could tell at the time that something had startled you, but it took me awhile to put together what it was."

Daniel drew a steadying breath and let the last useless wisps of denial fade away. "If you knew what I was going to do, why didn't you stop me?"

A shadow of unreadable emotion passed over Brannigan's face. "It was cruel of you to rope Nate into this."

"Nate isn't involved." Daniel realized instantly how stupid his words sounded. If Nate wasn't involved, then he was at this moment dutifully cremating the bodies of Ian Roshek and Alisa Kent. "He could have refused," Daniel amended.

"You knew he wouldn't refuse. You knew how miserable he was with the continual, needless loss of life due to a government more interested in its pet projects than in the health of its citizens. You knew he'd be outraged when you told him the truth about the Rosheks and Alisa Kent. He's never crossed the line before, but you dragged him along with you. Now he's put himself and Rebecca at risk."

Daniel mopped wet palms on his trousers. What could he say? He *had* been the cause of Nate Halbrook's leap into treason. But if Brannigan had known what Daniel was planning, why hadn't he stopped him?

Did he plan to finish Daniel's work for him? All he'd have to do would be to hold Daniel prisoner until cell deterioration made it impossible to revive Ian or Alisa Kent. Nate didn't have the expertise to do it without him. But Jill—what about Jill? The bewilderment and relief on Jill's face . . . her arms around his neck . . . the warm spatter of her tears . . . Brannigan *couldn't*, in cold blood . . .

Brannigan was watching him, reading his thoughts. "She's all right? There were no complications?"

"She's fine," Daniel said fiercely, as though saying the words could keep her that way.

Brannigan looked at the Tremont signet on his finger. "Up until tonight," he said, "I tried to convince myself that you were simply indulging in fantasy, that you wouldn't really do anything so crazily treasonous—"

"I don't believe that. You knew I was serious."

Brannigan sighed, looking pale and sick. "I owe you my life," he said. "You and Ian Roshek. And you've both committed crimes more than worthy of death."

"So turn us in. Call Colonel McLaughlin."

"Are you surrendering?"

"I'd rather not. But I'm not going to knock the phone out of your hand. If this is going to end, I'd rather have it end quickly, and I know Nate would too. I only ask that you plead with the Council one more time to spare Jill's life."

"I never thought you could be such a fool. Are you a believer now, Daniel?"

Daniel laughed shortly. "I don't know. But I know Ian Roshek—after everything I've watched him go through, I pretty well know him to the bone—and I'll tell you this: I'd sooner worship Roshek's God than kiss the feet of people who aren't satisfied just to lie about a man and publicly kill him, but have to taunt and torment him right before his death to provoke a little dramatic conflict for the spectators. No wonder they wouldn't let me tell him about Jill's death beforehand. They didn't want to dull the shock."

Brannigan pressed his lips together, his expression veiled.

"I'm sorry," Daniel said. "Sorry you were the one to figure it out, sorry you're disappointed with me. But I'm not sorry that I wouldn't go along with this mockery."

The limousine crawled through traffic. Brannigan and Daniel faced each other in silence, the tension in Brannigan's face gradually slackening to fatigue.

"To be honest," Brannigan said, "I don't know *what* to do with you."

"Let me go. Let us all go."

"And throw aside everything my father worked for. Everything James Tremont founded."

"Some things ought to be thrown aside. Dad was the most passionate admirer of James Tremont you could find, right up to imitating Tremont's tendencies to murder his way into power."

Brannigan opened his mouth to speak, then lapsed into silence. Daniel waited, surreally calm, watching Brannigan toy with the Tremont signet on his hand.

"I've always felt that reform can come from within," Brannigan said. "I thought you felt the same way."

"I did. But after what I've witnessed over the last few weeks, I've started to wonder if corruption in the system is the problem, or if the problem *is* the system—our whole philosophical framework, where the Council isn't accountable to any principles higher than its own decisions."

"Are you saying we should be accountable to Roshek's God?"

"I don't know what I'm saying. I just know I can't be part of what's happening here—not anymore. I don't think the Cadre is gone. Dad was too smart to give one man enough information to unravel his whole organization. I think there are still people in the government who are part of his inner circle, people Todd Kinnock didn't know about. But you know what? I don't think it makes a difference. The Council already has the same goals and uses the same tactics as the Cadre."

"Daniel!"

"It's true. And what if a majority of the Council decides that Dad's idea was a good one and votes to create their own version of the Liberty Cadre just to keep the nation submissive? Could you support that?"

"My loyalty to the Council is not the issue here." Brannigan's voice was thin.

"You have the same questions I do. If you didn't, you wouldn't have let me get this far."

"Daniel—"

Daniel read the pain and confusion now naked in Brannigan's eyes. "You didn't let me fake the executions because you fooled yourself into thinking I wasn't serious or because you couldn't stand the thought of turning me in. You let me go ahead because you wanted me to succeed."

"Daniel—"

"I don't know if Ian Roshek is right, but I'm willing to consider it. And I know this for certain—I don't want his blood on my hands."

Brannigan's face was taut. He removed his Tremont signet and held it between his thumb and forefinger, tilting it so the diamonds glittered in the car's interior lights.

"I suppose it *is* possible," he said quietly, "that James Tremont— and our fathers and mothers—were simply . . . wrong."

* * *

A voice. "Dan, he's waking up." Pools of light and color. Too befuddled to sort it out, Ian drifted back toward darkness.

"Stay with me, kid." A hand jiggled his shoulder. "Sleepy time is over. You ought to be awake by now."

Ian squinted at the face above him. Bulging, slate-colored eyes, white hair, chubby face . . . *Nathan Halbrook*. From the reception after Jill's concert. Director of the Tremont Euthanasia Center.

Euth Center. *The execution.* Ian tried to speak, but his mouth wouldn't cooperate.

"I know you're still confused," Halbrook soothed. "We'll explain everything."

Sweat drenched Ian's body, but his teeth chattered with cold. Where was he? Lemon-yellow walls. A lamp on a dresser top. The nightstand next to him was littered with medication vials, empty plastic packaging, and a couple of pieces of electronic equipment that Ian didn't recognize.

Nathan Halbrook stepped back and Ian blinked up at Daniel Lansbury. A hallucination at the moment of death. He was on a gurney in the Euth Center, poison flowing into his body. But this room with the yellow walls . . . Jill was here. No, that was a dream. Jill was dead.

Daniel was asking him questions. His name, the date, where he was, what he remembered happening. Ian heard himself responding to the first two questions, but couldn't answer the rest. Fragments of memory . . . Jill . . . Alisa Kent . . .

"I don't know . . . don't remember . . ."

"Don't worry about it. I didn't think you would. You've been awake a couple of times during the night, but you were pretty foggy." Daniel beckoned to someone else. A blurry blond figure rose from a chair.

"Jill." Ian's hand flopped like a slab of boneless meat as he reached toward her. *"Jill."*

"You look much better." Jill's cheeks were thin, but the joy in her smile was like sunshine. "How do you feel?"

"They told me . . . you were dead."

"I'm fine. We're at Mr. Halbrook's house. He and Daniel are— they're helping us."

Daniel Lansbury helping traitors? That was crazy . . .

Ian's gaze snagged on a woman in a white terry-cloth robe, sitting on a bed a few feet away. Her head was bowed and a tangle of black hair obscured her face.

"Alisa."

Alisa Kent didn't seem to hear him.

"She'll be all right," Daniel said. "She's just a bit disoriented."

"I can understand that," Ian mumbled.

"Time to get up." Daniel's eyes were bloodshot and his chin bristled with stubble. "You'll feel more alert if you move around. Are you hungry?"

"I . . . guess . . . I am. What time is it?"

"It's eight o'clock in the morning. What would you like first? Explanations or food?"

"Explanations."

"All right. Nate, help Alisa into the family room."

Standing up felt like trying to haul a backpack filled with rocks up a mountain, but with Daniel on one side and Jill on the other, Ian was finally able to shuffle into a living area furnished with pleasantly shabby couches and chairs. From the high, small windows—with curtains carefully drawn—Ian realized they must be in a basement.

Daniel guided him to the couch where Halbrook was seating Alisa Kent. Kent glanced at Ian and quickly looked away.

Ian touched her arm. "Alisa?"

She flinched.

"She'll be all right," Daniel repeated. "Just give her time."

Jill plopped into a padded wicker chair. Daniel sat on the floor in front of her and leaned back against her knees. "Ian, do you remember the night of Jill's concert when Nate mentioned a drug called Preserval?"

Ian scrounged through muddied memories. "Sure . . . biostasis."

"Do you remember anything more specific?"

"Uh . . . something about . . . keeps cells from dying even when the heart is not . . . *oh.*"

Daniel grinned. "Alisa, do you know anything about Preserval?"

Kent stared blankly past Daniel.

"Alisa. Answer my question. Do you know anything about Preserval?"

Kent's hands gripped together, milky flesh straining over sharp knuckles. "No," she whispered.

"Preserval is a drug that slows all biochemical processes to the point that cells will not degenerate, even in the absence of oxygen, food, and waste removal processes."

"President Ryce's elixir of perpetual youth," Halbrook said. "Daniel got the wacky idea that it might be useful for faking executions."

"How could you administer Preserval without anyone noticing?" Ian asked.

"It was astonishingly simple," Halbrook said. "I supervised the preparation of the public execution room, as well as the private room where Jill was to be terminated. It was easy for me to switch the drugs in the termination machines, and I did it before the police ever marched you into the Euth Center."

"Don't the police—check up on things like that?"

"Why would they? Executions are routine business at the Euth Center. The police just show up for the main event."

"Where did you get Preserval in the first place?"

"The Tremont Research Lab," Daniel said.

"So you pumped us full of Preserval, then killed us, then revived us?"

Daniel responded, "You were never dead. You were in stasis, with all biochemical processes slowed to the point that the monitors on the termination machines could no longer pick up any vital signs."

Halbrook spoke. "Because it takes Preserval a while to work, we started running it when we first started the saline drip. You were receiving a low dose all the way through President Ryce's speech."

Ian remembered the torpor that had weighed him down. "When you pushed the button to 'execute' us, what happened then?"

"Instead of injecting you with the usual Euth Center cocktail, we hit you with a massive slug of Preserval," Daniel said. "That was enough to make you appear clinically dead."

"Wasn't it obvious that we weren't . . . dying in the usual manner?"

"No," Daniel said, grinning.

"But all those heart monitors and stuff—didn't they show—"

"The only notable difference between your 'death' and a typical Euth Center execution was that at the beginning of the execution sequence, your heart rate and blood pressure were much lower than would normally be expected. But at that point, a medically knowledgeable viewer would probably just assume that fear of death had sent you into shock."

Ian still couldn't shake the sense that Daniel and Nathan Halbrook were both crazily overconfident. "But the people who were there—the witnesses, I mean—"

A glance passed between Daniel and Halbrook. "Relax, Ian," Daniel said. "Overall, your deaths looked like any other Euth Center death. You lost consciousness, then you stopped breathing, and your heart stopped beating."

Heart stopped beating. Ian restrained an urge to check his pulse to make sure his heart was working now. Alisa Kent's head was bowed, her body woodenly still. Ian wanted to reach out to her, but remembering Daniel's counsel to take it slowly, he turned back to Daniel and Halbrook.

"I think you're both nuts."

Daniel waved his hand impatiently. "If Preserval were a well-known drug, it would have been a lot more risky. But it's still experimental. Only a handful of people would have any hope of recognizing its physiological effects."

"And if one of those people . . . ?"

"You're just determined we're going to get caught, aren't you?" Daniel shook his head. "Think about the context of what took place last night. Do you really think someone is going to say, 'Hey, funny vital signs. I'll bet that Lansbury guy slipped his dad's murderer and the Newbold Bay bomber some Preserval?'"

"All right, all right," Ian conceded.

"Once I declared you dead," Daniel resumed the story, "Councilor Haines gave a speech about our duty to make sure that an anarchist gang like the Liberty Cadre never rises again. Then the ceremony was over. The spectators left and the police left—leaving your bodies to the care of the Euth Center staff."

"Which consisted of me," Halbrook added. "Colonel McLaughlin didn't want extra personnel around, either at your execution or at Jill's. I wheeled you to the cremation room and started the cycle, but instead of loading you into the crematory, I loaded you into the Euth Center van and brought you here."

"Do bodies usually, um, evaporate completely in your furnace?"

"When no one claims the bodies—which no one did for any of you, since none of your relatives wanted to admit they ever knew you—the ashes are not retrieved after the cycle, but are automatically swept into a mass collection box for later disposal. There's no way for anyone to know that your ashes aren't there, mixed up with the other unfortunates who had no one to claim them."

Jill moaned, looking queasy. "Do you have to ask for so many details, Ian?"

"Sorry." Ian gave her a brief smile and returned his attention to Halbrook. "How could you be sure no one would catch you loading us into the van?"

"The Center was closed both today and on the day of Jill's execution. The only people on site were janitorial crews that came on duty after the spectators left, but they were assigned only to clean the execution room and the gallery. They had no reason to venture down to the cremation room. And it was no problem getting you discreetly into the van, because the cremation room opens directly into the underground garage."

"You took an incredible risk," Ian said. "What if Lt. Peale or someone had decided to come to the cremation room to make sure you did the job right?"

"Roshek, do you have any idea how many executions I've assisted at? Even jerks like Peale don't care what happens to the body. That's like taking out the trash."

"They might have made an exception for such big-time criminals."

Halbrook chuckled. "What you're forgetting is that the police, with their own eyes, watched you *die*. You weren't breathing, all right? No heartbeat, all right? It's the responsibility of the Euth Center to deal with dead bodies, to cremate them or turn them over to the family for burial. It's not a police matter. Quit obsessing."

"It just seems like it—can't be that easy."

Daniel gave him a sour look. "It seems easy to you because you didn't even know it was happening until it had already worked. For those of us who beat our brains into scrambled eggs trying to figure out how to make the administration of Preserval mimic an execution—which it usually *doesn't*, because usually Preserval is administered at a steady, controlled rate, not as a trickle and then a gush—and who got to stand there wondering if this was really working or if you were dying under my hands, it didn't seem so easy."

"Sorry," Ian said meekly.

"The good news is that because no one has ever tried this before, there were no precautions in place to guard against it," Daniel said. "If McLaughlin had the slightest inkling that tampering with an execution was possible, she would immediately make tampering *im*possible."

"You still took an incredible risk."

"It was worth it." Daniel tilted his head back, and Jill leaned down for a kiss.

"Jill, what excuse did they invent for executing you?" Ian asked.

Jill played with Daniel's hair, curling light brown strands around her fingertips. "Colonel McLaughlin wanted me to speak at your execution, repeating their lies about you and saying how you deserved to die. I wouldn't do it."

"You . . . didn't believe what they told you about me?"

Jill rolled her eyes. "Don't be an idiot."

"You were willing to *die* rather than get up there and lie about me?"

Jill's hollowed cheeks blushed crimson. "If she had ordered you to lie about me, you wouldn't have done it."

Ian wished he had the strength to leap to his feet and snatch Jill into his arms. "You amaze me."

Jill's sapphire eyes sparkled.

Alisa Kent leaned back against the couch, her clenched hands loosening. Ian waited, hoping she would speak, but she didn't.

"You've told us how you did it," Ian said. "But you haven't told us why. I understand why you'd want to help Jill, though I never thought you'd go this far. But—" He glanced at Alisa Kent. "Why would you take this kind of risk to save a couple of traitors like us?"

Daniel yawned and pushed himself to his feet. "I don't know," he said. "Maybe after all that's happened, I just started to wonder if you might be right about a few things."

Speechless, Ian turned his gaze to Nathan Halbrook.

Halbrook tossed his hands into the air. "Hey, I was just glad to have the chance to do something I felt good about." He stood up. "Make yourselves comfortable. You'll be staying here until we can get you to the U.S."

"I don't suppose the border nets are still down?"

"Sorry, out of luck on that one," Daniel said. "But we *will* have some help."

"Help?"

Daniel and Halbrook exchanged a sheepish glance. "We didn't completely get away with what we did last night," Daniel admitted. "After it was over, I got cornered by someone who had reason to suspect I wasn't as devoted to duty as I pretended—and who, unfortunately, was familiar with Preserval."

Ian would have been frightened but for the grin on Daniel's face. "Who?"

"Someone who for a number of reasons couldn't bring himself to alert Colonel McLaughlin to an execution gone wrong." Daniel smiled wryly. "I wonder what your buddy Lt. Peale would say if he knew your influence has now corrupted a member of the Council."

"A member of—all right, now you *have* gone crazy."

"Spencer Brannigan, Ian," Daniel said.

Brannigan. Ian flashed back to the rigid, unhappy look Spencer Brannigan had worn at the execution. "He wants to—he's willing to help us?"

"He's not too happy about it. But he figures he's already involved just by keeping his mouth shut, so he might as well do what he can to get us out of New America before we get caught and get him arrested. There are several ways he might be able to accomplish it, but he'll have to move carefully."

So off-balance that he had to grip the arm of the couch to keep from toppling over, Ian managed to ask, "You're planning to come to the U.S. as well?"

"Yes." Daniel wrapped his arm around Jill.

"You look asleep on your feet, Lansbury," Halbrook said. "You were up all night babysitting your patients. Go get some rest."

"I'm all right. But I think I'll go take a shower."

"I was just going to see if I can help Becky with breakfast," Halbrook said. "Should I wait for—?"

"No, go ahead." Daniel gave Alisa Kent a thoughtful look, then turned to Jill. "Jill, you didn't get much rest last night either. Why don't you go lie down before breakfast?"

"Oh, I don't—" Jill paused as understanding flickered in her eyes. "Good idea." She headed down the hallway. Daniel and Nathan Halbrook exited in the opposite direction.

Ian sat listening to the quiet tread of feet ascending carpeted stairs. It took his overloaded mind a moment to realize that Daniel had just maneuvered to leave him alone with Alisa Kent.

Ian scanned her profile. Her cheekbone and jaw formed sharp, skeletal lines, and her eyes were sunken in purplish hollows. "How are you doing, Alisa?" he asked gently.

Kent turned and searched his face like she doubted she was really seeing him.

"This isn't exactly what we expected, is it?" Ian said.

"I didn't . . . trust . . . that it could happen." Kent drew a halting breath. "But I . . . I *knew.*"

"You knew?"

"It was . . . in the Annex . . ." Pain glazed her eyes and she lapsed into silence. Ian hesitated, reluctant to push her into reciting terrifying memories, but after a moment, she continued in a whisper.

"I had nothing left . . . no strength . . . it wasn't ending . . . there was nothing I could do . . . no way to—to wake from . . . they were there, all of them—all the pain that I—"

Ian folded his hands around her icy fingers. "Alisa . . ."

"Your book," she said. "Alma . . . the one who tried to destroy the church. He fought against God, yet when he was in agony, regretting the things that he . . ." Her hands trembled in Ian's grasp. "He called out . . . God heard him . . . I thought . . . maybe there was a chance . . ."

Tingling spread through Ian's chest. "You—prayed?"

"It was . . . insane to try . . . but He heard Alma . . ."

"What happened?" Ian asked softly.

"The pain wasn't gone . . . or the hallucinations. But I felt—calm. Strength, like I was being . . . supported, that I would be able to endure . . ." Awe rose in her face, luminescent and warm. "Also, very distinctly, that I would—live, that it wasn't time for—but I didn't see how it could happen—execution was inevitable . . . I thought I must be insane, that I'd only imagined . . ."

"You didn't imagine it," Ian said.

"I don't . . . understand why I would be . . . protected like this, when I—" Her fingers intertwined with Ian's, gripping hard.

"He heard me," she whispered.

ABOUT THE AUTHOR

Stephanie Black has loved books since she was old enough to grab the pages and has enjoyed creating stories since she and her sisters were playing make-believe games or writing plays for themselves and younger siblings. She graduated from Brigham Young University with a degree in history and secondary education. Born in Utah, she has also lived in Arkansas, Arizona, Massachusetts, and Limerick, Ireland, and now resides in northern California with her husband Brian and their five children.

Stephanie would enjoy hearing from her readers. She can be reached through Covenant e-mail at info@Covenant-lds.com or through snail-mail at Covenant Communications, Inc., Box 416, American Fork, UT 84003-0416.